Avon Books by
Kathleen E. Woodiwiss

EVERLASTING
THE RELUCTANT SUITOR
A SEASON BEYOND A KISS
THE ELUSIVE FLAME
PETALS ON THE RIVER
MARRIED AT MIDNIGHT
(with Jo Beverly, Tanya Anne Crosby and Samantha Jones)
FOREVER IN YOUR EMBRACE
SO WORTHY MY LOVE
COME LOVE A STRANGER
A ROSE IN WINTER
ASHES IN THE WIND
SHANNA
THE WOLF AND THE DOVE

KATHLEEN E. WOODIWISS

The Flame and the Flower

AVON

An Imprint of HarperCollinsPublishers

This is a work of fiction. Names, characters, places, and incidents are products of the author's imagination or are used fictitiously and are not to be construed as real. Any resemblance to actual events, locales, organizations, or persons, living or dead, is entirely coincidental.

AVON BOOKS
An Imprint of HarperCollins*Publishers*
10 East 53rd Street
New York, New York 10022-5299

Copyright © 1972 by Kathleen E. Woodiwiss
Excerpt from *The Reluctant Suitor* copyright © 2003 by Kathleen E. Woodiwiss
ISBN: 978-0-380-00525-3
ISBN-10: 0-380-00525-5
www.avonromance.com

First Avon Books paperback printing: April 1972

Avon Trademark Reg. U.S. Pat. Off. and in Other Countries, Marca Registrada, Hecho en U.S.A.
HarperCollins® is a registered trademark of HarperCollins Publishers.

Printed in the U.S.A.

114

For the flame will surely come,
And burn, and blacken, and lay bare the hill.
But with the first sweet breath of spring
They shy and lovely flower will again show
its face among the charred ruins.
It yields to the searing heat,
But with its persistent beauty
Far surpasses and finally tames the flame.

The Flame and the Flower

Chapter 1

June 23, 1799

Somewhere in the world, time no doubt whistled by on taut and widespread wings, but here in the English countryside it plodded slowly, painfully, as if it trod the rutted road that stretched across the moors on blistered feet. The hot sweltering air was motionless; dust hung above the road, still reminding the restless of a coach that had passed several hours before. A small farm squatted dismally beneath the humid haze that lay over the marsh. The thatched cottage stood between spindly yews and, with shutters open and door ajar, it seemed to stare as if aghast at some off-color jest. Nearby, a barn sagged in poor repair about its rough-hewn frame and beyond, a thin growth of wheat fought vainly in the boggy soil for each inch of growth.

Inside the house, Heather wearily turned potatoes against a dull worn knife that more scraped than peeled. Two years she had lived in this cottage, two years so miserable that they seemed to blot out her life. She could barely summon the happy times prior to that weary day she had been brought here, the softer days spilling over the years as she grew from baby to young woman, when her father, Richard, had been alive and she lived with

1

him in a comfortable London house, wearing stylish clothes, having enough food to eat. Oh yes, it was better then. Even the nights her father left her alone with servants didn't seem so frightening now. She could understand now his agonies, his loneliness for a wife long dead, the sweet, beautiful Irish lass whom he had fallen in love with and married and lost giving birth to their only child. Now Heather could even comprehend her father's need to gamble, that cruel sport which had robbed him of life and her of home and security, leaving her at the mercy of her only kin, a pluckless uncle and a shrewish aunt.

Heather wiped her brow and thought of Aunt Fanny lounging in the other room; the straw mattress would be flattened under her more than generous frame. Fanny was not a woman easy to get along with. Everything seemed to displease her. She was without friends. Not a soul ever came to call. She liked no one. She had thought the Irish woman her brother-in-law had married was inferior because of her people, a race she declared was always warring against the crown because it was their nature to fight, and now Heather bore the brunt of that malicious hatred. Not a day went by that it wasn't thrown up to Heather that she was half foreign. And with the prejudice was an emotion that ran deeper, twisting Fanny's reasoning until she half believed that like the mother, the daughter was part witch. Call it jealousy perhaps, for Fanny Simmons had never been pretty, not even remotely so, whereas the colleen, Brenna, had possessed great beauty and charm. Men's heads turned when she walked into a room. Heather had inherited her mother's exquisite loveliness and, sadly enough, the aunt's criticism along with it.

The gaming houses had claimed payment for Richard's losses at their tables, taking every material possession he had had but a few personal artifacts and some clothing. Fanny had hastened to London to declare her husband's right of blood, snatching up the orphaned niece and her meager inheritance before a protest could be made. She had grumbled because Richard had not shared his wealth nor left it behind for them, then sold the goods, all but one gown, a pink one that Heather was not even allowed to wear, and greedily pocketed the money.

Heather straightened her aching back and sighed.

"Heather Simmons!"

The words rang from the other room and the bed creaked as her aunt rose from it.

"You lazy flit, stop your daydreaming and get to work. Do you think your chores will be gettin' done while you mope around here? I swear a body would think that lady's school you went to would've taught you something useful instead of reading and all those high-handed notions what fill your head!"

The huge woman padded across the dirt floor into the room, and Heather mentally braced herself. She knew what was coming.

"See what good it done you—'aving to live off your only kin. Your pa were a fool, that he was, throwing away his money without a care o' nobody but hisself, all on account o' that flip he married   that Irish girl." She spat the words out in distaste as if she could think of nothing worse. "We tried to warn him against wedding her. But he wouldn't listen—'e had to have Brenna."

Heather lifted her gaze wearily from the shaft of sunlight drifting in from the open doorway to the large bulk of her aunt. She had heard the argument so often she knew it by heart; it failed to shake her kinder memories of her father.

"He was a good father," she said simply.

"That's a matter of opinion, missy," the woman sneered. "See what fix he left you in. No dowry an' eighteen you'll be next month. Ain't no man what'll marry you without one, though they'll be wanting you all right—to fill their beds. I got me poor hands full, trying to keep you decent. I ain't wanting you to spill no bastards in me home. Folks here is just waiting for that. They knows what trash your ma was."

Heather flinched, but her aunt ranted on, turning her narrowed eyes upon her and shaking a damning finger.

"The devil done his work when he made you just like her. A witch, she was. 'Taint natural for you to have the same looks. And so she ruined your pa, so you'll be ruining every man what lays his eyes on you. 'Tis the Lord's will what brought you to me. He knew I could save you from the fire an' brimstone you were meant for, and I done me duty in selling those fancy gowns you had. You were too vain an' uppity for your own good. Them old dresses of mine have done nicely for you."

Heather could almost laugh. If it weren't so sad she would. Her aunt's clothes hung about her worse than any sack, for the woman outweighed her twice over. This was all that she was permitted to wear, old rags that made a mockery of style or design. Fanny had even forbidden Heather to take in the seams to make them fit better, only to shorten the hems, so she wouldn't trip.

The woman caught Heather's contemplation of her hand-me-down and sneered. "Ungrateful little beggar. Just tell me where you'd have been today if your uncle an' me 'adn't taken you in? If your pa would 'ave 'ad good sense, he'd 'ave married you off with a nice dowry. But no, he kept you to hisself, thinking you too young to wed. Well, it's too late for you now. You'll be buried a spinster when you die—and a virgin, too, that I'll see to."

Fanny returned once more to the cottage's only other room, giving Heather a warning that she'd best hurry with her chores or suffer under the bite of a switch. Heather's fingers sped at their task. She had felt the sting of that branch. Red welts usually criss-crossed her back for days following a whipping. Fanny seemed to take special delight in marking Heather's bare flesh.

Heather dared not release another exhausted sigh, for fear it would draw her aunt's attention again, but she was weary of her labors. She had been up since before dawn, preparing a feast for Fanny's anxiously awaited brother, and she doubted her ability to last much longer. A letter had arrived several days before, informing Fanny that he would be coming this evening, and she had ordered Heather to start preparations immediately upon receipt of the note; she had even lifted a finger or two herself to arrange a treasured cup on a saucer. Heather knew the man was someone her aunt held very dear indeed. She had heard many glorious tales about him, and guessed that Fanny's brother was the only being, human or otherwise, that she cared anything about. Uncle John had confirmed Heather's beliefs when he told her there was nothing Fanny wouldn't do for the man. There had been only the two of them, and being ten years her brother's senior she had raised him from a babe. But it was very rare nowadays that he came to call.

The sun was a red ball flaming low in the west before everything lay ready. Fanny came to give her final approval and directed Heather to set out more candles to light later.

"It's five summers since I laid my poor eyes on my brother, and I want everything to be nice for him. My Willy's used to the best of London, and I won't be having him find fault with what's here. He ain't like that uncle of yours nor your pa. My brother's got lots of money cause he uses his head." She gestured to her own large head to make her point. "You don't see him in no gaming houses throwing away his wealth nor sitting on his prat like your uncle. He's a man what makes his own chances, he does. Ain't no finer clothier's shop than what he's got in London. He even has a man what works for him, he does."

She finally gave the blessed command for Heather to go and freshen up.

"An' Heather, wear that gown your pa give you. It'll do nicely. I want my brother's visit to be a happy occasion without the likes of those rags you're wearing marring it."

Heather turned around, eyes wide with surprise. For

two years her pink gown had remained tucked away, untouched and unworn. Now she would be allowed to wear it. Even if it was for the pleasure of her aunt's brother, she was delighted. It seemed an eternity since she had worn anything pretty, and now she smiled in anticipation.

"Aye, I see you're pleased. Always thinking how pretty you look in those fine dresses, you are." Fanny pressed close and wagged her finger under Heather's nose. "Satan is at his work again. Mind you, the Lord knows what a task you are for me." She sighed heavily, as if tired of her burden. "It's better that you were married and off me hands. But I pity the man who would wed you, though there ain't no chance of that without a dowry. You need a strong man to keep you tied down and burdened with his babe every year. You need it to take the witch from your evil soul."

Heather shrugged her shoulders and continued to smile. She longed for the nerve to frighten her aunt into believing she was really a witch. It would be a heathenish thing to do and the temptation would have been great for a braver person, but for her the idea quickly ebbed away. The consequences would not be light.

"Another thing, missy, wear your hair coiled round your head. It'll do nicely indeed," Aunt Fanny smirked slyly, knowing how much her niece disliked being told how to wear her hair.

The smile quickly faded from Heather's face, but she turned away murmuring an affirmative answer. Her aunt waited for disapproval of her commands to be expressed in the slightest way; she took it upon herself to hand out discipline with harsh methods.

Heather crossed the room and moved behind the curtain separating her small corner from the rest of the living area. She heard her aunt leave the cottage and it was only then she dared allow a mutinous pout to show. She was angry, but more at herself than at her aunt. She had always been a coward and the way things were going she would always be one.

The dreary cubicle held but the barest necessities, yet it was here she sought succor from the brutality of her aunt. She sighed and bent to light the short candle on the shoddy table beside the narrow rope cot.

"If only I were stronger and braver," she thought, "then I would set her back on her heels. If just once I could retort in kind to her needling." She flexed a slim arm with a wry smile fleeting across her lips. "But I'd have to be Samson to wrestle her!"

Earlier she had set an ewer of warm water and a wash-bowl in her room and now Heather stretched in antici-pation of the bath. With a distasteful grimace, she half tore the hated dress she wore from her body. Standing naked, she relaxed and ran her hands down her slender body, wincing when her fingers touched a bruise. Aunt Fanny had flown into a rage the day before when she had accidently knocked over a cup of tea, and before she could flee the woman had laid the bundle of a straw broom heavily across her buttocks.

With tender care Heather removed the pink gown from its bundle and hung it where her eyes could caress it as she bathed. The water was refreshing and she scrubbed vigorously until her skin blushed with a youthful glow. She worked the cloth over a small sliver of scented soap she had scavenged and lathered herself liberally, reveling in the pungent fragrance.

Her toilette complete, she drew the gown carefully over her shabby chemise. The bodice of the gown had been made for a younger girl. The fabric was tight across her breasts, and she pondered on her growth and consid-ered the daring swell above the low décolletage, then dismissed the problem with a shrug of her shoulders. It was her only gown and it was too late an hour to con-template alterations.

In delightful luxury, she brushed her hair until it gleamed in the candlelight. This had been her father's pride, something he had treasured and often stroked in absent thought as, she surmised, he had done with her mother. More than once he had stared at her as if dreaming and in deep longing, murmured his wife's name before he had consciously shaken himself and turned away with misty eyes.

As directed, she coiled her hair around her head, but left a few stray curls to tumble down the back in feigned disarray and another on each temple in rare defiance. She surveyed herself in the piece of broken glass that served as a mirror and nodded her head. She had done better than she expected with the crude materials at hand.

On the other side of the curtain, Heather heard someone enter the cottage and move about the room; there was a deep hacking cough. She stepped around the drapery, knowing it was her uncle. He was lighting his pipe with a wood splint from the fire and he coughed again as it took light. Swirls of smoke filled the room.

John Simmons was a broken man. He had little to care about in his life but his miserly guarded money and the doubtful companionship of Aunt Fanny and had ceased to worry about his appearance. His shirt was grease stained and dirt was thick under his nails. He had lost the good looks of his younger years and now stood before Heather a stooped and withered man who appeared well beyond his two score and ten years. His eyes held a lackluster film of broken dreams and crushed hopes and frustration-filled days under his wife's heckling. His hands were gnarled and twisted with the years of back-breaking labor eking a shallow subsistence from the marshy land, and his weather-thickened skin held the pain of the passing seasons etched in deep lines that furrowed his face.

He glanced up and saw the soft beauty of his niece and something of a new pain seemed to fleet across his features. He sat back in his chair and smiled.

"You're looking lovely this evening, child. I'm supposing it be for William's visit?"

"Aunt Fanny gave me permission, Uncle," she answered.

He sucked on the pipe a moment as his teeth tightened upon it. "Aye, I can believe that," he sighed. "She goes to great lengths to please him though he's a cold man. Once when she journeyed to London to see him he refused to speak with her. Now, she dare not go for fear of angering him, and he's satisfied with it thus. He has his wealthy friends and wouldn't think of claiming her his kin."

A slightly blurred portrait of his sister, William Court was even the same height as Fanny, which was a full head taller than Heather. Perhaps he was not quite as obese, but Heather surmised that difference would diminish in a few years. His pudgy face was ruddy, with heavy jowls, and he possessed a protruding underlip which was constantly wet with saliva. He dabbed at it continuously with a lacy handkerchief, making sniffing noises as if it were his nose he wiped. When he held Heather's hand in greeting his was sickeningly soft, and when he bent to kiss her hand, she had a vague feeling of revulsion.

The clothes he wore bespoke of elegant taste, but his mincing manner did little to enhance a masculine mien. The suit of soft gray, liberally piped with silver, and the white shirt and stock seemed to accentuate his pinkish hands and wheezing red face. William Court may have been wealthy, but Heather could find little to attract her. His trousers were extremely tight, almost to a point of discomfort it seemed, and it could be guessed that they had been deliberately cut thus to display to the casual eye his otherwise questionable manhood.

He had arrived in a rented landau with a precisely dressed coachman who was sent to the barn to bed down with his two dapple-gray horses. Heather sensed the driver was put out with his lowly accommodations since he himself was better dressed than the occupants of the cottage. The barn was hardly fit for his animals. But if he were annoyed he said nothing, going silently about his work, tending the horses and carriage.

Aunt Fanny, with her grey hair pulled tightly against her large head, looked like a forboding fortress in her stiffly starched gown and apron. In spite of her past ranting and raving about how fancy clothes were the work of the devil, she was openly pleased to see her brother prosperously dressed and bustled about him like a hen over a baby chick. Heather had never seen her so affectionate to any individual, and it was kindly received by William Court who obviously enjoyed being waited upon hand and foot. She ignored her aunt's drooling endearments and didn't attend closely to their conversation until at dinner it drifted to the current news from London. Then she began to listen intently in hopes of hearing news of old friends.

"Napoleon escaped and now everyone believes him to be on his way back to France after his defeat in Egypt. Nelson taught him a thing or two. He'll think twice before tangling with our seamen again, by Jove!" William Court swore.

Heather noted that his speech was considerably better than his sister's and she wondered if he had attended a school.

Aunt Fanny wiped her mouth with the back of her hand and snarled. "Pitt didn't know what he was talking about when he said leave the French be. Now he's up to his bloody neck with them and those Irish too. I say kill 'em all!"

Heather bit her lip.

"The Irish! Ha! Pack of animals they are, if you ask me! They don't know when they're happy and well off!" Aunt Fanny continued.

"Pitt is trying to form a union with them now. Perhaps next year it will go through," Uncle John said.

"Per'aps we'll have our throats slit by the bloody lot of them, too!"

Heather glanced hesitantly to her uncle, uneasy as always with her aunt's prejudice. John lowered his eyes and drained his ale in one breath. He sighed and cast a longing glance to the jug Fanny guarded, then set his mug upon the hearth and silently returned to his pipe.

"The Yankee's the same! They'll cut your throat rather than look at you. We'll have them to fight again, mark my word."

William chuckled, his jowls quivering with amusement. "It would do you no good to come to London then, dear sister, for they come into port as if they owned the place. A few get snatched for impressment, but they're a careful lot and stay to themselves. When they venture into the city they go in numbers. They don't like the idea of sailing on the British ships. Aye, they're a careful lot and some have the audacity to think themselves gentlemen. Look at that fellow Washington, for instance. And now they have that other fool, Adams, whom they've elected as their king. It's outrageous! But it won't last. They'll come back, whining like the dogs they are!"

Heather didn't know any Yankees. She was simply glad that her aunt and Mr. Court were discussing them instead of the Irish.

She let her attention slide from the conversation. As long as they did not talk of London society or her ancestors she was not interested. If she dared speak up and declare her loyalty to them or ask if there was social news of London, she knew her aunt would descend on her viciously. As it was, her thoughts wandered elsewhere and she sat for what seemed an eternity.

Aunt Fanny brought Heather out of her shell; she reached across the table and maliciously pinched her arm. Heather jumped. She rubbed her arm, where a red welt was forming, and looked up at her aunt, blinking back tears of pain.

"I asked you if you wanted to teach at Lady Cabot's finishing school. My brother thinks he may be able to find you work," Aunt Fanny snapped.

Heather could hardly believe her ears. "What?"

William Court laughed and explained. "I've very good connections with the school, and I know they're looking for a young lady of quality, and you do have excellent manners and good speech. You would, I believe, be perfect for the position, and I understand you also attended a school in London which will be of much help." He dabbed at his massive lips before continuing. "Perhaps in the future I could arrange a suitable marriage for you with a prominent family in town. It would seem a shame to waste such ladylike grace on a farm yokel here. Of course, if I do arrange such a contract, it would mean supplying you with a substantial dowry which I'll expect to be repaid when you have your man secure. It's a slight trick, but could be profitable to each of us. You're in want of a dowry, which I can supply, and I'd favor the interest on the loan which you can provide afterwards. No one need know of such an arrangement and I know you're wise enough to obtain the money after you're married. Would this position at Lady Cabot's be acceptable to you?"

Heather was not sure about William Court's marriage scheme, but—to get away from this farm, Aunt Fanny, her boring existence! To once again be near London society—it would be marvelous! If it weren't for the stinging of her arm, she would think she was still dreaming.

"Speak up, child. What is your answer?" plied William.

Hardly able to suppress her glee, she did not hesitate further. "The offer is most kind of you, sir, and I'll be happy to."

William laughed again. "Good! Good! You'll not regret your decision." He rubbed his hands together. "Now, we must journey to London tomorrow. I've been away from my business too long and I must get back to relieve my assistant. Do you think you can be ready, child?" He waved a lace handkerchief under his nose and dabbed once again at his thick lips.

"Oh, yes, sir. Whenever you choose to leave I'll be ready," she said happily.

"Good, good. It's all settled then."

Heather cleared the table and it was with a new feeling she did so, knowing it would be the last meal she would clean away in this cottage. She was too caught up in her happiness to bother making conversation with her aunt as the woman watched her, and when she was to herself behind her curtain she thought of all the delights of being free from Aunt Fanny. Any position in London would be superior to living under that woman's thumb and taking her abuse. Heather would be free of the harsh words, the violent anger, and maybe, somewhere, there'd be someone who cared.

Little preparation was necessary for the next day's journey for what she possessed was what she had worn that night and what she would wear again tomorrow. She slipped naked beneath the blanket on her cot. It was rough against her flesh and when the wind brought the chilled air of winter it failed to keep her sufficiently warm. She giggled with pleasure when she thought of not having to contend with it any longer. In less than a twelve month it would be a new century and she wondered what its years held for her now with this new chance to live and be happy.

The next afternoon they journeyed to London in William Court's carriage and Heather found it a most enjoyable ride. The countryside along the way was green and lush in June. She had not noticed the same moors when she traveled to her uncle's home two years before, but, now that she went south toward London, she thought it beyond comparison in its beauty.

Mr. Court proved a kind host and very attentive. She was able to talk with him at last about the current events of London society and she laughed gaily to hear his tales of the regency's court. Once she glanced up to find him watching her with an intensity she could not fathom, but he quickly looked away. For a moment she had some slight qualms about going to London with him alone since, after all, he was not a legal guardian but a most distant cousin. The uneasiness soon faded and she mused that he was studying her for what future marriage contract he could arrange.

It was dark when they reached the outskirts of London. The ride had made Heather uncomfortably sore and weary from being bumped around and thrown against the side of the coach every time they hit a sink hole. She was greatly relieved when they arrived at the shop.

Within the place, silks, muslins, lawns, velvets and satins of all colors and textures were stacked high on tables and shelves. There was everything a woman could desire for the making of a stylish gown. Heather was amazed at the vast selection, and in her excitement hurriedly felt one cloth, carefully examined another and failed to notice a man sitting at a desk near the rear of the shop.

William Court laughed as he watched her move about the room. "You'll have more time to examine everything later, my dear, but now you must meet my assistant, Mr. Thomas Hint."

Heather turned and saw a strange little man who she instantly decided was the ugliest creature she had ever seen. Large, liquid eyes bulged from a round face and the nose was a short, flattened thing with flaring nostrils. His tongue continually flicked over thick, scarred lips, reminding her of lizards she had seen on the farm. His grotesque, hunchback figure was clothed in a rich, scarlet silk that was spotted, like his shirt, with food stains. When he smiled at her it was lop-sided, with one whole side of his face compressing into a tight, horrible smirk. She thought he would look better if he didn't try to smile. In fact, she couldn't see why William had him in the shop. She was positive he frightened more customers away than he attracted, and if he attracted anyone they were persons whose minds were deranged.

As if in answer to her questioning thoughts, William

Court spoke. "People are used to Thomas. We have a good trade here because they know we're well skilled in our business. Is that not so, Thomas?"

He was answered with a non-committal grunt.

"Now, my dear," William continued, "I want to show you my apartments upstairs. I believe you will be pleased."

He led her toward the back of the shop, through a doorway hung with draperies and into a small room where a meager window gave off the only light. There was a stairway to one side and it led them to a dim little hallway with a single door leading from it. It was a massive wooden door, ornate compared to the dreariness of the hall. William smiled and opened it for her and Heather caught her breath in surprise at what lay behind it. The apartment was luxuriously furnished with pieces of Hepplewhite and Chippendale. A red velvet settee was grouped with two matching chairs upon a splendid Persian rug. Oil paintings and rich tapestries hung from light colored walls and a chandelier reflected prisms of light on red velvet draperies and their trim of gold braid and tassels. Fragile porcelain figurines were placed upon tables with candelabras of pewter, and toward the rear of the room was a place to dine. Every appointment had been carefully chosen and obviously no cost had been spared.

William opened another door within this room and stepped back to allow Heather to enter. Inside she found a large four-poster bed draped in royal blue velvet. A small commode was convenient to the bedside with a large candelabrum upon it and a bowl of fresh fruit. A silver-handled paring knife had been placed beside it.

"Oh, sir, it is elegant," she breathed.

He took a pinch of snuff and smiled slowly as he watched her move toward a mirror standing near the bed. "I pamper myself with a few luxuries, my dear."

If she had turned at that precise moment, Heather would have been aware of what he had taken care to conceal before. His desire for her was plainly visible in his eyes as they traveled down her slender body. He turned lest she swing round and find the lust within his gaze.

"You must be famished by now, Heather."

He went to a wardrobe and flung open the doors. A vivid and wide assortment of lady's gowns hung within and he searched among them until he found a beige gown of lace sewn with tiny sparkling beads and lined with a clinging flesh colored material. It was a gown of much cost and beauty.

"You may wear this for dinner, my dear," he smiled. "It was made for a young girl your size but she never came back for it. I've often wondered why she failed to, seeing it's one of the loveliest I've ever designed, but I suppose the girl found she couldn't afford it after all." He gazed at her from behind lowered eyelids. "It is her loss but your gain. It is my gift to you. Wear it tonight and you'll please me greatly."

He moved to the door and there turned again to her.

"I've sent Thomas to tell cook to fetch us dinner. It should be here shortly so I beg you not to keep your sweet company from me too long. If there are other articles of clothing you need, the wardrobe is at your disposal."

Heather smiled hesitantly, holding the treasured gown to her as if unable to believe it belonged to her. When William closed the door behind him, she turned slowly to her image in the mirror, still clutching the dress to her.

During the years she had lived with her aunt, Heather had not looked upon her reflection except for glimpsing it in the piece of broken glass and in occasional pools of water. She had almost forgotten the way she looked. She was now as she had seen her mother in her portrait, the very image of her. Yet she was perplexed over why people thought and remembered Brenna as being beautiful. The tall pale blond beauties who visited court and whom she had read about in her girlhood had always seemed to her to be the very essence of loveliness, not small, dark-haired women who looked like herself.

Heather washed the day's grime from her body and found a fresh chemise in the wardrobe. Donning it, she blushed at its indecent display of her body and felt more than a little wicked wearing it. It was of the softest batiste, transparent to the eye, and it completely revealed her body. Its low bodice barely covered her bosom. She was too accustomed to the childish garments of her younger years to be totally at ease in the chemise, yet she could not bear to even think of wearing her own badly frayed one under such a beautiful gown.

She smiled in amusement at herself.

Who will see me? Only my eyes will gaze upon this reckless creation, no one else's.

She laughed at the nonsense of it and gaily set about to do her hair. She twisted, twirled, curled and pinned the glossy black tresses into a fashionable coiffure, pulling it up and away from her face. Instead of a plain coiled hair-do, she chose to catch it into a mass of soft ringlets that cascaded over each other down the back. Concentrating a moment over her artistry, she picked up the paring knife from the table and began to cut little wisps of hair in front of her ears until each had a soft curl dangling in front of it. With a smile of satisfaction, she thought of how her aunt would shriek in rage and call her loathsome names if she could but see her.

Very gently she touched her finger to the knife to test its edge, as she idly thought of her aunt. At once a drop of blood stained the blade. Grimacing and holding her finger to her mouth, she put the instrument down, commenting to herself that she would be careful in the future if she wanted any fruit sliced or peeled.

The beige gown caused as much surprise as the undergarment she wore beneath. Wearing it she no longer looked the young girl but the woman full grown. Indeed, her eighteenth birthday the following month would prove she was. But there was something else about the gown that made her seem strangely different. As the chemise, it barely concealed her bosom, and the lining gave the illusion she was without even that questionable undergarment. She looked the temptress, seductive, without innocence, a woman knowing her way among men instead of a maiden still untouched as she was.

William was waiting for her when she came from the bedroom. He had taken some time with his own appearance, changing his traveling garb for richer, more elegant clothes and curling short wisps of his thinning hair around his fat face, succeeding only in making it appear rounder.

"My dear sweet Heather, your loveliness does make my heart wish for younger years. I have heard tales of such great beauty as yours, but never, never have I seen it with my own eyes."

Heather murmured a gracious comment before her attention slid to the food that had been brought. She sampled the tantalizing aromas that filled the air. The table had been set with crystal, china and silver and a feast lay on the sideboard. There she found roast game bird, wild rice, buttered shrimp, sweet pastries and candied fruits. A light wine was in a decanter conveniently placed at the head of the table.

William, at the moment, filled his eyes with other pleasures as he allowed his appraising gaze to sweep over Heather slowly, no longer attempting to hide his lust. His devouring stare remained momentarily upon the décolletage where the higher curves of her breasts swelled above the gown. His tongue passed over his thick lips as he surveyed those soft curves, impatiently anticipating the taste of that sweet, young flesh.

He held a chair for her near the head of the table and smiled. "Sit here, dear lady, and let me wait upon you."

Heather complied and watched as he filled their plates.

"Cook is a bashful sort," he commented, dipping a

generous portion of rice upon his plate. "She delivers my food promptly at my command then hurries away before I barely catch a glimpse of her. She whisks everything away again with the same silent efficiency and I've hardly known she's come. But as you will soon find out, she's a most excellent *chef de cuisine*."

They began the meal, and Heather was amazed at the amount of food the man consumed. She found herself wondering if he would be able to move when he finished. His bulging jaws continually worked to chew his food and as he devoured the delicious partridge and sweet tarts he licked his greasy fingers and almost incessantly smacked his lips. Several times he gave a loud belch, startling her.

"When you begin at Lady Cabot's, you'll have great opportunities to meet some of the men from the wealthier class of people, and with your beauty it will not take you long to become the most sought after girl that ever entered that establishment."

He laughed, peering glassy-eyed at her over his goblet.

"You are more than kind, sir," she replied politely, though she thought the wine had made him a little daft. Few men visited ladies' schools and those who did were usually well beyond marriageable age and had some business there.

"Yes," he grinned tipsily. "But I expect to be paid well for my efforts."

He looked at Heather hard now, but again she did not notice, watching instead the wine glass he held unsteadily in his hand. He spilled some of the drink down his waistcoat and some dribbled down his chin when he took a deep sip.

"You'll find Lady Cabot's quite a different place than you've ever known before," he slurred. "The madame and I are partners and we take care that only the comeliest maids live behind its doors. We must be very particular, for it's frequented by the very rich and they do have such high standards. But with you I think there's a fortune to be had.''

Heather decided the poor man was too inebriated to know what he was rambling about. She stifled a yawn, feeling the effects of the wine herself, and longed to crawl into bed.

William laughed. ''I fear I've exhausted you with my chatter, my dear. I had hoped you would not be too tired from our journey to permit us a long, friendly chat, but I see our conversation must continue tomorrow.'' He put up a hand when she tried graciously to protest. ''I'll hear no arguments. You must go to bed. As a matter of fact, I'm beginning to feel in need of that favored spot myself. It would please me greatly to know you're reclining upon those soft downy pillows.''

Heather more or less glided to her bedroom, the warmth of the wine relaxing every nerve, every limb. She heard William chuckling to himself as she closed the door behind her, and she leaned against it and laughed too, knowing all was changing in her life. She danced over to the mirror, feeling a little giddy, and bowed low before it.

''Tell me, Lady Cabot, how do you like my attire? If you view this with pleasure, you must see the gowns my aunt gave to me.''

Laughing, she whirled and threw open the doors of the wardrobe to inspect the assortment of gowns within, deciding William wouldn't mind if she feasted her eyes on them. She had always enjoyed beautiful clothes and it had been hateful wearing those old dresses of her aunt. She selected a few gowns to admire further, took them to hold before her in front of the mirror, dreaming a little of owning such fine clothes.

She did not hear the door open behind her, but as it was pushed wide she spun around with a start and saw William standing on the threshold, wearing a dressing gown. Doubt grew rapidly to sweep away her confidence. It dawned on her why he was there and it came as a great

surprise, having associated him with Aunt Fanny and her
rigid views of such matters. She stood staring at him,
stunned, feeling the weight of the trap he had sprung
upon her. She had fallen into it like a lamb for slaughter.
His eyes burned bright in his ruddy face and a repulsive
smile twisted his thick lips. He turned and locked the
door behind him and leisurely held the key to tantalize
her before he dropped it into his pocket. His gaze roamed
over her and he seemed to enjoy the fear he saw in her
face.

"What do you want?" she breathed.

He leered. "I've come to collect my due for taking
you away from that dreary life in the country. You are
such a tempting wench I couldn't resist you. And you
were so trusting it was easy to snatch you from my poor
sister. When I tire of you I shall allow you to join Lady
Cabot's lovely group. You'll not find boredom there. And
in time perhaps I'll even let you wed some rich soul who
fancies you." He came a step closer. "There'll be no
need for you to worry, child. Your husband will be a bit
disappointed when he takes you to his bed, but he'll not
complain too loudly."

He moved forward and Heather backed fearfully
against the table by the bed.

"I plan to have you, my dear," he said smugly. "So
there is no reason why you should fight me. I'm a very
strong man. I do enjoy force if that is what it is to be,
but I prefer willingness."

She shook her head. "No," she choked through her
fright. "No! You'll never have me! Never!"

William laughed in a terrifying way and Heather
braced herself to flee. He was deeply flushed from the
great amount of wine he had consumed and the fire raging through his veins. His raking gaze unclothed her and
she pressed her hand to her bosom as if to ward off his
penetrating gaze. She made to dart past him, but he was
quick despite his fleshy bulk and he caught her round the
waist. He pressed her backward over the table, enfolding

her in a bone crushing grip. His lips, wet and sticky with wine, sank to her throat, and a sick feeling of nausea rose within her. She struggled with him, but her strength was no match for his. As his lips traveled upward she strained her face from him and tried to kick out, but his weight increased, pinning her legs against the table. She was held in an iron grip that left her breathless, and she wondered if her ribs could stand the pressure without cracking. In a panic she remembered the candelabrum on the table behind her and reached for it to protect herself with. She almost had it within her grasp but she was too hasty and it fell to the floor. Then her hand brushed the knife and she clutched at it in desperation.

William was intent on spreading his hot, moist kisses over her throat and bosom, paying little heed to what she did until he felt something sharp press against his side. Glancing down he saw the knife and with a startled oath snatched at her arm. She winced in pain as his fingers closed cruelly about her wrist, yet she held on in blind desperation. His anger soared that this small slip of a girl should dare threaten his body. Heather fought back with all the strength she could muster. His obesity forced her backward until it felt as if her back would break. Her hand grew numb and she knew she must soon yield the blade to him. Pressing his weight against her, William freed his other hand and, reaching across, twisted the small knife from her. Fearing the worst, Heather ceased her struggle and fell to the floor at his feet; deprived of her support, less than agile William Court staggered forward and fell headlong upon the polished planks. He gave a growl with the impact. Heather had risen and stood poised to flee when William slowly rolled over. The small hilt of the fruit knife protruded from a slowly blooming spot of red on the shoulder of his gown.

"Pull . . . it out . . . ." he gasped.

She bent and put a cautious hand to the knife but shuddered and recoiled from him, twisting her hands against her mouth in blinding fear.

"Please," he croaked. "Help me."

She sank her teeth into her hand in panic and looked wildly about the room. He groaned, louder now; confusion shook her every fiber and fear and hatred raged within her body. If he were dying . . .

"Heather, help me. . . ."

His voice trailed off and his chin quivered as if with the effort of drawing another breath.

From some inner source, strength welled forth and calm returned. She leaned forward and drawing a ragged breath, took the knife with greater determination. Now she braced her other hand against his chest and pulled. The blade resisted a moment then slowly came out with a grating feel to it. Blood welled forth and with a gasp William fell back unconscious. Heather snatched a towel from the table, opened his robe and pressed it to the wound. Absently she laid her hand upon his chest and could detect no movement. Now she searched for some sign of life in earnest. Holding her hand beneath his nostrils she could feel no breath, and laying her ear to him she could hear no beat of his heart. Her own began pounding in her ears. She felt panic rise again and now could find no reason nor strength to battle it.

"Dear Lord, what have I done?" she murmured.

"I must get help!" The thought flared across her mind. But who would believe her, a stranger in this city now? Newgate was crowded with women who claimed men had tried to assault them—and the block got its share too. They'd not believe it was just an accident! In her mind she held a picture of a stern judge in a long wig sneering down from his high bench, and then the face beneath the white hair became that of Aunt Fanny, sternly pronouncing sentence.

". . . and at sunrise the next day following shall be taken to Newgate Square and there . . ."

Her mind would go no further, yet the echo of the stentorian voice fanned the flames of terror until they seared her very soul. Her body shook and had she not been kneeling she would have fallen. Her head slumped and for a long time she sat not even thinking, then at last she looked up and a thought came to her.

"I must get away from here."

It was as simple as that. She must escape. She musn't be here when they found William's body. She must flee.

Still gripped in panic, she forced herself to search his pockets for the key. She trembled, but it had to be done. Her own fear now fed her strength.

She wrapped her own clothes in a scarf she found and clutching it to her, hurried to the door. She paused there for a moment without opening it, picturing the scene behind her. Again fear gripped her. She flung open the door and began to run as fast as her legs could carry her, through the parlor, the hall doorway, down the stairs, and toward the curtained doorway to the shop. As she put out her hand to fling open the draperies her panic increased. Someone was there behind the curtain. Her already fast pace was quickened by sheer terror. Someone was after her. She ran swiftly, not daring to turn, her heart pounding hard in her bosom.

She tore down the street, fearful of glancing back. She had no idea where she was going. Perhaps if she lost herself she could lose whoever was behind her. But why couldn't she hear anyone running after her? Was her own heart beating so loudly in her ears that she could hear nothing else?

Through the streets of London she raced, past shops of business, past great houses that loomed large and menacing in the darkness, past houses of lesser importance. She did not pay any attention to the people who stopped and stared after her.

Soon she was exhausted, and in spite of her fear she stopped to lean against a rough-hewn stone wall. Her lungs burned with the effort of each breath she sobbed. Gradually she became aware of the tang of salt in her nostrils and the fetid smell of the waterfront. She raised her head and opened her eyes. Dense fog lay close upon the cobblestone street and the darkness pressed in until she could hardly breathe. A torch burned on a distant corner and she sought its light and could not bring herself to leave the small circle and go again into the dense black-grey night that surrounded her. Had she the courage, she knew not which way to flee. There was no hint of direction. She could hear the slow lap of water against the pier and the measured creaking of masts and an occasional muffled voice, but the sounds came to her from all around and she could see no spark of light anywhere.

"There she be, by Jove! That's the one! That's her! Come on, George. Let's get her."

Heather started and whirled about and saw what appeared to be two seamen coming toward her. They knew about her and were coming for her. They were the ones who had been following her. For some reason she had thought it was Mr. Hint. Her legs could not move. She could not flee. She had to wait there for them to take her.

"Hello, miss," the older one said and smiled at his companion. " 'Tis sure the cap'n will like 'er, eh Dickie?"

The other one passed his tongue over his lips and lowered his gaze to Heather's bosom. "Aye. This one will suit him fine."

Heather trembled under the scrutiny of the men, but from the present time on she knew she would have no liberties. The only thing left her was to be brave.

"Where are you taking me?" she managed.

Dickie laughed and punched the other in the ribs. "Kind o' receptive, ain't she? He'll like her all right. Makes me wish I was him an' could afford such."

"Just a little ways, miss," the older one replied. "On board the merchant ship, *Fleetwood*. Come on."

She followed the man and the younger fell in behind, giving her no chance to escape. She wondered why they must take her on board a ship. There must be a portreeve there. It didn't matter. Her life was nothing now. Meekly she climbed the gangplank after the fellow and received his hand as he helped her down from it. He led the way across the deck to a door which he opened and she was ushered through a short companionway and after a light knock, through the door at its end.

As they entered the captain's cabin, a man rose from the desk where he had been sitting and had it not been for her bruised state of mind, Heather would have noticed his tall, muscular build and piercing green eyes. Fawn colored breeches were fitted snug about his narrow hips and a white ruffled shirt, opened to the waist, revealed a chest wide and firmly muscled beneath a mat of crisp black hair. He had the look of a pirate about him, or even Satan himself, with his dark, curly hair and long sideburns that accentuated the lean, handsome features of his face. His nose was thin and straight except for a slight hook in its profile just below the bridge. His hair was raven black and his skin darkly tanned. White teeth flashed in contrast as he smiled and came forward, sweeping her with a bold gaze from top to toe.

"Aye, you've done a handsome night's work with this one, George. You must have searched hard and wide for her."

"Nay, cap'n," the old man returned. "We found her walking the streets of the waterfront. She came most willingly, cap'n."

The man nodded and walked slowly, deliberately, completely around Heather as she stood rooted to the floor, not touching her with anything but those emerald eyes and they were enough, boldly, rudely evaluating every angle of her visible assets. A coldness grew deep inside her and she clutched her small bundle to her bosom. She felt naked in the thin gown and wished for some sack of heavy black that would cover her from neck to wrist to toe. He paused before her for a moment, smiling, but her eyes would not meet his. She kept them cast downward and stood humbly awaiting some indication of her fate. Behind her the two men grinned, extremely pleased with themselves.

The tall man moved aside with them and the fellow, George, spoke in a low voice. Heather's eyes moved about the cabin but saw nothing. Outwardly she appeared calm, but the emotional strains raging within her further sapped her strength. She was exhausted, bone tired, confused. She found it difficult to reconcile a magistrate of the law on board a ship, but knowing little of the processes of justice, reasoned that she was probably to be sent to some penal colony, for in her own mind she was guilty of murder.

"Oh God," she thought, "that I should be raised from a sty by the temptation of a life of ease and for my sin plunged into a prison. I killed a man and I've been caught and I must now accept whatever fate decrees for me."

Her mind stopped and held and was trapped by these final facts. She was guilty. She was caught. Justice had done with her and she had no further word. She did not hear the door close behind her as the seamen left, but words from the man who stood before her roused her from her thoughts. He laughed gently and made a sweeping bow.

"Welcome back, m'lady, and I repeat, what is your name."

"Heather," she murmured softly. "Heather Simmons, sir."

"Ah," he sighed. "A small, tempting flower from the moors. It's a most lovely and fitting name, m'lady. Brandon Birmingham is my name. Most of my friends call me Bran. Have you dined this evening?"

She made a small nod.

"Then perhaps some wine—a very fine Madeira," he commented, lifting one of several decanters from a small table.

She shook her head slowly, dropping her gaze to the floor. He laughed softly and came forward to stand close before her. He took the bundle she clutched and tossed it in a nearby chair as he stared down at her, dazzled by her youthful beauty and the gown that seemed only a sparkling veil over her body. Her ivory skin glowed softly in the candlelight, and by the golden flames he saw before him a small woman, gracefully slender with breasts full and round, generously and temptingly swelling above her gown. They rose and fell slowly with her breath.

He moved closer and in a rapid movement slipped his arm about her narrow waist, nearly lifting her from the floor, and then covered her mouth with his, engulfing Heather in a heady scent, not unlike that of a brandy her father had been fond of. She was too surprised to resist and hung limp in his embrace. She saw herself as if from outside her body and felt with mild amusement his tongue parting her lips and thrusting within. From a low level of consciousness there grew a vague feeling of pleasure and, had the circumstances been different, she might have enjoyed the hard, masculine feel of his body against hers. He stepped back, still smiling, but with a new fire kindled in his eyes. As he took his hands from her she gasped in stunned surprise for her gown fell in a heap about her ankles. She stared at him for a split second before she hurriedly bent to retrieve the garment, but those hands caught her shoulders and straightened her and she was again enfolded in his arms. This time she fought, for with sudden clarity it dawned on her just what he had in mind. She realized her disadvantage as her exhausted body struggled weakly against him. If William Court's grip had been of iron, this man's entire being was of finely-tempered steel. She could not free herself and her hands pushed in vain against his chest. Her struggles pulled his shirt loose and then his furred chest lay bare against her with only the thin film of the chemise between them. She was left breathless each time his mouth took hers and passionate kisses seemed to cover her face and bosom. She felt his hands go up her back and with an easy tug he separated the shift and snatched it from her. Her naked breasts were crushed against his chest and in fearful panic she pushed hard and for a moment was free of him. He gave a deep throaty laugh and used the interlude to rid himself of boots and shirt and as he shed his breeches he grinned.

"A game well played, m'lady, but have no doubts as to the winner."

His eyes burned with passion's fire as he stood enjoying her now unbridled charms, far lovelier than he had imagined or even hoped, and she stared in horror at her first sight of a naked man. She stood fixed to the floor until he stepped forward and with a frightened squeak she turned to flee but found her arm seized in a grip that was gentle yet as unyielding as a band of steel. She ducked under his arm and sank her teeth into his wrist. He grunted in pain and she jerked away, but in her haste she stumbled and fell full length into his bunk. Almost immediately he was on top of her, pinning down her writhing body, and it seemed that every move she made only abetted his intent. Her hair came loose and seemed to stifle her in its mass.

"No!" she gasped. "Leave me alone! Let me be!"

He chuckled and murmured against her throat. "Oh no, my bloodthirsty little wench. Oh no, not now."

Then he moved upward and she was relieved of his heavy weight, but only briefly. She felt his hardness searching, probing between her thighs, then finding and entering that first tiny bit. In her panic to escape she surged upward. A half gasp, half shriek escaped her and a burning pain seemed to spread through her loins. Brandon started back in astonishment and stared down at her. She lay limp against the pillows, rolling her head back and forth upon them. He touched her cheek tenderly and murmured something low and inaudible, but she had her eyes closed and wouldn't look at him. He moved against her gently, kissing her hair and brow and caressing her body with his hands. She lay unresponsive, yet his long starved passions grew and soon he thrust deep within her, no longer able to contain himself. It seemed with each movement now she would be split asunder and tears came to her eyes.

The storm at its end, a long quiet moment slipped past as he relaxed against her, once more gentle. But when he finally withdrew, she turned to the wall and lay softly sobbing with the corner of the blanket pulled over her head and her now used body left bare to his gaze.

Brandon Birmingham rose in bewilderment and for a moment stared at the flecks of blood that stained the sheet on his bunk. His eyes coursed slowly over Heather's figure, now turned away from him. He could not but admire the well turned hips and graceful thighs that had, a moment past, been his. He almost reached out to caress the gently curving back, but his mind was confused by the turn of events—her calm, reserved acceptance of the situation when she first entered the cabin, her light and playful resistance, and then the sporadic, inexperienced assistance she had given him in bed and now this endless weeping and the blood on the sheet. Was she some girl compelled to take up this occupation by poverty? Her clothes and manner did not bear this out, yet her hands, though slender and white, were not soft as a lady of leisure's might be.

He shook his head and shrugged into his robe and went to pour himself a healthy glass of brandy. He took a long drink and stared pensively out the windows from which he had viewed much of the world. He was a foreigner to this land which his parents had once called home. It had ceased to be theirs shortly after their marriage when his father, an aristocrat but an adventurer at heart, had looked upon America with interest. Now they were both ten years dead, his mother of a swamp fever, his father only a few months later of a broken neck suffered when thrown from one of those wild horses he loved so much. They left behind them two sons and a goodly fortune— a plantation home and land to the eldest, being himself, and to their younger, Jeff, a share of the money and a prosperous warehouse in Charleston, a city which they

had loved and called home as he did now. Born to these
parents, a father who had been many times stubborn and
more than willful, and a mother whose quiet, serene gen-
tility had been the backbone of the family, he, Brandon
Birmingham, had known a rigorous, adventurous life. His
schooling had always come first but as a young lad, and
at his father's insistence, he had hired on as cabin boy
to a salty old sea captain. He had learned the ways of the
sea, ships, and the world, enabling him to take a com
manding position in that occupation when he had found
it useful. But not all his time had been spent sailing the
seas. Before that, he had been taught the workings of the
plantation, from soil to market, and had never ceased this
pleasant toil through his years of growing up.

That was his main interest now, at the age of five and
thirty—to settle down upon that land for good and enjoy
the everyday world of it. Before leaving Charleston he
had made a decision that this would be his last voyage.
With France as unsettled as she was, it might prove un-
profitable to continue. So he would take upon himself the
responsibilities of a plantation and begin raising a family
He would be content—he hoped.

He smiled thoughtfully to himself. Strange how fondness for a land could make a man do things which didn't
sit well within his mind. He was marrying Louisa Wells,
although he didn't love her and knew her morals were
not those of a genuine lady, for the simple reason he
wanted back the land she possessed that had once belonged to the Birmingham family. His father had been
granted the land that now made up the Wells and Birmingham estates from King George, and to begin building his plantation he had sold a small portion to that
family. Brandon's father had severed ties with Britain
years before the war, and because of his service as an
officer in that struggle against the crown had been able
to keep his estates. Now, since Louisa had been left alone
by the death of her parents a few years back, her land
was being neglected and misused. Louisa was badly in

debt. She had spent the fortune her father had left her and had sold all but a few of her slaves to keep up her high standard of living which had become only a front now. The merchants in Charleston had long ago refused her credit. So she was quite pleased with herself at having caught one of the city's richest, most eligible bachelors. But she had caught him, knowing the land was bait. Several times he had attempted to relieve her of it for a goodly sum, which she had needed badly, but she had refused and played her woman's part to the hilt. She acted the virgin when she enticed him to her bed, but he was not that kind of fool, and there was much gossip about this woman he and his younger brother had grown up with. Her experience in bed did prove entertaining, however, and he was not too displeased.

A frown wrinkled his brow. It seemed odd to come from a family where jealousy and possessiveness for one's mate were but a matter of fact and he, looking so much like the father who had possessed those traits, was not even jealous of the men who had shared his fiancée's bed. Was he too cold and unfeeling to love or be possessive about the woman he was to wed? It wasn't even comforting to know that he cared more for her than he had for any woman in his lifetime. But it wasn't love. If he had ever suffered the slightest twinge of jealousy when she looked at another man, he would feel different now, at least a little more hopeful of learning to love her. But since he had known her all of her life, some thirty-two years of it, he was skeptical of any radical changes after their marriage.

Jeff had declared him insane at the news of their engagement. Well, perhaps he was, but he had a mind of his own and if he hadn't inherited his father's jealous moods, he had inherited his stubbornness. His father's determination and willful disposition had always been his. Even when his parents had died, leaving him with a prosperous plantation and the wealth to back it, he had not sat back and reaped the harvest. Instead, he had asked

Jeff to take charge of the plantation and had bought this merchant ship and begun to sail the seas, bringing even more wealth to himself and his brother.

He looked across to his bunk, then moved closer to stand beside it. The sobbing had finally ceased and sleep had come in its stead, but it was not an untroubled slumber. It reminded him more of an exhausted one. He reached down and gently covered Heather's lovely body and pushed back the blanket from her head.

The last thing he had expected to walk through his cabin door this night was a virgin. Knowing they were a troublesome lot, he had made it a habit throughout his life to avoid them, playing his leisure time upon those well versed creatures of gay, carefree living, in and out of bawdy houses, expensive and otherwise. This night, his first night in port after a long voyage across the ocean, he had freed his men to seek their pleasures, keeping only his manservant, George, and Dickie on board. But the urge had already been strong within him and he had bade George find him some lively vixen for the night, with emphasis upon cleanliness and comeliness. No, he had not expected a virgin, and one so lovely, never. It was strange to find her here. Young innocents like her usually had marriage in mind, trying coyly to entice a man into that trap with their charms. How else had he managed so successfully to remain single through his years of manhood had he not known their ways and avoided them? But now when his bachelorhood was about to end and a marriage to begin to a woman well known by other men, he had had this fresh young thing for his pleasure and her reasons were still a mystery.

He slowly shook his head, then leaving his robe on a chair, doused the candles and stretched out beside her. The last thing he thought of before he dozed off was the gentle fragrance of her perfume and the warmth of her close beside him.

*   *   *

The first faint streaks of dawn had breeched the eastern sky when Heather roused and then came fully awake, aware of her surroundings. She stirred and sought to move her head but found her hair caught beneath Brandon's arm where it was bent under his dark head. His other arm was flung across her chest and his knee rode casually between hers. Cautiously she tried to ease herself from beneath his weight but succeeded only in awakening him. Before he was fully roused, she lay back and fearfully closed her eyes and breathed deeply as if in slumber.

Brandon opened his eyes and quietly studied the face beside his own, taking great pleasure in its fine beauty. Long, sooty black lashes lay on skin, fair and flawless, and fragile eyelids hid from his view eyes that were clear and deep and the color of sapphires. He remembered them well. They had a most captivating slant, as did the soft brows that were like straight, upward slashes across her face. Her mouth was gently curved, pink and temptingly soft, her nose straight and delicately boned. Louisa would turn green with envy if the two ever chanced to meet, which was highly improbable. He smiled at the thought. His fiancée was quite proud of her own good looks and would not like to take second place to this slight nymph. Some people had even claimed Louisa as the most beautiful woman in Charleston, though there were many beauties there. He hadn't thought of it much, but he supposed it could be true. Louisa's golden hair and warm brown eyes were quite easy to look upon and her tall, buxom figure pleasant to ride. Still, this Heather here, in her soft and delicate beauty, would leave no doubt in the city as to who was the fairest.

He leaned closer to kiss her ear and lightly nibble at its lobe. At his touch and before Heather could think, her eyes flew open.

"Good morning, love," he whispered softly and rose above her to kiss her lips.

She lay perfectly still, fearing any movement might stir

his passions. He needed no stirring. The fires in his loins were already burning high and growing hotter with each passing moment. His kisses passed from her lips, over her eyes, down her throat and paused at her shoulder where his teeth made tiny nibbles, sending shivers down her spine. She stared horrified as he pressed his bearded mouth to the pink crest of her breast and lightly teased it with his tongue.

"Don't!" she gasped. "Don't do that!"

He raised his heated gaze, smiling. "You'll have to get used to my caresses, *ma petite.*"

She withdrew from those amused eyes and fought to turn away, pleading with him. "No. Please, no. Not again. Don't hurt me again. Just let me go."

"I won't hurt you this time, sweet," he breathed against her ear, pressing soft kisses to it.

The weight of his body held her on her back in the bunk and now Heather began to fight in earnest. She held her knees tightly together while she sought to scratch or claw him anywhere she could, but always a hand or elbow was there to stem her effort. He laughed as if enjoying her struggles.

"You show considerably more spirit this morning, m'lady."

Then her arms were slowly drawn upward on either side of her head and held there easily in one of his hands. His other hand cupped a breast and he played with it to his pleasure while she twisted and fought against his overpowering strength. His knee slowly forced open her thighs and spread them and again she felt his manhood deep within her.

There were no tears this time, but a hatred and a fear began to build apace in her mind. When he rolled from her she scurried from him and cowered in the corner of the bunk, her eyes wide and filled with the hurt and fear of a wounded fawn. He watched her with a puzzled frown furrowing his brow and sat up close beside her. He reached out to caress her cheek, feeling the need to comfort her, but she cringed from his hand as if it were a red hot iron and he realized with some surprise that it was he who frightened her. His frown deepened and his fingers slid through her hair, gently combing the silken strands that seemed now only a wild mass of soft tangles.

"You've aroused my curiosity, Heather," he murmured gently. "You could have gotten a king's ransom for what you lost to me a few hours ago and yet you were wandering the streets like any ordinary strumpet and, so I hear, you came willingly, without even trying to bargain for your worth, nor did you last night even hint that you were still intact, a virgin, or try to set a price with me. The gown you wore is costly, valued at more than some creatures of the streets might make in a year, though you, I guarantee, are of a different status entirely—so different I can't even imagine why you peddled your virginity as you did, taking the chance that you might have been raped and lost it for nothing."

Heather stared at him speechless, unable to fully comprehend the impact of his words.

"You seem gently born and not the type to be wandering the streets or engaging in this profession. Your beauty is uncommon, few women have such, and you wear expensive clothes, and yet," he murmured, taking one of her hands into his and turning it over, "your hands show the effects of toil." He lightly ran a finger over her palm then pressed a kiss into it. Still gazing at it, he spoke again softly. "When you arrived last night you were calm and reserved, but just a moment ago you fought me tooth and nail and would not permit me to be gentle."

As he spoke her mind flew. He was not the law? Good God, what price had she paid for her fear and panic? It would have been better if she had stayed and faced the regency's men than to be here, deflowered and shamed to her very bone, or better yet to have remained where she was than to have sought the city at all.

"But you need have no fear, Heather. I'll provide well

for you and you'll live in comfort. I just arrived yesterday from the Carolinas and I'll be a long time in port. You'll stay with me while I'm here. I'll see that you're established in a house of your own before I . . ."

He was interrupted by a shriek of high, shrill, hysterical laughter, as Heather yielded to the shock of the situation. It dwindled gradually into sobs as tears streamed down her face. Her head dropped forward and her hair tumbled over her shoulders to mask her body. Tears fell on her hands folded in her lap as sobs jerked her tiny frame. Finally she threw her head back and looked at him with reddened eyes.

"I wasn't peddling my wares in the streets," she choked. "I was simply lost and couldn't find my way."

He stared at her a long moment in stunned silence before he frowned in confusion. "But you came with my men."

She shook her head in agony. He didn't know. He didn't know about her at all. He was just a seaman from a foreign country. She choked on her tears, vowing he must never know of her greater sin.

"I thought they were sent after me. I became separated from my cousin and lost my way. I thought your men were from my cousin's."

Her head fell back against the wall and tears made wet paths down her face and plunged to her naked bosom which quivered with her silent crying. He watched those pale round breasts and his frown deepened as he wondered what repercussions there would be for this deed. Perhaps she was kin to some high official. He could almost feel the cold steel of the ax biting into his neck. He rose from the bed and stood by its edge, his back turned to her.

"Who are your parents?" he asked hoarsely. "Someone as beautiful and well bred as you must have many friends at court or come from a very influential family."

Her head rolled wearily back and forth against the

wall. "My parents are dead and I've never been to court."

He walked to her gown where it lay on the floor. He picked it up and turned to her holding it. "You must have wealth. This gown cost no few pence."

She looked at him and laughed, a bit amused. "I'm without a farthing, sir. My cousin gave me the gown. I work for my mere existence."

He looked down at the sparkling beads on the gown. "Won't this cousin be worried about you and be out trying to find you?"

Heather grew silent as her eyes dropped to her nakedness. "No," she murmured. "I doubt that now. My cousin isn't one to worry long over the matter."

Brandon smiled in relief and draped the gown over the back of a chair. He walked to the washstand where he began to wash. He turned a few moments later to watch the girl rise from his bunk, and his eyes moved over her body slowly, taking in every detail of her alluring curves. She felt his gaze and clutched her arms before her to shield her womanhood from him, and he laughed softly and turned back to the mirror and prepared to shave while she hurriedly sought her old chemise from her bundle.

"There's no reason then, Heather, why you can't stay with me and be my mistress. I'll find you a house in town where you may live in comfort and where I may take my leisure. I'll furnish you with a goodly sum so you will not have to seek out other men nor would I allow you to do that. There'll be times in the future when I'll want to return and will need feminine companionship while I'm here. I'd like to think that matter is taken care of."

For a moment Heather was almost overcome by her hatred of the man. The emotion was beyond anything she had ever felt for anyone before. His casual attitude toward her and the whole affair infuriated her so much she wanted to shriek in rage and fling herself upon him and claw his handsome face to ribbons. But she thought better of it as she saw, now that he had his back to her and the door, her chance to escape. Wearing nothing more than her shift, she bit into her lip to keep it from quivering and eased her gown from the chair. She clutched her bundle to her. She stepped toward the door cautiously, her heart in her throat, and took another step.

"Heather!" he said sharply, startling her and sending all hopes of escape fleeing. She turned fearfully and found his fierce green eyes upon her as he casually stropped his razor, and she knew terror—horrible, soul-shaking terror.

"Do you think I'm going to let you sneak away from me? You're too unique to find a replacement for and I have no intentions of letting you slip through my fingers."

The deadly calm in his deep voice was more frightening than Aunt Fanny's violent shrieks had ever been. She trembled before him as the color drained from her face. He picked up the strop and the pounding of her heart almost drowned out the noise the leather made as he sharpened his razor. Her eyes grew round and she cringed fearfully away. A small, satanic smile curved his lips and he snapped his fingers and pointed to the bunk.

"Now get back in that."

She was well conditioned to taking orders and she did so now, terrified of what he might do if she didn't. Still clutching her bundle and gown, she sat down on the bunk and stared up at him as if she expected to be flogged. He dropped the strop on the table and wiping his face on a towel, came to the bunk and stood for a moment looking down at her. Then he threw the towel in a chair and took the things from her. He pointed to her shift.

"Get that off."

Heather swallowed hard. Her eyes flew down his body and widened even more. She was fast losing her innocence.

"Please—" she gasped.

"I'm not a patient man, Heather," he said and his voice was very menacing.

Her fingers shook as she untied the ribbons and unfastened the tiny buttons between her breasts. She caught the hem and raised it over her head. Her eyes lifted shamefully to his as she felt his fiery gaze upon her body.

"Now lie down," he directed.

She slid down into the bunk and her whole being quaked with fear of him and of what was to come. She tried to cover herself with her hands, feeling the awful humiliation of being naked and a coward.

"Don't," he said and slid in beside her and drew her quaking limbs to his.

"Please," she whimpered. "Aren't you satisfied that you've taken the one thing that was only mine to give. Must you keep torturing me again and again?"

"You might as well accept your lot as a paramour, my sweet, and become aware of the finer arts of the profession. The first thing I'm going to show you is that it doesn't necessarily have to be painful. You fought me twice now and the last time caused your own misery. This time you will relax and let me do as I want without a struggle and though you may not enjoy it yet, you'll see what I say is true."

"No! No!" she cried, trying to struggle free, but he clamped his hand tightly on her waist.

"Be still."

Again he commanded, again she obeyed. She hated him but her fear was greater by far. She trembled violently with it.

"Is this the way you treat your wife?" she asked miserably.

He smiled and bent over her lips. "I'm not married, sweet."

She had no more to say when his kiss ended but lay tense and waiting. He made no move to mount her. Instead he played gently with her, caressing, softly titillating, cupping her breasts and pressing kisses over her body.

"Relax," he murmured against her throat. "Just lie still and don't fight me. Later you can learn what pleases a man, but for now just lie still."

Her mind tumbled over itself in its frenzy and no words sought her tongue. As she lay and submitted to his pawing, her life passed before her as if she were dying, and she wondered what great evil she had done that the past years should have abused her so cruelly. Yet even Aunt Fanny's endless heckling would be better than having to lie here under this man's hands while he pleasured himself with her. Trapped! Caught! Like a bird in a snare and now, plump and roasted, she must wait on the platter while he whetted his knife for the carving. And when the feast was done, what then? The same table? The same dinner? Again and again? Surely no simple-minded fowl ever suffered its fate but once.

Her thighs were parted and she could not suppress a gasp as he drove home.

"Easy, sweet," he breathed.

She closed her eyes tightly and stilled her careening fears. There was nothing to do now but let him have his way. When he lay finished above her, he whispered against her hair.

"Any more bruises, m'lady?"

She kept her eyes shut and turned her head aside. She loathed the very thought of him. He moved against her, urging her answer.

"Did I hurt you this time?"

"No," she choked out.

He laughed softly and freeing her from his embrace, sat on the berth beside her and drew the sheet over her.

"You don't appear to be a cold wench, *ma petite*," he said, running his hand over the curve of her thigh and waist, "only for the moment a reluctant one. Soon you'll learn to enjoy it. For now just learn to accept it."

"Never!" she half sobbed. "I hate you! I loathe you! I despise you! Not in a million years!"

"You'll change your mind," he laughed. He stood up. "Someday you'll be begging for it."

She turned in a huff, presenting her back to him and jerked the sheet over her shoulder. He chuckled again and reaching down, caressed her buttock.

"Just wait, Heather, and we'll see which one of us is right."

Anger shook her. He was so confident of himself, of her, of the future. He had it all neatly planned. And what did she have to say in the matter? All she could do was beg for mercy and that would fall on deaf ears. But given the opportunity she would escape.

She smiled to herself, thinking of that, and her spirits rose if only slightly. Her chance would come sooner or later and she would not hesitate to take it. The mere thought of escape soothed her frayed nerves and she relaxed into the pillows, listening to Brandon move about the cabin behind her. Her eyelids grew heavy and sleep pushed aside even those more requitable thoughts.

When Heather woke, she opened her eyes without moving. The room was still and quiet and she thought herself alone at last, but when she rolled on her back she saw Brandon at his desk with quill in hand, reading over his ledgers. He was dressed and seemed for the moment to have forgotten her, engrossed in his work as he was. She might have been some stick of furniture for as much attention as he paid her. She watched him quietly. There was no denying that he was handsome, physically magnificent. She might have even dreamed once of such a man. But never in those innocent dreams of romance did she imagine that her love would fly to her on the wings of violence, or that she would be kept against her will to fulfill base desires.

"Are you feeling better?" he asked, looking up to find her eyes on him. He smiled and rose from the desk. "I hope you're hungry. I waited to breakfast with you.''

She sat up in the corner of the bed, clutching the sheet over her bosom, and her hair fell in soft disarray over her shoulders.

"I want to get dressed," she murmured, watching him cautiously as he came forward to lean against a timber above the bunk.

He smiled warmly. "If you must, my love." His eyes went over her. "Do you want any help?"

Heather almost climbed the wall to escape from him. "Don't you touch me!" she cried.

"Ah-h, I see my little kitten has her claws bared." He looked deep into her eyes. "Shall I make you purr, my sweet?"

"I'll scream," she whimpered. "So help me I will."

His white teeth flashed as he reached out and took her by the wrists and pulled her to him. His eyes held hers prisoner.

"Do you think that would do you any good?" he asked, as if amused. "Unless called for, my men stay away from this cabin when I'm entertaining. Besides, my dear, I can stop your screams quite easily with my kisses."

She shrank from him and a shudder of revulsion passed through her as his gaze went down her body, but he only laughed. Catching her around the waist, he swung her to her feet.

"You're very tempting, m'lady, but it isn't time for your second lesson yet. My servant is waiting to serve us our meal."

He left her to open a locker by the bed, and drew out a man's dressing gown which he handed to her.

"It's a trifle large, but it's the best I can offer at the moment." He smiled. "I'll take you this afternoon to purchase some clothes. If you're like most other women that should perk you up."

She quickly wrapped the robe around her and found herself lost in it. There was no doubt it was his and it was far too big for her. The sleeves trailed below her hands and the bottom dragged the floor, so she had to gather in a good foot of it to walk.

A smile played lightly about Brandon's lips and his eyes gleamed as he observed her. He helped her fold back the sleeves.

"If it's possible to be jealous of a simple garment, m'lady, then I am of this one, and if it had life I'd warrant it would be aquiver now with its good fortune."

She glanced away nervously. "May I be allowed privacy to wash, sir?" She clutched the robe tightly at her throat and whispered, "Please."

He made a sweeping bow and grinned. "Your slightest wish is my command, m'lady. There are matters concerning the cargo that need my attention anyway so you may have some time."

She eyed him covertly as he walked to the door and before he opened it he glanced back at her and grinned quite devilishly, then made his exit with a laugh.

Heather released a small sigh of relief and went to the washstand where she poured water in the bowl. She scrubbed every inch of her body until her skin glowed a healthy pink. She longed for a steaming tub bath so that she could soak in it and remove from her body every trace and remembrance of him, of the fine mist of sweat that had moistened his body and then hers, the feel of his hands upon her, the memory of his smothering kisses. Everything. Every tiniest bit of evidence that she had been his.

The cool water helped a little to revive her downtrodden spirits, and she donned her shabby shift and pink gown, feeling a trifle better. She raked her fingers through her hair, combing it as best she could in that manner, then returned his robe to the locker, noting as she did so the well chosen and obviously costly clothes within. It was irritating to think that she couldn't secretly laugh at his choice of apparel.

Her nerves stretched taut with her toilette complete,

and needing some task to occupy her thoughts, she began putting some order to the cabin, which was littered with clothing. His were thrown over the back of a chair, her beige gown in another. The torn chemise was still where he had dropped it after ripping it from her. She picked it up and found it irreparable.

His hands destroy well, she mused.

With renewed anger she marched to the bunk and began smoothing the sheets until her eyes fell on the blood that stained them, and she realized it was her blood, her proof of virginity. In a high rage, she jerked the sheets from the bed and threw them to the floor.

Her eyes bright and her cheeks flushed, she whirled around at a soft laugh from behind her and faced Brandon who stood in the open doorway. He had returned silently and without her knowing. His eyes dropped from her angry face to the sheets behind her, then he raised his eyes again as he closed the door and leaned against it. He smiled at her mockingly, and with an infuriated groan, Heather turned her back. She heard him laugh. He was laughing at her and she hated him. He was detestable.

He came up close behind her, slipped his arms about her waist and drew her back against him.

"Do you think you could have remained chaste for long with the face and body you have, my sweet?" he murmured against her hair. "You were meant for love, and I am not saddened because I snatched you before other men tried you, nor do I feel guilty over the pleasure you've given me. Pray do not blame me for being infatuated with your beauty and wanting you for my own. It would be a task for any man not to. You see, in truth, m'lady, I am your prisoner, caught in your spell."

She trembled as his searing lips pressed against her throat and beneath her breasts her heart thumped wildly.

"Are you void of a conscience?" she choked. "Doesn't it matter that I do not wish to be here? I am not one of your strumpets, nor do I have any desire to be."

"You do not wish it now, my love, but later you will. If I allowed you to go now I'd never see you again because of what has passed between us. If we had met differently, I could have courted you gently and wooed you into my bed with tender words. But here we started backwards and frightened you and as a bird flees from its captor, so would you fly from me. To keep you I must show you that it is not so bad being my mistress. You'll have everything your heart desires."

"I have heard tales of Yankees," she said snidely, "but I never guessed that all those aspersions could be true until I met you."

He threw back his head and laughed heartily. "Spoken like a true Englishwoman, m'lady."

She jerked angrily away and faced him. "Just tell me why you want me?" she demanded. She threw her arms wide. "Heaven above, tell me why I must suffer your affections when you can find many a maid more willing than I anywhere you should happen to look! Wouldn't your romps in bed be more entertaining with a woman who appreciates your advances than with one who loathes the very sight of you?"

He chuckled at her anger. "You have a sharp tongue, m'lady. You wound me to the quick. But the reasons are quite simple. Take a look at yourself and you'll see a very excellent one. You're like a breath of fresh spring air after a night in an overcrowded tavern."

He took a seat at his desk, relaxing in the chair as he regarded her.

"I find you very desirable, Heather, truly worth having—a jewel among pebbles. The challenge of winning you excites me. I've never been denied before."

"You should have been," she spat vindictively. "Perhaps then you would have learned to be a gentleman."

His eyes sparkled. "I've found with you, sweet, that when I want you badly enough I can overlook being a gentleman."

She turned her back on him in frustration. There was

no talking to the pompous, arrogant scoundrel. He made his own rules to fit his own games. She couldn't think of enough names to do justice to the way she felt about him. All she knew was that she'd leave him and his miserable cabin if it were the last thing she ever did.

A few moments later George entered the cabin, carrying a large tray laden with their morning meal. The servant smiled rather sheepishly at her as he placed the tray upon the table, but she glared at him and presented her back where in turn he looked to his captain, quite confused. A small smile curved Brandon's lips and he nodded to the servant to continue with what he was doing. When the table lay set, Brandon held a chair out for her.

"If you please, Heather," he smiled mockingly. "I can hardly dine while you stand and glower at me. Now sit and be a good girl for a change."

George looked between the two, becoming more perplexed, and hurriedly poured coffee in the mugs. Heather grudgingly took her place and adjusted a napkin irritably over her lap. She sipped the coffee, though she preferred tea, then grimaced at its strong taste and pushed it away from her. Lifting her eyes, she found Brandon watching her with an amused smile.

Nothing was said and she attacked her small steak of beef as if it needed yet to be slaughtered, though in truth it was quite tender. She found it strangely prepared, not boiled nor cut into tiny bits for a stew but simply cooked in its own juices and left still rare. She tried a small piece and found it tasty, but her appetite was far from hearty and she simply picked at it.

George watched her for a moment in indecision, wishing to please but not knowing how. He turned finally to leave, and noticing the sheets upon the floor, went to pick them up. His eyes widened as he saw the stains and he glanced quickly to his captain, who was watching him, then to Heather whose back was turned to him and once more to Brandon who met his look and nodded once to his unasked questions. The servant's eyes widened even more and he hurriedly gathered the sheets in his arms and made a hasty exit.

Brandon regarded Heather's display of temper and casually sliced off a bite of steak.

"I will not tolerate your spiteful mood at my table, Heather," he said calmly, "nor your treating my man unkindly. In his presence you will be a lady."

Fear rose within Heather and every muscle in her body drained of strength, leaving her quivering in her chair. She grew pale and even her small desire for nourishment left her. She folded her hands in her lap and gazed down at them, unable to meet his stare.

Brandon swallowed some of the hot coffee as he continued to study her, this time concentrating on the gown she wore. It was a garment a younger girl might wear and pretty though it was, he didn't care for its girlish lines. It made him feel uncomfortable, as if he had stolen a babe from its cradle. The only thing about it that found favor with him was the snug bodice which pressed her bosom upward, reassuring him that she was no child. But it was hardly the sort of gown he wanted his mistress to wear, and the frayed chemise he had seen on her earlier would have to go. She was too beautiful to wear rags.

The meal at its end, he returned to his desk to work at his ledgers while Heather, not knowing what to do with herself, paced the floor or fidgeted at the window seat and felt like climbing the walls. He left the cabin for a time, long enough for her to gather courage to try the door, but her thought of escape was badly timed for she found him in the companionway giving orders to one of his crew. Angrily she slammed the door closed when he glanced up and smiled at her mockingly.

When George came with the noon meal she was polite, but not to the point of being gracious. Silently she cursed the man.

Brandon pushed his chair back from the table, a time later, his hunger for food satisfied, and Heather felt his eyes sweep her. A silence filled the room and she swallowed hard, keeping her gaze averted. She knew his affections had warmed again and her heart refused to slow to a regular beat. His voice when he spoke was low and rich with passion.

"Come here, Heather."

She froze in the chair. She would not go to him. She would stay where she was. He could not bully her. She shook her head and managed to croak a weak, "No."

His eyelids lowered and he smiled slowly. "I admire your spirit, *ma cherie*, but do you think it wise to resist me? You know as well as I that you do not possess the strength to stop me from taking what I want. Would it not be better to acknowledge defeat and come willingly?"

Heather shook and terror could not be denied. Her courage failed her. Slowly she rose on trembling legs, her teeth tugging nervously at her bottom lip, and went to stand before him. He smiled at her leisurely and sliding his hand up her arm, pulled her between his legs and down upon his knee where she sat rigidly as he pressed his lips against her throat.

"Don't be afraid," he breathed. "I won't hurt you."

His mouth moved over her shaking lips and parted them as his arms slid tightly around her, one hand settling on her back while the other sought her hip. With a half sob, Heather went limp against his chest, trembling violently within his grasp. His kisses went on it seemed to her without end. When his hand slid from her hip to her thigh and moved slowly upward along the inside, caressing it, she groaned under his kiss and strained against his chest. But the embrace could not be broken. His lips left hers to kiss the corners of her mouth, her chin, her ear.

"Don't fight me," he murmured. "Let yourself enjoy it."

"I can't," she choked.

"Yes, you can."

His lips as they traveled from her throat to the rounded curves above her gown were moist, parted, drinking in

the sweetness of her flesh. They caressed her breasts unhurriedly, moving from the deep valley between to the
pointed peaks which rose up beneath her gown. His
breath came more rapidly and touched her skin like a hot
iron. Aroused, he unfastened her bodice and pressed passionate kisses on her naked flesh.

From the cabin door came a hesitant knocking and a
black scowl crossed Brandon's face. Heather frantically
clutched her garments together over her bosom in shame
and tried to leave his knee when he loosened his hold
upon her, but he tightened it again, forcing her to stay
where she was. When he called out to the intruder, there
was no doubt of his irritation.

"Blast you, come in!"

George opened the door and stood red-faced as he
looked across the cabin at them, shuffling his feet in embarrassment.

"Beggin' your pardon, cap'n, but a messenger's come
from a merchant who wants to speak with you about the
cargo. His man says he's interested in buying the whole
lot of rice and indigo if the two o' you can meet and
agree."

"He wants me to go to him?" Brandon asked, almost
incredulously. "Why in hell's name can't he come here
to the *Fleetwood* as the others do?"

"The man's crippled, so his messenger says, cap'n,"
the servant replied. "If you're willing, his man will look
over the cargo to see its value and then take you to him."

Brandon muttered an oath and the scowl deepened.
"Ask Mr. Boniface to give him a tour, will you, George?
Then send the man in here when he's through."

George skittered out, closing the door behind him and
Brandon reluctantly turned Heather loose. She ran to the
window seat and hurriedly fastened her clothes as he
moved behind his desk and sat down. She felt his eyes
on her and the color rose high to her cheeks.

Some time later the messenger was admitted and she
turned her back to the occupants of the room and sank

to the cushions of the seat. That anyone should find her in Captain Birmingham's cabin embarrassed her to the bone. Her face flaming with the shame of it, she wanted very much to die. Through the windows she watched the water lap against the sides of a merchantman docked nearby and mused how, if she but had the nerve, the water might put her problems to an end. She thought she might welcome its liquid fingers snuffing out her life. She leaned forward to gaze more intently at the dark swirling river, unaware that the messenger had left and that Brandon had come up behind her. He dropped a hand to her shoulder and she jumped with a start. He laughed softly and sank down beside her on the cushions and touched a curl over her breast.

"I'm afraid I must leave for a few hours, Heather, but I'll return as soon as I'm able. George has been instructed to keep an eye upon you so I beg you not to make it difficult for him. He's a gentle soul where ladies are concerned despite what you may have thought last night. I have informed him that I want you here when I return, so do not try to get away. I'll have his skin if you succeed and I'd find you again if I had to tear down all of London."

"I don't care in the least if you skin your man," she replied heatedly. "But if the opportunity to escape presents itself, I'll take it."

Brandon raised an eyebrow. "In that case, Heather, I shall take you with me."

She almost panicked. "Oh, don't!" she cried. "Please. I beg of you, I would die of shame if you did. Oh, please do not. If you wish, I'll read while you're away. I swear."

Brandon studied her with a great deal of interest. "You can read?" he asked.

"Yes," she returned softly.

He smiled down at her. Not many women could read, and he felt a new respect for the girl.

"Very well," he said finally. "I will leave you here,

and I'll stop at a clothier's on the way back so that you may look like a woman. Now stand up and let me judge your size.''

Self-consciously, Heather complied and slowly turned around before him as he directed. His eyes moved over her appreciatively.

"You're hardly bigger than a mite.''

"Some people say I'm thin,'' she commented softly, remembering some of her aunt's insulting remarks.

Brandon laughed, "I can imagine the jealous old crones who said that. They were probably wallowing in their own fat.''

A small smile broke across Heather's features as he seemed to describe her aunt, and then it was gone, almost as quickly as it had come, but it did not go unnoticed.

"Ah-h,'' he grinned. "I knew I could make you do that sooner or later.''

Heather turned away and lifted her nose high in the air. "Because of you, I have little to be happy about.''

"Now it's that again, is it?'' he chuckled. "Your moods are very changeable, m'lady.'' He rose and came to stand behind her. "Now let us see if some of that ice has thawed from your lips. I wish to feel some warmth for a change. Come, kiss me as a mistress should. I've not time for more.''

Heather released a quivering sigh of relief at not having a repeat performance of his lovemaking. She concluded a bit of effort on her part, as if yielding to his protestations, would do much to allay whatever fears or suspicions he might be harboring over leaving her. She turned and with a new determination, slid her arms behind his neck and pulled his head down to hers. His brows lifted as if he were considering this new change in her and Heather, not wanting him to dwell too long upon the matter, pressed moist, warm lips upon his and seizing upon her meager experience, kissed him long and in a loving fashion, arching her body against his.

Brandon savored the honey taste of her lips and the

intoxicating nearness of her body and all logical thinking fled his mind. His arms went around her and held her tightly as he enjoyed the unexpected warmth of her response. His body demanded he do more with her. She was too tempting, this slight wisp of a girl. Her lips were too warm, her body too desirable. It was becoming extremely difficult to think of leaving her. Damned if it wasn't.

With an effort he set her from him.

"I will be hard put to go anywhere if you kiss me like that," he said huskily.

Heather's face pinkened. The kiss had held some surprises for her, too, for she had not found it such a loathsome task.

"And now I fear my departure will be delayed after all. These tight breeches leave nothing to the imagination," he grinned.

Her eyes traveled downward innocently to his pants. She was instantly sorry. Her face flooded with color and she jerked around with a moan, mortified.

Brandon chuckled behind her and then with a pensive sigh, turned to the business of dressing, mumbling wistfully, "Had I but the time, madam——"

Seething, Heather began stacking dirty dishes at the table, thinking many ill thoughts of the man behind her. She decided he was more than detestable.

Brandon was giving a last adjustment to his stock when Heather turned to him again, her temper somewhat abated. For all the hatred she felt for him, she could not deny what a fine specimen of a man he was. His garments were immaculate and well chosen, in the height of fashion, and they fit his tall, broad shouldered frame superbly. His breeches were tailored so well they clung nearly as tightly as his skin. They did nothing to disguise the bulge of his manhood.

"He's so handsome he probably has to fight the women off," she thought bitterly.

He came forward and, in a casual but possessive and

intimate manner, pressed a light kiss upon her lips and gave her buttock a fond pat.

"I'll be back soon, sweet," he smiled.

Heather could hardly hold her tongue, wanting to scream at him in rage. She watched him leave, all too confident of himself for her state of mind, and then heard the click of the lock on the door. With frustrated anger rising in her veins, she whipped her arm across the table and sent the stacked dishes flying.

Chapter 2

*H*eather wasted no time in her determination to flee the ship. If Captain Birmingham returned before she left, her opportunity would be greatly diminished. She tried to think of ways George could be tricked and wondered if he could be bribed with money? But what would she use for that scarce item? Her beige gown was the only thing of value she possessed and she pondered whether it would be sufficient temptation to bring him over to her side. Then she thought of the man who had used her body for his pleasure and her ideas of bribery died away. The servant would either be too loyal to that pompous cad of a sea captain or too afraid of him to endanger himself with any temptation of bribery. No, that would not do at all. She'd have to think of something better.

Many plans flickered through her mind, but none would take finite shape. She could not bribe him, so she would have to use force. But what could a mere girl do against a man who was without a doubt much stronger than she? His stringy muscles could easily keep her detained for his captain.

She began searching the cabin for anything that would help persuade the man to hand over the keys to the cabin door, jerking open the desk drawers, frantically searching through papers and books, even in Brandon's sea chest. She found only a bag of coins. Wearily she sank into the chair behind the desk. Her eyes wandered about the cabin, hunting through each corner and shadow of the room.

"He must have some weapon here," she bit off, disgruntled because time was against her.

Her eyes fell on the locker, and leaping from the chair, she dashed across the room and flung open its doors. She searched frantically through every garment hung within but again she found nothing. With a despairing sob, she began yanking the contents from the closet until her eyes fell on a box wrapped in cloth upon the floor of that tiny compartment.

"Probably his jewels," she thought testily as she picked it up.

She pulled the box from its protective cloth. She had no interest in his jewels, if that was what the box held, but the container itself interested her. Made of fine-grained leather, it was elaborately tooled and inlaid with gold with a large "B" dominating the top. It wasn't a very deep or large box, but she was sure it held something of value. Curiosity began spreading within her, and she couldn't stop her fingers from opening the catch and lifting the lid.

Heather gasped in surprise, and she gave a silent prayer of thanksgiving. There, lying in a bed of red velvet, were two of the most beautifully executed flintlocks of French design she had ever seen. She knew little of firearms, but her father had possessed one of this type, only not so finely made. Their butts were of smooth English oak, oiled to a rich luster and bound with heavy brass rings to blue steel barrels. The trigger guards and butt plates were of lightly worked brass, and the locks were of hand-wrought iron, well oiled against the ravages of time.

She examined the pistols, failing to fathom their mechanisms. Her father had never shown her how. She knew

the lock pulled back to cock it, yet how it was loaded
was a complete mystery. Silently she damned her ignorance and closed the cover on those fine weapons, trying
to think of some way to even her odds with George. She
cast glances about for anything. Perhaps something to hit
him over the head would do. But she realized as she
searched that she probably couldn't hope to more than
daze him. Unless he was restrained in some fashion, she
wouldn't have time to get away.

Opening the box again, she took out one of the heavy
pistols and examined it again. Would he know that she
didn't have the slightest idea how to use the pistol? Just
as long as she pretended how, it might frighten him
enough to hand over the key to the door.

She began to take heart now and a smile broke upon
her face. Going to the desk and sitting down, she took
out pen and paper and began scratching out a note to
Captain Birmingham. She would have need of money,
but she would never allow herself to be accused of selling
her body for it. She would take one pound from the bag
of money she had found earlier and leave in its stead the
beige gown. It was more than a fair trade.

She folded the note and left it on top of the gown and
then carefully hid one of the pistols beneath the pile of
maps and papers where it would be easily accessible to
her when George returned with the tea she had requested
as he cleaned up the broken dishes from the floor. He
had seemed anxious to please despite the mess and said
there would only be a small delay while he sent a man
to buy the leaves. It had worked perfectly, giving her
time to search the cabin in his absence. Now she hid the
monogramed box in a desk drawer and straightened the
cabin so the servant wouldn't become suspicious when
he entered and found it had been searched. After doing
this, she sat and read from a book she found on the desk.
It was the least she could do, since she had promised.
She would show Captain Birmingham she was not a person to be kept against her will. She laughed, anticipating

the rage that would descend upon George, for whom she could feel nothing but hatred. After all, he had brought her to this disgrace. A fitting reward, she thought.

Shakespeare's *Hamlet* was not very quieting to her already frayed nerves. She began to feel apprehensive at the delay of George's return and at times would put the book aside to pace the floor. After a few moments, she would snatch up the book again and force herself to read. When he finally did unlock the door and rap, she dropped the book and shot out of her seat in pure nervousness. She made herself sit again and calmly called admittance. He opened the door, stepped in and turned to lock it. In his hand was a tray bearing her tea.

"I brought you the tea, miss. It's good and 'ot." He smiled and started to come forward to bring it to her.

Now was her chance. She raised the pistol from the desk and pulled back the lock.

"Don't move, George, or I shall have to shoot," she said. Her voice sounded strange to her ears.

George glanced up from the tray and found the huge bore staring at him. He didn't think a gun in a woman's hand was a laughing matter. They never realized the full danger of one. He turned a few shades paler.

"Please drop the keys on the table, George, and do be careful," she pleaded. She watched as he did so, leaning against the desk to ease her shaking limbs.

"Now very carefully walk to the window seat," she directed and did not take her eyes off him as he made his way hence.

He moved slowly, deliberately, and with a great deal of caution across the room. He knew when to be careful. When he stood in front of the window, Heather's breath slipped from her in a long sigh.

"Please sit," she commanded, feeling a bit of confidence return.

She moved to the table, picked up the keys, not taking her eyes from the old man facing her and backed to the door. Without turning, she felt for the lock and thrust the key in and turned it. The feeling of prison slid away with the latch.

"Please, George, to the locker and inside. And don't try anything for I'm quite nervous and the pistol is really very delicate."

George dropped his idea of quick assault. It was true, she was nervous. She had trouble holding the gun steady in her hands and she had her lip tightly clenched between her teeth. She would shoot if he made a move to stop her, he concluded. He wondered if the pain of his captain's rage would be less than that of a shot from the pistol the girl held in her hands. He knew the man's anger could burn to great heights when provoked. He had been with him for a long time. He was fond of his captain and admired him; he was also afraid of him at times. But he doubted if Captain Birmingham would kill him and he was sure the pistol could easily send him to his grave if he tried to take it from the frightened girl. He walked to the locker, stepped into the cramped space and pulled the door closed behind him.

Heather had stood watching the servant, ready to run if he made a move toward her. She breathed a sigh of relief when he was safely closeted and crept to the door of the locker and pushed it closed until she heard a click. It had no latch on the inside so she would have time to get away before an alarm could be sounded. She went to the desk and opened the drawer where she had found the bag of money and took her one pound, leaving the empty pistol on top of the desk.

It didn't take her long to reach the door. It opened very quietly. No one was about in the companionway and she hurried to the door at its end. She had not thought about getting off the deck of the ship, and when she cracked the door a slit, her escape looked impossible. There were many people aboard, and she would not go without notice. These must be merchants inspecting the cargo, she presumed, for quite a few prosperous looking gentlemen wandered about.

Closing the door, she rested her head against the cool wood of the ship, feeling despair.

What would happen when she tried to leave the ship? Only the captain and a couple of his men knew that she was aboard. What did these men here know of her? Why not be brave for a change, she argued with herself. Just walk out in the midst of them.

Fledgling hope returned. This time without hesitation she opened the door. Her heart beat so, it threatened to burst within her breast. Forcing a smile, she passed into the crowd with an air of queenly grace. She held her head high, nodding it ever so slightly to the men who turned to gape at her. They grinned at her and brought her to the attention of their companions. A hushed quiet fell over the deck of the ship as the men followed her openly with admiring stares. They were interested, but none made a move to stop her. When she lifted her skirts a small degree, their eyes went to the pretty ankles and dainty small slender feet. A tall, middle-aged gentleman with dark skin, white hair and goatee offered his hand to her. She smiled sweetly at him and took it and as she walked away from him down the plank, felt his eyes upon her. Before she stepped off she turned and smiled again. He returned her smile and bowed gracefully, sweeping his hat before his chest.

She knew she was flirting shamelessly but the thought that her departure from the ship would be reported to Captain Birmingham in detail warmed her with pleasure. She had outwitted him!

Many were waiting to help when she stepped off the ramp. They swarmed around to be the one who took her hand. She selected the most handsome, expensively dressed one among them and coyly placed her hand in his. She asked him sweetly if he would find her a carriage and was amazed when, with great abandon, he charged off in search of one. He was back shortly, questing if he might escort her to where she was going. She refused politely, and reluctantly he handed her into the waiting carriage. She thanked him graciously for his assistance. He asked where she lived, but she could not tell him, and it did him little good to insist. She remained polite but silent, and with a sigh he dropped her hand and closed the door. When the carriage started moving she smiled at him but shook her head when he apparently thought her smile was an encouragement and made to run after her.

When the carriage turned the corner, Heather leaned back against the seat and smiled. She felt hysterical laughter rise, so great was her relief. She relaxed and closed her eyes and some time later they pulled up at the coach house on the outskirts of London. She went immediately to reserve a seat on the coach that would take her back to her aunt's.

She had decided earlier she would go back. There was no other place to go. Aunt Fanny and Uncle John couldn't possibly know what had happened to William for a long time, if ever. She doubted that any of William's friends in London knew of a sister living on a small, dreary farm. It was hopeful thinking on her part, yet after seeing William living in such grandeur, she didn't believe he had made much mention of his sister. And she had to leave London while Captain Birmingham was still in port. Her uncle's farm was the safest place for her to be.

She would stay with her aunt just long enough to find a position of work elsewhere. She would become independent of the woman whose brother was dead because of her. It was hard to go back, but to remain in London was impossible.

On the coach trip back, her mind was tortured by the events of the day before. She tried to quell the thoughts that plagued her. Still they persisted, haunting her ruthlessly. She tried to convince herself that none of it was her fault, but it did little to still the pain of all that had happened to her. She was not the same person of the day before, an innocent who had ridden to London dreaming of great things to come her way. She was a woman now, no longer ignorant of a man's caresses, no longer a girl.

She vowed with great determination this would not change her. Marriage now would only bring disgrace. But if she was to remain a spinster, she would at least be an independent one. Above all, she would not be dependent. Then later, employment would be found elsewhere.

The problem now was what she would tell Aunt Fanny and Uncle John. She needed a reason for coming back. Not being on the best of terms with her kinsfolk, she couldn't return and say she had missed them so much in a day's time she found she couldn't bear to live away from them. That would surely make her aunt suspicious. No, it had to be some believable lie.

When the coach came to the village crossroads near her uncle's farm, it stopped only long enough to allow Heather to get off. She descended without a glance behind and remembered nothing of her companions on the journey.

She took the road leading eastward out of the village, the sun now making long shadows before her. Unconsciously, the nearer she got to the small farm, the slower her step became. When she finally arrived, the sky was pitch black and meal time was long passed. She walked slowly to the door and lightly rapped on it.

"Uncle John, it's Heather. May I come in?"

She heard scrambling from within the cottage and then the door was flung open. She had hoped to see her uncle first, but it was not to be so. Her aunt stood in the doorway, a look of surprise on her face.

"What are you doing here?" the woman questioned in astonishment.

It was time to tell another lie, and it bothered Heather to think that just since the day before she had been reduced to lying about everything.

"Your brother found when he returned to London that he had to journey to Liverpool and inspect some silks he wanted to buy. He didn't feel that it was appropriate for me to be in the city unchaperoned.'' She almost choked on the words, for the lie tasted bitter in her mouth.

"Well now, a bit disappointed you are, eh?" Aunt Fanny smirked. "Going all that way to London expecting the whole world. Serves you right for being such a snooty little beggar. Always thinkin' yourself a queen. Leaving here in such a grand fluff, I could of thought you to be one. Now I'm supposin' you're here to take up your chores again after you've been away.''

"If it pleases you, Aunt," Heather replied meekly, knowing that life with the woman would be harder now. But anything would be better than what Captain Birmingham had had in mind for her.

"It pleases me fine, missy, and you're going to appreciate being home, you are," Aunt Fanny sneered, meaning just the opposite.

Heather understood but made no reply. She would accept the way the woman treated her without complaints. It was probably what she deserved for being so vain to think that a life of wealth in London was something she had been created for. The only thing for her to do now would be to humble herself and make amends.

"Well, get to bed with you, for when morn comes you'll have to be up and working. Your uncle is already to bed.''

Heather dared not mention food, but her stomach growled so, she was sure her aunt noticed it. The woman made no reference to it, and Heather knew she would not. She had eaten little that day with Captain Birmingham sitting across from her. Her mouth watered now as she remembered how tasty the food could have been if that fiend of a madman hadn't been there.

Without a word she moved to her corner and behind the curtain where she disrobed. The blanket was as rough as it had been before and it was likely to prove as incapable of keeping out the cold as it had in the past, unless—unless she could find a position of work elsewhere.

It would mean she'd have to go to the village and scan the town's posted paper which usually advertised for young girls to fill occupations of maid, tutor and the like. It wouldn't be hard to find something, she was sure.

Despite the hunger that gnawed at her stomach, she drifted into a dreamless sleep. Morning came for her in swift, harsh movements and cruel words when her aunt tore back the curtain and threw the old hand-me-down dress into her sleeping face. The woman reached down and shook her with ruthless hands.

"Get up, you lazy chit. You'll be having to make up for the chores not done the two days you be gone. Get up with you now," she snorted.

Startled out of her slumber, Heather sat up in her cot, blinking the sleep from her eyes. Her aunt looked more like a witch than she remembered, alarming her. With trembling body she quickly jumped out of bed and pulled the old dress over her head under the watchful eyes of her aunt.

She only had time to grab a piece of stale bread before Aunt Fanny sent her to fetch firewood. When she went out to get it, she found Uncle John preoccupied with his own thoughts and not even interested enough to speak to her. He was chopping the wood and when he saw her, he ducked his head over his work. She could not mistake the effort he made not to speak to her and it hurt deeply. She wondered why he tried to ignore her. It was as if she possessed two heads and he wished not to look upon her. An uneasiness crept through her suddenly and made her begin to wonder if he suspected anything. But how could he?

Through the day she grew certain something was troubling him. Though he never spoke to her, he watched her closely, as if he were trying to read her mind. Becoming uneasy under these stares, she would move out of his range of vision. She could not fathom what was bothering him, and she dared not ask.

By bedtime she was completely exhausted and fell into

her cot, too tired to move. Her thoughts were not so in-
active however. She saw William Court's prostrate form
as clearly as if she were again standing at the door looking back at him. But that vision quickly faded when Captain Birmingham's face loomed up above her in the
darkness. She saw his mocking grin, his strong brown
hands reaching out for her. She heard his amused laughter once again, and with a strangled cry, she rolled over
and buried her face into the pillow to smother the sobs
that shook her, remembering too well the feel of his
hands upon her body.

Morning dawned and she was up and working before
her aunt stirred. She had vowed after those sleepless
hours she spent in her cot that she would labor and toil
until not one thought or memory remained that could
torment her. She would find the joy of sleep through
extreme fatigue.

When Aunt Fanny came from the other room, fastening her homespun dress over her enormous bosom,
Heather was down on her knees cleaning cinders from
the hearth. The woman came to the hob, snatched up an
oatcake and frowned down at Heather.

"You look a bit pale this morn, missy," Aunt Fanny
sneered. "Could it be you're not happy with being
here?"

Heather dumped the rest of the ashes into the wooden
pail and stood up, brushing a strand of hair from her face.
Soot was smudged across her cheek and the oversize
dress she wore hung loosely from her slender shoulders,
exposing much of one round breast where the neck opening had fallen. She wiped her hands on her skirt, leaving
it smeared with soot.

"I'm satisfied with being here," she murmured, glancing away.

Aunt Fanny reached out and jerked Heather's face
around, her fat fingers bruising her niece's tender flesh.
"Your eyes are swollen. I thought I heard you cryin' in
your pillow last night, and I see I was right. You're mourn-

in' cause you're not in London, I'm supposing.''

"No," Heather whispered. "I'm content."

"You lie! You hate it here! You want to live in London in the grand manner you think is due you!''

Heather shook her head in denial. She didn't want to go back. Not yet anyway, not when Captain Birmingham was still there and likely carrying out his threat to search the city for her. He might be there for three or four months yet, getting rid of his cargo and buying more. She couldn't go back.

Aunt Fanny pinched her viciously on the arm. "Don't you lie to me, girl!''

"Please—'' Heather gasped.

"Let the child alone, Fanny," Uncle John said, standing in the curtained doorway of their bedroom.

Aunt Fanny turned on him with a snarl. "Look who's givin' orders so early this morning. You're no better than she, moonin' o'er somethin' you ain't got, always wishin' for what you had but lost!''

"Please, Fanny, not again," he sighed wearily, hanging his head in despair.

"Not again you say. Yet you live with that woman's memory every day you live. The only reason you took me for your wife is 'cause you could naught have her! She loved another besides you.''

He flinched under the cruelty of Fanny's words and moved away, his shoulders drooping more with his defeat.

Aunt Fanny wheeled around on Heather and gave her an angry shove. "Get on with your work and stop dillydallying!''

With a quick, pitying glance toward her uncle, Heather grabbed up the pail from the floor and hurried across the room to the door. She could not bear the sight of her uncle's sagging shoulders.

A week went by, then two, the last seeming even longer than the first. No matter how hard she toiled, Heather could not push her disturbing memories aside.

She was plagued night and day. Many times she would wake in the darkness of night with a cold sweat moistening her brow, having dreamt again that Captain Birmingham was with her, holding her against his long, lean body in a fierce, passionate embrace. In other dreams he would appear as the devil, laughing heartily at her quivering form, and she would awaken with her hands crushed to her ears. Dreams of William Court were just as frightening. She would always see herself standing above him, holding the fruit knife in her hand, and from her fingers blood would be dripping.

Another two weeks drifted by without relief, and it was beginning to tell on her. Her appetite fluctuated from complete lack of hunger to nausea to insatiable cravings. She suffered from drowsiness, an unforgiveable sin in her aunt's opinion. She had received enough bruises to be aware of that. And she did awkward things, such as carelessly dropping dishes or burning her fingers on hot kettles. It was enough to drive a person mad. It threw her aunt into a frenzy, especially after she broke a treasured bowl.

"What do you think you're doing to my home, you vicious little bitch, breaking everything in sight like you are? Do you want me to take a stick to you?" she screeched, giving her niece a slap across the face.

Heather fell to her knees, trembling violently, her face stinging from the blow, and began to pick up the shattered dish. "I'm sorry, Aunt Fanny," she croaked, tears scalding her cheeks. "I don't know what's come over me. I can't seem to do anything right anymore."

"As if you ever did," sneered the woman contemptuously.

"I'll sell my pink gown and buy you another."

"And what will you sell to pay for the rest of the things broken?" Aunt Fanny inquired sarcastically, knowing well that the gown was worth more than all the broken items put together.

"I have nothing more." Heather whispered miserably, rising to her feet. "Only my shift."

"It ain't worth a farthing, and I won't be having your tits poppin' out of those old dresses of mine when you go to the village."

Blushing deeply, Heather pulled the neck of the gown up for the hundredth time that day. The dress was so large that what had been modest for her aunt was just the opposite for her. When she bent over, the monstrous neckline revealed a great deal. If not for the string tied around her waist it would divulge everything, right down to her knees, especially since she had nothing to wear underneath. For modesty's sake, she had to save her chemise to wear when she went to the village.

It was less than a month later when she finally received permission to go with her uncle to the village. Though she had waited anxiously through the weeks for the authorization from her aunt, she was leery of going because her uncle still continued to watch her. It made her jittery to have him stare at her so. She feared that once out of Aunt Fanny's sight he would be tempted to ask questions, wanting to know about William Court, and she wondered if going to the little hamlet was worth them finding out that the man was dead; however accidentally it had been, she was still to blame. But she had to go. It was the only way she could read the town paper that was posted in the village square. The sooner she found employment elsewhere, the better. Besides, her aunt was expecting a lovely gift from the bartered gown.

White-washed cottages with thatched roofs nested cozily by the village pond, and an inn near the crossroads invited strangers to stop and enjoy the peaceful serenity of the country hamlet. Late summer flowers adorned window boxes and flowerbeds, and trimmed hedges made do as fences between the cottages. It was by far a nicer place to live than London, where filth, beggars and sinfulness predominated.

When they arrived in the hamlet, Heather and her uncle went immediately to the village common, a piece of land a chain or so square in the center of which a posting board stood. Uncle John made a habit of going there first. It was his only contact with the world outside the boundaries of the village and his farm. There Heather discreetly scanned the notices. A scullery maid was needed, she read, but she cringed at the thought. Someone desired a governess, making her heart thump wildly in her bosom, but she read further and found they specified an older woman, no younger than forty. Her eyes ran over the notices again as she prayed desperately to find one she had missed which would be suitable. She was willing to work as a maid, but if there was something better, she would be happier. But there was nothing more. Her hopes fell, and when her uncle turned to go, she followed in his path with tear-filled eyes.

He led her next to a shop where she could select a replacement for Aunt Fanny's broken dish. She did so listlessly, feeling now in the lowest of spirits. When her uncle had pulled the little cart to a halt near the square, she had been wonderfully elated because he had not questioned her. Now, though still thankful for his unasking silence, she wanted to go somewhere alone and cry. She chided herself for being so impatient. There was bound to be a notice later that she would find agreeable. But her aunt let her come so rarely with Uncle John that it might be ages before she could return, and that would mean having to stay with her aunt just that much longer.

Mr. Peeves, the shopkeeper, took the dish she handed to him. "Will there be anything else, Maid Heather—a new gown perhaps?"

Her face flushed with color. It was not the first time he made mention of a new gown. She knew how everyone stared at her with pitying glances behind her back and how the young girls made merry of her oversize clothes. She had too much pride not to be embarrassed. But as long as she had life left in her body she would hold her head high and pretend it didn't matter.

"No," she replied. "I just want the bowl."

"A very lovely dish it is too, well worth the money. That'll be six shillings, Maid Heather."

She dug the knotted kerchief from her pocket and untied it. She counted out the money carefully and gave it to him. It left her with seven shillings, which she knew her aunt would eventually be getting. Her eyes went longingly to some colorful ribbons on a nearby table.

"The blue would go pretty in your hair, Maid Heather," Mr. Peeves suggested, having sharp eyes in his head. He took up the ribbon and handed it to her. "Try it on, why don't you?"

Glancing uncertainly at her uncle, Heather let the shopkeeper press it into her hand. She turned slowly to the mirror, the only one in the village, and raised her eyes. It was the first time she had looked at herself in a mirror dressed as she was. Her hair was neatly braided and looped heavily from above each ear, and she was well-scrubbed and her clothes clean, but it made little difference in the absurdity of her dress. Her aunt's gown fit worse than any sack, making her slight figure appear even smaller.

No wonder people stare at me and laugh, she thought wearily.

The door of the shop opened and she dragged her eyes from her reflection. It was Henry Whitesmith, a tall, thin lad of one and twenty who had long been infatuated with John Simmons' niece. Though Heather had never encouraged him, he was always near when she was about, gazing upon her with adoring eyes, taking her hand whenever possible. She was fond of him, but only in a sisterly way. He came immediately to where she stood and grinned down at her.

"I saw your uncle's cart outside. I was in hopes you would be with him."

She smiled at him warmly. "It's nice to see you, Henry."

He blushed with pleasure. "Where've you been? I've missed you."

She shrugged her shoulders, glancing away. "Nowhere, Henry. I've just been staying at home with Aunt Fanny." She didn't want to speak of her trip to London. She felt her uncle's eyes on her, but she didn't care.

The door opened once again, and Heather sensed the identity of the person before she looked up, knowing that Henry was never without a tagtail. The new arrival advanced toward him but came to an abrupt halt when she spied Heather. The expression on her face changed, and Heather shivered under the withering stare.

It wasn't the first time Sarah had glared at Heather, being as jealous as she was of Henry's attentiveness to another girl. Sarah would have gladly done more if it had brought Henry down on his knees before her. Their families had already discussed the dowry she would be bringing to him when they were married, but he stood stubbornly opposed to being wed, and Sarah knew his infatuation with Heather to be the reason. It didn't matter how much she made fun of Heather's odd dress with the other village girls, she was still well aware, as were they, that beside Heather Simmons, even dressed as she was, they were found lacking. Even her own father had commented often of the uncommon beauty the Simmons girl possessed. All the men, young and old, were smitten with the Irish girl.

Henry scowled at Sarah before he turned back to Heather. "I have to talk with you," he whispered urgently, reaching out to touch her arm. "Could you meet me by the pond later?"

"I don't know, Henry," Heather replied softly. "I have to stay with my uncle. Aunt Fanny doesn't like me wandering off alone."

"If he can keep an eye on you, can you still talk with me?" he asked hopefully.

She frowned slightly, confused. "I suppose so, but not for very long."

"Have him bring you to the pond before you leave," he said in a rush. "I'll be waiting."

He left her without saying more and brushed past Sarah on his way from the shop. It wasn't long before the girl followed him out.

Later, when Uncle John stopped his cart by the pond, Heather descended and went to where Henry stood by a tree. The young man was unable to speak for a moment as he gazed at her with adoring eyes, tracing lovingly each detail of her small, perfect features. When he did, his voice was uncertain and quavered with emotion.

"Heather," he choked out. "Do you think your aunt would ill-favor me. I mean—would she think me not good enough for to court you?"

Heather looked up at him, surprised. "But, Henry, I have no dowry."

"Ah-h, Heather, I care naught that you have none. I love you, not what you can bring me."

She could hardly believe her ears. Here, indeed, was the suitor she thought she would never have because she possessed no dowry. But he was too late. She was no longer a virgin. She could never bring herself to marry any man now, sullied as she was.

"Henry, you know as well as I that your family would never let you marry me without a dowry. It's just not done."

"I'll naught marry if I can't have you, Heather, and my family wants my children. They'll come round soon enough for us."

Heather's gaze dropped to her clenched hands. "Henry, I can't marry you."

The boy frowned. "Why, Heather? Are you afraid of having a man bed you? If that be it, rest at ease. I would naught touch you lest you felt ready for me."

She smiled sadly. Here was patience and love offered to her and she could not take them. Captain Birmingham had seen to that. What a difference there was between the two men. She couldn't feature the bearded captain of the *Fleetwood* being so patient with a woman. It was a pity she couldn't marry Henry and lead a normal quiet life here in the village and raise children they both could love. But that was out of the question now.

"Henry," she whispered softly, "you would do well to notice Sarah. She loves you very much and she would make you a good wife."

"Sarah don't know who she loves," Henry snapped. "She's always chasing after some boy and right now it happens to be me."

She chided him gently. "Henry, that isn't so. She sees no one but you. She wants to marry you very much."

Henry wasn't having any of it. "But I want you for my wife, Heather, not some simple-minded, plain girl like Sarah."

"You shouldn't say things that aren't true, Henry," she said in the same soft, reproving voice. "Sarah would make a far better wife than I."

"Please! Don't speak more of her!" Henry cried. His face had taken on a tormented expression, not so different from the one that had been on Sarah's face. "I want only to look at and think of you. Please, Heather, I must have your uncle's permission to court you. I can't wait much longer to make you my wife."

Here it was, a plea for her hand. Her aunt perhaps would be surprised. But it was too late. Now she had to convince this gentle man that she couldn't marry him. But he would not listen. What was she expected to do—tell him what had happened to her? Then he would be repulsed, sickened, and she would be shamed.

"Henry, I won't ask my aunt if she will allow it. I cannot marry you. It wouldn't be fair to you. I could never be happy here. Don't you see, Henry? I was brought up much differently. I'm used to having everything done for me and being dressed in the finest clothes. I can't be content being a mere cobbler's wife."

The look on his face plunged a sharp pain through her bosom, yet Heather knew it was best this way. He would soon be able to lick his wounds and realize he had a life to live without her. She watched in agony as he staggered from her, blinded by his tears.

"Oh my God!" he cried. "I loved you the moment I saw you. I naught could think of no one but you these two years past. And now, you say I'm not good enough for you. You're a black-hearted wench, Heather Simmons! May God have mercy on your soul!"

Heather stretched out a hand to him pleadingly, but he was gone, not caring where he ran, stumbling, then rising again. Tears welled up in her eyes and rolled down her cheeks as she watched him run away.

"I'm cruel," she thought. "I've hurt him deeply and now he will despise me."

She turned toward the cart and walked slowly back. Her uncle was watching her. He always watched her now. Was he ever to stop?

"What's the matter with young Henry?" he wanted to know when he reached down to pull her into the cart. His fingers closed over her upper arm, and he lifted her up as she clung to his shoulder.

"He asked to court me," she murmured, taking a place beside him on the narrow seat. She wished not to discuss it. Her stomach quivered and she felt sick.

"And you told him no?" he questioned.

She nodded her head slowly as though an incautious movement might make her retch. She shuddered and was silent, and he, thankfully, stared off into the distance over the head of the old horse that pulled them, lost in thought.

The first of October passed and the weather grew cooler. Here and there a stray leaf drifted to the ground and came to rest on grass still green. Squirrels could be seen scurrying along limbs of trees in search of food to hoard for the winter. Soon it would be time for slaughter and Heather dreaded even the thought. She needed no further encouragement to be ill. Each morning she rose, dragging herself from the cot with an effort, feeling sick and list-

less and wondering if she would ever get well. With the
extra load of chores her aunt had thrust upon her, she
was finding it hard to keep her illness a secret. She had
vowed never to allow her aunt to see her ailing, but it
was becoming difficult. Sometimes she felt so faint she
expected to collapse any moment. She had hoped in time
that those tormenting memories which made her ill would
leave her in peace. But still they remained with her, and
so did her troubled stomach and frayed nerves.

"Stop your mopin' around and finish those dishes,
missy."

Heather shook off the daze that enveloped her and hurriedly wiped another wooden bowl. In just a moment
more, she would be able to relax in a warm bath and
soothe her aching body. She was tired and weary, and
there was a dull ache in the small of her back. She had
done the washing earlier in the day and her strength had
been sapped away with the lifting, the scrubbing, the
beating, the reaching. And later she had almost swooned
when carrying in a load of firewood.

She put the dishes away and dragged out the wooden
tub for her bath. Watching her, Aunt Fanny picked up
another sweet tart from the table and stuffed a great part
of it into her large mouth. Heather shuddered, wondering
how the woman could eat so much. It seemed her aunt's
favorite pastime.

She wished the woman would go to bed as Uncle John
had done. She would prefer to bathe in peace. But her
aunt wasn't budging, so Heather filled the tub and tested
the water. It was pleasantly hot. She unfastened her dress
and let it slide from her shoulders down to the floor.

She stood before the hearth, totally unclad, her smooth
skin glowing in the light of the fire, and her slender body
was clearly silhouetted in its glow. Her breasts rose heavier now and were taut, and there was a slight rounding
curve to her abdomen.

Suddenly Aunt Fanny choked on the tart she was swallowing. With a strangled cry she leapt from her chair,

alarming her niece who whirled around to look at her. The woman's eyes were wide, staring at her in horror, and her face had gone from beet red to ashen gray. Aunt Fanny charged across the room toward her and Heather cringed away, thinking her aunt had gone mad. She was seized viciously by the arms.

"Who are you breeding by, missy? What jackal have you hooked yourself to?" the woman screeched.

Cold, dreaded shock seized Heather's every nerve. Her eyes grew very wide and her face very pale. In her innocence she had not thought of this. As she had lain under Captain Birmingham and struggled with him, she had not considered the consequences of his act. She had reasoned her failure to come sick at her normal times to be because she was so upset with everything that had happened to her. But now she knew differently. She was going to have a baby—a baby by that scoundrel of a sea captain. That cad! Madman! Lunatic! Oh God, she thought, why? Why?

Livid with rage, Aunt Fanny shook Heather until her head threatened to snap off.

"Who is it? Who's the bloody toad?" she cried. Her hands tightened around Heather's arms until it brought an outcry of pain from the girl's lips. "Tell me or by me God I'll wring it out of you!"

Heather found it impossible to think. She was dulled, senseless with shock.

"Please—oh, please let me go," she murmured in confusion.

A look of enlightenment crossed Aunt Fanny's face, and she shoved Heather into a nearby chair. "Henry— that's who it is, ain't it? Your uncle said he was sweet on you, and now I know the reason. He's the father of the babe. If he thinks he'll ruin my good name in the village and go flitting off clean, he thinks wrong. I told you if you ever sinned, you'd be found to reckon with and now you're going to wed Henry. The filthy good-for-nothing! He'll pay for it, he will!"

Slowly some sense seeped through Heather's trauma. She became aware of what her aunt was saying, of Henry's name spoken. Shivering and addled, she forced herself to some semblance of awareness. Whatever she did, she could not let Henry take the blame. She could not hurt him like that and have him despise her more. Trembling, she picked up her gown from the floor and pulled it to her naked body.

"It wasn't Henry," she said softly.

Her aunt swung round. "Eh? What you say, girl?"

Heather sat unmoving, staring into the fire. "It wasn't Henry," she repeated.

"And who was it if it weren't the cobbler?" the woman questioned fiercely,

"It was a sea captain from the colonies," Heather sighed listlessly, dropping her cheek against the tall, crude back of the chair she sat in. The flames from the fire illuminated her small face. "His men found me and took me to him and he forced himself upon me, God's truth."

What did it matter now if she told of the defilement she had suffered in the hands of that man? Everyone would know in a few months of her pregnancy unless her aunt decided to keep her at the cottage and not allow her to go into the village. Even then, how would they explain the baby's presence after the child was born?

Her aunt's brow knitted in confusion. "What are you saying? Found you when? Where was this?"

Heather could not bring herself to tell the woman of William's death. "I was lost from your brother and the Yankee seamen found me," she murmured, still staring into the crackling fire. "They gave me to their captain for his pleasure, and he wouldn't let me go. It was only through my threat to shoot his man that I gained my freedom. I came here straightaway."

"How did you get lost from William?"

Heather closed her eyes. "We went—to a fair—and somehow we became separated. I didn't tell you before because I couldn't see the need. It's the Yankee's child I carry, not Henry's. But the man won't marry me. He's one who takes and does what he pleases and he won't be pleased to marry me.''

The frown was wiped away from Aunt Fanny's face, and a slow menacing smile replaced it. "We'll see about that. Now, tell me, didn't your pa have a friend who be magistrate judge in London? Lord Hampton was his name, weren't it? And didn't he control the investigation of all the ships suspected of smuggling?''

Again confusion swept over Heather. Her thoughts were too muddled to grant her any explanation for her aunt's questioning. She answered hesitantly.

"Yes, Lord Hampton did and still does as far as I know. But why—''

The smile deepened. "Ne'er you mind with the reasons. I want to know more of Lord Hampton. Did he know you and was he very good friends with your pa?''

A frown touched Heather's smooth brow. "Lord Hampton was one of my father's closest friends. He used to come to our home often. He's known me since I was a baby.''

"Well, all you need know right now, missy, is that he is going to help you get wed,'' Aunt Fanny said, a cold, calculating expression on her face. "Now get your bath and go to bed. We're going to London tomorrow, and we'll be having to rise early so we won't be missin' the coach going through the village. It won't do to go in a cart when we'll be callin' on Lord Hampton. Now hurry with you.''

Heather got to her feet with an effort, completely baffled by her aunt. Why the woman wanted to know about Lord Hampton she didn't know, but Aunt Fanny was a master schemer of devious plans, and it wouldn't do to question her. Obediently Heather slid into the wooden tub, feeling a heaviness in her lower abdomen as though she were just now with child, and all the time before, unscathed.

There was no doubt whatsoever in her mind that she was breeding. She should have expected just such as this from the Yankee bull. Strong, potent, full-blooded, he had done a man's due with an ease she found maddening. How was it when a great many men sweated over their mates month after month with little to show for it, that she had to have the misfortune to be taken to bed by such a virile male being.

Oooohh, he is abominable! She cried inwardly and added, quivering, *He is a devil.*

A stifled cry came from her lips, and she shuddered more violently, realizing what it would mean to her if he were forced to marry her. Her soul and life would be lost, married to the blackguard. She would be damned.

But at least the child would have a name and perhaps some good would come of that.

Her thoughts strayed to the unborn child. He was destined to be dark-haired, with both his parents being so, and he would likely be handsome if he took after his father. Poor child, it would be better if he were born ugly than to be a handsome scoundrel like his sire.

But what if the child were a girl? It would be a great blow to the man's confidence if such a thing happened, great manly beast that he was. If she married him, Heather thought venomously, she would pray for a girl.

Before she finished bathing Heather heard her uncle begin to stir in the other room where Aunt Fanny had gone when leaving her. Their muffled voices had come to her as she bathed. The woman would never have waited until morning to tell him of Heather's predicament.

Heather rose from the tub and clutched the towel over her bosom just as her uncle came from the tiny room. He appeared to have aged ten years.

"Heather, girl, I have to speak with you, please."

She blushed crimson, hugging the towel to cover her nakedness. He seemed not to notice that she was without clothes.

"Heather, are you tellin' the truth? Was it this Yankee who planted his seed in you?"

"Why do you ask?" she inquired cautiously, fearfully.

John Simmons rubbed his brow with a shaking hand. "Heather—Heather, did William ever touch you? Did he ever hurt you in any way, girl?"

Now Heather knew why her uncle had watched her so closely after she returned from London. He knew William, and had been worried about her. She could do nothing but reassure him now.

"No, Uncle, he didn't hurt me. We became separated at the fair. You see, there was a fair and I wanted to go, and he was kind enough to take me. But I got lost and couldn't find him. That's when these men found me and took me to their captain. The Yankee is the father."

A sigh of relief escaped the man, and a small, quivery smile crossed his face. "I thought—never mind. Just say I worried about you, but now we must find the man who be the sire, and this time I won't fail you. Me brother's child, I cannot fail again."

Heather managed a smile for her uncle. She couldn't tell him it would do no good to go to London to talk with Captain Birmingham because the man would not marry her. She was silent.

When they reached London, they took up lodging at an inn. Uncle John immediately sent a message to Lord Hampton asking to be granted an appointment and the next day was received by the man in his home. Heather and her aunt remained behind at the inn to await the outcome of the meeting. Heather dared not ask what they were about, but she was more than curious. When Uncle John came back, he went directly into conference with his wife. It seemed to Heather that whatever they were planning, it was going well because her uncle was in better spirits than when he had left.

She was told to go to bed early that night after her uncle had taken it upon himself to reassure her that Lord Hampton would be helping to solve their problem.

"He's only to see we're telling the truth and he will do what he must. And your Yankee won't be refusing to wed you lest he wants to lose everything he has and be thrown into prison."

Heather didn't understand anything. They couldn't put a man into prison because he refused to marry a woman he had gotten in the family way. There were too many bastards walking around for that to be so. No, they were going to threaten him with something else, and she could only think of the consequences to herself if he were forced into marriage. Her life would be pure hell and no other word would do so well to describe it. But she had no voice in the matter. They had taken it out of her hands. And she could not think which was worse, being married to the devil or having to raise a bastard child.

It was almost midnight of that same night when she was awakened rudely from a sound sleep by Aunt Fanny's large, insistent hands shaking her.

"Get up, you evil chit. Your uncle wants to speak with you."

Heather sat up groggily and looked at her aunt who stood beside the bed, holding a lighted candle high above her head.

"Hurry with you. We've naught all night."

Her aunt whirled into the shadows and left the room and Heather stared after her for a moment, blinking away sleep. Reluctantly she pushed the covers from herself. Her white body gleamed in the blackness and her hair, falling to below her waist, was lost in darkness. For the first time in many weeks she had slept without dreaming. The pitter-patter of rain on the windows had lulled her troubled thoughts to a peaceful quietness and she had curled into the downy softness of the bed and drifted into sweet oblivion. Her unwillingness to hasten from the bed now was understandable. But she must obey her aunt or suffer the consequences.

She slid drowsily from the cozy warmth and picked up her aunt's old dress and pulled it over her head. She didn't bother fastening it. In another moment she would just be taking it off again. She had an idea why they wanted to speak with her. She was well prepared to hear them say that Captain Birmingham had refused to be coerced into marriage. It would come as no surprise. They could have saved themselves a trip to London if they had asked her about the man. It would not take them long to tell her what he had said.

At her first timid rap on the door across the hall it was flung open by her aunt. The woman motioned her in with a hateful glower. As she moved into the room she was aware of its darkness. A small fire glowed in the hearth and only one candle burned on the table where her uncle and another man were sitting, quaffing ale from pewter tankards. The rest of the room was obscure and shadows were deep. She came closer cautiously to see whom the visitor might be and saw that he was no stranger but an old friend of the family, Lord Hampton.

With a cry of relief, Heather flew gratefully into the arms he held open to her.

"Heather!" he choked. "My little Heather."

She clung to him and sobs flooded from the bottom of her soul to be softened against his shoulder. Second to her father, this man was the one she had loved most from childhood. He had been exceedingly kind to her and was more of an uncle than her own. He and his wife had wanted her to live with them after her father had died, but Aunt Fanny had insisted that she live with her only kinsfolk.

"It's been long since last I saw you, child," he murmured, pulling her from him so he could see her better. His kindly blue eyes twinkled at her. "I remember when you were but a tiny tot and you would crawl up on my knee, looking for sweets." He grinned widely as he lifted her exquisite chin. "And now look at you, a portrait of beauty. Never have I seen such fairness before, never. You are even more lovely than your mother, beauty that she was. It's a pity I never had sons for you to marry. I

would have enjoyed you in the family. Since I have no
daughters either, perhaps I can say you are mine.''

She reached up to press her lips to his cheek. "I would
be honored to be your daughter," she replied softly.

Lord Hampton smiled with pleasure and held out a
chair for her to sit down in, but Aunt Fanny shoved
Heather away and proceeded to sit there herself.

"Let her stand. It'll do her good," she sneered, fitting
her monstrous shape between the arms of the chair. It
squeaked and strained in protest.

Caught off guard by the rudeness of the woman, Lord
Hampton gazed at her for a moment, wide-eyed. Then he
motioned toward a chair at the end of the table.

"Perhaps you would be more comfortable here, my
dear," he said to Heather, moving to draw the chair from
the table.

"No," Aunt Fanny barked. She gestured to a darkened
corner. "That chair is for him."

Heather glanced up in surprise. She hadn't known anybody else was in the room. The man sat in the shadows,
shrouded in darkness, and his silence gave no clue to his
identity.

"Come and join us, Captain Birmingʼam," Aunt
Fanny crowed. " 'Tis a fitting place for a Yankee."

Heather's heart gave a fearful leap and she swayed on
her feet.

"No, thank you, madam," a slow, confident voice replied. "I'm content where I am."

With the familiar voice burning across her brain,
Heather's knees buckled and she sought solace in a blissful faint. With a cry, Lord Hampton leapt to cushion her
fall.

"She's had a bad shock," he declared, swinging her
up into his aging arms. He lowered her with much gentleness into the chair declined by Captain Birmingham
and nervously seized a small cloth, dampened it, and
pressed it to the pale brow as he bent over her.

"Are you all right?" he questioned anxiously when her eyes fluttered open.

"Don't spoil the girl, Lord Hampton," Aunt Fanny suggested with a sneer. "She'll go lazy on you."

"I'm sure she would be entitled to a rest after living with you," he snapped, angered by the woman's indifference.

"Please," Heather breathed. "I'm all right."

He brushed her hair from her brow with trembling fingers. "You gave my old heart a start," he laughed shakily.

"I'm sorry," she murmured. "I didn't mean to. I'm better now."

But still she was trembling, conscious of those searing eyes upon her. With unsteady fingers she clutched her gown closer over her bosom, remembering that powerful gaze which seemed to peel clothes from her and leave bare the tender body beneath.

"Come on and let's get on with it," Aunt Fanny demanded. "Let's hear what the girl has to say."

Lord Hampton eyed Heather uncertainly, fearing she would swoon again. Her lips managed a weak smile of reassurance for him, and he left her unwillingly to return to his place at the other end of the table.

"Now, with taking the action he's going to, missy," Aunt Fanny began, "Lord Hampton wants to assure himself he's naught doing your captain an injustice by makin' him claim another man's child."

Heather's eyes shifted slowly from her aunt to the small, elderly man. She was feeling too dazed to understand completely what they were saying. Lord Hampton scowled at her aunt.

"Madam, perhaps unknown to you, I have a tongue in my head, and I vow it more eloquent than your garbled speech. If you don't mind, I shall speak for myself."

Huffily Aunt Fanny snapped her mouth closed and sat back in her chair.

"Thank you," Lord Hampton said curtly before he turned to look at Heather again.

"My dear," he began unhurriedly. "Since I am a man of honor, I cannot force Captain Birmingham to claim your child unless I know for certain he is the father. If you've been put upon by someone else—"

"There's been no one else," she assured him quietly, staring down at her hands. She related the details as if she had memorized them. "After I escaped from him, I took the coach back to my uncle's. There's only one coach leaving during the day to go through the village. It arrived at the village at dusk and I walked the rest of the way home. I met no one on the way nor would there have been time to tarry. My aunt can vouch for the time I reached the cottage."

"And she ain't been out of my sight one second since," the woman offered triumphantly.

Lord Hampton glanced at Uncle John to receive his verifying nod, then he turned back.

"What about before, Heather?" he persisted hesitantly.

She blushed hotly and could give no answer. From the shadows came the same self-possessed voice.

"The child is mine," Brandon stated flatly.

A pleased cackle came from Aunt Fanny, and she turned to Lord Hampton with a victorious smirk.

"Now what do you say to that? Will you do it?"

"Yes," he sighed wearily. "To undo the great impropriety inflicted upon Heather because of your wretched carelessness, woman, I must. I lament the day I allowed you to take her under your roof. You should have guarded more carefully this priceless gem." His angry gaze turned to Uncle John who sat very quietly in his shame. "And you who are of the same blood are worthless in my eyes. You disgust me."

"Well, what about her?" Aunt Fanny cried. "It was her doing. She was the one who crawled into bed with the bloke."

"No!" Heather gasped.

The involuntary denial escaped her before she realized she had spoken. With a growl, Aunt Fanny turned and viciously slapped Heather across the face, hitting her so hard the soft, bottom lip was bloodied and her cheek bruised.

In the darkness behind Heather a tankard of ale was slammed down on a table in rage. Before her, Heather saw through tears of pain that Lord Hampton had leapt to his feet. He leaned forward and planted his hands firmly on the table and spoke threateningly to her aunt.

"Madam, your actions are of the vilest nature! You have the manners of a barbarian, and were you a man, I'd surely demand satisfaction for what you have just done. Now I think it best that Heather go back to bed. It is clear she is upset with the whole matter."

Thinking herself dismissed, Heather rose from the chair and made to walk to the door, but her aunt snatched her by the front of the dress and snarled.

"No! For once she's going to stand and take her due. No decent girl would get herself in trouble with a man. I've tried to do my best to put the fear of God in her, but she's the devil's handmaiden. Just look at what he give her."

Ruthlessly Fanny ripped the old garment from Heather's back in one cruel, brutal swipe, leaving for all to see the beauty of her body.

In the shadows a chair was overturned as Captain Birmingham came angrily to his feet. He strode across the room in long, irate strides, and Fanny fell back, seeing the tall form swathed in a black cloak and the angry face red in the glow of the fire. Her eyes widened and her feet were frozen to the floor. She recalled accusing Heather of being born a witch and was sure that this man before her was Satan incarnate. She threw up her hands as if to defend herself, but instead the Yankee whipped the rain moistened cloak from his shoulders and dragged it around Heather as she tried desperately to hide her nakedness. He enfolded her quaking slightness in the flowing garment, making Heather tremble more violently with fright. The proximity of his long, muscular body was terror in itself.

Above her dark head, a muscle twitched furiously in Brandon's cheek as his angry glare took in the three startled people staring at him.

"Enough of this useless prattle," he demanded coldly. "Since the girl carries my child, her livelihood will be my responsibility. I will delay my trip home to see that Heather is comfortably settled in a house of her own with servants to care for her." He looked at Lord Hampton. "You have my guarantee that she and the child will be supported in a manner suitable to her upbringing. It is certain she must no longer live with her kinsfolk, nor would I allow my child to be subjected to the malice of this woman who calls herself an aunt. I had planned for this to be my last voyage here, but under the circumstances I will continue coming every year so that I may see to their welfare. Tomorrow morning I will set about finding suitable accommodations for the girl, then later I will return here for her and take her to a clothier's so she may be aptly dressed. Now, sir, I wish to get back to my ship. If you have more to say to these people, I will wait in your carriage until you have concluded your business." He turned his gaze directly to Auny Fanny and spoke dangerously slow and precisely. "I suggest, madam, that you keep your hands to yourself while this girl is still in your care or you will greatly wish that you had."

With that, he walked from them to the door, and Heather caught a glimpse of his angry, aristocratic profile and tall, lean body elegantly clothed in deep red velvet, then he was gone with only a pledge to sustain his bastard child and its mother. No one had even brought the subject of marriage to his consideration. He was going to make her a kept woman.

"He won't be so high and mighty when we finish with him," Aunt Fanny sneered.

Lord Hampton looked at her with cold eyes. "It is with considerable distaste that I must appear to satisfy your vengeful whim," he ground out flatly. "If not for Heather, I would put the matter from me and have done with it. But I must, for her sake, bring this man to the altar. But you are to be warned, madam, the man has a temper. You will do well to heed his words."

"He has no right to tell me how to treat the girl."

"You are wrong there, madam," he replied slowly. "He is the father of her babe and in a few hours he will be her husband."

Chapter 3

*T*he sun came in rays of sparkling light through the water-speckled windows and touched on Heather's face to awaken her. She stirred in half awakened ecstasy and stretched and rolled over, snuggling deeper into the downy bed as she hugged a pillow to her. She had been dreaming she was again in the home of her father. Now a soft, rain-sweetened breeze flirted with a curtain where a window had been left ajar and drifted to the bed to caress her cheek. Heather inhaled deeply and released her breath with a grateful sigh. The usual morning queasiness was in absence, letting her enjoy the smell of autumn in the air. She opened her eyes, then sat up with a start.

Captain Birmingham's cloak was slung over the back of a chair near the bed, and it sent her thoughts racing with a fleetness that only fear could provoke.

"The arrogant fool!" she hissed with venom. "Does he think he can put me in a house of his procuring and make me his mistress? I'll whelp in the gutter before I accept his half-witted proposal!"

Even now, she thought shrewishly, he's probably thinking how tender it will be when he takes me to the house and carries me to the bedchamber. He will think me grateful for his generosity and that I will submit to him accordingly. I would be no better than a harlot! No!

Rather that I slit my throat from ear to ear than let him make me his mistress. He cannot touch my belly with his vile hands and know his bastard son grows within me! No! Never will I submit to him in that way!

But what would happen to her if they forced him to marry her, she wondered frantically. She would have to yield to him then and obey him. And he would not be so gentle when full of rage.

"Oh, pray that he doesn't hurt me too much," she uttered, a shudder of fright passing through her body.

A moment later there came a knock on the door, and rather than wear his hated cloak again, she tore the sheet from the bed and wrapped it around her body, flipping the end over her shoulder. So garmented, she opened the door and found a gray-haired woman standing in the doorway and behind her, two girls of an age no more than herself, carrying an assortment of cases.

"Maid Heather," the older woman said with a smile. "I'm Mrs. Todd and these two girls are my assistants. We've come from Lord Hampton, and be here to fix you for your wedding."

Something cold and fearful gripped Heather's heart and sent a shivery spasm through her body. She clung to a nearby chair for support, fearing her knees would give way. Mrs. Todd noticed nothing of her pallor or her shaking hands. She was too busy ushering the two girls in with their cases.

"Have you eaten this morning, love?" she asked, turning to Heather at last.

Heather shook her head. "No," she whispered.

"Oh, well, don't you worry about a thing, love. I'll send one of the girls down to fetch breakfast. We'd not have you fainting from hunger when the betrothals are being said, would we? And we do have a lot to do 'til then. You'll be needing your strength, slight lass that you are."

"When will the wedding be?" Heather managed to ask.

The woman showed no surprise at the strange question asked by the young bride. "This afternoon, love."

Heather slithered into a chair with a weak, "Oh."

"Someone should have told you, love, but with everything so rushed I can see how they forgot to. His lordship says the groom is anxious to wed and will not brook a delay. Most certainly I can see his reason for impatience. Such a beauty you are, love."

But Heather wasn't listening. Her imagination was already sweeping her to the coming night when she would lie beside Captain Birmingham and feel his panting breath against her mouth and his strong, ruthless hands upon her body. Her face burned at the thought. He would not care how he bruised her, and she wondered if she would be able to still her trembling body and not anger him more by struggling.

She jumped from the chair in a quick, nervous movement and went to the window, fearing that she would not be able to. Her teeth tugged at her bottom lip as she felt the tension begin to mount. She had hoped for more time. She hadn't dreamed they would force the marriage so soon. How could she possibly go to him now calmly and let him do with her what he might?

Much to her alarm, her moments of freedom slid away with frightening speed. As in a daze, she found herself fed, bathed, perfumed and groomed, all against her stunned will. No moment of that morning was hers. As they tugged and pulled and goaded, she thought she might scream in rage at them to leave her be. The noon meal came and though she was not hungry, she pretended to eat so they would give her rest, dropping the food from the window to a hungry mongrel when they weren't looking. But as soon as the tray was taken away, everything began again. No part of her body was left untouched, no matter what shame it caused her, and when she tried to protest, the three argued.

"But, lass, a touch of essence here or there will make a strong, grand man from a shy, bashful sort."

And Heather thought wildly that just the opposite was needed for the man she was to marry.

Finally she was readied and for the first time allowed to gaze upon herself. What she saw was herself, yet not the Heather she had always seen. She had never looked this way before. For a frightening moment she caught a glimpse of the beauty that others saw and found uncommon. Her hair, brushed to a silky sheen, was coiled intricately through itself and around the top of her head to resemble the coiffure of a Greek goddess. A tiara of golden spikes and pearls crowned her head, and below it, blue feline eyes stared back at her in alarm. The definite slant of her eyes fringed by the long, sooty lashes was made even more noticeable by the manner of hairstyle which was drawn tightly from her face. Her cheekbones, fragile and high, allowing for a slight hollowness beneath them, had been pinched and were no longer pale. Her soft, pink mouth was slightly opened with her awe.

"A lass more fair than you does not live, Maid Heather."

The moment was lost for Heather and again she surveyed her raiments. With love, Lady Hampton had sent as a gift her own wedding gown, an elegant garment resembling somewhat a monk's habit complete with hood. It was ice blue in color and made of rich, heavy satin cut in simple, slender lines. The sleeves reached to the wrist and were, as the skirt of the gown, slightly flared. Elaborate golden embroidery and countless seed pearls embellished the hood and sleeves, and placed about the hips was a girdle of great beauty and considerable fortune. It was of gold leather and was richly sewn with pearls and rubies. A train a good arm's length longer than herself waited to be attached with gold chains and its heavy satin was richly embroidered and embellished with the gold and seed pearls.

A costume fit for a queen, Heather thought drearily.

She frowned suddenly and moved to the window again. The hour of her doom was growing near. Time was fast draining away and still she trembled.

"For once in my life," she prayed silently, "please—
oh, please let me be brave."

Behind her the door swung open and Aunt Fanny
marched in.

"Well now, I see you're all dressed in your finery,"
the woman sneered. "And I'm supposin' you be thinkin'
you look pretty, ain't you? But you look no better'n what
you did in my old dress."

Mrs. Todd stiffened her spine as if the insult had been
directed at her. "I beg your pardon, madam!"

"Oh, hush your mouth," Aunt Fanny snapped at the
woman.

"Please, Aunt Fanny," Heather pleaded softly. "Mrs.
Todd has worked hard."

"Aye, I'm sure she had to with you."

"Madam," Mrs. Todd said coldly. "The girl is not
deserving of criticism. She be by far the comeliest maid
I've ever had the pleasure to attend or have ever seen for
that matter."

"She's the daughter of Satan," Aunt Fanny hissed.
"Her beauty is his doing, and 'cause of it, no man will
find peace with himself after he's seen her. It's the devil's
way of makin' man lust after a witch, and to me she's
ugly. That man she's marryin' is her just mate. The two
of them be of the devil!"

"That's nonsense!" Mrs. Todd cried. "The girl is an
angel."

"Angel, is it? I don't suppose she told you why she's
gettin' wedded so soon, did she?"

From the open doorway where he had come to stand
and listen, Uncle John spoke with a slow but steady
voice. "It's 'cause Captain Birmingham wants her without delay, ain't it, Fanny?"

The obese woman turned in a huff, ready to snarl a
denial at him, but something, perhaps her fear of the Yankee sea captain, made her silence the angry words that
came to her lips before they were spoken. Instead, she

whirled on her niece and made as if to pinch her, but Heather quickly glided out of her way, reasoning the less pain she suffered now, the better prepared she would be for it later.

"I can say I'll be happy to get you off my hands," Aunt Fanny spat. "You've naught been a pleasure to have around."

Heather flinched under the biting remark. Tears came to her eyes as she turned once again to the window. All her life she had lacked the love of her kinsfolk. What her father had given to her had been marred by unhappiness, and now she was destined to go through life without knowing of another. Even the son, if it was to be a son, whom she was carrying would probably be encouraged to hate his mother by a father who was forced to be one. There would never be another chance for love in her life.

An hour later, stiff and unsmiling, Heather descended from the steps of the rented carriage with the aid of Uncle John. The mighty cathedral loomed upward, over-powering in its immensity, and she, small and insignificant before it, mounted the steps, clinging to her uncle's arm. She was numb to the world about her. She did things mechanically. She put one foot in front of the other as she was towed along by her uncle. Mrs. Todd, who had come along for last minute assistance, walked beside her, fussing with the bridal cape that she held draped over her arms. The woman would have swooned if some harm had come to it. She worried and clucked like a mother hen over her brood, but Heather scarcely noticed her. She stared straight ahead toward the high, main portal of the cathedral, coming closer with each step she was taking. It gaped dark and sinister, waiting with maddening patience to swallow her life. Then she was under its arched frame, moving into the vestry, and she stopped because her uncle stopped. The organ music drummed on her heart and sounded loud in her ears. Mrs. Todd flitted about her, straightening the hood over her head, attaching the long train at her shoulders with the gold chains, spreading it out behind to its full length. Someone handed her a small, white Bible with a golden cross stamped in the soft leather, and she took it without thinking.

"Pinch your cheeks, Heather," Aunt Fanny scolded harshly from somewhere near. "And stop lookin' so frightened or I'll pinch you myself."

Mrs. Todd glared at the woman, then did her duty by bringing some life to Heather's cheeks herself.

"You're the queen of the day, love," she whispered to Heather and gave a final adjustment to the crown and hood.

The music changed and so did the beat of Heather's heart. The shock brought her out of her daze.

" 'Tis time, love," Mrs. Todd said quietly.

"Is—is he in there?" Heather murmured to the woman, hoping greatly that he had refused finally to come.

"Who, love?" the woman questioned.

"She's talkin' about the Yankee," Aunt Fanny hissed.

"Yes, pet," Mrs. Todd replied kindly. "He's standing before the altar waiting for you. And a high handsome man he is too, from what I can see of him."

Heather swayed weakly against Mrs. Todd and the older woman steadied her with a helping arm and a smile and walked her to the door.

"It will all be over in a moment, love," she said, giving a final encouragement before the door swung open.

Then Lord Hampton was offering his arm to her and she took it mechanically, moving on her own quaking limbs beside him down the aisle. She could feel the pounding of her heart inside her breast and the weight of the Bible in her hand. The heavy burden of the train tugged at her shoulders, seeming to hold her back, but she moved on as the great organ drowned out all other sounds, even the beat of her heart.

The candles at the altar burned beyond the group standing there, making them dark shadows in a dimly-lit church. But she knew which one was her husband-to-be by his height. No one in the world seemed as tall as he at the moment.

She came closer and the candlelight touched on his face, and for a split second Heather was halted by the cold, stark features. She had an overwhelming desire to flee. Her bottom lip quivered, and she caught at it nervously with her teeth to still its cowardly shaking as Lord Hampton moved away from her, leaving her alone. The green eyes before her roamed insultingly over her person, divesting her of her bridal gown in a cruel, heartless way, and Heather trembled more violently. The Yankee stretched out a strong, brown hand and offered it to her as his leer brought a deep blush to her pale face. Reluctantly she lifted her hand, which was cold as ice, and placed it in his much larger, much warmer one, and he drew her the remainder of the way to the altar steps.

Tall and powerful he stood, garmented regally in black velvet and flawless white. He was Satan to her. Handsome. Ruthless. Evil. He could draw her soul from her body and never feel remorse.

If she were brave, she would turn now before the vows were spoken and fly from the insanity of what they were doing to her. Every day women gave birth to bastard sons and raised them in the streets. Why was she not so courageous? Surely having to beg for food and being destitute were lesser evils than being thrown into the fires of hell.

But even as she argued with herself, she slid to her knees with the man beside her and bowed her head to pray for the blessings of God.

Time stood still as they were swept into the marriage ceremony, and all the while every nerve, every sense she possessed screamed of the presence beside her. The lean, well manicured hands held her gaze and the closeness of his body lent to her nostrils a scent of his cologne, not overpowering like so many strong perfumes meant to cover the stench of unwashed bodies, but fleeting and inoffensive, a clean, masculine smell.

"At least he is well washed," she mused.

She heard him respond to the priest's urging in a firm, steady voice.

"I, Brandon Clayton Birmingham, take you, Heather Brianna Simmons, to be my lawful wedded wife—"

Thankfully appearing not to falter, she spoke the same words, pledging herself to this man in soft tones. It seemed only a moment later that he was sliding a gold band upon her finger and they were again bowing their heads before the priest.

She rose finally on shaky limbs as her new husband drew to his full height. He looked down at her unkindly, his green eyes freezing to her hesitant gaze.

"I believe it is customary for the groom to kiss the bride," he said.

She replied in a nervous strained voice. "Yes."

She feared she would faint under his stare. Her heart raged so turbulently that her gown fluttered over her heart. His long, brown fingers moved around the delicate bones of her jaw and gripped it firmly so she could not move her face away while his other arm slid behind her back under the loose, flowing train. He crushed her to him suddenly in a fierce, possessive embrace, and Heather's eyes widened and her face drained of color. She felt the eyes of the others on them, but he seemed not to mind. On the contrary, he seemed to welcome their stares. His arm was like a band of iron around her, squeezing the life from her small body, pressing her tighter against him. His head lowered and his parted lips moved over hers in a passionate kiss. His open mouth was wet and searing, demanding and insulting, leaving her little dignity. Her hand struggled up and strained against him piteously.

From somewhere near she heard Lord Hampton cough uncomfortably and her uncle murmur something unintelligible. Finally the priest touched Brandon's arm and spoke awkwardly.

"You will have time for that later, my son. The others are waiting to congratulate you."

At last his grip slackened and she could breathe. Her quivering mouth burned from his blistering lips and an imprint of his fingers was clearly marked upon her fair skin. She turned on wobbly knees and smiled tremulously as Lord and Lady Hampton came up to her. The kindly man gave her a fatherly kiss upon the brow.

"I hope I have not done wrongly with you, Heather," he said uncertainly, glancing up at Captain Birmingham who stood stiff and unyielding beside her. "My intentions were to see you cared for, but—"

"Please," she murmured, reaching out to place shaking fingers against his lips.

She couldn't let him finish. If she heard her fears put into words, she would run shrieking from them all, tearing at her garments and hair in an excess of insane passion.

Lady Hampton glanced up timorously at the Yankee captain who stared coldly ahead, his mighty seaman's legs planted firmly under him, his hands clasped behind his back. He appeared to be standing on the deck of a ship, staring out across an ocean. Her hands trembled uncontrollably as she embraced Heather and tears moistened her eyes. The two women, both small and slight, clung to each other in their distress.

As if the thought just occurred to him, Lord Hampton quickly made a proposal. "You will stay the night at Hampshire Hall. There will be more room there for you than in the ship's cabin."

He didn't add that any room there would be easily accessible to him if Heather screamed while in the hands of her new husband.

Brandon turned his frigid gaze upon the smaller man. "And of course you insist upon that also," he growled.

His lordship faced him with an unwavering stare. "Yes, I do," he said calmly.

A muscle twitched angrily in Brandon's cheek, but he

said nothing, not even when his lordship suggested it was time they left for the wedding feast at Hampshire Hall. He just took his bride's arm in a firm, solid grasp and allowed the others to precede them from the church.

Heather, nervous and jittery with his hand at her elbow, would have preferred going out on Lord Hampton's arm, but Brandon clearly had no intentions of letting her do so. His mastery over her had already begun and she knew that she would never again belong to herself. His possession of her was complete—except for perhaps her soul, but he would not stop until that too belonged to him.

Much to her dismay, she was halted by the sudden refusal of her cape to be drawn with her up the aisle. Frantically she looked over her shoulder to see what was binding it, and Brandon turned his black scowl on her as she appeared to tug away from his unrelenting grasp.

"Please," she started in a quavery voice, lifting a hand to explain her seeming reluctance to move forward.

His eyes went past her toward the garment caught on a splintered pew, and he grinned down at her sardonically and went back to release it. Heather watched him nervously, clasping the Bible she held in both hands. Her palms were moist and her fingers twitched. She glanced at the gold band that stamped her as his. It was rather loose and slid around her finger easily. Just to look at it brought more fear to her heart, knowing what it would mean.

Brandon detached the golden embroidery from the rough splinter and tossed the end of the cape over his arm in a careless manner and came back to her. Again his hand slid under her arm.

"There's no need to distress yourself, my love," he said mockingly. "The garment is intact."

"Thank you," she murmured softly, raising her eyes uncertainly to his.

His taunting smile seared her and brought a rush of color to her face. He was cruelly laughing at her and her stung pride would not allow that. It brought her chin up defiantly. She glared at him through the tears that sprang to her eyes.

"Were I a man you would not smirk so easily," she spat, hating him.

He raised a finely arched eyebrow and chuckled unmercifully at her. "Were you a man, my dear, you wouldn't be in this situation."

Her blush deepened. Infuriated and seething with anger and humiliation, she tried to wrench free from his long fingers but he only tightened them around her arm.

"You cannot escape me again, my beauty," he said easily, seeming to enjoy her distress. "You are now forever and for always mine. Marriage with me is what you wanted and that is what you shall have for the rest of your life—unless by chance you are widowed. But do not fear, love, I have no desire to leave you too soon."

Her face turned ashen under his careless gibe, and she swayed on her feet, feeling faint. He steadied her by drawing her near, and he raised her chin so he could gaze down into her eyes. His own burned like coals of green fire.

"Not even your Lord Hampton will be able to save you from me now, though I see he will try. But what is one night in many?"

The words sent a quivery spasm of fright rushing through her body, and her head fell back weakly against his arm.

"What a beauty you are, my sweet," he said huskily. "I shan't grow tired of you too soon."

Lord Hampton, tense and nervous at their long delay with coming from the church, could not wait a moment longer. He hurried back in to find Heather clutched in her husband's arms, her head thrown back, her eyes closed, her face very pale.

"Has she fainted?" he asked anxiously, coming to them.

The fire in Brandon's eyes died and he glanced at the

smaller man briefly. "No," he replied and returned his gaze to his wife. "She will be better in a moment."

"Then come," his lordship said irritably. "The carriage is waiting."

He turned and left them, and Brandon's arm tightened around his wife.

"Shall I carry you, my love," he asked mockingly, an evil jeering grin twisting his handsome mouth.

Heather's eyes flew open.

"No!" she cried, flinging herself from him in a sudden burst of pride and energy. His laugh straightened her spine even more. With a toss of her head she walked from him, but he still held her train over his arm and she came up short when the extra length ran out. She glanced back audaciously and glared at him when he would not release it. The corner of his mouth went up scornfully as he came to her side again.

"Your escape is impossible, my love. I have a very possessive nature."

"Then bed me here if you must," she hissed, hate giving virulence to her tongue. "But do it quickly, for the others wait."

His jaw tightened and his eyes grew cold. "No," he said, taking her arm. "I shall take my pleasure of you slowly and at my leisure. Now come, for as you say, the others wait."

Outside the church, they were met by a shower of wheat. Sparse as the wedding party was, Lady Hampton would not let the simple custom go undone. Later they moved to the waiting carriage. Aunt Fanny was silent with the Yankee so near. Uncle John, hesitant and unsure of himself, helped Lady Hampton down the steps of the cathedral and her husband, Lord Hampton, hung back, watching Captain Birmingham assist his young bride.

Uncle John handed his wife and Lady Hampton into the carriage and climbed in after them. As Heather drew near she found the three squeezed together on one side, Lady Hampton suffering greatly by being in the middle.

The poor woman's complaints went unuttered however, and permitting herself a small smile after all that she had been through, Heather lifted her skirts to climb up into the landau. She was greatly surprised when she found herself being slung up in her husband's arms and placed aboard. Without thanking him for embarrassing her, she sank down on the vacant seat and gave him a withering glare which he could not see. He climbed in and threw his weight down beside her, and she was squeezed unmercifully when Lord Hampton got in also. To allow herself more room she tried to sit up on the edge of the seat, but she found herself unable to move because her husband was sitting on her skirt. She glanced up at him, but he was staring out the window and the muscles in the side of his face were tense with anger. An unintelligible, cowardly murmur escaped her lips as she pushed back against the seat again, fear catching at her heart. Their bodies were so close, his shoulder overlapped hers and the back of his arm rubbed against her breast. The full length of her thigh was pressed to the granite-hard muscles of his.

As the chaise rolled along the cobbled streets, she made an awkward attempt to converse with Lord and Lady Hampton although they were just as tense as she. Her tone was almost inaudible when she spoke and cracked with nervousness. To save face she soon fell silent, afraid to trust her voice any longer.

The ride seemed endless. They were jostled and bounced and Heather wondered frantically if any bone in her body would be left unbroken. Though Lord Hampton was not a big man, he was still larger than she and between her husband, whose tall broad-shouldered frame gave no inch, and his lordship's, she, being much smaller than the two, endured much. The pressure of Brandon's arm against her breast alone was sending her into a state of shock.

Finally the carriage drew up before Hampshire Hall. Brandon descended first and with capable hands reached up, clasped her under the arms and swung her down beside him. She straightened her clothes with a jerk and flung her long train over her arm with an arrogant toss of her head. Inside the mansion she stopped to discard the heavy cape and, much to her displeasure, was helped by her husband who unfastened the gold chains from her shoulders. His long fingers worked with great dexterity.

The wedding feast was already laid upon the table when they entered the dining room. Lord and Lady Hampton took their places at the ends of the table and motioned for Heather and Brandon to sit on one side, Uncle John and Aunt Fanny on the other. They lifted their glasses in toast to the young couple.

"To a most happy and rewarding marriage despite what has here before taken place," his lordship offered. Then he added as an afterthought, "And may the child be a fine boy."

A red glow spread over Heather's features as she lifted her glass to her lips. But she did not drink. She would not hope for a boy and give this man more confidence in himself. She noticed, however, that he drank the champagne down quite easily, and she eyed him distastefully.

The meal went too quickly for Heather's peace of mind, though by the time they left the table it was past the hour of eleven. The men took their brandies into the drawing room as Lady Hampton propelled Aunt Fanny off to her sleeping quarters and drew Heather to the bedchamber prepared for her and the Yankee. Two giggly young maids were waiting for the young bride, and a night garment of transparent filmy blue cloth lay on the bed. Heather blanched white at the sight of it, but Lady Hampton led her to a bench in front of a huge mirror and pressed her down into it.

"I shall return with some wine when you're ready," the woman murmured, kissing Heather's brow. "Perhaps it will help."

As the maid drew her bridal gown from her and uncoiled her hair, Heather knew nothing would protect her from her fear. She would have to be unconscious before she would not quake with fright.

"I might as well be a virgin," she thought with some surprise, "as much as I tremble."

Brushed a hundred strokes, her hair was left loose and flowing, reaching down to her hips. Her clothes were taken away—not even a robe was left—and Heather, sitting on her heels in the middle of the bed and wearing only a gown of gossamer to veil her nakedness, tried to still her trembling body and calm herself for the ordeal that was to come.

Outside the bedroom, footsteps clicked against the marble floors, but she breathed a sigh of relief. They belonged to a woman.

Lady Hampton opened the door and came in, carrying a tray bearing a wine decanter and two glasses. She set it down upon a table beside the bed and poured Heather a glass as she inspected the work the girls had done. She nodded with approval.

"You are even more beautiful now, my dear, than you were in your bridal gown, impossible though it may seem. You were a vision. I felt so proud. I just wish there would have been more time to invite guests. You needed to be shown off. I could have told them you were my own sweet. How I grieve that your mother died so soon and never knew you. She would have been proud of you."

"Proud of me?" Heather asked forlornly, looking down at her stomach. "I've brought disgrace to you all," she said tearfully.

Lady Hampton smiled at her gently. "Nonsense, my dear. Sometimes a girl cannot help the things that happen to her. She's just a victim of circumstances."

"Or of Yankees," Heather murmured.

Her ladyship laughed softly. "Yes, or of Yankees, but at least he's young and handsome and clean. When my husband first told me of your predicament and said a Yankee seaman was to blame, I was sick with worry. I thought he would be old and lecherous. Even your aunt confided that she expected the man to be so. It was probably a great disappointment to her that he was not, considering what you've suffered in her hands. But he's so magnificent. Truly all your babies will be fine and beautiful and I suppose you'll have many.''

Lady Hampton's voice dwindled off to barely a whisper as she remembered the passionate embrace Captain Birmingham had given his young bride and the rock hard expression that had been on his face afterward.

''Yes,'' Heather breathed silently. She swallowed hard and said aloud, ''Yes, I suppose we'll be having many.''

She was thinking of the ease with which Brandon had planted his seed in her. She would no doubt be giving birth to many.

Lady Hampton rose to go and Heather looked up pleadingly.

''Must you go now?'' she asked in a quavery voice.

The woman nodded her head slowly. ''Yes, my dear. We've held him at bay long enough. We cannot any longer. But if you should need us, we will be near.''

The woman's meaning was not lost upon Heather. She knew if she called out for assistance they would come, despite the fact that they had no right to interfere.

Again she was alone and frightened. But after she had tasted bitterly her husband's mockery, she was determined now not to cringe and cower from him.

''Let him see that I am willing,'' she thought cunningly. ''He will not choose to hurt me then.''

Her waiting came to an abrupt end, startling her when the sound of his footfalls came in the hall. Her face flamed as she saw the door open, and then she found herself staring across the width of the room into his green eyes. His gaze lowered and a fire was kindled as he raked her body with his stare.

Heather sat awkwardly, her heart beating wildly. The bedcovers had been drawn to the end of the bed out of her reach and she longed to pull them to her. The gown she wore was like a soft blue veil over her body, more alluring and revealing than bare flesh. It was tied with soft ribbons at the waist on each side, but from the waist up and the waist down it was slit with no further ornament to hold it together. As a result the sides of her breasts were exposed and the long, slender limbs were laid bare to his gaze. The hardest thing she ever had to do in her life was to sit calmly before him and let him look at her as he was doing.

"You're very beautiful, my love," he said hoarsely, coming forward to the bed. His eyes were like flames of fire, scorching her. He reached out and pulled her to her knees. "You're even more lovely than I remembered."

Still on her knees, she came reluctantly to him as he drew her into his embrace. His hands slid carelessly under her gown and over her buttocks as he bent his head slowly to her, and trembling, Heather waited for his kiss. But before his lips pressed upon hers, he drew away the slightest degree and laughed softly in his mocking way.

"You are more willing now, my love, than you were before. Does marriage make it so different? Was that the price you were selling your body for? And here I thought at last was a woman pure in heart who would willingly give her body to no man for a price, only for love."

"Oh, you horrible wretch!" she cried angrily, trying to snatch free. "What do I have to say in the matter? You will rape me as you did before, whether I struggle or not."

"Be quiet," he said quickly, jerking her closer and forcing her to be still. "Do you want the others to hear and break down the door? Lord Hampton is just waiting for the invitation."

"What do you care?" she taunted viciously. "You are stronger than he. What will it matter if you have to throw him out before you finish your business with me?"

A muscle twitched in Brandon's cheek and already Heather knew that slight movement meant danger. He glared down at her, his green eyes fierce and frigid.

"I wouldn't assert my husbandly rights upon you to-night if you were the last woman in the world," he sneered.

Heather stopped struggling immediately and raised her eyes to his in surprise, wondering if she had heard him correctly. His eyelids lowered and his jeering grin reap-peared, showing startling white teeth against the darkness of his skin and beard.

"You heard right, my dear. I have no intention of mak-ing love to you in this house tonight." He ignored the expression of relief on her face and went on. "When I take my pleasure of you, my love, it will be in my own way, in my own house or on my own ship, and not where another man is waiting anxiously to barge in and pull us apart, and certainly not when that man is holding an axe over my head."

"An axe?" she repeated innocently, relaxing against him.

"Don't tell me you don't know. Surely you knew of their plan. I cannot believe you were not in with them."

"I don't know what you're talking about," she said cautiously.

He laughed bitterly. "Always innocent, aren't you, sweet?" His eyes dropped to her bosom and he ran his fingers over the side of her breast where the filmy gown left it bare. His thumb brushed her nipple underneath. "Always innocent," he said softly. "Always beautiful. Always cold."

She allowed his hands to caress her. They were gentle and as long as nothing would follow and he was her husband, she would not take the chance to stir his anger by refusing him this much. But she persisted with her questioning. She wanted to know what axe they had used.

"How did they make you marry me?" she inquired softly.

His lips touched her hair and moved to her throat and Heather shivered involuntarily at their burning intensity. His hand stroked her breast still and seemed not to want to stop. Nervously she pulled away, fearing he would not keep his word. She reached and drew the bedcovers over her and sank down again in the middle of the bed.

"Are you going to tell me?" she whispered, staring at him.

His mood was again mocking, cruel, angry. "Why should I? You've heard it all before. But if it matters so much to hear it from my lips I shall tell you. Your dear lordship was going to convict me of smuggling and selling arms to the French, despite the fact I'm lily white. I would have been sent to prison, my ship taken from me, and God only knows what would have happened to my plantation back home. Very crafty of your friend, I must say."

He yanked off his coat and threw it into a chair and began untying his stock.

"Do you know I am—or shall I say, I *was* engaged to be married when I returned home? What am I supposed to tell her—my fiancée? That I saw you and couldn't help myself?"

He paused a moment, pulling his shirt from his brown shoulders. He gazed at her angrily.

"I don't like being forced, my dear. It goes against my grain. If you had come to me when you first learned of your pregnancy, I would have helped you. I may have even married you if you had acted as if you desired marriage with me, but to send your mighty friend and threaten me, it was a most unwise thing for such a little girl to do."

Wide-eyed and fearful, Heather huddled under the sheet as if it would give her protection from his savage hands if he turned on her. He moved about the room, blowing out candles and she watched him cautiously. He had stripped to the waist and did not appear to have any thought of stopping there. But for the moment he settled down in a chair by the bed.

"You know you're very beautiful, don't you?" he said, coldly appraising her. "You could have had any man of your choosing, and yet you had to have me. I would like to know the truth, if you don't mind. Did you perhaps learn that I have wealth?''

She looked at him strangely, seeing no need for him to ask. ''I know nothing of your financial situation,'' she replied softly. ''You were just the man who—who took my virginity. I couldn't go to another man, sullied as I was and with your child in me. I would have given birth to a bastard before stooping so low.''

''Your honorable nature is to be applauded, madam,'' he said in a light, bantering tone, and his scoffing burned her.

''Why should you have been allowed to go merrily upon your way and not made to right the wrong you did?'' she cried.

He was beside her in an instant.

''Please, my dear,'' he said uneasily. ''Refrain from raising your voice above a whisper or we'll find ourselves with company. I have no desire to be thrown into prison by your Lord Hampton because he thinks I am mistreating you—especially since I've already made you my wife.''

His anxiety pleased her, but she went on in a hushed whisper. ''You say you dislike force. Well, I loathe it, but I could do nothing to stop you from taking your pleasure of me. Now you're angry because you've had to pay the piper, yet you do not think of the child I carry—what it might have suffered, born a bastard.''

''The child would have been well cared for and so would you have been.''

She laughed ungraciously. ''As your bastard and your mistress? No, thank you. I'd have slit my throat before consenting to that proposal.''

The tic in his cheek returned and he stared at her for such a long time she sat transfixed like a bird before a snake, then lids lowered slightly over mocking eyes.

''A woman who is kept by a man is usually better

tended than his wife. I would have been kind and more than generous with you.''

''Meaning you will not be now,'' she said with sarcasm.

''Exactly,'' he answered smoothly, heartlessly terrifying her. He got up from the bed and stared down at her. ''As I've said, I don't like being blackmailed, and for you I've chosen a fitting punishment. You wanted security and a name for our child. You will have them, my dear—but you'll not have one damned thing more. You'll be hardly better than a servant in my home. You'll have the name you wanted, but you'll have to beg and plead to have me grant your slightest wish. You won't have any money nor will you lead a normal life, though I will be careful to save you the embarrassment of others knowing of your situation. In other words, my dear, the position you thought so honorable will be no more than your own special prison. You won't even share with me the more tender moments of marriage. You'll be just another servant in my eyes. As my mistress you would have been treated as a queen, but you will now know me as master and nothing more.''

''You mean we won't be—intimate?'' she asked with much surprise.

''You've caught on quickly, my love. And you needn't worry about me in that respect. I won't be cutting my own throat to spite my face. You're only one woman among many, and for a man it is easy to find relief for his baser needs.''

Heather sighed with the joy of the disburdened and smiled, gloating over her good fortune. ''Sir, nothing could please me more, I assure you.''

He sneered at her coldly. ''Yes, I can see that you're pleased now. But your hell has only begun, m'lady. I'm not termed a pleasant sort to live with. I have a foul temper which can snap up a small tart like you without a second's notice. So be warned, my beauty. Do not tempt it. Tread lightly and perhaps you will survive. Do you understand?''

She nodded, no longer licking her lips over her blessings.

''Now go to sleep. It will be some time before I'm able to do the same.''

Quick to obey, lest he should find fault with her so soon, she slid down into the bed with haste and drew the covers under her chin, watching him warily as he moved across the room to the balcony doors. He opened them and stepped out into the moonlight. Not taking her eyes from him, Heather turned on her side carefully so she would not draw his attention back to her. Again he had taken up the stance of a sailor looking out to sea and the moon touched on his handsome face and broad shoulders. His smooth, brown skin gleamed in its light, and she drifted to sleep staring out at him.

Heather awakened abruptly when Brandon fell back on the pillow beside her, and drugged with sleep, she thought he would do some harm to her. She sat up with a startled cry on her lips and flung up an arm as if to ward him off. But he caught it with a snarl and jerked her back to her pillow.

''Be quiet, you little fool!'' he growled, leaning over her. ''I had no intentions of spending the night in a chair and leaving you the bed.''

A tremor of fright passed through her body as he held her down. He was just above her in the darkness and his warm breath touched her face. The moonlight streaming in from the balcony etched his angry profile.

''I didn't mean to cry out,'' she whispered fearfully. ''I was just startled.''

''For God's sake, be startled some other time,'' he snapped. ''I have an aversion to prisons.''

''Lord Hampton wouldn't—'' she began softly.

''The hell he wouldn't! Now that you have my name, your honor is restored, but if he thought he acted unwisely in giving you to me, he would go ahead with his threat and toss me into prison just to keep me from you. So despite what you feel about me, if you want our child to grow up with a father, please don't offer him any encouragement.''

"I hadn't intended to," she replied in a whisper.

"You couldn't have proved it by me," he retorted.

"Oh, you!" she hissed, trying to struggle free from his grasp. "Why was I so unlucky to be put upon by you! You're—you're abominable!''

He laughed softly as he held her down. "Some women wouldn't agree with you, my dear.''

"Oh, you cad!" she panted breathlessly. "You vile, uncouth, loathsome rapist—defiler of women! I loathe and detest you.''

He caught her to him, his lean, hard body immensely threatening to her small frame, and gave her a quick, silencing, bone-breaking squeeze.

"Be careful, my beauty, or you will find yourself with your hands full. I can stop your screams quite easily. It will not discomfort me in the least to act the husband.''

She gasped with pain as his grip tightened again, and Heather thought she would be crushed in his brutal arms. She felt his thighs against her own quaking, cowardly limbs and realized that she was the only one even partially clothed. But the gown was little comfort. It was wound around her waist and bared a breast whose fullness was now crushed to his chest. There was no question to his desires.

"Please," she whimpered as his hold became more harrowing. "I will be good. Do not hurt me so.''

His deep chuckle made a shiver of fright pass through her body as he continued to hold her, then quite suddenly he released her and dropped her back to the pillow.

"Go to sleep. I won't bother you.''

She drew the covers under her chin with quivering fingers and curled on her side facing him, shaking uncontrollably. The moonlight made the room bright and she saw that his eyes were open and he lay flat on his back with his hands under his head, staring up at the ceiling. Even in the dimness of the room she thought she saw his cheek vibrate with rage.

"Where is your home?" she questioned softly, a long while later.

He sighed heavily. "Charleston of the Carolinas."

"Is it very beautiful there?" she ventured again.

"To me it is. You may not like it," he replied stiffly.

She dared not ask more of what was to be her home. She had braved enough as it was.

A chilling breeze came through the opened balcony doors and woke her at the first break of dawn. At just awakening, she was out of sorts, not being able to recognize her surroundings. But she soon became aware of the man she pressed to for warmth. Her left hand lay across his chest over the crisp, dark hair covering it, and her cheek rested against his sturdy shoulder. He slept soundly, his face turned slightly toward her, relaxed in slumber.

Not moving for fear of awakening him, she studied him at her leisure. Her eyes traced the firm, straight mouth, now softened with sleep, and the long, dark lashes which lay on brown cheeks.

"He is a handsome man," she thought. "Perhaps it would not be so bad to have a son like him."

He stirred slightly and turned his face away, leaving her to stare at the back of his rumpled head and the broad expanse of his chest where her hand lay. She gazed at the ring on her third finger and marveled at the brightness of the gold. It looked strange on her hand and what was even more odd was the way she suddenly felt. The thought of being this man's wife seeped through with new realization. It was something he had said the day before—forever and for always she would be his. And now she mused: "Even in eternity I will belong to him."

Very slowly and carefully, so as not to awaken him, she drew the covers over his chest, but she soon realized her mistake with thinking him chilled. It didn't take long for him to kick the covers away completely, making her blush profusely.

His body lay bare to her gaze now, but she did not turn away though her face flamed with her own temerity. Instead she let her eyes roam over him slowly and with much interest, satisfying her curiosity. There was no need of others to tell her what she could see herself—that he was magnificently made, like some wild, grand beast of the forests. Long, flexible muscles were superbly conditioned, his belly flat and hard, his hips narrow. Her hand, slim and white, appeared out of place upon his brown and hairy chest.

Disturbed by the strange stirring within her, she eased from him and moved toward her side of the bed. She turned away, trying not to think how her eyes had lingered on his body, and she saw a leaf fall to the floor of the balcony. She huddled under the covers, wishing she were as warm-blooded as the man beside her.

The mantel clock had long before struck nine chimes when the two giggly girls returned to dress her. They rapped on the wood lightly and she heard their snickering through the door. It maddened her and brought a bright flush of color to her face as she slid from the bed. She glanced back over her shoulder at her husband and found him still asleep and undraped. Very cautiously she went around the bed and pulled the sheet up carefully over his nakedness. He awakened instantly, startling her so much she jumped. She drew back her hands as if she had just touched fire and went a few shades redder as his gaze swept her, making her extremely conscious of the filmy garment she wore and of its even more revealing slits. A slow, amused smile curved his lips and made her tremble, and she turned uncertainly and went to the door, knowing his eyes followed her.

The two twittering, sniggering maids came in together, one carrying a tray of food. They glanced about the room curiously as though they expected to see some secrets of

the night before unfolded in front of their eyes. Seeing
Brandon propping himself up on the pillows with only a
sheet drawn up over his lap, they were sent into renewed
giggles. He chuckled with amusement at their nervousness, but Heather desired greatly to give each a pinch,
especially when they kept right on staring at her husband
with such a hungry look in their eyes, giving her to wonder if they were so chaste as their fidgeting implied. They
went together to the bedside to show him the great assortment of food on the tray, and Heather waited impatiently as they cooed over him, spreading a napkin over
his lap with maddening slowness and pouring him tea.
In the midst of all this, his eyes lifted to her own bright,
angry face and mocked her, and she turned away smol-
dering.

Finally the maidservants remembered their duties and
returned to attend her, preparing a rose-scented bath and
laying out her bridal gown again, it being the only gown
she possessed. Under the interested and observing eyes
of her husband, they stripped the blue veil from her and
helped her into the bath. Their giggling did not cease as
they scrubbed her back and arms, but when they began
to wash her shoulders and bosom, she could not endure
it any longer. She snatched the sponge and soap from
their hands impatiently and snapped at them to leave her
be. She immediately regretted not being more tolerant
when Brandon laughed at her with mirth, throwing his
splendid head up high with his glee. She glowered at him,
feeling intense hatred rise up once more within her. But
she did not dare hiss the words at him she wished to,
fearing he would silence her again with his fierce, heartless hands. Besides, she would not give the two skinny,
homely girls the satisfaction of knowing she and the
handsome beast were anything but newly wedded and in
love.

Rising from the tub in shimmery wet splendor, she
allowed them once more to assist her, standing motionless as they patted her body dry under Brandon's unre-

lenting gaze. He watched with such a slow, unhurried regard that her skin burned from its intensity. She was more than willing to don her shift though its transparence and immodest décolletage were hardly very comforting. As they brushed and combed her hair, she found herself as fidgety as the young girls, and she cursed herself silently for allowing Brandon's appraisal to make her nervous. But it was almost more than she could bear to have him lounging back against the satin pillows watching her, and the two servants seemed to take forever doing her hair. When they stepped back to compliment each other on their artistry, she breathed a sigh of relief. But her short lived comfort came to an abrupt end when Brandon swung his long legs over the side of the bed and stood up, dragging the sheet with him. He managed deftly to wrap it around him without revealing more of himself to the girls, and he came to her, holding the sheet around his narrow hips. He dropped a kiss on one round breast just above the lace of her shift.

"A rewarding experience, my love," he murmured easily. "I must admit I've never had the honor before of being present at a lady's toilette."

For a moment their eyes met in the mirror, his warm and devouring, hers nervous and uncertain. But under his openly admiring regard, she flushed crimson and dropped her eyes to her lap, still feeling the brush of his lips upon her breast and the strange tremor which they had evoked. She heard his soft laugh and then he turned and made a show of kissing each maid's hand, and he might as well have been fully garmented the way he acted. He was completely at ease and terribly confident of himself.

"You truly have done well, my ladies," he purred to them. "My wife is greatly appreciative."

The two almost swooned, never having such a thing happen to them before and certainly never by such a fine specimen of a man. They fell against each other giggling unceasingly and ran to ready his bath. When they finally left the room, Heather sprang up from the bench and flounced angrily to the bed for her dress.

"What need was there for that?" she snapped. "They should have been severely reprimanded for the way they acted, and you only encouraged them to be worse."

He smiled slowly, his gaze moving appreciatively over her back. "I'm sorry, my love. I wasn't aware that you were so jealous."

Her blue eyes flashing, Heather spun around in a rage, prepared to send a string of insults flying at his head, but Brandon only laughed and dropped the sheet to the floor.

"Attend to my bath, will you, sweet? I have trouble reaching my back."

She could do nothing but splutter and spew and turn a bright red. His odious manner riled her blood to the boiling point. Yet as he was, standing unclothed before her and daring her to speak with amused patience, she had to back down. She could not stand and curse him for the wretch he was, when both of them were conscious first of all of his nakedness. He waited for her answer in a relaxed stance, hands on hips, one knee bent and slightly forward. She hated him for his coolness, his mocking gaze, but she would not call him names.

Holding her teeth clenched tight, she brushed past him and picked up the sponge and soap and waited for him to get in the tub, her back as rigid as stone. She heard his amused chuckle and she gritted her teeth more. Then he was easing into the tub of hot water in front of her.

She hesitated but a moment over his back, then with frigid determination she bent over him and began to lather the soap over it. She scrubbed hard, venting her anger into the strokes she used. But when she had gladly concluded that task, he just grinned.

"You're not finished, pet. I would like to be washed all over."

"All over?" she squeaked weakly, incredulously.

"Of course, sweet. I'm very lazy."

She damned him with unuttered words, knowing he

was making her bathe him because it satisfied his need for vengeance. His excuse of being lazy was meant only to flaunt his mastery over her. He was most aware that having to touch him in any way was agony for her, and he had chosen the intimate chore of bathing him as punishment. She'd have gladly taken a beating rather than to do it and he knew this well.

Despising him, she jerked up the sponge again and bent to her task as he leaned back in the tub. She ran the soap through the mat of hair on his chest and over his broad shoulders, her face burning under his casual scrutiny. His unflinching stare caressed her white arms, the long, slender neck, and finally her bosom whose beauty was revealed even more as she worked over him, exposing part of one round breast.

"Did you have someone you were fond of in your uncle's village?" he asked suddenly, a frown wrinkling his brow.

"No," she said sharply, then rebuked herself for not being more cunning.

The frown vanished. He ran a wet finger across her breasts and smiled. "I'm sure there were many who were smitten with you."

Angrily she snatched her shift up high over her bosom and rubbed it against her flesh where the water trickled down between her breasts. When she let go again, the garment returned to its place, now quite damp.

"There were a few, but you needn't worry. They weren't like you. They were gentlemen."

"I'm not worried at all, my pet," he answered easily. "You were well guarded."

"Yes," she retorted sarcastically. "That is, from everybody but you."

He chuckled and swept her again with his burning gaze. "It was my pleasure, sweet."

She went livid with rage. "I suppose it pleases your male ego too, to have me breeding now! You must surely be proud of yourself!"

His grin was mocking. "I'm not displeased. I happen to like babies."

"Oh, you—you—" she sputtered, seething.

The grin was gone with frightening speed. "Finish attending your husband's bath, my dear," he said sarcastically.

She choked off a sob and squeezed the sponge out over his knee. There was nothing left to wash now but the lower half of his body, and she could not bring herself to be that familiar with him. Tears sparkled in her long lashes and fell from her cheeks.

"I can't," she murmured.

He reached under her chin and lifted it up gently. His gaze went deep into her eyes. "If I choose, you know you will do it, don't you?" he asked softly.

She closed her eyes in agony and nodded her head. "Yes," she whispered miserably, tears falling freely now.

His hand caressed her fragile cheek. "Gather my clothes then, will you, sweet? I'm sure everyone is waiting to see how you have fared."

She went gladly and collected his clothes from about the room, more than grateful because he had been lenient with her. It would be a long time before she'd dare call him names again or flare up in anger at him. She would have to remember he disliked insolence and would not stand for it. She had been effectively disciplined and would do his will as an obedient wife. Cowardly she was, and she hadn't the nerve to do anything else.

When they left the bedroom, she walked beside him silently, completely docile. She even managed a timid smile when he slid his hand behind her back to her waist and glanced down at her.

In the drawing room the two older couples waited anxiously, though Aunt Fanny for an entirely different reason. She was hoping for the worst, but she frowned blackly as her niece came in seeming at ease with the man beside her. His lordship went to Heather immediately and embraced her.

"You're looking radiant as always, my child," he said with relief in his voice.

"Did you expect anything else, my Lord?" Brandon asked coldly.

Lord Hampton laughed softly. "Do not hold a grudge against me, my son. To me, Heather's happiness comes first."

"Yes, you've made that abundantly clear. Now, will I be allowed to take her to my ship today or must we again have your hospitality forced upon us?"

In good spirits, his lordship was not easily vexed. "By all means, take her with my good blessings. But first, would you be opposed to eating the noon meal with us? It's not a command, but an invitation. If you're not so inclined, we will understand. It's just that we hate to see Heather go. She's like our own child."

"I suppose it will do no harm to stay," Brandon answered stiffly. "But I must get back to my ship soon after. I've been away too long as it is."

"Of course. Of course. We understand. But I desired to talk with you about Heather's dowry. We are prepared to settle the matter ourselves—generously."

"I wish nothing from you, sir."

His reply drew shocked attention and most of all from Heather. His lordship stared at the Yankee captain for a moment, completely baffled.

"Did I hear you correctly, sir?"

"You did," Brandon said formally. "I have no intentions of taking payment for marrying my wife."

"But it's expected! I mean, a woman should bring to her husband some form of dowry. I am more than willing—"

"The dowry she will bring is the child she is carrying, nothing more. I'm quite capable of taking care of my own without gifts. Just the same, thank you for the offer."

Heather closed her mouth and moved to sit down, feeling more than stunned.

"Crazy Yankee," Aunt Fanny muttered.

Brandon clicked his heels together and bowed formally before her. "From you, madam, that is truly a compliment."

She glared at him and made as if to sneer an insult but thought better of the idea, much to her credit. Instead, she clamped her mouth shut and jerked her face away from his mocking gaze.

"As you are well aware, madam," he said to her back, "what I say is true. I do take care of my own—and their debts."

The meaning of what he said was lost upon Heather, but Fanny Simmons grew very pale and very nervous. She refused to look at him. She was still silent when a servant came to announce that luncheon was served.

Chapter 4

A cold October thunderstorm had washed the autumn
air and left the day with occasional squalls chasing
themselves across London. The wheels clattered over the
cobblestones and splashed through mud holes as the landau lurched and jolted its way toward the docks. Heather
sat quietly by Lady Hampton in the rear seat. The woman
spoke softly to her and now and then smoothed a glossy
black curl lovingly, or lightly touched her hand. It was
the only indication of nervousness displayed despite the
sorrow of the approaching moment. But often Heather's
eyes were drawn hesitantly to the stoical face of her husband who sat beside Lord Hampton across from her. He
was braced in the corner against the bumps and his eyes
moved slowly and impassively about the carriage, falling
on her for a moment then sliding away with the same
ease with which they had touched her. Lord Hampton
made sporadic attempts to engage him in conversation,
but was rewarded with brief, noncommittal answers uttered only for the sake of politeness.

The carriage made a careening turn and swept down a
narrow waterfront street, crossed an open muddy court,
and drew up in the lee of a building. A small sign rattled
and clapped above a door, labeling the structure: *Charleston Enterprises Warehouse*.

Brandon stepped lightly from the carriage and turned to Heather. "You'll have several moments to say your farewells. I must have the warehouse agent signal my ship for a lighter."

With this he strode away, the wind ruffling his close-cropped hair and the lace at his cuffs. Heather's gaze followed him into the building, then she slowly turned to Lady Hampton and found tears brimming in the woman's eyes. Their parting sorrows could no longer be withheld. She fell into the woman's arms and through their tears their hearts communed—a motherless girl, a childless woman. Lord Hampton rather hoarsely cleared his throat. It was a brief moment's passing before Heather sat upright again and he took her hand into his.

"Rest easy, child," he comforted. "It is the way of the world that few partings are forever. Who knows when our paths may meet once more and we might share another moment of life. Take care, my child. Take very special care."

Impulsively Heather hugged his neck and brushed his leathery cheek with her lips. "Won't you please come and see me again before we sail?" she pleaded.

"No, we mustn't, Heather. Your husband's ire has been strained enough. It's best we bid farewell here. Perhaps he will later forgive us, but for now, God speed, my very own."

She threw her arms around Lady Hampton again. "I'll miss you both," she gasped, tears flowing freely.

Her ladyship clasped the girl firmly to her. "You will have your husband, my love, and soon a child. You'll have precious little time to think of us. But something tells me you'll be happier with him than you were here. Now go, my dear. Go seek your angry man. And Heather—remember that anger and love are but a whit apart."

Reluctantly Heather drew from Lady Hampton's embrace and moved to the door of the landau. She heard her husband's voice just outside as he spoke briskly to a lounging tar, and she realized he had returned and was now standing by the horses waiting for her. Brushing the tears from her face, she opened the door and lifted her skirts to descend from the carriage. Brandon hurried to assist her and slid his hands to her waist. Their eyes met, and for once, thankfully, he did not mock her tears. He lifted her down gently, then reached into the carriage as Lord Hampton handed him their cloaks and the small bundle of gifts from Lady Hampton. She moved away as he spoke in a low voice to the Hamptons.

The *Fleetwood* stood out in open harbor several hundred yards from the dock awaiting her turn at loading. Just pulling around the bow, a whaleboat skimmed toward them, four deckhands straining at the oars. A small, elderly, somewhat agitated man stood in the stern, urging them on, no doubt with colorful phrases.

Closer around her the dock was alive in a chaos of sound, sight and smell. Idle sailors loafed about with the stench of the prior evening's revelries still upon them, and drab, unwashed strumpets quite boldly hawked their wares, hoping to make a shilling or two or an evening's bed and board. A group of rats squealed stridently over garbage in the open gutter, then fled as a rock flung by an urchin thumped among them. Shrill laughter rang as several unwashed ragamuffins skittered across the dock, leaped over the gutter and disappeared in an alleyway.

Heather shuddered, remembering how she had thought of giving birth to a bastard and letting him grow up knowing this life of the streets. At least now the child would have an existence above this. What did it matter that she was neither loved nor wanted as a wife? Her child would have a father and something of a home despite having a sire who sailed the sea.

This was the life of a merchant captain—this squalid, filthy scene around her and that small ship yonder. What part she would play in her husband's life she did not know as yet, only that she would be the mother of his child. Whether he took her with him on other voyages in the future or left her conveniently behind was his decision and one in which she would have little or no say. But as she faced the wind that brought the scent of the sea to her nostrils, so she must face life—head on, taking whatever small pleasure her husband allowed her and being content. In time, perhaps, she would not care that love had passed her by.

At the touch of her husband's hand on her back, Heather's thoughts fled swiftly. He had come with a noiseless tread, startling her. Feeling her slight body quiver, Brandon drew his cloak over her shoulders.

"We must go now and meet the boat," he murmured.

Taking her arm, he guided her through stacks of cargo, coiled ropes and nets as the whaleboat approached the end of the pier. When the craft first touched the dock, the small man leaped ashore and scurried to meet them. He snatched the round stock cap from his head, and Heather realized with a start that it was George, her husband's cabin boy and manservant. The man bowed in a jerky manner and addressed his master.

"We thought you were to come back yesterday, cap'n. We almost give you up for lost. I was about to form up the hands and beat through the city for you thinkin' you'd fallen ill to the 'pressment gangs. You give us quite a worry, cap'n." And with a bob and hardly a pause. "Hello, mum."

"We were detained at Lord Hampton's for a bit," Brandon replied.

With a nod and another jerky bob, George resettled his hat over his shiny pate, relieved his captain of the bundles and walked behind as they proceeded to the boat. Brandon descended first to the craft, then swung his young bride down beside him and settled her in the bow. George tossed him the bundles and painter, slid down the ladder, assumed his place in the stern and set the tiller.

"Look lively, mates," he demanded. "We're under way now. Push off. Port oars awash, not stroke, lads— stroke—stroke. Now both and bend your backs to it, lads.

'Twill be a cold enough journey for the mum yet we drag it out. So hump, laddies, make it good.''

The small craft slid beneath the stern of a moored merchantman and headed out across open water to the *Fleetwood*. There was a light chop rolling before the breeze and a chill spray of water struck Heather's face, snatching her breath and sending a cold shiver through her. She pulled Brandon's cloak tightly about her and huddled deeper into its warm folds. Any comfort was short lived, however, for the elements combined in a concerted effort to effect renewed discomfort.

The whaleboat's prow broke the back of each wave, swung high then slid down into the trough. The unaccustomed motion upset Heather's stomach, and each new plunge seemed to raise her gorge a bit higher. She cast an uneasy glance to her husband who sat with his face into the wind, seeming to enjoy the feel of the salt spray, and pressed her hand to the base of her throat.

''If I retch now, I'll hate myself forever,'' she thought wildly.

Her knuckles grew white but her face gradually assumed the greenish shade of the sea. Her battle was nearly won, yet as they drew near the ship, she raised her eyes to the tall masts, lurching back and forth above her in direct opposition to the motions she felt. A miserable groan escaped her lips at the confusion of movement and drew Brandon's immediate attention. He looked for one brief moment at the pale, distressed face and the slender hand struggling for control and acted swiftly. Sliding his arm around in front of her, he lowered her head carefully over the gunwale and let nature resolve itself in the sea.

A few moments later Heather gave a last shudder and straightened, loathing herself. Shamed and humiliated, she dared not raise her eyes. Beside her, Brandon wet a handkerchief and pressed it to her brow.

''Are you feeling better now?'' he asked gently.

The motion had died away and the craft now stood in

the lee of the ship. She managed a weak nod as George eased the boat against the curved belly of the barque.

As Brandon secured the bow painter on the chains the older man did likewise aft. The captain then braced his foot on the ladder and turning, gestured to Heather.

"Come, *ma petite*, I'll help you aboard."

She came cautiously and made to set her foot on the ladder beside his. His arm went about her and, taking her slight weight against him, he climbed up to the deck of his ship. He set her down and for a moment his attention returned to the whaleboat, leaving Heather to gaze about. She found herself standing at the bottom of a seemingly confused tangle of ropes, cables and spars, and through them all, the great, raked masts lunged skyward, now swaying with a soft, gentle rhythm against the clouds. From the bowels of the ship came an almost musical squeaking, creaking and groaning. The tempo of sound and motion matched and almost made the ship a living, breathing thing beneath her. It had a clean, salty smell, and as she looked she realized each item was neatly in its place, ropes coiled at hand, pins and buckets stowed. A sense of order lay about the ship.

Brandon returned to her side. "You will need to change your gown, Heather. I purchased a few things for you before I found you had disappeared. They're in my cabin." And with a mocking eyebrow raised, he added, "I believe you know the way."

She blushed profusely and glanced hesitantly toward one of the doors beneath the quarter-deck.

"Yes, I can see that you do," he murmured, watching her. "You will find the clothes in my trunk. I will be along in a moment."

So dismissed, she moved away from him to the door. Before she opened it, however, her gaze went back for one brief moment to her husband and found him deep in conversation with George. It seemed he had already forgotten her.

The cabin was as she remembered it, compact and

small, occupying as little of the precious cargo space as possible. The day's dreariness made it a deep twilight within as only soft hazy light came from the windows at the stern. Before she moved to the trunk she lit a candle on the table and hung her husband's cloak on a peg by the door. Then she knelt before the trunk and her fingers touched the latch and lifted the lid.

A startled gasp escaped her as she saw the beige gown neatly folded on top. Memories came flooding back, reminding her of William Court and of the night spent in this very cabin.

Her eyes were drawn reluctantly to the bunk where she had lost her virginity and she gazed at it for a moment, remembering the struggles that had taken place there, the passionate and fiery lips against her flesh, and lastly of the defeat. Her hand slid to her belly with a will of its own and her face burned.

She started when the door behind her opened and Brandon walked in. Hastily she pushed the beige dress aside and pulled out a deep red velvet gown that was beneath. It possessed a neckline cut low, and sleeves, fitted and long, trimmed with white lace at the wrists. It was a gown made for a woman with no childish affectations to mar its simplicity and beauty.

As Brandon pulled his coat off and threw it on the bunk, she rose and began unfastening her gown with trembling fingers. She stepped out of it carefully and put it away in the trunk.

"There's an inn nearby," said her husband behind her. "It will be more comfortable for you there than it is here."

A small frown touched her brow as she turned and looked at him. He had unbuttoned his shirt and was already engrossed in his ledgers at his desk. As easily as he dismissed her from his ship could he dismiss her from his mind. Perhaps he would even leave her behind when he sailed. There was no guarantee that he would not, and she would be left destitute.

"I am not unaccustomed to discomfort," she replied in a soft voice. "I will be content to stay here. You need not take me to an inn."

He glanced up at her. "You are very agreeable, my love," he flung with a short, scornful laugh. "But it is I who make the decisions here. The inn will be more suitable to your needs."

She had not thought of this, that he would so cruelly leave her behind. She felt a coldness begin to grow in the depth of her body.

"Is this truly to be my fate?" she wondered forlornly. "To be left on the waterfront to fare as I might in childbirth at the hands of midwives who know nothing more than filth and squalor? Is my son to have a name and still to live his life as an urchin in a gutter?" She turned and a shiver of apprehension went through her.

Was there no mercy in this man? If he wanted her to beg, she would gladly go down on her knees before him and plead for her child's life. But he did not seem to want that. He had made up his mind coldly and without emotion. She was to go to an inn.

Trying to calm her fears, she drew the red gown up over her shoulders and went to where he sat. His attention fell on her and a strange expression crossed his face. The deep rich color of the gown had darkened her eyes until they appeared as midnight blue, and the flawless skin shone startling white against the red. Her bosom was generously and beautifully displayed, the gown barely covering the pinkness at its peaks.

Terribly afraid and unsure of how he would react to doing this small labor for her, Heather turned her back to him.

"I'm not able to fasten it," she murmured softly as her stomach fluttered and her consternation grew. "Do you mind?"

She felt his fingers on the back of the gown, and she bent her head forward and waited, scarcely breathing, until he finished, then she moved away, casting an uncertain glance over her shoulder at him as she did. He was again studying the books, but now there was a black scowl on his face.

As she went quietly about the room, putting her bridal cape away, gathering the clothes she would need at the inn, and hanging his discarded coat on a peg inside his locker, she eyed him covertly, fearing that she would do some small thing to irritate him, but he seemed absorbed in his books and oblivious to her.

The time dragged slowly and silently by. There was only a moment's respite when George brought coffee and tea. But he served his captain with hardly a murmur and brought the tea to her where she sat in the gallery behind her husband's chair. Then the servant was gone again, leaving her to listen to the gentle sighing of the ship and the dull thud of her heart.

The time was nearly ten of the hour when Brandon pushed his chair from the desk and looked at her once more. His eyes dropped to her bosom and he frowned again.

"You had better wear my cloak to the inn," he said brusquely. "I have no desire to be waylaid once we're ashore by some petty whoremonger who thinks you'll bring him a pretty price."

The color flew to Heather's face and her eyes fell from his gaze. She murmured an obedient answer, slid from the cushions and brushed past him to get the cloak.

A few moments later they were in the boat waiting for George to descend. The servant dropped her bundle and a duffel bag to the boat, then climbed down and gave orders to the sailors to push off. On shore he walked behind them, looking cautiously over his shoulders for would-be thieves or other dangerous characters.

They arrived at the inn without incident and entered to the strains of a melancholy tune a sailor was singing. The man was small and thinly fleshed, but his voice was a full baritone of gentle touch. Near him, a few men sat quaffing ale and listening, enthralled by the magic of his voice. A fire crackled in the hearth and an aroma of roast pig rose into the air, making Heather's mouth water. She closed her eyes and tried not to think of the hunger that gnawed at her stomach.

Brandon murmured something to George and the servant went off quickly to talk with the innkeeper as Heather followed her husband to a table in the corner. She slid into the chair he held for her, and a moment later they were being served food and drink which Heather accepted gratefully as her stomach growled for nourishment.

She did not notice the stares she drew from the men nor the cloak slipping away from her shoulders nor two seedy-looking men who sat across the room from them talking in low whispers to one another. Her attention was divided between her food and listening to the song of "Greensleeves" the tar was singing. With a start she felt her husband lean over her. He drew the cloak again over her shoulders and her face flamed as she lifted her eyes to his.

"I bought the gown for my private admiration, my love," he said softly, "I didn't mean to have you pleasure other men with the sight of your lovely bosom. It is not wise to do so either. You are causing a stir among these men."

Heather pulled the cloak together and glancing about cautiously, she realized what he said was true. She seemed the center of attention. Even the sailor had stopped singing for a moment as he gazed at her. Shortly he began again.

> *Black is the color of my true love's hair*
> *Her looks are something wondrous fair,*
> *The purest eyes and the softest hands*
> *I love the grass on where she stands*
> *I love my love and well she knows,*
> *I love the grass on where she goes.*

If she on earth no more could stay
My life would quickly pass away.

Heather glanced at her husband and saw that he was irritated with the sailor's song. His eyelids had lowered over his eyes as he attended his meal, but in his cheek a small muscle twitched. As before, she grew silent and fearful when she sensed his anger.

After dinner, the innkeeper showed them to the room for which George had made arrangements. The servant carried the bundles in, then removed himself with the innkeeper. For a few moments Heather waited for Brandon to leave also, never to be seen again, but he lounged in a chair and seemed in no hurry to go, so she went to him and had him unfasten her gown, and she began to undress as if she expected him to stay. She took down her hair and ran her fingers through it to smooth the curls because she possessed no brush or comb. Aware of her husband's eyes on her, she slipped out of her gown and shift and laid them over a chair and donned a nightdress Lady Hampton had given her.

The gown was of a thin white batiste with inserts of lace over the bosom, and a neckline cut round and very low. Beneath the breasts a narrow ribbon was drawn through lace and tied. The sleeves were full and long and a ruffle edged with lace fell over her hands. Though less filmy than the gown of her wedding night, this one, like the other, was meant to give a man pleasure, but as she moved in front of a candle's glow, it brought an angry oath from Brandon's lips. Heather glanced up with a start to see him striding toward the door.

"I'll be back in an hour or two," he growled, opening the door. Then he was gone and Heather sank to the floor as tearful, frightened sobs choked her.

"He cannot even speak the truth," she gasped. "He will never return."

Each moment then that passed was longer than the one before. She paced the floor, wondering what she was to

do and where she was to go. She could not go again to
her aunt's and allow her child to grow up under the
woman's hateful hand, nor could she go to Lord Hampton and ask him to help her. She had too much pride to
cast her troubles upon them again. Perhaps if life were
merciful she would find work as a maid here at the inn.
She would ask tomorrow, but for the night she would
sleep if she could.

The night aged and try though Heather may to calm
her fears and push her doubts aside, sleep did not come.
It seemed an eternity had passed when she heard a bell
toll the hour of one. With a cry she jumped from the bed
and ran to the window to slam it closed. She dropped her
head against its frame and her slender shoulders shook
with sobs. Just outside her door she heard a man's voice
and another in reply. Her fear doubled, and when the
door opened, the color drained from her face. But the
light in the hall touched on George's face and silhouetted
her husband's tall, broad-shouldered frame.

"You came back!" she breathed.

His face turned her way before he closed the door and
they were again lost in blackness.

"Why aren't you in bed?" he asked, moving in the
darkness toward the bed. There was a scratch of flint and
steel. The tinder caught and he lit a candle on the table
then looked at her. "Are you ill?"

She came toward him from the shadows and the candlelight made the tears sparkle in her eyes. "I thought
you had left me," she murmured. "I thought I would
never see you again."

For a moment he gazed at her with some surprise, then
he smiled gently and drew her near. "And you were
frightened?"

She nodded her head piteously and tried to choke back
a sob but it ended sounding like a hoarse croak. He
brushed her hair from her face tenderly and touched his
lips to her brow to quiet her trembling.

"You were never alone, *ma petite*. George was outside

the door all the time, guarding it. He's just now gone to get some sleep, but do you think me the cad to leave you, not assured of your safety?''

"I didn't know what to believe," she whispered. "I feared you would never come back."

"My God! You are not very complimentary to me— nor to yourself. I would not leave a lady to her own defense in such a place and more certainly my own wife and she heavy with my child. But if it will calm your fears, I'll not leave you again while we're here."

She lifted her eyes to his and saw a kindly warmth in them. "No, there is no need," she murmured. "I'll not be frightened again."

He cupped her chin in his hand. "Then let us go to bed. The day has been long and I am tired."

Wiping the tears from her cheeks, she climbed into bed on the side nearest the door and watched him quietly as he opened the bundle George had carried in with her own. Her eyes widened as he took out the box of Flint-lock pistols with which she had once threatened the servant. He brought it with him to the bed where she lay, and dropping down beside her, took out the pistols and began to load them.

"Do you expect trouble?" she questioned softly, sitting up.

He glanced at her and smiled. "It's just a precaution I sometimes take when I'm not at ease with things around me. You needn't worry, my love."

She watched curiously as he loaded one, remembering her own distress when she had tried to determine how and had not been able to. Seeing her interest, Brandon laughed softly.

"Do you wish now to learn how to load these?" he asked, smiling. "You do very well as it is with them empty. George was quite embarrassed when he found that you had tricked him. The fact that a mere wisp of femininity had made him quake with fright before an empty gun injured his pride. He was impossible for some time after. So was I for that matter,'' he added gruffly, remembering the way he had viciously hurled a string of oaths at the servant when he had returned to the *Fleetwood* and found the girl gone. His disposition had not improved any when he also found that she had disappeared without a trace.

He took her arm and pulled her to the edge of the bed beside him. ''But it is of no importance now. If you desire to learn how a pistol is loaded, I will teach you.'' Then he looked into her eyes and warned, ''But don't ever make the mistake of thinking you can turn these on me and not use them. I am not George and you would have to kill me before you could escape.'' He laughed again softly. ''And as for that, I doubt that you have it in you to kill a man, so I think I would be safe in taking these from you.''

Heather swallowed hard. She stared up at him silently, with eyes round as moons. She believed every word he said. He was not one to make idle threats.

They sat very close together on the edge of the bed, so close their bodies touched—her thigh against his, her arm pressed to his side. His arm was braced behind her, his hand resting on the bed very near her buttocks. Her composure was sorely strained. Nervously she dropped her gaze and pushed the hem of her gown demurely over her thighs and knees, realizing it had slid up almost to her hips when he pulled her to him.

''May I try to load this one,'' she asked, hesitantly touching the pistol he held in his other hand.

''If you wish,'' he replied, handing it to her.

The flintlock was heavy and meant for a man's hand. She found it uncomfortable in hers. Laying it across her knees, she took up the powder horn and lifted the muzzle of the pistol to pour the gun powder down it.

''Turn it away from your face,'' Brandon directed.

She obeyed and poured a small amount of the gray powder into the muzzle. As she had seen him do, she stuffed a piece of paper in and with the rod rammed it down the barrel, then wrapped a lead ball in a patch of oiled cloth and pushed it down the muzzle also. It was done.

"You learn very quickly," Brandon murmured as he took the pistol from her and laid it with the other on the table. "Perhaps you will be another Molly Pitcher."

Glancing up at him, she frowned slightly. "Who is she, Brandon?" she asked softly, not realizing that she had spoken his name for the first time.

He smiled and reached up to touch one of her glossy curls. "It was a name given to women who helped carry water to American soldiers in battle and to one woman in particular who helped to hold the line against the British at Monmouth."

"But you are English too, Brandon, are you not?" she asked, gazing up at him with curious eyes.

He laughed, "Indeed no, madam. I'm an American. My family came from here, it is true, but long before they died they considered themselves loyal Americans. My father helped fight the British and as a boy so did I. You will have to get used to the idea that your beloved England is not so beloved where we're going."

"But you trade with us," she said in much astonishment. "You sail here and do business with the people you once fought."

He shrugged his shoulders. "I am a man of business. I sell my cotton and goods to the English for a profit. They sell me what my people will buy for more profit. I never hold grudges if I think it will interfere with the business of making money. Besides, I do a service for my country in bringing back the things that are needed and are not yet obtainable."

"Do you come here every year then?"

"I have been for the last ten years, but this will be my last year. I have a plantation to run. I can't neglect it any longer. And now I have other responsibilities on the way. I'll be selling the *Fleetwood* when I get home."

Something caught at Heather's heart. Was it possible

he meant never to sail again, to settle down and be a
father to their child? Perhaps she would even be allowed
a nominal position in his household. The very thought
flooded her being with warmth and she almost relaxed
against him. But cold reality and doubt chilled the dream.

"Will I live on your plantation too?" she asked, almost fearing the answer.

"Of course," he replied, rather amazed at her question. "Where did you think you would live?"

She shrugged her shoulders nervously. "I—I didn't
know. You didn't say."

He chuckled. "So now you know. Now do be a good
girl and get into bed and go to sleep. Your chattering has
worn me out."

She crawled into bed again as he stood up and began
to undress. When he had stripped, he motioned her across
the bed.

"It's best I sleep nearest the door," he said.

She quickly moved to the other side of the bed and
did not ask why she must. It was clear he expected something to happen.

He blew out the candle and lay down beside her. A
dingy lantern hung aglow in the courtyard below and in
the gusty evening breeze, cast its bouncing shadows
dimly into the room. To her dismay, Heather found that
her hair was streaming across Brandon's pillow and was
caught beneath him. She waited for him to free her, but
a long time passed and he did not and then she knew he
would not for he had fallen asleep with his cheek against
her soft curls. With a sigh of resignation, she settled herself to pass the night in bondage, but with his presence
close beside her, she found security and she sank into the
nether realms of slumber.

From the depths of sleep she struggled with terror's spurs
goading her to full awareness. A hand pressed tightly
over her mouth, smothering screams bred of panic. Her
eyes flew open and in frenzied reaction she clawed at the

hand. Then her husband's face loomed up close above hers in the darkness, and with senses returning, her fear passed and she sank back to the pillow. She stared up at him in confusion, her eyes wide and searching.

"Lie still," he whispered softly. "Don't move. Don't make a sound. Pretend to be asleep."

She nodded her head to let him know she would obey. His hand slid away and he sank down again beside her. His breath came slow and even, as if he were asleep, and from beyond the door she could hear a muffled voice and an odd picking and scratching at the door itself. The bar slowly began to lift, and she struggled to control her own breathing. With the fluttering in her chest it was no easy task.

A dim thread of light appeared and grew wider as the door swung open. Through slitted eyes she watched and saw a head appear. She heard a whisper.

"They're asleep. Come on."

Two dark figures stole into the room, and the door was pushed shut. Heather gritted her teeth as the men moved forward and almost jumped when the floor creaked beneath their feet. An angry whisper came.

"Do not wake the bloke, you fool, or we may not get the girl. He's not a wee one."

"She's across the bed," the other whispered a little louder.

"Sh-sh," the first hissed. "Don't you ken, I kin see that with me own two eyes."

They approached almost to the foot of the bed when Brandon snaked the pistols from beneath the sheets and sat up.

"Hold your pace, lads," he demanded. "You've been found out. And do stand very still for these worthy pieces have two leaden balls to hole your hides."

The two froze in mid stride, one half turned as if to flee with the other holding his companion's arm.

"Heather, light the candle that we might set faces to our midnight visitors," Brandon urged.

She crawled behind him quickly and lit the candle on the commode. The glow of its flame spread over the room softly and touched on the men's faces, proving them to be the same two who had huddled across the room from them at mealtime.

"We meant no real 'arm," one spluttered. "We wouldn't 'urt the girl."

The other intended kidnaper was bolder. "We can guarantee you a tidy sum for 'er, cap'n. She'll bring more'n 'er weight in gold from a certain duke we know. It won't matter that she's no virgin even." His eyes went to Heather and he grinned, showing badly rotted teeth. "She's well worth the price, cap'n. We'll split three ways, we will."

Trembling, Heather pressed closer to her husband and drew the bedcovers up under her chin. She disliked the way the men leered at her. She knew if they had been successful in taking her she would have been used many times by both of them before she'd have ever been presented to the duke. They were akin to William Court, intent upon satisfying their own lusts first.

Brandon laughed dangerously as he stood up and faced the men. He was casually unconcerned with his state of undress and bore the pistols with a careless swagger which did not ease the two thieves' nervousness.

Heather felt the heat rising to her face. It was one thing to be alone with Brandon when he was naked, but to have others present—it was something else entirely. His male nudity seemed all the more startlingly bare to her with these men here.

"I must disappoint you good gentlemen," he said lightly. "This girl carries my child, and I am a selfish man."

"It won't matter about 'er, cap'n," the timid one interrupted. "The dukie will bed 'er in the ninth month, and seeing she's so comely, it won't be difficult for him. 'E'll give her a few hours to whelp, then 'e'll be on her again. 'E'll pay the same for 'er now, an' we'll give you half seeing you'll be needing to find another wench to warm your bed."

Brandon's eyes burned coldly and his knuckles grew white about the pistols. A small tic began to show itself in his cheek.

"There's a foul odor in this room that almost smothers me," he drawled, a forced grin twisting his lips. "Step over to the window, laddies, and open it for me. And do be gentle as you go, for my hands grow weary."

The two men scrambled to obey, then turned again to the Yankee smiling.

"And now, my hearties, I must once more explain before you take your departures," Brandon began in a slow, precise way, almost gently. Then his voice became very menacing and dreadful with his rage apparent in each separate word. "This girl is *my* wife and carries *my* child. She belongs to *me,* and what is *mine,* I *keep!*"

The last words seemed to blast all thoughts of gain from the brigands. Their jaws dropped, their eyes widened in fear, and small beads of sweat dappled their brows. They now became deeply concerned with their continued longevity.

"But, cap'n, she—we—"

They both stuttered in their attempts to placate him. The bolder one finally managed to speak clearly.

"But, cap'n, we didn't know. No common wife would seem so fine to bed. I mean, sir—"

"Be gone with you," Brandon roared. "Take your leave before I throttle you both!"

They started toward the door, but were halted as Brandon chuckled wickedly.

"Oh no, laddies. The window will do sufficiently well."

They gawked and spluttered at him. "But, Cap'n, would ye 'ave us break our necks on the cobblestones?"

"Out!"

The pistols threatened and the two men scrambled to comply. They scuffled briefly and the bolder one plunged through the window, whether aided or not was uncertain. A meaty thud, then strangled curses and groans were heard from below.

"I think I've broken both my poor legs, you sea scurvy bastard!" was the man's cry.

The meeker one gazed backwards, but Brandon gestured and the man made his reluctant departure. Upon his arrival below, a cacophony of angry shrieks, oaths and moans became an original account of the many possibilities of what might have occurred on Brandon's family tree. But their shrieks only drew an amused chuckle from the second-story window as Brandon closed it. He barred the door again and secured the bar so it could not be lifted again from without. The sounds outside dwindled off as the two thieves hobbled away.

Still chuckling, Brandon slid into bed beside Heather who now sat in the middle of it, watching him quietly, her eyes a little wide. He grinned at her.

"I wonder what damage befell the last one. He screamed the loudest, don't you agree, my pet?"

She met his gaze, then as she nodded, a soft ripple of musical laughter escaped her.

"Oh, I do indeed agree," she laughed. "And I suppose I must feel honored that they lied about what I should bring. No man would pay such a price for a woman."

He looked at her for a moment in a queer manner, listening to the sound of her voice, watching the bright, happy smile. His gaze fell to the smooth, silky breasts rising full and tantalizing above her gown and to the soft transparency of her dress which concealed very little of her slender body. Moisture broke from his brow as he experienced once again a familiar tightening. A muscle in his cheek flexed as he turned away, and a sudden impulse to hurt her surged upward within him.

"Considering what you must weigh it wouldn't have been very much," he said harshly before he blew out the candle, and in the dark he added coldly, "If they had offered more I might have been tempted."

Bewildered by his sudden change of mood, Heather crept to her pillow and lay down. She did not know what she had done or said to cause him to want to hurt her so cruelly. He was so unpredictable. How could she understand him? One moment he was gentle and kind as he had been earlier, the next she was left speechless by his irascible disposition.

Morning found Brandon in absence and Heather quickly jumped from the bed. She washed and threw on her clothes, leaving the red gown unfastened because she could not reach the hooks. Quite bravely she searched through Brandon's duffle until she found a brush. Wondering what her chastisement would be if she dared use it, she bit her lip and almost put it back. But there was no other and her hair looked quite impossible. There was a likelihood he might never notice its use if she were quick, and in an effort to have the task done before discovery, she started brushing vigorously. But much to her dismay he came in just as she was giving her hair a few final strokes. She jerked around to face him, looking very guilty with the brush in her hand. She saw immediately that he was in a foul temper and that she had chosen a bad day to be brave.

"I'm sorry," she said. "I don't have a brush of my own. My aunt has the few things that were mine."

"Since you took it upon yourself to use it without my permission," he growled low, "you might as well have the pleasure of doing so."

She put the brush down hastily as he moved toward the window beyond her and she sidled away from him with caution. She cast a furtive glance over her shoulder at him as she began braiding her hair, to assure herself he was staying by the window. Her look fled elsewhere when she saw that he was watching her. She began to tremble and with her fingers shaking it was difficult to plait her hair neatly. She had to start over several times before she was satisfied with the results, and always she was conscious of his green eyes on her. She managed somehow to double the heavy braids and tie them above each ear so that the loops hung freely and brushed her shoulders as she moved.

"I'm taking you to a clothier's this afternoon," Brandon said flatly, turning away to stare out the window. "You'll be needing gowns more modest than what you have on."

Holding the dress in place, Heather eyed him warily. He was dressed in a casual manner, not yet having donned his coat. His breeches were fawn colored and tightly fitting and he wore a waistcoat of the same hue. His shirt was white, as were his stockings, and full sleeved with a ruffle edged with lace falling over his brown hands. As always his clothes were immaculate and in excellent taste. She had noticed that once he dressed himself to suit his own personal high standards, he did not fuss nor bother about his attire. He was no mincing fop.

His attention seemed now concentrated on the world outside their room, and she saw by his profile that his brows were drawn down in a heavy scowl. The sounds of carts and carriages rolling over cobblestones came now and then from the streets below, but it was mostly only the cries of beggars and urchins that drifted in.

She went to the bed and made it up, moving as noiselessly as she could around it. After that task was done, she sat on its edge and waited for time to pass or for her husband to move or give her a command. She waited an eternity. Her back began to ache and she leaned her head against the bedpost. She closed her eyes, but they fluttered open again with nervousness. Her stomach gnawed at her backbone. Finally Brandon moved and she straightened, drawing the falling gown up over her shoulders again. His eyes raked over her dispassionately.

"Are you intent upon going about in that manner till night or are you going to come here and let me fasten you? If you want to eat, you'd better come quickly."

She slid from the bed hastily, not daring to do otherwise, and went to him, her teeth tugging at her bottom lip. Her heart thumped heavily as she raised her eyes to his.

"I didn't mean to displease you about the brush," she said uneasily. "My hair was so tangled from letting it go unbrushed last night. I couldn't do anything with it."

He gazed down at her for a moment, his face void of any expression, then suddenly the scowl reappeared. "It is of no bother," he said curtly. "Just turn around so I can hook the dress."

She obeyed as the color drained from her face, her eyes full of bewilderment. Disregarding his displeasure over the use of his brush, she sensed he was still vexed with her over last night though she possessed not the slightest reason why he should be.

When they went down to eat, George gave her a quick bob and a "Hello, mum," and pulled out a chair for her, then spoke to his captain briefly and hurried away. Heather's eyes followed him to the door. Frowning slightly, she wondered how many of her husband's men the servant had already told of her earlier presence aboard the *Fleetwood* and of everything that had followed. He seemed to know quite a lot of his captain's business.

But brief though her expression was, it did not escape Brandon's notice.

"You need not worry about George, my love," he reassured her abruptly. "He is very discreet. It is enough to say that he knows that you were no woman of the streets and is regretful for the trouble he has caused you. And though you may wish to disagree, he is not a stupid man. He saw the stains of your virginity when he carried the bedclothes from my cabin that day. He safely assumed you had been deflowered."

Heather felt she would die of shame. There was nothing left to do. She could never face the manservant again, knowing this. A little groan escaped her as she hid her scarlet face in her hands.

"Please do not distress yourself, my dear," he said lightly, a one-sided grin curving his handsome mouth. "It is certainly nothing to be ashamed of. There are many women who wish they could offer such proof of purity to their husbands when they are first taken to bed by them. It pleases a man to know there have been no others before him."

"And were you pleased?" she snapped, her eyes flying to his face. He was laughing at her again and that riled her.

His grin widened as his eyelids drooped lazily. "I am as other men, my pet. I was pleased. But I had no need to be shown proof of your virginity. You know yourself when I became aware of it. It gave me quite a shock, to say the least. I might have pulled away and begged for forgiveness if I had possessed any inkling that you were not willingly beginning in that business." And he added with a soft laugh as if in apology, "But I'm afraid you made logical thinking impossible."

"Where was the need then?" she asked bitterly. "You had already done your damage."

He chuckled and his gaze devoured her as it had the previous day. "Not quite, my love. I had not then given you the part of me you carry with you now. If I had withdrawn from you then, there would have been no pregnancy. But as it happened, you have a life growing in you now, and I am to blame. Your aunt and uncle made it easy for me to be certain that the child is mine."

"I could, however, be lying about my condition," she replied with bravado, wanting to shatter his cocksureness if just for a brief moment. She lifted her lovely little nose and dared to meet his gaze.

"You're not," he said flatly, smashing her efforts without a moment's hesitation.

"You have no proof—" she began.

"Don't I?" he drawled, one mocking eyebrow raised.

Then she knew she had charged fullbore into her own defeat.

"You forget, *ma belle*," he said lightly. "I have seen you in your natural state, and though it's not at first apparent, you do have a lovely little stomach growing. In a month's time it will be quite obvious."

She fell silent as the serving maid came to their table. There was nothing more to say anyway. How could she argue against the truth?

After the meal, George came back again.

"Would you be wantin' me to hail a livery now, cap'n?" he asked.

Brandon glanced at Heather. "If you are ready, my pet?"

"I must beg to be excused a moment," she replied softly, not wanting to look at him. He must surely be aware now that her needs arose more often than his. With his almost constant companionship since the wedding, her many pleas to be excused must have struck him odd.

He turned to George and spoke in a low voice. "We'll be along in a moment.

When the manservant had gone, Brandon stood up and helped her from her chair. "I'm sorry, my love," he murmured, smiling. "I thought of other things and not of your delicate condition. Please forgive me."

So, he had noticed the frequency of her trips after all and related them as was due to her pregnancy. Was there nothing that escaped him? And was there nothing he did not know of women?

She glanced up and saw his grin, and for a fleeting moment her eyes met his. But under his warm gaze her cheeks grew pink and she became flustered. He laughed softly when her look went chasing off and his arm slid behind her back. He squeezed her waist gently before his hand fell away again.

She was walking back to the door where Brandon stood waiting when she heard her name spoken by a familiar voice. She turned with a start to see Henry Whitesmith rushing toward her holding a full tankard of ale in his hand and wearing the garb of a merchant seaman.

Apparently he had entered with a group of sailors while she was out. Surprised at seeing him, she was unable to speak for a moment as he hurriedly set down the tankard and took her hands into his.

"Heather, my love," he cried happily. "I thought I would naught see you again afore I left. But what are you doing here, and where's your aunt? Did you come to see me off?"

"Off?" she said stupidly, not knowing what he meant. She frowned. "Henry, what are you doing here? Where's Sarah? Why are you wearing those clothes?"

"Don't you know, Heather? I've signed onto the *Merriweather* of the British Tea Company. We sail within a fortnight for the Orient. I'll be gone two years."

"But why, Henry?" she asked, stunned. "What has become of Sarah?"

"I couldn't marry her, Heather. I love you, and I won't marry anyone but you. So I come here to London to seek my fortune and get rich like you said you'd have a man. I have a chance now to do it. When I return from the Orient, I'll be gettin' a full three an' a half shares. Why, Heather, do you know I'll come back a wealthy man. I could even have as much as five hundred pounds in my pockets."

"Oh, Henry," she sighed miserably, dragging her hands from his.

Once more he gazed upon her with adoration. His smile was broad and his eyes bright with joy. He did not notice her distress.

"You look grand, Heather. I've ne'er seen you looking so fit." He reached out and touched her cheek gently and his hand trembled. "Will you wait for me, Heather? Will you say you'll be mine? Would you even marry me now an' send me off a happy man?" His gaze dropped to her breasts, and his voice was unsteady and the words seemed to catch in his throat as he spoke. "I want you, Heather. I love you, an' I want you badly."

"Please—" she gasped. She glanced past him and saw

Brandon coming toward them, a heavy scowl on his face. She looked back at Henry nervously and then he was upon them.

"If you are ready now, my love, we must be going." Brandon said, dragging his cloak over her shoulders to hide her bosom from Henry's gaze. "The carriage is waiting."

Henry stared at Brandon incredulously and watched his arm go about Heather's shoulders. He was filled with a sudden rage, seeing another man touch his beloved.

"Heather, who is this man, this—this Yankee?" he demanded. "What are you doing here with him? Where's your aunt? And why do you let this man put his hands on you like that?"

"Henry, you must listen to me," she begged. She did not want to break the news to him like this, not in this public place, not at this time, not so cruelly. Her insides were cold with dread. "I had not meant this to happen, Henry. Please believe me. You should have taken me at my word when I said I couldn't marry you. It was impossible." Her eyes lifted to her husband's and in her own there was a plea for understanding. This boy must not be made to suffer from Brandon's sharp tongue. "Henry, this is my husband, Captain Birmingham of the American ship, *Fleetwood*."

"Your husband?" Henry cried. He stared at Brandon in horror. "Oh, my God, you don't mean it, Heather! Tell me you're jesting with me! You wouldn't marry a Yankee!" His eyes fell in dismay on the other man's dress and richness of cloth. His own rough sea garb wouldn't have been worth the man's stockings. "Not a Yankee, Heather!"

"I would not be so cruel to jest with you, Henry," she replied softly. "He is my husband."

"When—when did you wed," he choked out, tears brimming over in his eyes.

"Two days ago," Heather whispered, her gaze dropping. She could not bear his tears. If she had to stand much longer and talk with Henry she would lose control and run from them sobbing. Her whole body was rigid with her efforts to keep from doing so, and having Brandon's arm around her did not help. It only reminded her that he was to blame for all this. But his silence was a blessing.

"Can you tell me why you married him—a Yankee, an' not me, Heather?" he questioned miserably.

She raised her eyes to his. "What need is there of that, Henry? I am married now and it cannot be undone. Let us say farewell now and part. You will forget me soon."

"You won't tell me?" he asked.

She shook her head and tears blurred her vision. "No, I cannot. I must go now."

"I won't forget you, Heather, you know that. I love you an' no other woman will do."

Despite Brandon's presence, she rose on her toes and pressed a kiss to Henry's cheek.

"Goodbye," she whispered, then she turned and let Brandon draw her away and lead her outside.

In the carriage she stared out the window glumly and did not care at the moment that Brandon watched her and was in an angry mood.

"When did this boy ask you to marry him?" he asked abruptly, after the carriage was on its way.

She turned from the window and sighed. "After I met you," she replied.

His brows drew together in a fierce scowl, and he was silent for a moment. When he spoke again his voice had a sharpness to it that gave evidence of his irritation.

"Would you have married him if you had still been a virgin?"

She looked at him and caution made her speak the truth. "I had no dowry. His parents would have resented me for that reason. I wouldn't have married him."

"You do not speak of love," he said slowly.

"Love has no place in marriage," she said bitterly. "Marriages are arranged for profit or gain. Those who are in love go find their pleasures in haystacks or meadows. They throw caution to the wind to have each other. It is beyond me to know their reasons.''

Brandon studied her leisurely. ''Now I know you have never been in love, nor been tempted by it, and as I also know, you are still innocent of love's joys, virginal as a matter of speaking.''

She met his gaze. ''I know nothing of what you speak of,'' she said shortly. ''I am no virgin. You are talking in riddles.''

He laughed softly. ''You almost tempt me to show you what I mean. But that would only be giving you pleasure, and you have yet to pay for your part in blackmailing me.''

She glared at him. ''You still speak in riddles,'' she snapped. ''And in lies. I am guiltless of the plan to blackmail you. Must I tell you again?''

''Oh, please spare me,'' he replied with a heavy sigh. ''I have no use for mendacity.''

''Mendacity!'' she shrieked. ''Who are you to accuse me of being mendacious, you—you—''

He jerked her to him sharply. ''Careful, Heather,'' he warned. ''Your Irish temper is showing.''

She swallowed hard as his cold, green eyes bore into hers. It had not taken her long to throw good judgment aside and flare up at him. She must learn to control her feelings better.

''I'm sorry,'' she murmured in a weak voice. She loathed herself for apologizing and for being a coward. Another woman might hiss insults at him anyway, or go beyond good thinking and slap his handsome face. But she couldn't feature herself doing such a thing, and she hated to think what he might do to her if she tried. Even now, to be caught to him as she was with his hands biting into her arms, she was filled with a fear that made her quake. And his fierce, piercing gaze tore from her what little courage there remained. She was a pluckless female who quailed at a mere glance from him.

He let her go and laughed scornfully. "You should take special care to bite your tongue sooner, my dear. You will grow tired of pleading for my pardon if you do not."

"It is difficult to be silent when you taunt and insult me as you do," she murmured disconcertedly, dropping her gaze to her hands folded in her lap. "You leave me little pride."

"I never said I would," he said sharply, turning to stare out the window. "I told you what to expect. Did you think I lied?"

She shook her head slowly. A tear fell on her hand and then another, and she brushed them away.

Not glancing around, Brandon swore and impatiently drew a handkerchief from inside his coat and handed it to her.

"Here," he said shortly. "You will need this. And if you insist upon weeping all the time, it would pleasure me beyond belief if you would remember to carry your own handkerchief. It annoys me considerably to find mine gone when I need it."

"Yes, Brandon," she whispered faintly, not daring to remind him that she had no handkerchief to carry.

For the continuation of the journey, Brandon sat and stared stonily out the window, leaving a cold silence to fill the carriage and a great dread crushing Heather's chest.

Madame Fontaineau greeted them at the door of her shop with a charming smile. Captain Birmingham was a regular customer when he was in port. She liked the tall Yankee. The handsome rascal had a way with women and she was still young enough to appreciate it.

He drew the cloak from the young girl's shoulders, and her eyes slid over the red gown. She smiled with pleasure, deciding no other mademoiselle could have worn it so well. Her curiosity had been aroused when he bought this dress and other clothes for a girl so dainty. She assumed he had found a new mistress. The gowns he had purchased during the two years preceding had been made for a taller woman, more statuesque. This slip of a girl, still in the youthful bloom of womanhood, could never have filled those ample dimensions, and there was something blasé yet naïve in this girl's manner, almost innocent, refreshingly unique. It was enough to set her to wondering. Many of the more successful courtesans frequented her shop and on their wagging tongues Captain Birmingham's name was often bandied with the most complimentary phrases. Thus she knew considerably more of the man's personal life than he guessed. But here was something new and quite different, a small, trim mademoiselle such as one might choose for a wife. Heaven forbid!

She was French herself, certainly not too old, and still very appreciative of a man who could be called a man. She had often regarded Captain Birmingham with more than a business eye, though she had always been careful to leave it at that. She was wise enough to know he would disappear from her world forever if she even suggested they become more than just friends. Out of kindness to an aging and susceptible heart, and lacking interest in an older woman, he would turn her down and never be seen again.

It was then that her eyes fell to the gold band the girl was wearing.

"Madame Fontaineau, may I present my wife."

The woman's mouth dropped open in surprise, but she quickly spoke to hide her astonishment.

"I am pleased to make your acquaintance, Madame Birmingham. Your husband is a favorite customer of mine for a long time. He is an expert on women. You are most beautiful."

Brandon frowned slightly. "My wife must be outfitted with a complete wardrobe, Madame Fontaineau, if you please."

"Oui, monsieur, I will do my best," she said hurriedly, realizing her blunder. Men did not like their amorous activities to be common knowledge, especially to their wives. But the shock had been too much for her. She had forgotten herself when she spied the ring.

Madame Fontaineau moved her eyes over the girl and watched her walk away to look at the materials stacked on the tables. The young madame had a body slender as a reed, yet soft and alluring. A man's hand would ache to touch it. No wonder the Yankee captain had married her. She was quite a beauty, and they made a pair, these two. They were to be envied.

With resignation she glanced up at the Yankee. "Elle est perfection, eh, monsieur?"

Brandon's eyes lifted slowly to his wife's back. "Oui madame. Magnifique."

Heather did not understand the conversation, nor did she try. She noticed, however, that Brandon had replied easily. He was full of surprises. They were conversing now in French, leaving her to wander about the room as she might. She moved aimlessly between the tables, eyeing her husband and the woman secretly. They seemed to know each other well. He laughed with her and the couturière casually touched him on the arm, something she, his wife, could not bring herself to do. She frowned, remembering with clarity what the dressmaker had said. It seemed she was just one of many women he had purchased clothes for.

She turned quickly, vexed with Brandon for bringing her here. He could have spared her this awkward situation.

She lifted a sketch from a nearby easel and looked at the drawing, forcing herself to concentrate on it instead of the man and woman behind her. It did not hold her interest for long. It was a sketch of a gown fashionably up to date, with a high waist but amply embellished with bows and giggaws, one a woman of loose virtue might wear. She didn't like it.

Raising her eyes from the sketch, she found herself being appraised by a young man who had apparently come through the curtain at the rear of the shop just a moment before. His eyes were roving greedily down the front of her dress as if he could see right through it. He licked his lips and moved toward her. She stood for a moment, immobilized in confusion. The lad, mistaking her pause, was heartened. He smiled broadly, and it was his complete misfortune that Brandon looked up from his conversation and saw him approaching his wife with this over-eager attitude.

It was a small straw, but for Brandon it was the one that laid the camel flat. First thieves, then an old flame, now a stripling lad. The girl was his and not some public piece to be petted or gloated over. His patience was at an end. He'd be damned if he'd stand for another man feasting his eyes upon Heather.

Filled with almost uncontrollable rage, he crossed the room in the time it takes to blink an eye. Heather saw him coming and with a frightened squeak jumped out of his way. He seized the lad by his coat and lifting him clear of the floor, shook him like a dog shakes a rat.

"You gutter-licking scum. You'll learn quickly to keep your distance from my wife. I'll smear you from one end of this shop to the other."

The poor boy's eyes almost bugged out of his head, and he squealed in helplessness. Heather stood petrified, all senses stunned, but Madame Fontaineau flew to Brandon and seized his arm.

"Monsieur! Monsieur!" she pleaded. "Monsieur Birmingham. Please. He is but a child! He meant no insult, monsieur. Please let him go! I beg you."

Brandon complied slowly, but his jaw still worked with rage. His hands slid from the boy and Madame Fontaineau seized the lad none too gently and hustled him to the back, chattering the while in angry French. Just before brushing the curtain aside, she was seen to land a stinging cuff upon the unhappy youth's ear. Neither Brandon nor Heather had moved when a moment later the woman returned.

"I apologize, Monsieur Birmingham," Madame Fontaineau said humbly to Brandon. Brushing past him, she went to Heather and took the girl's trembling hands. "Madame Birmingham, he is my nephew and a sometimes doltish child. But ah-h, madame," she added with a shrug of her shoulders. "He is unmistakenly French, is he not?"

As the woman laughed Heather glanced at her husband, her eyes still very wide and uncertain. He met her gaze and raised a mocking eyebrow, but he did not smile and she knew he was still angry.

"Please step this way, Madame Birmingham," the dressmaker smiled, taking Heather's arm. "We will begin with the selection of material for chemises." She pulled Heather with her to some shelves stacked with bolts of sheer muslins, linens and batistes. "May I perhaps suggest the muslin for everyday and the delicate batistes for special wear? They are very soft to lovely skin such as yours."

Again Heather's eyes lifted to her husband's face. He stood nearby and was leaning back against the table with his arms folded across his chest. His expression did not change as she looked at him, and she feared he was angry with her. Her gaze fell nervously and she turned back to the woman.

"It is of no matter," she murmured softly. "Whatever you think best."

Madame Fontaineau glanced up at Brandon to receive his nod of approval, and she grinned, remembering the care with which he had selected underclothing for this girl. The chemises had to be of the finest fabric, soft and transparent to meet his approval. She would not forget when making these new ones.

"He is very possessive with his young wife," she thought, remembering his sudden explosion. "And he will have to fight many men to keep them from her. She has the look of sweet innocence in her face yet she is a temptress. Better that he had fallen in love with me."

"Captain Birmingham, if you will bring madame to the fitting room, we can begin selecting for the gowns. I have some nice sketches which are of the latest styles."

She whirled briskly and led the way to the back of the shop, through the curtains into a hallway, and finally into a small room cluttered with materials and sewing. She brought out a chair and motioned Brandon to sit down, turning as he did so to Heather.

"Madame, if you will allow me, I will unhook you and we may begin measuring as soon as this lovely gown is removed, eh?"

Turning her back to Madame Fontaineau, Heather waited quietly as the woman unfastened the gown for her. The whole room was hardly bigger than the size of a bed and so cluttered with sewing, there was barely room for the three of them. In those close quarters, her skirts brushed Brandon's knees as she moved and there was no place to go but in front of him. He had only to reach out a hand to touch her.

The couturière was most exact in her measuring, using her tape skillfully. Heather found herself lifting her arms, straightening her spine, raising her shift, all at the woman's command.

"Will the madame hold in her stomach now," the dressmaker continued, placing the tape around Heather's hips.

Heather glanced up and saw a silent chuckle shake Brandon's shoulders. She glared at him over the woman's head, not caring any longer that he might have been vexed with her. Disgruntled, she replied to the woman.

"It is impossible."

Madame Fontaineau sat back on her heels where she was kneeling in front of Heather and thought about the matter, how la petite madame could have this slight problem. Finally her eyes rose and a knowing smile curved her lips.

"The madame has a wee one coming, yes?" she asked.

"Yes," Heather admitted begrudgingly with her face glowing pink.

"Ah-h, that is wonderful," Madame Fontaineau murmured. She gave Brandon a sidelong glance. "The monsieur is a proud papa, yes?"

"Most assuredly, Madame Fontaineau."

The dressmaker laughed softly. She thought, "So, he has no doubt it is his. He replies easily and without delay. Perhaps the girl is as innocent as she looks."

Aloud she said, "Ah-h, monsieur, you do my heart good. You do not flush nor stutter with embarrassment when admitting you will be a father. It is good. There is no shame in a man claiming what he has done." She gave Heather a quick, appraising glance before she turned again to him. "And your wife will be a most charming mother, eh, monsieur?"

Brandon's eyes moved over his wife slowly and glowed with a strange light. "Most charming," he agreed warmly.

"Ah-h, look at him!" Madame Fontaineau thought with a sigh. "Already he is impatient to get her back to their bed. La petite madame will never go long without a child of his making in her belly. He will use her well. Ohhh, to be she!"

"Madame looks beautiful in the chemise I made, eh?" she inquired, watching his eyes almost devour the girl. "She has the body of a goddess—full breasts, the slender waist to fit a man's hands, and the hips and legs—oo-la-la!"

Heather closed her eyes, shamed to the very depth of her soul. She felt like a slave being sold to a man—this man—for the purpose of giving him pleasure. One could expect to be pinched and examined any moment. But it was her body Madame Fontaineau spoke of so freely, not a slave's. The woman had no right to degrade her or her person in this manner. A woman's body was something sacred, something private, to be given respect and not sullied by those who would make it so. It was not meant for a slave's block, to be sold nor bartered.

She gritted her teeth angrily and opened her eyes, only to find herself being watched in the mirror by Brandon. Time stood motionless as he caught and held her gaze and would not free it. Even when his eyes lowered to her body, making her acutely aware of the transparency of her undergarment, she could not look away from his face. Then once again his eyes held hers and a small tremor passed through her body and left her feeling weak and giddy and terribly strange.

With no answer from the Yankee to encourage her to continue with her appraisal of the girl, Madame Fontaineau rose to her feet, once again the business woman.

"I will go get the sketches now. If the madame wishes to put on her gown now, I will fasten it when I come back."

She swept out of the room and Heather dragged her eyes from the mirror and reached for her gown. As if in a daze she stepped into it and pulled it up. She slid her arms through the sleeves and crossed them to hold up the gown until Madame Fontaineau's return but glanced up with a start when Brandon reached out and caught her skirt and drew her between the spread of his legs. She stared at him in astonishment, her eyes wide, her mouth open slightly. Her heart pounded fiercely with emotion. The movement did not escape Brandon's observant eye, and he laughed softly as he watched her breasts tremble.

"Why so frightened, my little rabbit?" he grinned. "All I intended to do was fasten your gown."

In a nervous reaction she tried to shield her breasts from his gaze by spreading her hands across them above the neck of the gown, but he only drew them away and grinned mockingly.

"There is no need to cover yourself, my love. No eyes but mine are here to see."

"Please," she whispered breathlessly. "Madame Fontaineau will come."

He laughed softly. "If you will oblige me by turning

around, all she will see is a man fastening his wife's gown. Otherwise—''

She spun around quickly and heard his amused chuckle as he lifted his hands to her gown. He was still fastening it when Madame Fontaineau returned.

''I have brought all the sketches that I have. There are many to choose from, as you will see.''

The woman swept a low tabletop clear and dropped the stack of drawings on it then pulled the table before them, imprisoning Heather between Brandon's knees. When he finished hooking her dress, she sank to the floor and began to study the drawings. These were more to her taste, but she doubted that her husband would want to spend on her the amount these gowns would cost. She looked at them longingly, then sighed.

''Do you not have sketches of plainer gowns, less costly than these?'' she asked the woman.

Madame Fontaineau stuttered in surprise and Brandon quickly sat forward in his chair and leaned over his wife, dropping a hand to her bare shoulder.

''My love, I'm quite capable of buying these for you,'' he said, glancing at the sketches.

Madame Fontaineau breathed a sigh of relief. The captain had excellent— and expensive—taste in clothes. He was not going to let his wife think of pennies at a time like this. And since he was able to purchase a more costly wardrobe, what was the girl's purpose? If the positions were reversed, she would be grabbing the finest clothes she could.

''Since you appear timid of spending my money,'' Brandon said softly to his wife, ''I will help you select the wardrobe—if you have no objections.''

Heather shook her head quickly, feeling jittery with his hand on her. His long fingers seemed like tongues of fire on her bare flesh. Yet they rested on her casually, over her collarbone and the beginning swell of her breast, not seeming to know what they did to her, not seeming to feel her labored breathing under their grip.

"But he must be aware of it and is only tormenting me. He knows I fear him," Heather thought.

She was surrounded by him, his thigh was a hard rock against her shoulder blade, his hand a lead weight holding her at his feet, his head and shoulders looming above her to keep her from rising. She was caught in his trap like a fly in a web, yet to all outward appearances she sat lovingly at his feet and was happy to have his hand on her.

Brandon pointed to one of the sketches. "This will go well in a blue silk the exact color of my wife's eyes. It must match. Do you have the shade?"

Madame Fontaineau first studied Heather's eyes as they lifted to her, then she smiled broadly. "Oui, monsieur, it is the color of sapphire blue. It will be as you wish."

"Excellent," he replied, then gestured to another drawing. "Take that away. She would be lost in all those ruffles."

"Oui, monsieur," Madame Fontaineau agreed. As always he was choosing well. But then, when did he not? The man knew how to dress a woman in the best.

Another drawing was passed over with an explanation that the gown was too gaudy. Five more were chosen. Another two declined.

Heather watched, fascinated, unable to speak. Everything he selected she more than agreed with, and those discarded she had prayed would be. His sense of color astounded her. The man was gifted. She had to admit he chose better than she.

Many more gowns were decided upon at a rapid pace and swatches of material were tagged to them. Nothing went undone. Silks, woolens, velvets were chosen, brocades, muslins, voiles. Heather lost count. Ribbons, jets, beads, furs were accepted for trim and adornments. Laces were carefully examined and ordered. She was aghast at the amount of clothes he bought for her, certainly a great deal more than she had expected. She would never have selected so many for herself if given a free hand, and she found it hard to believe he could be this generous with her. Yet, the gowns were ordered.

"Does everything meet with your approval, my dear?" he asked lightly, and she knew he wouldn't have cared if they had not. He had bought the gowns to please himself, to have her dressed the way he wanted her to be. But everything did meet with her approval. How could it not when it had been chosen so well?

She nodded. "You have been more than generous," she murmured.

Brandon glanced down at her. His position above permitted him the unrestricted view of her bosom as the gown gapped away from her. His hand ached to move downward under the garment and caress that silky flesh.

"My wife is in need of another gown that she may wear now," he said, dragging his eyes from her once again. "Do you have something to fit her that is more conservative than the gown she has on?"

Madame Fontaineau nodded. "Oui, monsieur. There is a little dress I finished just the other day. I'll get it now. It might be what you have in mind."

She hurried from the room and returned shortly with a gown of blue velvet. It had long snug sleeves and a very demure white satin collar which fitted closely about the throat. White satin cuffs trimmed the wrists.

"Is this what you had in mind?" she asked, holding it up.

"Aye," Brandon replied. "Wrap it up and we'll take it with us. Now we must attend to the accessories. You will, of course, have everything ready in ten days."

The woman's mouth dropped open in surprise. "But, monsieur, it is impossible! A month at least, please."

"I am sorry, madame. In a fortnight I set sail. In five days I shall return with my wife for fittings and in ten I want everything delivered to me finished aboard my ship. There will be an extra profit for you if they are ready and well sewn. If not, it is your loss. Can you do this?"

Madame Fontaineau couldn't let such an order go. Even if she had to share some of the profits with other couturières, she would still make quite a large sum. She would have all her friends and family sewing from now until that time, but she would have them ready. The man struck a hard bargain, yet he was accustomed to giving orders and having them obeyed. He was to be admired, for he would accept nothing but the finest work.

"It will be as you wish, monsieur," she said.

"It is settled then," Brandon said. He gave Heather's shoulder a quick squeeze. "We must go now, my love, and see to finishing your wardrobe."

He helped her rise and drew his cloak over her shoulders again. A few moments later they were leaving. Madame Fontaineau stood at the door of her shop watching them go.

"La petite madame is smarter than I," she concluded silently. "By asking first for less she was given more. And he is happy to have purchased the best for her. All women should be so wily."

Then she turned and clapped her hands loudly. "Claudette, Michele, Roaul, Marie. Come quick. We have work to do."

Chapter 5

Well dressed ladies and fine gentlemen crowded the shops of London and pushed and shoved to get where they were going. Remembering her childhood pleasure of going with her father to these same shops, Heather felt her spirits rise. She chatted gaily with shopkeepers, tried on silly bonnets, giggled at herself in mirrors, danced about and completely charmed those persons who could be charmed. Brandon stood back and watched her and was silent. He only nodded to the shopkeepers when she tried on something that met with his approval and paid out the necessary coin. Even when unthinkingly she dared to catch his hand and pull him along with her into a shop, he allowed it and did not rebuke her. But never did she ask for anything nor expect it. She had fun in just looking. She had not been able to do so for a long time. She watched as grand ladies paraded in front of her and laughed to see fat, little husbands trying to catch up. Her eyes shone and her smile was quick and easy. She swirled gaily and turned her head with a carefree air, making her braids swing and causing men to follow her with their eyes.

It was only toward dusk, when her eyes fell on a wooden cradle in a shop, that she suddenly became very quiet and thoughtful. She touched the tiny cradle with trembling fingers and ran her hand over the smooth wood. As her teeth tugged at her bottom lip her eyes raised slowly to his. She was again uncertain.

Brandon came to her side and studied the crib as if considering its purchase. He tested it for sturdiness.

"There is a finer one in my home," he said at last, still inspecting it. "It was mine but it is yet strong and capable of supporting a child. Hatti has been wanting to see it used for a long time."

"Hatti?" she inquired.

"She's the Negress in charge of my home," he answered. "She was there before I was born."

He turned and walked slowly from the shop, and Heather followed and came to his side as he motioned for a livery. His voice was gruff when he spoke again.

"Hatti has been waiting impatiently at least fifteen years for me to wed and sire children." He peered at her obliquely. "I'm sure she'll be overjoyed to see you on first sight considering you'll be quite rounded when we arrive home."

Self-consciously Heather overlapped the cloak in front of her. "You were to be married when you returned. What is to happen? Hatti will surely resent me for taking your fiancée's place."

"No, she won't," he replied brusquely and glanced toward the approaching carriage.

His manner didn't allow further questions and Heather was left wondering why he was so positive the Negress would not resent her. It did not seem right.

The livery stopped before them and Brandon gave the name of their inn to the driver, then tossed the packages in and handed her up. Heather sank wearily to the seat, feeling suddenly very tired and exhausted. The shopping had sapped her strength and now she longed to crawl into bed and drift into restful slumber.

Brandon studied the small, dark head on his shoulder a long time before he slipped his arm around his wife and eased her head to his chest. She sighed contentedly in her sleep as her hand moved to his lap. The breath caught in Brandon's throat. He went pale and suddenly began to shake. He cursed himself for letting a mere girl affect him this way. She played havoc with his insides. He felt as if he were again a virgin, about to experience his first woman. He was hot and sweating one moment, cold and shaking another, a sensation not normal for him, a man who had always enjoyed a woman casually, had her at his whim, made love to her for his pleasure. Now this girl needed to be taught a lesson and he could hardly keep his hands off her. Where was his cold, logical wit, his easy self-control? Had it all flown out the window when he swore to her never to treat her as his wife, then knowing that he mustn't touch her, she had suddenly become the one thing he must have? But he had desired her all along, even when he thought she would never be seen again.

What, pray, was the matter with him? She was barely a woman, hardly old enough to be carrying his child. She should have been somewhere safe with someone mothering her, instead of being here with him and soon to become a mother herself.

But the fact was undeniable. He wanted to make love to her. He wanted to take her immediately, did not want to keep himself in restraint another moment. How much more could he endure of having her near and seeing her in various stages of undress without throwing her down and satisfying himself with her?

Yet he couldn't let himself make love to her, no matter how much he wanted to. He couldn't let his threats slide. He swore she would pay for intimidating him and, by damned, she would! No one could blackmail him, then be happy and content after doing so. It was the devil in him that wouldn't let him be bested, and pride was the devil's name.

She was just a woman and women were all alike. She could be forced from his mind. He had never known one who couldn't be.

But Heather *was* different and it wasn't fair for him to say that she wasn't. The others had all been willing and eager partners in the games of love, knowing well what they were about. This girl was an innocent whose virginity he had taken by force and who knew nothing of men and romance. Now she was his wife, and pregnant with his child. That alone made her different. How was he to forget his own wife? He hadn't been able to forget her when she left him. If she were homely, perhaps it could be possible to push her from his mind. But how could he when she was so beautiful, so completely desirable, and now always so close under his hand?

Before he could answer his own question, the carriage drew up in front of the inn. It was night now and gay laughter and singing could be heard from within, and in his arms his wife still slept.

"Heather," he murmured quietly with his lips against her hair. "Do you wish me to carry you to our room?"

Her head moved on his chest.

"What?" she asked in her sleep.

"Do you want to be carried through the inn?"

Her eyelids fluttered open slowly, but she was drugged with drowsiness.

"No," she replied sleepily. She made no effort to rise.

He laughed softly as he reached down to cover her hand with his. "If you insist, my love, we can go for another ride through the city."

With a strangled cry Heather came awake instantly and snatched her hand from him, jerking upright. His leering grin sent the color burning deeper into her face and made her want to die. She stumbled over him to get out of the carriage and almost fell out head first as she flung open the door. It was only his quick action that saved her when he saw her begin to tumble. With a cry he caught her and swooped his arm around in front of her and hauled her back into the carriage and onto his lap.

"What were you trying to do?" he barked. "Kill yourself?"

She flung an arm over her face. "Oh, leave me be!" she cried. "Leave me be! I hate you! I hate you!"

Brandon's face went rigid. "I'm sure that you do, my dear," he sneered. "After all, if you hadn't met me, you'd still be living with that fat aunt of yours, taking her abuse, trying to hide your nakedness with gowns twelve times your size, scrubbing and scouring until your back broke, taking what bit of food she threw at you, content to hovel in your corner and grow old with your maidenhood still intact, never knowing what it means to be a mother! Yes, I have been cruel to take you from that pleasant life. You were happy there and I should be damned for forcing you from it." He paused only a second before he went on more brutally. "You don't know how sorely I regret letting myself be tempted by your woman's body without first learning that you were still a child. Now I have you slung around my neck for all eternity and it doesn't please me one damned bit when I think of it. Oh, but to have been gelded long ago and allowed to live in peace forever!"

Heather's shoulders slumped forward suddenly and she began to cry as though all the misery in the world was pent up inside her. Her whole body shook with her weeping, and she squalled in her arm as any child would who is lost and forlorn. She didn't want to be a yoke around anybody's neck. She didn't want to be a burden, a dead weight to be endured, hated and unwanted. She had not meant to be such.

Watching her slender body quiver with sobs, Brandon lost all desire to hurt her more. His face was grim and his mouth was drawn downward at the corners. A great heaviness lay upon his chest as he searched unsuccessfully in his coat for his handkerchief.

"Where did you put the kerchief?" he asked with a heavy sigh. "I can't find it."

She shook her head in her arm and caught her breath as she sat upright on his lap. "I don't know," she muttered miserably, not able to think clearly.

She wiped her tears on the hem of her gown as he searched her dress for pockets. As he did so the driver of the livery stepped cautiously to the door and peered in.

"Is there anything I can do for the lady?" he offered uncertainly. "I heard her crying, and it breaks me heart to hear a woman weep."

Brandon frowned at the man slightly as he continued the search for his handkerchief. "There is no need for your assistance, sir," he replied politely. "My wife is just a little upset with me because I won't let her mother come live with us. She'll be all right when she learns her tears haven't changed my decision."

The driver grinned. "In that case, sir, I'll be leaving you to her. I know what it's like to have your wife's mother living with you. I should have been as strong as you when I first married my wife. Then I wouldn't be having the old witch in my house now."

He wandered back to his horses as Brandon finally located his handkerchief between Heather's breasts. He drew it out and wiped her tears and held it as she blew her nose into it.

"Are you feeling better?" he questioned. "Can we go to our room now?"

A sigh escaped her as she nodded and he stuffed the handkerchief down her dress again and gave her a little pat on the rump.

"Let me get up then, and I'll help you out of the carriage."

The inn was noisy and alive with drunken tars and bawdy women whose shrill laughter rang out over the coarse, ribald humor of the sailors. Holding Heather's hand behind him and walking just ahead to hide her tear-streaked face from the stares of the curious, Brandon led her through the room. George had been sitting by the fire but jumped up when he saw them and followed behind to their room. As Brandon opened the door for Heather and allowed her to slip in, the servant listened attentively to his orders and went off again to do as bidded when his captain stepped into the bedroom. Brandon closed the door behind him and glanced at his wife who was bending over the washbowl splashing water on her face.

"George has gone to fetch a tray of food. I won't be staying to eat. And I would prefer that you not leave the room while I'm gone. It wouldn't be safe for you without my escort. If you want anything, George will be just outside the door. Tell him what you want."

She cast an uncertain glance over her shoulder at him. "Thank you," she murmured.

Then he was gone without another word, leaving her to stare dejectedly at the closed door.

The fluttering was like a movement of a butterfly's wings, seeming unreal because of its faintness. She lay very still under the quilt, afraid to move lest it would go away and never come again that night. And in the dark she smiled a little to herself. Once more it came, this time more insistent. Her hand slid to her belly as if beckoned and her thoughts suddenly cleared.

"It does not make it easier knowing he's right. It would have been impossible to get from the cottage unseen, no matter how desperately I planned and hoped. They watched me too closely. I would have spent a lifetime there if he had not already taken me to him and given me his baby."

The stirring was felt beneath her hand.

"So now I am to be a mother, and he is to be hated and cursed because he made me so. But must it be this way? Is it too difficult to show him kindness and gratitude though I know he loathes the ground on which I walk and would prefer to be no man at all than have me chained to him. He has been kind despite his hatred of me. Now I must show him I am not a child and I am thankful. But it will not be easy. He frightens me and I am such a coward."

The sounds of his returning came in the deep darkness of night. He moved quietly about the room as he disrobed and only the lantern outside in the courtyard showed him his way. He eased into bed beside her, turning on his side to face the door. And again the room was still. There was only the sound of his breathing that came to her ear.

Before she opened her eyes the next morning, she heard the rain, a heavy, pouring rain that drove the peasants from the streets and the birds from the air, a clean, drenching rain that washed everything anew. It was the season for rain and sometimes one thought it would never end.

The man beside her moved and she opened her eyes as he pushed away the sheet and sat up. She did likewise and slid out of bed, drawing his attention to her. He frowned heavily.

"There's no need for you to get up now," he said irritably. "I must see to a few last things about the cargo, and I won't be able to take you with me."

"Are you going right away," she asked uncertainly, fearing his frown.

"No. Not immediately. I'll bathe and breakfast before I go."

"Then if it would not displease you," she said softly, "I would prefer to rise."

"Do whatever you wish," he growled low. "It makes no difference to me."

Hot water for his bath was carried in, and he lowered himself into the brass tub when the two of them were alone again in the room. He was in a black, untalkative mood and as Heather came hesitantly to the tub, she was fearful of offering him her services. She was so nervous she couldn't speak, and her hands trembled as she reached out to take the sponge from his hand. He looked up with some surprise when she did.

"What is it you want?" he asked impatiently. "Do you have a tongue in your head?"

She took a deep breath and nodded her head. "I—I wish to help you bathe," she managed.

His scowl deepened. "It is not necessary," he

growled. "Go dress, and if you so desire, you may break-fast with me downstairs."

She stepped back from the tub nervously and turned away. He wanted nothing to do with her this morning, it was plain to see. To keep from aggravating him more she must stay out of his way and not bother him with her presence.

Moving quietly about the room, she gathered the underclothing she had washed after her bath the night before and folded it away, still a little damp. She took off her nightgown in a corner behind him and dressed, putting on the new blue gown he had bought for her. But as the red gown, it fastened down the back, and though she tried she could not manage more than a few of the hooks.

"It will just have to go undone," she decided stubbornly. "I am not going to him. I won't be a nuisance."

She was trying to comb the tangles out of her hair with her fingers when he finished his bath and got out. He toweled himself off briskly without a glance in her direction and began to dress. He only turned her way when he came after a fresh shirt from a table behind her, and with her heart in her throat Heather glided away from him cautiously, fearing he would notice her. The movement, however, brought not only his attention but his anger as well.

"Do you have to be so damned skittish?" he snapped. "I'm not going to hurt you."

Heather stood trembling before his glare. "I'm—I'm sorry," she murmured fearfully. "I just didn't want to get in your way."

He swore under his breath and snatched up his shirt. "I don't mind you getting in my way nearly as much as I do seeing you scurrying out of it. I assure you I won't give you the back of my hand as your aunt was fond of doing. I have yet to hit a woman."

She looked at him uncertainly, not knowing now whether to move or stay where she was. He was tying his stock, jerking at it in his anger and not doing well in the mood he was in. On an impulse, she went to him and pushed his hands aside. He stared down at her warily, but she wouldn't meet his gaze. With nervous fingers she rewrapped the stock about his neck and tied it as she had done many times for her father. When it was neat and in place she picked up his waistcoat from the chair and held it up, while he, still scowling, slid his arms into it. Bravely she went even further and buttoned it for him, though she sensed he was restless and would have preferred doing it himself. When she started to get his coat he waved her away.

"Never mind," he said hoarsely. "I can put it on myself. Get the brush and do your hair."

She obeyed quickly and as she was brushing it he came up behind her and fastened her gown. When he was done, she thanked him, smiling timidly as he gazed down at her, and both the day and her heart grew considerably lighter.

In the several days that followed she spent most of her time in their room, knowing that George was somewhere near. She saw her husband in the mornings when he rose to bathe and dress, and they would descend to breakfast together. He would then leave and be gone until late at night, long after she had retired. He always came in quietly and disrobed in the dark, being careful not to awaken her, but each time she would rouse for a few moments and feel secure in knowing he was back.

It was the fifth morning hence and the usual routine had become relaxed, almost second hand. His dour rising temper was softened by the hot bath each morning and he would even sit still for long moments while she scrubbed his back, a dear concession indeed. These early interludes were gentle and peaceful for Heather. She enjoyed the almost silent companionship they shared. An occasional spoken word and these small services performed one unto the other started her day easily and made them bearable. Even Brandon proved tractable, and

on parting after breakfast below he would place a husbandly peck upon her brow and leave about his affairs.

This late October morning began the same, and with
her hand upon his arm they went down to the common
room to have their meal. He seated her at the familiar
table in the corner and placed himself beside her. As went
the rote, the bovine mistress of the inn yawningly brought
them French coffee to sip before their meal. Brandon
swallowed his black while Heather heavily creamed and
sugared the vile brew. Soon the morning's fare was
placed before them. A large bowl of cold pork pudding
and two ample plates of potatoes hashed with eggs and
ham comprised the meal. There was also soft warm bread
with newly-churned butter and honey, rich and mellow,
to spread upon it.

Heather faced the pudding and plate and shuddered as
she pushed them away. She chose instead a small crust
of bread to spread and nibble. The coffee served to soothe
her uneasy stomach though she was not fond of the drink,
and she sipped it slowly.

"Your fitting is set for this afternoon," Brandon said,
breaking his bread. "I'll be here to take you at two hours
after noon. Ask George to have a carriage waiting for
us."

She murmured an obedient answer as he glanced at
her and bent her head over her cup of coffee when his
gaze caressed her casually. Her composure always
slipped a little when his eyes fell on her, leaving her
feverish and awkward under his careless regard. When
he was near she usually found her tongue tied and intel-
ligent answers came hard.

She sat quietly as he ate, watching him covertly. He
was clothed in dark blue, and the high, stiff collar of his
coat was embroidered with gold thread. His shirt and
stock, almost painfully white, were freshly donned and
held only the lightest hint of cologne. He was impeccably
groomed, as always, and so handsome he made a woman

feel weak just looking at him. Heather realized with some surprise that even she was not unaffected.

"I tore the cuff of the shirt I wore yesterday," he said, pushing his plate from him and wiping his lips. "It would please me if you would mend it. George is not very talented with a needle." He turned her way with a raised eyebrow. "I assume you are."

She smiled and blushed, pleased that he should need her services. "Needlework is one of the first things every English girl learns."

"All prim and proper," he muttered, half to himself.

"What?" she asked hesitantly. She feared he was being snide with her again, and she wondered why he should lose patience with her after these days of tranquility.

But he laughed softly and reached up to tease one of the curls lying over her shoulder. She had washed her hair the day before and today had pulled it back and caught it with a ribbon, allowing loose ringlets to fall down her back. The curls were too much of a temptation for him to leave untouched.

"Nothing, my sweet. I was just thinking how well you are learned in the ways of a woman."

She felt that he was making fun of her, but she was unsure and there was no way of knowing.

The front door of the inn opened and a tall, young man in braided tricorn and blue coat entered the inn. His gaze settled on Brandon, and he crossed the room, doffing his hat. As he approached Brandon looked up, then rose from his chair.

"Good morn'n, suh," the young man drawled. He dipped his head slightly to Heather. "Morn'n, ma'am."

Brandon introduced the man as James Boniface, the purser of the *Fleetwood*. As he presented her, Heather noticed that Mr. Boniface showed not a flicker of surprise when she was identified as his captain's wife. There was no doubt he had already been told of the sudden marriage. In what degree of detail she did not know, but she hoped he was left ignorant of most of the facts and most certainly the date the wedding took place though that indeed would be pleading for a miracle. When she began to show her pregnancy there would be much finger counting and the men of the *Fleetwood* would wonder if their captain and she had been lovers before their marriage.

Mr. Boniface smiled broadly. "It's a pleasure to make your acquaintance, ma'am."

She acknowledged his greeting, and Brandon motioned him to take a seat. "Is it too much to hope that you bring good news from the docks this morning hour, or is there some matter in dire need of my attention?"

Mr. Boniface shook his head and grinned, settling across the table from them as he accepted the proffered coffee. Brandon resumed his seat and leaned back, propping an arm on the back of Heather's chair.

"You may rest at ease, suh," Mr. Boniface assured him. "All goes well. A day from the morrow the slip for the Charleston stores will be open for us, and we can birth and load. The manager says since it's a heavy rush with winter almost on the northern sea, we'll be a full six days to lifting iron and setting sail. It's the best we can expect with a dearth of seasoned hands about the docks."

Brandon breathed a sigh of relief. "I'd nearly yielded hope at ever leaving this port. The hands must be sought out and we must see to the ship. It's too long we've been here. They'll be ready to go home."

"Yes, suh," Mr. Boniface eagerly agreed.

Heather could not share the young man's enthusiasm. She experienced dread and uncertainty instead. She thought no more of what the man might know. This was her home. It was not easy leaving it and going to a strange land. But in her husband's voice she heard a tone that was lighter and warmer than she had ever heard before, and she knew he was more than ready to be going home.

The two men left and she went again to the room to

stay the hours her husband was gone. At her request, George fetched her a needle and thread and sewing scissors, then she set about mending her husband's shirt, a chore she found strangely comforting. With his shirt in her lap and his baby moving within her, she felt a soft contentment and for a few moments very much like a wife. She paused in her task, thoughtful for a moment, and her peace of mind faded. She must soon pack her possessions and leave what had been her home for a perilous voyage to a new land. She faced a great unknown with a man sworn to vengeance on her. She would bear her child among unfamiliar people who might well be resentful at her very presence. She would be like a stripling oak, torn from the forest and planted in a new land. She had no hint of whether she would grow and flourish or wither and die among strangers.

Tears threatened to spill, but she wiped them away and raised her eyes to the window. She rose and went to stand before it and gazed out upon the city she had known. She thought of the shame and the grief she would leave behind and her head lifted higher. For so long now, each day presented her with almost insurmountable challenges that seemed to tear her self-confidence to shreds. At least this was a clean unknown and if God gave her courage, which she needed desperately, and strength, she might shape it into something better. She must deal with each day as it came and trust to the future to be kind.

She returned to the mending, no longer content, but with a new strength forming in her, just as the child formed.

Heather finished the shirt and placed it neatly folded on the bureau. George had brought her a small lunch earlier and afterward she had tidied herself for the outing. She now waited for her husband's return. George came in briefly to report that the carriage had arrived and was waiting in the courtyard. Somewhere in the city a bell tolled twice and as its echoes died away, she heard Brandon's voice from the street below. Soon she heard his footsteps on the stairs, and the door opened. She smiled as he entered and greeted him warmly.

"I see that you're ready," he said gruffly, frowning slightly as he gave her a sidelong glance. He was carrying a gray velvet cloak over his arm and he came to her, lifting it from his arm.

She shrugged. "There wasn't much to delay me, Brandon," she murmured.

"Then here," he said, handing her the cloak. "The air has a chill today and you'll need a cloak. I thought this would suit you better than mine."

She took the cloak from him, thinking it a garment of his. But as she spread it about her shoulders, she realized it was a woman's cloak, and very costly. She had never possessed one so fine before, not even when she lived with her father. She touched it, feeling rather in awe of it, and smoothed the fabric over her skirt.

"Oh, Brandon," she gasped at last. "It's so lovely."

Still frowning he reached up to fasten the silken frogs at her throat, but she was most intent upon the garment and wouldn't stand still in her excitement. She bent from side to side, trying to see it and finally drew an amused chuckle from Brandon.

"Hold still, you little squirrel, and let me do these," he grinned. "It's harder than trying to harness a bee to get these fastened."

She giggled happily and bent her head to look over his hands at the fine cloak. The top of her head brushed his chest and a sweet fragrance rose from her hair.

"And now I can't even see what I'm doing," he teased softly.

A fit of laughter seized her as she tilted her head up. Her gaiety was presented in full countenance, and a smile softened his face as he enjoyed her obvious pleasure with the unexpected gift. His eyes darkened. Unthinkingly, Heather had placed a hand upon his chest, and the contact was electric. Their eyes met and held and the smiles faded. His hands seemed to finish their task of their own accord, then as if moved by some other force, they slid over her shoulders to her back, almost pressing her to him. Heather suddenly felt very weak. Her legs began to tremble and breathing was almost impossible. But still the green eyes held her prisoner, and in the room time seemed to hang suspended. Then a whinny and a shout from the courtyard shattered the spell. Brandon withdrew his hands and mentally shook himself. He smiled again and taking her hand, placed it within the crook of his arm.

"Come, sweet," he urged softly. "We must hurry."

Turning toward the door, he guided her from the room and down the stairs and out to the waiting carriage. It was a small livery, pulled by only one horse, and as they approached George apologized for not finding a roomier and more comfortable one.

"It seems the bigger liveries were taken, cap'n," he said.

Brandon waved his apologies aside and handed Heather in. "There's no need of a larger one, George. This will suffice. We'll be gone several hours I would expect, so have a table set in our room for dinner. Also there's a matter that needs be tended. My wife is in need of a sea chest. Find her an ample one and have it taken upstairs." He drew a small pouch from his pocket and tossed it to the servant. "A nice one, George."

The man grinned and bobbed his head. "Aye, cap'n."

Brandon climbed in and took his seat as Heather carefully held her cloak aside. With a jerk and a lurch the carriage started off, and the stiff-sprung vehicle jolted its way through the crowded streets. Rather than be thrown about between Brandon and the wall, Heather chose to lean against her husband, and at sight of his usually neat lapel standing up, she reached up and smoothed it into place. Brandon accepted her attention passively and for the remainder of the journey sat silent and pensive. He was acutely aware of her presence beside him, the soft curves of her body pressed ever so lightly against him.

The fresh clean scent of soap and rose water that clung to her filled his senses and set his mind to spinning.

Madame Fontaineau met them at the door of the shop with a gay burst of chatter and led them immediately to the fitting room.

"Everything is going well, Captain Birmingham," she assured him. "Much better than I had expected. There will be no problem finishing the clothes on time."

"It is well then, madame," Brandon said, sitting in the proffered chair. "We sail a week from today."

The woman laughed. "Don't worry, monsieur. I do not intend to see you sail without clothes for the madame."

As the woman began sorting through the basted gowns, Heather moved to Brandon and turned around, pulling her hair out of his way so he could unfasten her. A strange expression crossed his face as he lifted his hands to her gown, and his fingers were a little clumsier than usual. She stepped out of the gown, and Madame Fontaineau helped her into the first dress to be fitted.

"It is fortunate," the woman chirped, "that the styles are as they are. You will have no difficulty wearing them for several months with the waistlines high as they are, and we are leaving a good seam in some to allow for your last months."

Brandon's brows drew downward suddenly, and his eyes fell to his wife's abdomen. For a few moments today he had forgotten her condition and the circumstances dealing with their marriage.

"Do you think this gown will meet with your approval, monsieur?" Madame Fontaineau asked of the next dress. "The color is most attractive, eh?"

Brandon moved his eyes down his wife's slender body and then up again, hardly noticing the rose-pink gown that clothed her. He murmured an agreeable answer and looked away.

The gown was removed a short time later and Heather spoke with the woman quietly about the fitting as Brandon watched her furtively. The strap of her shift had fallen over her shoulder but she seemed not to have noticed. From under his brow he stared at the full curve of her breast and the smooth skin of her shoulder, and he stirred in his chair, realizing he was becoming physically affected by the sight.

"Oh, this black gown is my favorite, monsieur," the couturière piped several minutes later as Heather stood bedecked in another basted gown. "Who would have thought black could be so elegant but you, monsieur. The madame looks most radiant, does she not, monsieur?"

Brandon grunted a reply and moved in his chair, beginning to perspire. Just a while earlier at the inn he had been precariously close to breaking his promises with no thought whatsoever of them. With little encouragement he would have forgotten his pride, his honor, and allowed his word to mean nothing. He would have picked Heather up and carried her to the bed, and no one and nothing would have interfered with his making love to her. Now, sorely aggravated watching her dress and undress, he was about at his limits. He couldn't stand much more. His pride and his passions were waging a terrible war, and the outcome was most uncertain.

Scowling, he brushed a fleck of lint from his coat and looked about the room. He did not watch when the dress was removed again.

If they didn't soon finish he was going to prove himself no better than an animal. He would need nothing more than the partial privacy of the carriage to show Heather that he was. And it would do her little good to protest, the way he was feeling now, so wrought up inside it felt as if his vitals were being wrenched from him; and she would just hate him that much more. She seemed so damned pleased with the present arrangement, she would probably fight like a cat if he even suggested she'd have to let him make love to her. After her first experience who could blame her? But he didn't want it to be like that again. He would have to be gentle with her, and show her he could give her pleasure too.

Several more gowns were tried on, much to his discomfort, and he cursed himself for buying so many. His scowl grew ominous and his replies to Madame Fontaineau shorter. Heather and the dressmaker both cast wary glances in his direction.

"Monsieur is perhaps not pleased with the gowns?" the woman inquired hesitantly.

"The work is perfectly satisfactory, madame," he replied stiffly. "It is the everlasting puttering that sets my nerves on edge."

Madame Fontaineau breathed a little sigh of relief. He was just growing weary of the tedious fittings, as any man would.

Brandon looked away again and shifted his position in the chair. At least the gown Heather wore now covered her bosom and he was safe for a while if he chose to glance back at her. She was standing there so innocently, wondering why he was agitated. Didn't she know what she did to a man? Couldn't she guess? Just because he had given his word never to touch her, it didn't mean that he wasn't affected by the sight of her in a shift that left nothing to the imagination and gapped away from her bosom every time she bent over.

Madame helped Heather into another gown and instantly began a stream of rapid French. The gown's bodice was so tight that Heather's breasts swelled more than generously over the low neckline and seemed eager to overflow. In his chair Brandon squirmed and swore silently. A cold sweat broke from his brow and the muscle in his jaw began to tic.

"Ah-h, that Marie!" Madame Fontaineau spat angrily. "She will never learn to sew. Or perhaps she thinks all women are flat like she, oui? Or perhaps la petite madame is a child instead of a woman full grown. She must see her mistake. I must show her."

The woman flounced out of the tiny room, leaving Heather barely able to breathe in the pin-riddled dress. She moved her arm and winced with pain.

"Oh, Brandon, will you see?" she pleaded miserably, moving to him. "I feel like a pincushion. The girl must have left all her pins in the dress. I can't breathe without one sticking me."

She held her arm out of the way, and Brandon paled as she moved guilelessly between his knees. There was an ugly scratch marring the white skin of her underarm, and a long vicious-looking pin protruded from the material at the side of her breast, but the head of the pin was inside her gown and it couldn't be freed from without. Most reluctantly he reached up and slid two fingers inside her bodice against the soft warm flesh of her breast as she stood obediently motionless and watched him with trusting eyes. His gaze caught hers for a second, and amazingly his face flushed red.

"What the hell!" he thought angrily. "She has me blushing like an unsullied virgin!"

He jerked his hand away as if he had been burned. "You'll have to wait until Madam Fontaineau returns," he growled. "I can't reach it."

Heather stood bewildered at his brusque manner. His discomfort was obvious as he sat awkwardly and avoided her gaze. She moved away hesitantly and was greatly relieved when Madame Fontaineau returned with Marie, a thin, gawky girl of no more than fifteen.

"See! See what you've done!" the woman flung at the little girl.

"Madame, please," Heather begged despairingly. "I must get out of this dress. It is full of pins."

"Bon Dieu!" the couturière gasped. "Ah, Madame Birmingham, I am so sorry. This Marie is still a child." She turned to the girl and waved her away. "Shoo! Shoo! I will speak with you later. Now I must attend the madame." At last the dress was unhooked and Heather was grateful. It was the final gown to be fitted, and to Brandon's intense relief, in just a few moments they were out of the tiny fitting room and ready to leave the shop.

On the carriage ride back Brandon was completely uncommunicative. His frown was now a fierce scowl and his cheek twitched spasmodically. When they arrived at the inn it was almost dark, and he swung Heather down rather roughly from the carriage and reached in for the bundles they had collected. He opened the door for her and they entered the inn, noisy as usual with fun-seeking sailors and harlots. As Heather passed through their midst, holding her cloak tightly about her, one brave but drunken soul made to approach her. He retreated rapidly when he saw Brandon and the look on his face. They proceeded without further incident to the room where Brandon threw the packages down on the bed and moved toward the window. A large chest bound with bright brass straps was pushed against the foot of the bed. He frowned down at it as he passed, then scowling over his shoulder at his wife indicated the chest.

"This is yours," he said gruffly. "You might as well put your things in it now. You'll be packing anyway in the next few days."

He proceeded to the window as Heather removed her cloak. She lit a squat candle on the commode and noticed a table had been set with linen and service for two. It had been such an active afternoon she hadn't realized she had grown so hungry. Now just the thought of food made her mouth water and she looked forward with anticipation to its coming. Her stomach gnawed at her as she hung her cloak beside Brandon's on a peg near the door. She was straightening the bundles on the bed when a light rap was heard on the door, and at a gruff "Aye" from Brandon, it was pushed open by George. Two boys followed him carrying platters of food and a bottle of wine. They placed them on the table, then departed as George lit the candles. At the door the servant cast one last quizzical glance at his captain's back and peered at Heather, then took his leave with a perplexed frown. After the door was closed, Heather moved to the table and began serving the plates with the tender roast beef and boiled vegetables. Not aware that Brandon watched her

over his shoulder, she struggled for some moments with
the wine bottle, trying to get it open. Finally he took it
from her and drew the cork with one exasperated movement. He returned the bottle to her and she murmured
her thanks and filled the goblets. When he made no move
toward the table but stood staring at her instead, she
raised dubious eyes to his.

"May we eat now, Brandon?" she pleaded softly. "I
fear I'm starving."

He bowed stiffly and pulled her chair from the table.
As she moved into it his gaze ran down her back, the
sweet curve of it tempting his hand, and he almost
reached out. Then she sat down and for a moment he
stood tensely gripping the chair. At last he seated himself
and took a liberal draught of the wine and tasted a small
piece of meat. Heather, feeling the drain of two bodies,
addressed herself with delicate precision to the meal.
Several times she felt Brandon's eyes upon her, but when
glancing at him found his gaze elsewhere. He picked at
his food with preoccupation and ate little, though often
he refilled his glass with the heady wine.

The dinner was finished and no word spoken though
Brandon still struggled with his weighty problem. Not
wishing to draw some cruel retort, Heather rose and went
to the bed where she began opening the bundles and sorting the contents to put them away in the trunk. She up-
wrapped a rich fox muff and did not resist the urge to
tuck her hands into it. She blew on the fur and rubbed
her nose into its softness without knowing that Brandon
had drawn near and stood watching her. He stretched out
a hand and gently lifted a curl from her shoulder, and
she glanced up to find him close beside her. There was
an odd look in his eyes, half way between pain and pleasure, and he made as if to speak but the words caught in
his throat. He gritted his teeth and a scowl darkened his
features. Dropping the curl, he spun on his heels and his
angry stride took him across the room. He began to pace
the floor like a caged cat, and Heather watched him and

grew more bewildered. His voice startled her when he spoke and she jumped.

"Dammit, Heather, there are some things you must learn about a man. I can't—"

His jaw clamped shut and the small tic showed in his cheek when he turned to face the light. He stopped his pacing before the window and stared once more into the darkness.

After she had waited a long while for him to speak again, Heather gathered the things from the bed and packed them carefully into the trays of the chest. She puttered about the room for some time, casting occasional apprehensive glances at her husband and finally settled herself in a large chair and began to work on a sampler Madame Fontaineau had given her that afternoon. Brandon turned from the window and strode to the table. He picked up his glass and mumbled an oath when he found the bottle empty, then slammed the glass back to the table, causing Heather to start and prick her finger on the needle. He stood by the table a short time, then finally came to her dragging a chair with him. He sat down before her as she put the sampler down in her lap and looked up at him expectantly. He struggled for a moment with what he wanted to say. His hands moved to her knees and smoothed the velvet fabric over them.

"Heather," he finally murmured. "It's a long voyage to America. We'll be together most of the time in a room much smaller than this and sleeping together in a bed half the size of the one that's here. It will be miserably cold and uncomfortable and it won't be pleasant for you at all, especially since you'll be the only woman aboard. You won't be able to wander about freely aboard ship, or leave my side when you're out of the cabin. It would be dangerous for you to do so. You must understand, Heather—sailors long from shore can't look at a woman without becoming—aroused. If repeatedly aggravated they become desperate." He studied her closely to see if she understood what he was trying to say. She was gazing at him intently, listening to his every word, but he doubted that she associated any of this with him. He sighed heavily and began again. "Heather, if a man watches a beautiful woman and is around her for a long period of time without reprieve, he gets a strong urge to bed her. If he can't it becomes painful for him. He must . . ."

He couldn't seem to finish the sentence. Her cheeks had grown pink and she picked at the sampler in her lap nervously.

"I will stay in the cabin as much as possible, Brandon," she said softly, not looking at him. "I'll try not to get in anyone's way."

Brandon swore silently and the muscle jerked in his cheek. "My God, Heather," he rasped, rising to his feet. "What I'm trying to say is—it's going to be a long voyage without—without—dammit, you're going to have to let me—"

He didn't finish. His pride won out, and with a vicious curse he threw the chair out of his way and stormed across the room to the door.

"Don't go downstairs or leave this room," he snapped over his shoulder. "George will be here to watch after you."

He jerked open the door and strode out swearing, and for a moment Heather sat stunned, unable to comprehend exactly what had happened. He had lost his temper with her so quickly, when all she had been trying to do was understand. She heard him growling orders to George, and a moment later the servant came to the door looking as confused as she. He came in with her permission and began clearing the table, and with a small sigh she rose from the chair and went to stand by the window. Brandon's tricorn lay on the sill and she picked it up and smoothed it tenderly, almost lovingly. She turned, still caressing it.

"He forgot his hat, George," she murmured wistfully,

tracing her finger over the braid. "Did he say when he'd be back?"

The servant glanced up from the dishes and looked at her. "Nay, mum," he replied almost apologetically. "Not a word." Then slowly, as if the words came with great difficulty, he added, "Mum, the cap'n sometimes takes with an odd notion, but if you wait a bit he'll usually straighten himself out. Have a bit of patience with him, mum. He's a hard man, but a good one."

Shamefaced, as if embarrassed by his own verbosity, George continued stacking dishes on the tray, and Heather smiled softly, holding Brandon's tricorn pressed to her.

"Thank you, George," she murmured.

At the door he glanced back at her over his shoulder. "Would you be wanting hot water for your bath as usual, mum?"

She nodded her head slowly, still smiling. "Yes, George. As usual."

Heather roused from sleep slowly. Brandon was in the room again, and she stirred under the downy quilt and smiled a little to herself. She blinked sleepily, moving a hand toward his pillow, then sat up with a start. It was almost dawn. The sky was light and the stars were gone. Her eyes flew to he door and there Brandon stood slumped against the sill, staring at her. His eyes were red and watery, his stock loose and his jacket askew. A drunken grin twisted his lips as if he were amused with himself.

"Brandon?" she gasped. "Are you all right?"

This was a side of him she had never considered. He was stinking, reeling drunk. He lurched forward and the reek of issue rum and cheap perfume struck her as if a solid thing. She recoiled slightly and watched him warily.

"You privy wench," he leered. "With your high-curved breasts and your rosy butt, you tempt a man even when you're asleep."

His arm swept out suddenly to clear the top of the nightstand with an angry swipe, and Heather sidled away cautiously, beginning to feel afraid.

"Aaah, damn you precious virgins!" he snarled. "You're all alike, every bleeding one. You castrate a man within his own mind and make him unable to bed another. You rake his pride from his heart with careless claws, then primp and prance and strut about like a hen before a rooster and parade your innocence upon the world with your fine noses high in the air." He stumbled forward unsteadily and locked his arm about the bedpost. He gestured wide as if presenting her to the world. "And here before me sits the queen of virgins, poised upon her throne of ice and surrounded by a moat of purity. And what of me? I played the game and won the prize, and now I have it home and cannot touch the bow."

He grasped the bedpost with both hands and rubbed his brow against it as if rubbing out some pain. "Oh, virgin wife, why weren't you made thin and ugly, then I could ignore you as you wish. But of all the women in London town, my weak-minded self chose you, the finest bit of fluff that ever tempted any man's eye. And you treat me not like a man but as some old buck, too worn to seek a doe. You play and pose before me and expect my spirits not to rise. You tempt and taunt then deny me husband's rights. My God, you wench! Do you think me some safe eunuch? A shilling buys more kindness than I get from you!"

He leaned toward her and peered intently at her face. "But I'll teach you, my lusty vixen," he ground out, jabbing his finger at her. "I'll take you when and where my little heart desires." His eyes raked over her and his voice deepened. "By damned, I'll take you now."

He lunged across the bed, his hands outstretched, intending to seize her by the waist. Heather squealed in fright and scrambled away from him, leaping to her feet in a flurry of nightgown. There was a rending tear, and Brandon lay sprawled across the bed, staring stupidly at a handful of fabric clenched tightly in his hand. He raised on an elbow and lifted his eyes to her in bewilderment and stared at her nakedness, her flesh gleaming white in dawn's light. Then slowly he sank to the bed as his alcoholic stupor overcame him. His hand relaxed and the gown fell to the floor.

Heather watched him cautiously for a moment, expecting him to rise again and come after her. When he did not she came a step closer and peered over his arm at his face half buried in the quilt. His eyes were closed and his breathing regular.

"Brandon?" she said, distrustfully.

He did not move. His eyes remained shut. She reached out gingerly and touched his hand, ready to spring away if he made to catch her. It swung limply as his arm dangled over the bed. She came still closer and stared down at him and moved his arm onto the bed, realizing that she was quite safe now. She bent and picked up her gown from the floor and laid it over the end of the bed, then turned again to him and tried to pull off his coat. It was not as simple as it appeared. He was too heavy to be moved by her alone. There was only one thing left to do and that was to get George. She put on her shift and threw her cloak about her and leaving their room, went down the hall a short way to the servant's. At her knock she heard some dire mumblings from within, then a stumbling. The door creaked open and George appeared, rubbing his eyes. His great nightshirt almost masked the bandy legs thrusting from the bottom. His toes curled away from the chill floor, and from his head a long knit nightcap dangled. His eyes widened when he saw her through his drowsiness, and he hurriedly placed his lower half behind the door. He cast a jaundiced eye to the dawn streaming through the window, then looked at her again.

"Mum! What be you doing this hour?"

"Will you come, George?" she asked softly. "The captain has taken ill of spirits and I need your assistance in moving him."

He frowned his confusion at her but replied, "Aye, mum. Be but a moment."

Heather returned to the room and George followed a short time later with his trousers properly in place. He saw Brandon sprawled on the bed and his eyes widened in surprise.

"Oh, the cap'n's really outdone himself this time," he gasped. He cast a glance awry at his mistress. "It's not a normal thing for 'im, mum, I assure you."

She didn't reply but turned to Brandon and began easing a shoe from his foot. George's gaze went past her to the torn gown tossed over the foot of the bed, and he hurriedly attended his captain without another word. He straightened him about and together they removed his coat, stock and waistcoat. Except for an occasional groan or sigh, Brandon did not wake from his drunken dreams. Only his breeches remained when Heather's eyes met George's in indecision, and they silently agreed to leave him thus. They pulled the sheet over him and before George left he set the night bucket beside the bed, close to Brandon's head. He paused at the door.

"It will be nigh on to noon before he rouses, mum. I'll bring you a little something to ease his head before then." And with a quick glance out the window at the broadening day he murmured, "Good day, mum."

Heather closed the door behind him and returned her cloak to the peg. Dragging a quilt from the bed she went to the large chair in the room and curled into it, tucking her feet under her, and began working on her sampler. Slowly the shock of Brandon's return wore off and in its stead came rising anger. The sampler no longer was stitched with slow, calm motion. The needle was jabbed in it and jerked through as if in vengeance upon the cloth.

"He roams the streets and finds no purchased paramour lively enough to meet his taste," she hissed to herself, "And then he stumbles here and seeks to make me again his nanny goat!"

She glared at Brandon as he slept soundly on his pillow, looking as innocent as a well fed baby, and stabbed the needle through the sampler again.

"You horny fool!" She yanked the thread. "It's only when you've sacked the town you turn to me. And then you posture *me* the villain who tempted your soul!"

His lack of response drew her courage further out. It was rare indeed that she had a chance to display her anger and sarcasm without fear of retribution. She whipped the needle through again.

"You curse all virgins now but not so long ago you found it met your mood to take me."

She flew out of the chair, throwing the sampler on the floor and in a highly agitated state began to pace the room.

"What does he think me? That I would wait humbly and when he snaps his fingers, fall into bed like a well-trained bitch?"

Her eyes fell on the coat hanging over the back of a chair, the shoulders broad, the waist narrow.

"Does he think I dote upon him and plan to spend my life serving his whimsy?"

She whirled and strode to the side of the bed to look down at him, still uncommunicative in his dreams.

"You blithering ninny, I am a woman. What I had I was holding for the man I'd have chosen and you stripped me of even that. I'm a living, breathing human being, and I do have some pride."

With an infuriated groan she spun about and stormed to her chair again, flinging the quilt about her as she sat down. A small snide smile twisted her lips as she gazed at his handsome face. Ah, but he was a magnificent man!

It was past ten of the morning when she woke from a nap in the chair. Brandon still slept soundly, and as she rose she gave him a contemptuous sneer before going about the business of getting dressed. George brought her a cup of tea and a muffin, and after she ate she tidied the room and returned to her sampler to wait the waking of her husband. Noon had long since passed when the first groan was heard from the bed, and in a calm way she continued stitching, watching him as he sat up cautiously on the side of the bed. He put his tousled head in his hands as if it were a weight too burdensome for his shoulders and moaned. Then he caught a glimpse of her shoulders of the corner of his eye and he straightened painfully.

"Get my robe," he growled.

She put her sampler down and went to the wardrobe. He glared at her as she came to him and took it from her. Refusing her help, he put it on and stood up slowly. In agony he walked toward the door and opened it.

"Have my bath ready when I get back," he snarled. "And it best be hot or I'll chew your little rump."

After he closed the door behind him she allowed herself a smile of satisfaction at his discomfort, but she hurriedly saw to his bath, knowing it was safer to obey him. When he came back he was paler, but he was walking a little easier as though he thought his head might stay on. He shed his trousers, handed them to her without a glance and stepped carefully into the steamy bath. He drew in his breath as he eased himself into the hot water and gave a long sigh when he settled comfortably against the back of the brass tub. He sat quite still for the longest time, his eyes closed, his head resting back on the rim, then there was a knock on the door and his eyes flew open angrily.

"Blast it, stop that hammering!" he bellowed, then he grimaced and in a lower voice continued. "Come in if you must!"

Carrying a small tray bearing a snifter filled with a liberal portion of brandy, George tiptoed gingerly into the room with his head slunk low on his shoulders. He exchanged a hurried glance with Heather to see how she was faring and decided she was weathering the storm very well. He handed his captain the drink and beat a hasty retreat.

Brandon swallowed half the contents of the glass in one gulp and eased his head back to the tub again, feeling the brandy spread its glow. Heather readied his towel and clothes, then moved to the side of the tub to help him bathe. For a moment she stood staring down at him, holding the sponge and soap in her hands. Sweat rolled from him freely as he sat in the hot water, taking the evening's poisons with it. He had his eyes closed and his arms lay on the rim of the tub, and he looked almost content. Too content. Feeling an urge to interrupt his reverie, she reached out and dropped the soap and sponge into the water. He started slightly as water splattered on his face, and he opened one eye and peered at her. The water trickled down his face and into his beard but he made no move to wipe it away. The eye bore into her as if he contemplated her slow dismemberment, and Heather lost courage when he opened the other. She quickly glided away to a safe distance and busied herself with inconsequential chores as he stared at her.

She returned, though somewhat cautiously, to help when he finally sat up to bathe. He saw her reaching for the soap and lost his temper.

"Get the hell out of here, you blasted wench!" he yelled. "Get out of my sight! I can wash myself. I never could stand a she-cat scratching at my back anyway!"

Heather dropped the soap with a start and hurriedly skittered away. She went to the door and had opened it when he inquired snidely:

"And where do you think you're going like that?"

Her hand went over her shoulder to the back of her dress; she had forgotten her half-dressed state. She raised her nose into the air. "I'm going down the hall to have George fasten my gown," she replied with a stately air.

She quickly closed the door before he could comment, but she gathered from the outburst of oaths and curses coming through that he was none too pleased with her. As it happened, a chambermaid passed as she moved down the hall, and Heather requested her assistance in hooking the gown.

It was the Sabbath and the inn was quiet, the common room almost empty. Heather ordered tea as she sat down at their usual table and spoke casually with the innkeeper's wife. She had not long to wait before Brandon joined her. He scowled as he came in and took his seat without a word. It was only after the mistress of the inn served them their meal and went again about her business that he growled at her in a low voice.

"Unless you want me to turn you across my knee, madam, and throw up your skirts to paddle your bare backside, I suggest that you take care with what you do."

She turned round, innocent, blue eyes to his, feigning complete ignorance to the cause of his anger. "Whatever is it, my love, that makes you want to beat your wife, and she carrying your child?"

His jaw twitched. "Heather," he ground out. "Do not play coy with me. You would see I am not in a jesting mood."

Heather swallowed hard and turned her attention to her plate. Just that small movement in his cheek was enough to dissuade her. Again she was completely cowed.

It was only when they were retiring for bed that night that he noticed the torn gown hanging in the wardrobe. He fingered it lightly and frowned, then watched Heather climb into bed in her shift. He blew out the candle and undressed in the dark and lay for a long time staring at the ceiling with his hands under his head. There was a slight movement beside him and he glanced Heather's way. She lay on her side with her back to him as far away as she could manage without falling off the bed. She had pulled the quilt over her shoulders as if it would give her protection against him. With a silent oath he turned from her, deciding that nothing had happened after all because she seemed too well pleased with herself and he did not feel relief within his body.

The next morning Brandon hauled his wife out of bed

before dawn, giving her no time to protest.

"Hurry up, wench, I have not time to delay. We're bringing the *Fleetwood* in this morning and I must get out to her."

He helped her dress as he threw on his own clothes, then pulled her along with him downstairs and ate a hurried meal as she drank tea and tried not to yawn. Afterward he escorted her outside through the darkness to the convenience behind the inn and waited until she was done. He deposited her safely in their room and gave George his orders. Then he left and didn't return until the wee hours of morning, and as before, he undressed in the dark and crawled into bed beside her, taking care not to wake her. The following days the schedule was the same, and except for those moments in the morning Heather did not speak to Brandon. She stayed in their room while he was gone and occupied her time as best she could. She ate her meals there or, if few sailors were about, in the common room under George's guard.

It was the fourth night of the week when Brandon came back early. She was in the bath, not expecting him at that hour of the evening, and when the door opened she gasped.

Brandon hesitated a moment at the door, surveying with pleasure this charmingly domestic and most attractive scene. She sat upright with her arms folded demurely across her, her blue eyes wide and only now recovering from surprise. Her skin glistened wet and shimmered in the soft candlelight, and with her hair piled on her head, a few loose curls dropping coyly to her shoulders, she was a fetching sight, by far the loveliest thing he had seen that day.

A small stool stood beside the brass tub to assist in entering and upon it sat a bottle of bath oil and a large bar of scented soap. He smiled tenderly and leaned against the door, closing it. With measured tread he crossed to the tub and placing one hand on the far side, leaned down as if to kiss her.

"Good evening, sweet," he murmured softly.

Confused by his gentle manner and feeling trapped, Heather sank slowly into the tub until the water was about her shoulders. She made an attempt to return his smile but her lips were unsteady. He chuckled softly at her effort and straightened and his face was replaced by his hand holding a bar of soap. The soap hit the water in front of her face and the drenching splash left her spluttering and gasping for breath. She opened her eyes to find a towel being held close to her.

"Wipe your face, sweet," he chided. "It's all wet."

In a rage she snatched the towel and pressed it to her eyes. "Oh, you—you—" she choked angrily.

He laughed softly and walked away, and when she again looked at him he was sitting in a chair with his feet stretched out before him, watching her with a contented smile on his face. She glared at him and his smile only deepened.

"Enjoy your bath, love," he said, then he leaned forward as if to get up. "Would you care to have me scrub your back?"

She gritted her teeth in frustration and started to rise from the tub, but he settled back in his chair and waved her back down.

"Do relax, Heather, and enjoy it," he admonished more seriously. "It's likely to be the last good one you'll have for some time to come."

She sat back and turned to him with a bewildered look, thinking that he had chosen a new way to discipline her. "Brandon—I beg of you. My pleasures are small and this one I particularly cherish." She looked at him pleadingly. "I beseech your kindness, Brandon, not to take this from me. Oh, please. I do enjoy it so."

She bit a quivering bottom lip and dropped her gaze. The grin faded from Brandon's face and he rose and came to the foot of the tub. He leaned his hands upon it and stood looking at her. She sat with her eyes cast down, dejected, like a child expecting to be chastised. When he spoke it was most gently.

"You do me grave injustice, Heather, to imply that I, in spite, would deny you such joy. I spoke only of this: that tomorrow we go aboard the ship as we will sail some three days hence."

She raised her head to meet his gaze and her breasts caught the glow of the candles and glistened in the light.

"Oh, Brandon, I am sorry," she murmured humbly. "It was shrewish of me to underrate you so."

She paused, noticing that his gaze no longer met hers but was directed lower. His lips were white and the tic returned to his cheek as she watched. She blushed deeply, and with an inarticulate murmur of apology drew the large sponge to her breasts. Brandon turned away abruptly and went to stand before the window.

"If you will extract yourself from the tub, madam," he said gruffly over his shoulder, "we might dine in more civilized circumstances. And you'd best hurry, I sent George to fetch a small supper."

Heather complied with considerable haste.

It seemed only a few moments after she had gone to sleep that Brandon was shaking her awake. It was still dark outside, but he was already dressed. He pulled her from the bed and handed clothes to her. She slid into her gown and he helped her yank it down into place and began hooking it while she brushed her hair into order. He wrapped her cloak about her and stood by the door as she rubbed the last traces of sleep from her face with a damp cloth. Then they descended to eat a quick meal and a short time later were walking the few blocks to the ship.

The crew was already astir, making the ship ready for the day's loading, and the men paused to watch the captain and his lady board, and their eyes followed them until they disappeared through the door under the quarter-deck.

Once in the captain's cabin, Heather discarded her

cloak and curled up in his bunk and went back to sleep, not even waking when Brandon drew a quilt over her. After finishing a small lunch which he brought her at noon she climbed up to the deck and stood by the rail to watch the activity of the sailors and the port. Vendors swarmed about the docks selling fresh fruit and vegetables to sailors craving a break in their monotonous diet of salt pork, beans and sea biscuits. Rich merchants, dressed nattily in their finery, rubbed shoulders with beggars and thieves who tried to reduce the size of their purses. Sailors strolled along with harlots, caressing them openly, and liveries with their straight-backed drivers were waiting for hire. Vivid colors mixed with the dull to dress the seaport in its every day splendor. Ships were being loaded and unloaded and the sound of sailors' swearing mingled with peddlers' cries and the voices of merchants' bargaining. Two seamen from the *Fleetwood* kept the dock area clear where the wagons drew up to unload their supplies. She had never seen a place so bustling with activity, and she watched a little breathlessly, leaning over the ship's railing to get a better view of the things that went on below her. She could hear Brandon's deep, authoritative voice every now and then, from different parts of the ship, giving orders to his men as they laid cargo aboard. At intervals she would see him talking with Mr. Boniface or the bo'sun or the mate. On other occasions he would be down on the dock speaking with merchants.

It was late afternoon when she saw George drive up in a horse-drawn cart loaded down with her trunk, Brandon's duffle bag and, to her surprise, the brass tub from the inn. Confused, she watched him unload the items from the cart and bring them aboard. When he set the tub down, he turned to smile up at her, and then she knew that Brandon had bought the tub for her. Her eyes went past George to her husband who stood beyond him with Mr. Boniface. He had glanced around to watch the servant bring the tub aboard and now his eyes lifted to hers.

Their gaze met across the space between them, and Heather felt suddenly very happy and alive. No gift of greater beauty or fortune could have pleased her so well as this old brass tub. The corners of her mouth lifted and the smile was soft and warm and beautiful, and gazing up at her, Brandon was held for a moment in its spell, then James Boniface cleared his throat and repeated his question.

It was evening before Madame Fontaineau and two of her assistants brought Heather's clothes. After they had found everything satisfactory, Brandon brought an iron strongbox from his sea chest and began counting out the necessary sum. The couturière sidled around to look over the top of the box at the contents and gasped audibly at the great amount of money which it contained. Brandon raised an eyebrow at the woman, sending her back to her place across the desk, then continued with his counting.

Madame Fontaineau glanced at Heather, who was kneeling beside her trunk packing the gowns and other items away, then turned again to Brandon, smiling with a calculating gleam in her eye. The sight of money always made her a little reckless.

"Will the madame be returning with you next year, monsieur?"

"No," Brandon answered.

Madame Fontaineau's smile broadened and she smoothed her hair. "When you return you will of course come to my shop to buy her new clothes, will you not, monsieur? I will be looking forward to sewing again for her." And then she cooed. "My talents will be at your disposal, monsieur."

The remark passed Heather's innocent ears without notice, and she didn't glance up from her task, but Brandon understood clearly the woman's intent. His eyes raised slowly to Madame Fontaineau and he regarded her for some moments passively, then very coldly his gaze traveled down her as if appraising her for her worth, stopping momentarily on the somewhat matronly bosom and the broadening hips. His eyes dropped again to the money.

"You misunderstand me, madame. I mean that I will not be returning to England again. This is my last voyage here."

The woman stepped back in shock. Brandon reached across the desk a moment later and handed her the money due in a pouch and Madame Fontaineau didn't stop to count it. She whirled and left without another word.

Brandon was preoccupied with other things at the evening meal so that there was hardly a word exchanged between them, and long after Heather retired to the bunk he worked at his desk with ledgers, receipts and bills. It was past the hour of midnight before he blew out the candles, undressed in the dark and climbed in beside her. Still awake, Heather rolled over to make room for him but there was not much space to spare. Brandon turned on his side away from her and she on hers away from him, and each for different reasons tried not to think of what had taken place when they had last occupied the bunk together.

The next two days passed quickly. The loading was finished, the provisioning completed, the last hatch battened down and final farewells spoken. Long boats came to tow the *Fleetwood* out into the harbor where she could spread her sails and catch the evening's offshore breeze. All aboard grew quiet and thoughtful, yet the ship seemed to cluck impatiently for that fresh zephyr to set her on the way home.

It was a calm evening, the water glassy smooth. The ship sat with her topsails and topgallants spread but hanging slack, waiting for the first breath of wind. The sun was half down behind the rooftops of London when a topsail flapped loudly in the quiet. All eyes drew immediately aloft. The sun was gone now, and a chill breeze stirred against Heather's face as she stood beside Brandon on the quarter-deck. The sails flapped again, and then filled as the breeze strengthened and Brandon's voice rang out.

"Weigh anchor. Look lively, hearties, we're sailing home."

The anchor winch began to clank from the forecastle and Brandon's voice took on an almost gay note.

"Ease off those port tacks. Take in the starboard."

The anchor splashed free of the Thames, and the ship began to gather headway. Heather watched the lights recede in the darkness and there was a tightness in her throat.

It was the wee hours of the morning before Brandon came to the cabin to sleep, and at breakfast he told her what was expected of her on the voyage.

"As far as I'm concerned, Heather, the decks belong to the men until a reasonable hour of the morning. If you venture out too early, you might find yourself blushing. I advise you to stay in the cabin until a late hour."

She murmured an obedient answer, keeping her gaze fixed on her plate, and her cheeks took on a rosy hue.

"And below decks is completely off limits to you," he continued. "The living quarters of the men are there, and you are too tempting a prize for a man on a long voyage. I wouldn't want to have to kill any of my men because they forgot themselves. Therefore, you will stay from there and out of their way."

He glanced up at her over his cup of coffee as she picked up her own cup of tea and stared down into it, her face still flushed. Her slender hands were wrapped around the cup and the gold wedding band, sliding loose on her finger, caught the light of the morning sun. He frowned slightly and his gaze dropped.

Late afternoon, shortly after four, Heather heard the lookout call.

"Land's end, ahoy. Fore quarter starboard."

The day was wintry gray with low clouds scudding across the sky. The wind was blowing a brisk nor'easter as she climbed to the quarter-deck. Brandon stood beside the wheel watching the south of England sweeping by and when land's end stood behind them, he turned to the man at the wheel.

"Helmsman, bring her about. Steady on due west." And then he bellowed to the tops. "Watch those gallants, lads, and take another reef in the mainsail."

He stood for some time with his hands behind him and his feet braced apart, feeling the deck beneath him and watching the rigging, masts and sails until satisfied his ship stood neatly trimmed with the wind on her heels. The sun sat low and red upon the horizon, painting the clouds a golden hue and splattering the sea in red. Land's end stood behind them now, all black and gold beyond the mists. With an aching in her chest, Heather watched the last of England fade from view and from her life.

Chapter 6

*T*he sun rose cold and bleak on the fourth day out and the easterly winds began to pick up. The first two days had been relatively mild and with every inch of canvas spread the *Fleetwood* had plowed along over lightly rolling seas. Now the rigging sang in the wind and the ship strained as it chopped its way through frothy white caps. The ship was heavily laden and rolled low in the water, yet she handled well and responded smoothly to the helm.

Brandon cast a weather eye ahead to a low bank of clouds on the horizon, stowed his sextant and folded away his charts. The wind was biting cold this morning and boded ill weather ahead, yet he smiled to himself as he went below for they were making good time, almost forty leagues a day. He entered the cabin, put away the charts and sextant and poured himself a mug of coffee from the pot on the small stove. As he sipped the hot brew he looked at Heather still asleep in his bunk. Her hand, partly concealed by the lace on the sleeve of her gown, lay across his pillow and her softly curling hair was caught beneath it. He thought of her warm and soft against him, and he wondered briefly how much of a fight she'd put up if he tried to take her now. She stirred slightly as if aware that she was being watched, and he forced the thought from his mind. She stretched lazily under the quilts, and her eyes fluttered open slowly. She saw him and smiled a timid morning greeting.

At that moment George knocked gently on the door, and she flew out of the bunk, giving Brandon a glimpse of a slender thigh before she snatched the gown down and hurriedly pulled on a wrapper. At Brandon's call the servant entered with a tray bearing their morning meal. From his pocket George passed Heather an orange, and she thanked him graciously. Brandon, seeing this movement over his shoulder, raised an eyebrow, wondering if the servant was becoming enamored with his wife's beguiling innocence.

"We'll be having guests for dinner tonight, George," he said abruptly, turning round. He felt Heather's surprise but he didn't look at her. "I have asked Mr. Boniface and the mate, Tory MacTavish, to join us. You will attend to it please."

"Aye, cap'n," the servant replied as he cast a quick glance at Heather. She had already turned away and seemed intent now on warming her hands above the stove. But there was no mistaking that she was upset, and George shook his head in consternation at the younger man's boorish manner. The captain could not stubbornly maintain his independent bachelorish ways as a family man.

The night seemed colder and Heather stood arrayed in one of her new gowns with her back to the little stove, waiting for Brandon to finish dressing. She had chosen the gown more for warmth than anything else. It was of a burgundy velvet with long sleeves and a high, close fitting neck and a bodice embellished liberally with black jets and tiny sparkling beads. She had swept her hair into a fashionable coiffure, and she presented now a most enchanting contrast in this otherwise totally masculine setting. As he gave her a critical appraisal Brandon decided she made a very fetching sea captain's wife. He smiled with amusement as she sidled closer to the stove and lifted her skirts to let the heat rise under them.

"The way you're hugging that stove, madam, I doubt if you'll favor the weather that lies ahead."

He glanced down at her slim ankles appearing beneath the lifted hem and thought of the icy winds that would ruffle her skirts and send her shivering to find warmth. Her daintily made chemises would be little protection when the wind billowed under them and touched on her bareness. He made a mental note to himself that he'd do something about that later.

"Will it be that much colder, Brandon?" she inquired, a little forlornly.

He laughed softly. "Indeed, madam. We are taking the northern route just south of Newfoundland so that we may gather time lost in our delay at leaving England. As it is, I do not expect to be home before the new year, though I have reasons to hope that we might make it before then."

The mate and the purser seemed to enjoy the evening and in particular her presence aboard the ship. If they were aware of her circumstances they gave no indication. Upon entering the cabin they had presented her with a tiny replica of the *Fleetwood* and thanked her graciously for her invitation. Brandon was somewhat taken aback by their assumption that the invitation had come from her and stood aside half mockingly as she accepted the gift, saying that she would cherish it.

The evening progressed smoothly as they entertained her with amusing tales from the English Court. They seemed eager to make the event gay and engaged in light-hearted buffoonery as they made mock battle of retrieving a napkin she had dropped and positioning her chair at the table. Occasionally she felt Brandon's scowl upon her as she giggled her delight with their humor and sensed his strange possessiveness. Under cover of the meal she glanced often to his face and pondered on his moods. His rage at a boy in a dressmaker's shop, his cold anger with two thieves who would steal her from him and with herself when she would have a servant fasten her gown. Yet on every turn of hand he left no doubt that he felt no great love for her. Indeed that he sorely felt the bite of ball and chain. What reason then? Greed? Hardly. She had ample proof of his generosity. The lavish wardrobe, the food they dined upon. The best wines graced the table, the best cigars waited to be smoked. No. It was not greed. But some strange anger grew when other men enjoyed her gay companionship and lightest repartee. What manner of man was she to? Would life with him ever be a normal thing, or just a game of guess with her always wrong?

The meal was over, the table cleared, the cigars now lit with profuse apologies to her, and the talk turned to business. Mr. Boniface asked if it would not be safer to take a southern route. Brandon sipped his wine thoughtfully for a moment and then replied.

"A week before we lifted anchor," he told the younger man, "two merchant vessels left for Charleston with their holds full. Each took the southern route. If they reach port before us our cargo will be worth half of what it will be if we can beat them. It is my hope that we reach our destination prior to their arrival. This is my last voyage and I plan to make a good profit from it for all concerned."

"That's fair thinking, captain," Tory MacTavish grinned, being a man fond of money.

Jamie Boniface nodded his agreement.

"Jeff and I both invested heavily in the cargo," Brandon continued. "I'd like to see our money doubled. If we make it back in time it will be."

Mr. MacTavish fingered his heavy, tawny mustache. "Aye, captain. It's worth the gamble. My own share will be a lot bonnier if we make it on time."

"As mine will be," the purser admitted, smiling.

"Will Jeffie be settling down now that you've taken yourself a bride, captain?" MacTavish inquired with a lively sparkle in his blue eyes.

Brandon quickly glanced across the table at Heather before he chuckled and shook his head. "As far as I know, MacTavish, he prefers to lead the bachelor life despite Hatti's constant nagging for him to do otherwise."

"Seeing that you've done so well for yourself, captain," Mr. MacTavish replied, turning a warm, friendly smile upon Heather, "he may be tempted to change his mind."

Her cheeks pinkening, Heather returned the smile. She felt Brandon's gaze fall on her and stay as if he were contemplating this statement and studying her for its truth. Her hands began to tremble and finally her eyes raised to his, and their gaze met across the table.

Mr. Boniface and Mr. MacTavish exchanged knowing grins. The two men silently agreed not to delay their departure. But when the door was closed behind them, Brandon once more returned to his desk and his books and Heather to her sampler, sitting as close to the heat as she could. The small iron stove was insufficient, and she shifted her position often in an effort to keep all parts at a reasonable temperature. Her movements finally distracted Brandon, and putting away his quill, he turned away from his work. For a while he sat glowering at her with his elbow on the desk and his other hand upon his knee. Finally he rose and came to stand over her, and with his hands folded behind his back, his feet braced apart, he stood for some time while Heather grew increasingly apprehensive at this undue attention. She laid aside the sampler and looked up at him.

"Is there something wrong, Brandon?" she questioned, no longer able to bear his perusal.

He didn't seem to hear her. He turned on his heels and went to his sea chest and raised the lid. He began to remove bundles from within, placing them carelessly on the floor until he came to a small one with which he rose and returned to her.

"You may find these uncomfortable at first, madam,

but I think their refinements will soon become apparent.''

She opened the bundle cautiously and stared in complete confusion at the contents. Grinning at her dumbfoundedness, Brandon reached down and lifted one of the lightly quilted garments from the stack and held the piece up for her inspection.

Totally bewildered, she asked, ''M'lord, you doubt my chastity? You'd bind me up in these?''

His shoulders shook with laughter. ''They're like a pair of men's breeches, but they're to be worn under your gowns to keep you warm.''

She just stared at them.

''You don't know the difficulty I had getting these made for you,'' he grinned. ''Every tailor thought me mad when I described what I wanted, and no one believed that I desired to put them on a woman. I had to pay a good sum to have them made.''

''You say I'm to wear these under my gowns?'' she inquired incredulously.

He nodded, amused at her dismay. ''Unless you prefer to feel the cold wind up your skirts, madam. I assure you I had these made with all good intentions in mind. You need not fear that I make sport of you. I wish only to see you warm.''

She touched the garment in wonder and finally a timid smile shaped her lips. ''Thank you,'' she murmured.

Another five days went by and as each day passed the weather grew colder. Heather no longer doubted the comfort of the odd garments Brandon had given her. She was more than grateful for them now. The first day she had worn them she laughed quite hard at herself when she put them on, never having seen anything so strange before. They reached to her ankles and were tightened at the waist with a drawstring. To her they looked quite ridiculous. She had still been laughing when Brandon came down for lunch, and she had lifted her skirts to show him while he admired the sight with glowing eyes.

It was only where she was now, in bed, that she did

not wear the undergarments, and there was no need with Brandon's warmth near. His body heat was like a magnet, drawing her close while she slept, and often she found herself snuggled against his back if she woke during the night. Several times she had awakened to find him lying on his back and she with her head on his shoulder or her knee raised and resting across his legs. This caused her some shock and dismay, that she could abandon herself so completely to sleep. He was on his back now, but they were both awake. They had retired early to combat the coldness in the cabin, finding the bunk a cozy haven they could share when the little stove was not enough to warm them. This night she had told him of her life before they met, though she suspected he had learned a great deal about her from Lord Hampton, but he listened with interest and asked questions now and then to make the story more complete in his own mind.

"But how did you come to be in London that night we met?" he inquired when she had concluded her story. He turned his head on his pillow to gaze at her and lifted a glossy curl from her shoulder to play with it.

Heather swallowed hard and averted her eyes. "I came with my aunt's brother," she murmured. "He was going to help me get a position at a school for girls, but I got lost when he took me to see a fair the night we arrived in London."

"What manner of man was he that your uncle let you go with him?" he asked abruptly.

She shrugged her shoulders nervously. "A prosperous one, Brandon."

"Blast it, that's not what I mean, Heather. Was your uncle the fool to let this man take you with only his word that he would find you work? Don't you know he could have sold you to men or even used you himself? It is perhaps best he lost you."

Heather lay very still beside him, listening to his anger. She began to wonder if he might be the one person to understand about William Court. She was safe from England now and prison. But would he take kindly to the thought that his wife was a murderess?

Fear chased the thought of confiding in him away, and the truth of that awful night stayed within her. What more could one expect of a coward?

"We just put into port that morning," he murmured softly, winding his finger through a curl. "I might have thought more clearly if it had been otherwise. But I was feeling restless so I bade George find me a little sport. His choice has been full of surprises—a very fertile virgin with influential friends."

Heather blushed profusely and turned her face from him, and Brandon's eyes ran to the nape of her neck where the fairness of her skin shone against her dark hair. It was a most tempting spot and one he craved to press his mouth to. It was difficult to think coldly at times and forget that she was his. He owned that soft, delicate spot he wanted very much to caress, to kiss.

"Now I will have to explain you to my brother," he said softly.

She turned back to him with the surprise of learning she possessed a brother-in-law.

"I didn't know you had a brother," she said.

Brandon raised an eyebrow and regarded her for a few moments impassively. "I'm quite aware of that, madam. There is yet a lot you have to learn of me. I do not blurt out my life's story as you seem fond of doing."

Heather did not take kindly to the insult. Letting out an infuriated groan, she snatched her hair from his grasp and rolled from him as far as she could go. She lay seething while he laughed at her, and tears of rage filled her eyes. She cursed him silently.

Brandon came awake slowly, as if swimming upward from the bottom of a deep pool. His mind was filled with the feel of Heather warm and soft against him. Those tender breasts seemed to bore holes in his back. Her thighs were snuggled under his buttocks and her silken limbs were bare against him. His manhood rose as he thought of taking her, not with force, but with gentle coercion. Her face swam in a vision before him with eyes dark and sultry, and small tongue darting about moist lips. In his half dream her hair seemed to beckon him closer and caress him as he kissed her. Her arms were open and welcoming and her fingers caressed him as his hands found those sensuous breasts and titillated them to excited peaks. He pressed his entry home and she arched her back and writhed in ecstasy as their fervor mounted.

His manhood and mind linked to betray him. Honor, pride, vengeance became as wisps of grass before the whirlwind of his passions. He started to roll over, determined to relieve his masculine persuasion. His hip pressed against her small, rounding belly and there a faint movement caught his attention. He slid his hand over her abdomen and felt it again, this time stronger. His baby kicked within her as if in protest to his thoughts. The hot blood waned and a cold consciousness replaced it. He recoiled with some distaste at having nearly lost his self-control.

He rose from the bunk, taking care not to disturb Heather and donned his robe. The moon was bright and there was no need of a candle to show him his way. He poured himself a brandy and began to pace the room, now wide awake and greatly disturbed. His body commanded him where his mind did not, and lately these dreams were recurring with more and more frequency. If he wasn't careful, he was going to wake one night after the thing was done.

He found himself beside the bunk with his elbow braced upon a beam above his head, and gazing down, he saw her innocent and tender, still deep in slumber. He thought of the cruelty and violence that had bred such gentleness, like iron which, when subjected to extremes, blends and emerges finely-tempered steel. She had withstood the worst he could offer in anger and the abuse of

Aunt Fanny, yet there was a naïve gentleness that seemed inborn to her.

Louisa came to mind, the full-blown woman awaiting his return. She was of a different mold from this slender girl occupying his bunk and not only in physical stature. Having had everything given to her at her asking by doting parents, she had never known cruelty nor violence. Her personality was open and easy, almost nothing could insult her. She was almost bold where men were concerned and enjoyed most thoroughly the pleasures that could be found in a bed, while Heather had expressed her complete contentment at not having to perform the more intimate duties of a wife. And it seemed strange, now that he thought of it, that all the times he had bedded Louisa she had never come with child. The direct opposite had been true here. The first time he had laid hand upon this unwilling creature before him his seed had struck fertile ground.

Now here he stood. All his worldly ways and high self-esteem had been set aside, and he was trapped by a guileless virgin like a young farm lad barely old enough to stroll alone from stable to store. And each day her unsought hold upon his very thoughts grew stronger, and he would before long be hard pressed to withhold his more amorous attentions.

In the bunk Heather stirred and began to shiver, no longer having his warmth beside her. She wrapped her arms about herself and huddled deeper under the quilt.

Brandon smiled wryly and removed his robe. Taking care not to wake her, he slid under the quilts again and took her into his arms to warm her. For this brief time he would forget his passions and his vengeance and just think of her as a little girl in need of someone to care for her.

He was gone from the cabin when Heather woke the next morning. Another quilt had been drawn over her, and noticing it, she smiled a little to herself, thinking how kind he could be sometimes. He came down for lunch in a quiet, thoughtful mood, and hardly a word was spoken between them as they ate. His face was reddened by the cold wind, and he wore a bulky seaman's sweater with a rolled collar, dark breeches and polished boots. He had put aside a knit cap on entering and had taken off a heavy wool coat. He was ruggedly dressed but Heather realized suddenly that clothes had little to do with his good looks. He was handsome in anything he wore, be they these or rich garments, and if anything these rough clothes seemed to accentuate his manliness.

Later that afternoon Heather left the cabin with a heavy cloak wrapped tightly about her and climbed to the quarter-deck. He was nowhere to be seen. She moved to the taffrail beside the helmsman, a sturdy youth with a fine fuzz of a youthful beard upon his face. Bashfully the young man kept his eyes upon the compass and pretended that she was not there. She almost had to shout to be heard above the wind.

"I thought the captain was on watch."

The helmsman raised his arm and pointed upward, and following his direction, she saw Brandon straddling the main topyard, closely inspecting the ropes that held it in place. She gasped and stepped backward, frightened at the dizzy height of his perch. To her the high mast appeared spindly, scarcely able to bear his weight. Her heart seemed to rise in her throat as she stood transfixed with sudden fear. She watched, unable to drag her eyes away. A gust of wind caught the sails and made them clap loudly. The ship heeled slightly and Brandon, caught unawares, grabbed for support. She pressed the back of her hand to her mouth, swallowing a scream, and bit into a knuckle.

Brandon, looking down toward the helmsman with a scowl, spied her and stopped his work immediately. He shinnied down the mast to the crosstree where he seized two back stays and wrapping his legs around them, slid slowly to the rail and then jumped lightly to the main deck. Coming aft, he climbed to the quarter-deck where he spoke rather gruffly to the young sailor at the helm.

"Let's watch those gusts, man. We'll be putting her through a test soon enough without straining her now."

"Aye, aye, sir," the seaman mumbled, shamefaced and quite put down.

Brandon swung his coat from the taffrail and shrugged it on as Heather found her breath.

"Oh, Brandon, what were you doing up there?" she asked, almost angrily. The scare had brought her near tears.

Somewhat surprised at her tone of voice, Brandon glanced at her and saw the distraught face. He stared at her for a moment in wonder at the emotion he saw and then he chuckled.

"Calm your fears, madam, I was in no real danger. I was merely inspecting the rigging."

She frowned in confusion. "Inspecting the rigging?"

"Aye, madam," he replied. Lifting his head, he squinted at the horizon. "Before three days are out we'll be in a good roaring storm, and I'd rather not be surprised by a parting cable then."

"But can't somebody else do that?" she quested worriedly.

His gaze dropped to her again and he grinned as he reached to snuggle her cloak about her chin. "It's a captain's worry, sweet, so therefore it's a captain's job."

Heather wasn't sure she was satisfied with his answer but she could not plead with him to stay from there. "You will be careful, won't you, Brandon?"

His eyes gleamed as he looked down at her. "I intend to, madam. You are far too lovely to be made a widow."

The next day dawned with a blood red sun, an ominous portent of the storm to come. The wind blew brisk but changeable and the men were sent again and again into the rigging to retrim the sails, to reef this one or let out that one. The sea ran choppy and contrary and the heavily ladened ship lurched and bucked. Low clouds boiled and raced. The sun shone through in fitful spurts, lighting the hazy gray sea with spots of translucent green. The night came ebony black and the only light on deck came from a lantern above the helmsman.

Heather ventured out once to the main deck. It was pitch black and she could hardly see her hand before her face. She stumbled across the lurching planks to the main mast and clung to it. She looked back toward the quarter-deck and gazed upon an eerie scene. The mate and the helmsman stood beneath the lantern by the wheel, and as the *Fleetwood* tossed, they seemed to float about against the darkness as if detached from the ship. She swallowed convulsively and hurried back to the cabin, determined to venture out no more until the storm had passed.

Before dawn the winds died and the new day was her-alded only by a gradual lightening. Dense black gave way to shades of gray. The sails flapped loosely in the near calm wind, and the sea heaved smooth and glassy as if heavy grease floated upon its surface. No horizon was visible for the sea blended into the clouds, and occasional low layers of mist obscured the topsails. The ship barely made headway and rolled with a sickening motion on the low swells. Night crept in on silent feet and a tense air pervaded the *Fleetwood* as the men rested for the battle ahead.

The wind gained ground as the night grew old. It seemed a long and restless night, and several times as the wind grew stronger, the crew was roused and sent up to take in sail. The ship was tended carefully that she might be kept in the best possible trim as the storm built around her. When the morning watch came on deck the seas were running high and the craft ran gallantly before the ever stronger gusts, clawing through the crest of each wave, then sliding down into the troughs. To Heather the ship became a world unto itself, a small outpost cast adrift in the churning elements of a crashing, surging chaos. The final sails were set and lashed tightly in place, ropes were strung across the decks to provide hand holds for those who must venture upon them. The main topsail only was spread full and the topgallants were taken in to the last reef, a single sprit sail forward to keep her heels to the wind, and thus she would ride out the storm. From now until the gale was spent no man would dare climb the rigging.

The day wore on and the seas grew higher and the wind raked cruelly everything it could touch. Inside the ship the timbers creaked and moaned as the *Fleetwood* tossed upon this seething mass between sea and cloud.

Heather ceased to know where day began or darkness reigned. It seemed that every rag of cloth aboard was damp and cold, and she rarely saw Brandon except when he stumbled in shivering and chilled to the marrow of his bones. Getting little sleep, he ate and drank his coffee as if in a stupor. When he entered the cabin she would help him strip away his sodden clothes and wrap him in a blanket that she kept warm before the stove. His eyes grew red with strain and his temper jagged. She quietly did what she could to ease his hardship, and when he dozed she let him rest. Usually he soon roused himself to dress and go again on deck to guide his ship between the crushing blows of the rampant sea.

Several days so passed when rising to another angry dawn, she found the deck was thick with slippery slush. The wind blew snow and sleet upon the straining ship and great, long festoons of ice bedecked the rigging. Brandon came below with frost upon his brows. His cheeks were white and stiff and a long time thawing. He sat close to the stove, huddled in the blanket with his hands wrapped around a steaming mug of rum-laced coffee. The brew was finished before his joints began to soften and it no longer took a great effort to move.

Heather was turning the clothes spread to dry before the stove when she was startled by a loud thump and turned to see the mug rolling gently to and fro on the floor. Brandon sat slumped in exhausted slumber. Very carefully she drew another quilt over him, and when MacTavish entered to speak with his captain, she shushed the man and sent him out again. Only the creaking of the ship could be heard in the cabin as she sat with her sampler, jealously guarding her husband's sleep. It was several hours before he stirred and stared blankly about the cabin then finally rose to full awareness. He set himself somewhat refreshed to his duty and his ship, leaving Heather satisfied in knowing that he had rested.

Darkness had descended when George came to tell her the storm was finally beginning to abate and they were heading out of the worst of it. Brandon came in long after midnight to get some badly needed sleep, and waking, she made to rise from the bunk to help him undress, but he told her gruffly to stay where she was. A moment later he slid shivering under the quilts, and she pressed close to help warm him. Gratefully he accepted her efforts, drawing her even nearer as he shook with the cold. Gradually his trembling subsided and he drifted to sleep, too tired even to turn on his side away from her.

At dawn he woke and dressed while she still slept and once more returned to his work. Though the storm still raged that afternoon he came down to the cabin and did not hasten back. He sat before the stove, knees spread, coat wide, enjoying the heat, but Heather had sidled closer to the stove and stood now in her favorite stance, the back of her skirts raised high, exposing her pantalets to the warmth. Brandon casually watched her through half-closed eyes, feeling vaguely sorry he had bought her the underwear. At a knock on the door she dropped her hem and whirled to face the stove. Brandon called out for admittance and George hurried in with a fresh pot of coffee and several mugs on a tray. He poured his captain a cup and turned to her.

"I'll be brewing you some tea in a moment, mum."

Brandon scowled at the servant, thinking how the man pampered her, and turned the same expression on Heather. She felt his tacit disapproval and hurried to smooth his temper.

"I'll just have coffee this time, George."

The servant poured her a cup, looking at her doubtfully. He knew she did not favor the brew.

Conscious of both men's eyes on her, Heather stirred sugar into the coffee and bravely gulped a mouthful, then fought back the shudder that followed. Unthinkingly she looked at George with a distressed smile and asked:

"May I have cream, George?"

Brandon choked and blew a mouthful of coffee back into his mug as he came upright in his chair.

"What, madam?" he choked. "Do you think we'll find a herd of cows in the middle of the North Atlantic?"

She started at his brusque manner and turning away, bent her head low over the cup to hide the rush of tears that welled up within her. He had no right to speak to her in that manner, especially before a servant.

Brandon drained his cup in one long pull as George glanced from one to the other in confusion, wanting to comfort his mistress, yet not daring to. He decided it was time to beat a tactful retreat and picked up the tray and left. Brandon stood up and slammed his cup down on the table and as he followed his man from the cabin he buttoned his coat and muttered something about women under his breath.

When Heather heard the door slam behind him, she sniffed and glared at the offending portal, then snatched up her needlework and began to sew, venting her anger again upon the poor sampler.

"He treats me like a child," she fussed, her lips pouting. "The stupid oaf expects me to know all about his ships and seas! He rants and raves at me in front of others as if I were expected not to feel the jibe."

She threw her sampler aside, seeing that she was ruining it and came to her feet angrily, tears almost blinding her. She fought to control herself, realizing this was not the mood to have him find her in. She must learn to think of her child only and bear what hardships she herself might encounter.

But it was not easy to play the docile wife when her

emotions raged as turbulently as the storm without. When he returned to the cabin late in the day, she was still smarting from the bite of his words. He shed his storm-soaked clothes and donned a robe, stretching himself in a chair before the stove to warm himself, while behind his back Heather glowered at him. Before him her manner was cool and uncommunicative. She hardly spoke to him, only to answer when he asked a direct question.

The evening meal came and went without a murmur from her, and George, seeing her untouched plate, for the first time in his captain's service, doubted the wisdom of the man he had so loyally served. The table was cleared away and she sat down again beside the stove and began to undo the havoc she had heaped on the sampler. Brandon contemplated this task with a sidelong gaze, watching her slender fingers pick the threads from the piece and wondered what had brought about this foul mood of hers.

Some time later she rose and went to her sea chest when he made no move to dress and go again on deck but sat instead before the stove reading a book. Turning away from him, she slid out of her gown and chemise, and Brandon's eyes lifted from the pages of the book and viewed her disrobing with a slow, unhurried regard. Her slender back was bared to the waist and there was a glimpse of a round breast when she bent to pick up her nightgown, and the flame within his eyes burned still brighter, then she quickly drew on the garment and wrapper and let the pantalets fall to the floor, and his eyes went back to the book.

She came back to the stove to brush her hair after turning down the covers on the bunk, and Brandon, losing interest in the book, closed it and put it aside. He watched her openly, enjoying this moment when she freed her hair and allowed it to fall in loose curls about her shoulders and down her back. The candles behind her on the desk silhouetted her slender shape as she stood in profile to him, and his attention was drawn to her abdomen, and for the first time he realized she was beginning to show her pregnancy. By the time they arrived home there would be no mistaking her condition, and questions would be aroused in people's minds, seeing her that far along with child. They would soon decide that he hadn't wasted any time getting her that way after reaching the port of London. He could just imagine their startled faces when he presented her to them. But those who were friends or acquaintances would not dare inquire about her for fear of tempting his anger. It was just family and fiancée who would ask, and what would he tell them, considering she had conceived within twenty-four hours of his arriving in port?

He chuckled over his thoughts and got up and went to her side, giving her a start. The brushing stopped and she turned wide eyes up to him. He grinned at her and put his hand on her belly, resting it there.

"You're rounding quite well, madam," he teased. "Charleston will know I wasted no time in mounting you. It will be most difficult explaining you to my fiancée."

Heather gave a quick, infuriated shriek, decidedly miffed at his words, and shoved his hand away angrily. "Oh, you beast!" she raged. "How dare you speak of explaining me to your fiancée! Had you a heart you'd be explaining her to me! I'm your wife, mother of your child, and you treat me like the dirt you tread upon!"

She brushed past him but whirled again to face him, her blue eyes flashing. "It matters little to me what you speak of to her. I'm sure your words will be soft and sweet as you tell how I forced you to wed me, a woman already breeding. You will paint yourself the innocent, taken advantage of by a scheming woman, and you will not care about your child. Be sure to say, too, my love, that you dragged me from the gutters and gave me your name only because you were blackmailed into doing so. Your words will be very convincing, I have no doubt;

and before you end, you may have won her virginity
too!''

He scowled at her and took a step forward, and
Heather quickly skittered about to put a chair safely between her and him.

''Don't you lay a hand on me!'' she cried. ''If you do,
I swear I will throw myself overboard.''

Brandon reached out and sent the chair sliding away
and Heather backed away fearfully as he advanced. She
stopped only when she could go no further with the wall
to her back.

''Please,'' she whimpered as he took her by the arms.
''Please don't hurt me, Brandon. You must think of the
child.''

''I have no intentions of hurting you, madam,'' he
growled. ''But your waspish tongue does sting my anger.
Be warned, wife. I have other ways to make you miserable.''

Heather swallowed hard. Her eyes were wide and uncertain and her mouth quivered. Seeing her fear, Brandon
turned her loose with an oath and went to the bunk.

''Come now to bed, madam. I have been too long
without sleep, and I intend this night to get my rest.''

Heather's head snapped up as anger replaced her fear.
How dare he suggest she lie beside him after all he had
said to her that day. She was not without some pride.

Though there were tears in her eyes she held her chin
defiantly high and went to the bunk beside him and
dragged her pillow and quilt from it. She took them to
the stern gallery, and Brandon turned with a raised eyebrow and watched her over his shoulder as she spread
them upon the window seat.

''Do you intend to sleep there, madam?'' he inquired
with disbelief.

''Yes,'' she murmured, taking her wrapper off. She
settled herself down on the cushions and pulled the quilt
about her.

''It's not a fit place for you to stay the night,'' he

informed her quickly. "The storm is not over. The window is damp and cold. You'll not find comfort there."

"I will manage," she said.

Brandon swore under his breath and shrugged his robe off and threw it down in a chair. He turned and sat down on the edge of the bunk and stared at her. She twitched and turned, trying to get comfortable, and a sudden lurch of the ship almost deposited her on the floor. Brandon chuckled despite himself, and she glowered at him and snatched the quilt tighter about her. She wedged herself between the beams, bracing against them to hold her precarious perch. She achieved some security, but her position was anything but comfortable.

Brandon sat for a long time watching her before he finally turned to lie down. He saw the empty space where she had slept since the start of this voyage home, and he suddenly realized that he was going to miss her beside him. Just the night before she had shared her body's heat to take the chill from him.

He turned again to look at her and his voice was hoarse when he spoke. "Madam, there's precious little heat to waste aboard this ship. I suggest we combine ours beneath the blankets here."

She lifted her nose primly and settled her shoulders into the corner. "I am so dumb, sir, that I believe there are cows in the middle of the Atlantic and my poor simple brain does not prompt me to rise from this window seat and spend the night in bed with you."

Brandon threw the quilts back angrily. "Well then, my fine feathered lass," he retorted, "I'm sure you and the icy sea will find ample companionship on that oaken sill. I will not beg you again to join me. Just let me know when you've had enough of playing games and I will make room for you. You'll not last long there."

Heather seethed with rage. She would freeze to death before she'd crawl back to his bed and let him mock her.

The night aged and the quilt about Heather slowly soaked in the dampness that seeped in through the window. She began to feel the cold and she huddled deeper in the wet cover to seek warmth. She clenched her teeth to keep them from chattering and every muscle in her body tensed to stop her trembling. She longed for the warmth of the bunk, but her pride whipped anew the memories of his cruelty and would not let her go to its comfort. Her nightgown was no protection against the sodden chill and soon was plastered to her body. Near dawn she finally dozed fitfully, but only because she was near exhaustion.

She roused with a jerk as the cabin door banged shut and through bleary eyes she saw the bunk deserted and her husband gone. She strained to sit up and the cabin rocked and pitched more violently than could be explained by the heavy seas without. She felt no coldness, indeed a dry warmth seemed to enfold her. She sought to fling the sodden quilt aside but it was caught beneath her and her arms began to tremble at the effort. She cleverly changed her tactics and slid her feet to the floor and there she sat while the cabin lurched and swung, then finally slowed to a gentle rhythm. She thought she could manage then. She fought to stand up and shrug away from the quilt, but it clung with the determination of a living thing, and she slid to her knees and found herself beneath its weight upon the floor. Breathing hard from the struggle, she lay still to regain her strength. A chill seeped through from the deck below and the quilt above and she began to shake and shiver violently. She raised her head wearily and spied the stove and thought of its warmth. There was a chair near it. If she could but stand erect, this icy weight would leave her. She dragged herself across the heaving deck. The chair seemed to swim in a fog and retreat before her. The struggle drained her but she fought on, the quilt still clinging like a frosty mantle upon her back. She reached the chair and grasped its legs and painfully drew herself up until she could rest her head upon the seat, and there she lay panting with exhaustion. The room reeled about her and she saw it as if through a long, dark tunnel. She seemed to fall down that tunnel until only a pinpoint of light remained and then it too vanished with a startling abruptness.

Brandon came down from the quarter-deck, somewhat improved in mood. His luck had held and his gamble had paid off. The storm had pushed them south but gained them several days. Having vented its fury upon the ship, it passed beyond, leaving the weather cold and the seas rough but grudgingly breathing its winds upon their sails to speed them on. Yet for all his good fortune, he remembered the night before and his temper turned. He smiled darkly to himself. He'd not allow that stubborn twit to vent her wrath upon him and dance away. She had a lesson still to learn if wife to a Birmingham she sought to be.

He snapped at George to hurry the meal as he passed the galley, and stalked to the cabin door, determined to set her back upon her heels and lay the law before her. He pushed the door open, his face black with rage, then stopped short, all anger draining away as he saw Heather sitting on the floor with her head and arm lying limply in the seat of a chair, a quilt twisted about her hips and her other hand lying palm up upon the floor.

She opened her eyes as he gasped her name and saw him rush toward her. She lifted her head and tried to speak, but her shuddering made her speech incoherent. He dragged the heavy quilt from her and picked her up in his arms. Her head rolled listlessly before dropping on his shoulder. She heard him yell for George and then he was placing her in the bunk and drawing quilts over her. The servant came running in and Brandon turned and barked orders to him, but Heather's muddled mind heard only a jumble of words. Again he was bending over her, this time pushing the covers away. Still shaking violently, she whimpered and fought weakly to keep them over her, thinking he meant to punish her. He was always punishing her.

"Let me, Heather," he said hoarsely. "Your gown is damp. You will be warmer without it."

Her fingers relaxed their grip and she lay unresisting as he unfastened her gown and slid it from her shoulders and down her body. Then once more she was wrapped in the bedcovers.

Heather felt a hand placed to her brow and its coolness was to be treasured. She opened her eyes slowly to look at Brandon, but it was not he who stood above her with his hand on her brow. It was her father.

"Heather Brianna," he coaxed. "Finish your broth like a good child or papa will not be pleased."

"But I do not wish it, papa."

"How do you think you will grow into a fine young lady if you do not eat, Heather Brianna? You are much too thin for a child of six."

The vision blurred and cleared again.

"Must you go again, papa?"

He smiled at her. "You'll be all right here with the servants. This is your tenth birthday. What child that age fears to be left alone?"

She watched his receding back, and her bottom lip quivered and her eyes filled. "I do, papa. I do. Come back, papa. Please."

"Your father is dead, child. He died at the gaming tables. Don't you remember?"

"Don't take my mother's portrait. It's all I have of her."

"It must go to pay the debts. Your father's portrait, too. Everything must be taken."

"We've come for you, Heather. You're to live with your aunt and me."

"So you're the girl. 'Tain't likely you'll be doin' your share of work, lookin' as frail as you do. My dresses will do for you fine. You'll bear no bastards in my home. I won't be letting you out of my sight. You're a witch, Heather Simmons."

"No. I'm not a witch!"

"This is my brother, William. He's come to take you to London."

"How sweet looking you are, child. Meet my assistant, Thomas Hint. He's not the sort who tempts a woman with his beauty."

"Please stay away from me. Don't touch me!"

"I plan to have you, my dear, so there is no reason why you should fight me."

"He fell on the knife. It was an accident. He tried to rape me. Somebody is after me. He does not know I killed a man. He thinks I'm from the streets."

"Do you think I'm going to let you sneak away from me?"

"It was the Yankee who took me. It's his child I carry. No one else has laid hand upon me. He thinks to make me his mistress and have me bear his bastard child while he weds another in his land. He is so pompous. Let it be a girl. I did not mean to cry out. You startled me. Please don't hurt me. He left his hat, George. Will he be back soon?"

"The captain is a good man."

"Oh Brandon, what were you doing up there? He treats me like a child. He pats my belly, then talks of his fiancée."

The heat was unbearable. She thrashed about to escape it. Something cool and wet slid over her body again and again with slow, unhurried motion. She was turned by strong yet gentle hands and her back exposed to the cooling caresses.

"Swallow," she heard a voice. "Swallow."

She saw her father again holding a cup to her lips as he held her up, and always obeying his slightest wish, she drank the warm broth.

Aunt Fanny appeared before her and she screamed as she saw the woman holding her dead brother in her arms, a knife plunged firmly in his chest. She tried to explain that it was an accident, that she really didn't kill him, that he fell on the knife. Thomas Hint came to her aunt's side and shook his head and pointed a finger at her accusingly. She saw the executioner's axe and saw his hooded head and his bared chest. He pressed her head down on the block and smoothed her hair from her neck. The cooling movements returned and her father brushed her long hair up from the back of her neck.

"Swallow. Swallow."

"Is she any better, cap'n?"

She was possessed by shivering. She was cold. Something warm was placed around her, and she was weighted down once more by heavy quilts.

"Papa? Don't leave me, papa. Henry, I cannot marry you. Please don't ask the reasons. There is so much blood. It was only a small wound."

William Court laughed and leered drunkenly at her. Mr. Hint was by his side and they were coming for her. Their claws reached out to catch her, and she whirled and ran from them straight into the Yankee's arms.

"Save me, please! Don't let them take me! I'm your wife!"

"You're no wife to me."

She tossed about in suffocating heat and the cooling motion began again. She saw Brandon above her and he stroked her body with a cool, wet cloth.

"Don't let my baby die, Brandon!"

His large hand slid over her belly and he looked at her. "It lives, my love."

Aunt Fanny laughed behind him. "Do you hear that, missy? Your bastard still lives."

The faces of William Court, Thomas Hint, Aunt Fanny and Uncle John bore down on her, all laughing loudly with their mouths gaping wide.

"Murderess! Murderess! Murderess!"

She flung her hands over her ears and thrashed about wildly. "I'm not! I'm not! *I am not!*"

"Swallow this. You must."

"Don't leave me, papa," she whimpered.

The fields were green with spring grass, and she laughed as she ran from the person behind her. She was caught and swung upward in sturdy arms, and laughing gaily she looped her arms about the man's neck in gleeful abandonment, and his face pressed close as he bent to kiss her. A scream was torn from her as she recognized Thomas Hint. She fought the arms about her waist and turning, saw the figure of a man retreat across the brow of a distant hill.

"Don't leave me! Don't leave me here with him! Don't leave me!"

She was being drawn down into darkness, peaceful, peaceful darkness. She floated, she glided, she swayed, and a mist rolled upward around her and consumed her.

Heather opened her eyes and saw the timbers of the bunk above her and everything was calm and peaceful, only the slight creaking of the ship could be heard. She lay unmoving for a moment, trying to recall what had happened. She had been trying to reach the bunk, but she must have fallen. She moved slightly and winced. She felt bruised, as if every inch of her had been beaten, and she was so weak. She turned her head on the pillow and saw Brandon. He was asleep in a hammock hung between the quarter-deck beams.

A hammock? Here? In the cabin? And he looked so gaunt. There were dark circles under his eyes and his hair was badly mussed and shaggy. Strange, he usually took great pains with them.

Her frown deepened as her eyes went about the room. It lay in complete disorder. Clothing was flung over chairs and boots lay askew on the floor. There was a pan of water near the bunk and rags hung on lines above the stove. She mused vaguely at what disaster had swept the place and why George had not tidied up.

With a painful effort she rose on an elbow and instantly Brandon's eyes flew open. He swung himself from the hammock and hurried toward the bunk but slowed when she looked up at him with sanity in her eyes. He smiled broadly and came to sit down on the edge of the bunk. He reached to feel her brow.

"The fever is gone," he said, as if in relief.

"What has happened?" she asked softly. "I feel so tired and I ache all over. Did I fall?"

He smoothed her hair from her face. "You've been ill, sweet, for several days now. This is the sixth day."

"Sixth day!" she gasped. Everything was a flurry of confusion with her. Six days had gone by. It seemed but a few hours.

Suddenly her eyes widened with fright and she grabbed for the quilt over her belly. "The baby! I've lost the baby, haven't I?" she cried. Frightened tears sprang to her eyes and panic bleached her soul. "Oh, Brandon, tell me true. Oh, Brandon!"

He smiled gently and placed his hand upon hers. "No," he murmured. "The child is still with us. He moves often."

She choked on tears and would have hugged him for his answer had she not caught herself. She brushed the wetness from her cheeks and smiled at him as she relaxed and lay back in the bunk, feeling relieved but exhausted.

He grinned. "I'd never have forgiven you, madam, if you had lost my son after all I've been through with you," he teased. "I have great plans for him."

She searched his face, hardly able to believe what her ears had heard. "You have plans for him?" she questioned. "You will be proud of him—of my child?"

"Of our child, my dear," he corrected warmly. "Did you think I would not be—my own son? Fie on you, madam, for believing otherwise. I told you once I was fond of children—and of my own I will be doubly so."

She continued to stare at him, her eyes wide and uncertain, then for the first time her lips spoke of a matter which had haunted her of late.

"Brandon, am I the first—" she began hesitantly. "Is

this your first—I mean, have you ever sired a child before by another woman?''

He sat back and raised a startled eyebrow at her, making her flush scarlet. She quickly dropped her gaze and murmured an apology.

"I'm sorry, Brandon. I didn't mean to pry. I don't know why I asked, really I don't. Please forgive me."

He chuckled suddenly and her eyes met his again as he drew her chin up. "For a man five and thirty years, I can't very well say I've never bedded another woman, can I?" He grinned. "But with reasonable certainty I can assure you that no woman before you has ever borne a child of mine. I pay no support for bastard children to any woman. Does that please you, my sweet?"

She smiled brightly. For some strange reason it pleased her very much. "Yes," she replied happily.

Feeling much better now, she struggled to sit up, and he quickly slid his hands behind her back to help her, and she clung to him as he drew her up and fluffed the pillows behind her.

"Are you hungry?" he questioned softly, still holding her. The quilt had fallen from her, leaving her bare to the waist with her hair streaming wildly over her shoulders and breasts. He was reluctant to turn her loose. "You should try to eat. You've lost a little flesh."

Her eyes lifted to his face. "So have you," she whispered.

He chuckled then and helped her back to the pillows as she drew the quilt over her breasts. "I'll tell George to prepare us both a lunch. He'll be quite pleased to see that you're better. He has become quite attached to you, and I'm afraid you worried ten years off his lifetime." His eyes sparkled. "Needless to say, my sweet, you won't be sleeping in the window again."

She giggled. "I've never had a more horrible night," she admitted.

"You have a most stubborn nature, madam," he grinned. "But next time you'll have little chance to prove it." He grew serious again. "From now on I shall allow my better judgment to dictate, and will enforce it accordingly."

She smiled uncertainly, knowing he was not jesting. Another thought crossed her mind as he rose and turned to leave. Halfway to the door she stopped him.

"Brandon?"

He turned and waited for her to continue. In confusion she wrung the quilt in her hands, not wishing to broach the subject, fearing his reaction, yet knowing she must. Again she murmured.

"Brandon—I—" She summoned her courage and looked straight at him. "Will you tell your family that you were forced to marry me?"

He stared stonily at her for several seconds, then without word or nod, turned on his heels and left. Heather rolled her head to face the wall in embarrassment at having asked the question. He had not answered her and the reply was now most clear. She wondered if she could bear the shame she would suffer.

When Brandon returned she had recovered herself and had vowed never to reopen the subject. He took one of her nightgowns from her sea chest and brought it with him to the bunk.

"Heather, if you will allow me, I'll help you put this on."

She let him draw it over her head, and as he pulled it together over her breasts and fastened it her eyes moved over his face. He looked so tired and so ill kept. His hair had always been neatly trimmed before, and the dark circles under his eyes were deep. He hadn't taken care of himself at all, and now she longed to reach out and touch his face and smooth away the lines of fatigue.

"George hasn't been taking care of you," she murmured softly. "I must speak with him about that."

He ducked his head away from her hand, embarrassed by his unsightly state, and stepped away from the bunk. He turned his back, but his attention returned again when she moved in the bunk, trying to get comfortable. He saw her wince.

"Ugh," she grimaced. "This bed has made me sore." She raised her eyes to his. "May I sit up please, Brandon?"

He took a quilt from the bunk and smoothed it upon a chair by the stove, bringing back her slippers which he placed upon her feet. He gathered her up into his arms, and Heather did not resist this time, looping her arms about his neck. She was rather sorry it was such a short distance to the chair. He was just tucking the quilt about her when George knocked on the door. The servant entered, carrying a tray of food and smiling broadly.

"Aye, mum, you had us all frantic, you did," he said, gently rebuking her. "We thought sure it were the last of you, and the poor cap'n never left your side one moment night or day, mum. He wouldn't let no other touch you."

Brandon scowled at the servant. "You have a loose tongue, George," he growled.

The man grinned at him. "Aye, cap'n," he replied, not greatly rebuffed, and set about placing the meal before them.

Heather felt no urge to eat although the soup sat temptingly before her, but in good manner she took a taste and then another. A gnawing appetite grew within her, and she ate with increasing gusto. She paused and found the eyes of both men quietly upon her and felt daintily disposed at this display of her own hunger. She lowered the spoon and feeling the need to say something, raised an eyebrow to the servant.

"By what I can see, George," she said, nodding to the disheveled room, "you've not been taking good care of your captain."

Brandon snorted and turned away, and George shuffled his feet and rubbed his hands together.

"Aye, mum. 'Twas a terrible fit he was in. He wouldn't even let me past the door." And nodding rapidly to emphasize his point, he said again. " 'Twas only himself what tended you and brought you through, mum."

A low growl came from Brandon, and he stepped forward as if to seize the grinning man who bobbing, hastily withdrew on a parting comment.

" 'Tis good to see you up and about, mum, and I'll be bringing you some harder vittles later."

Heather tasted the soup and began to eat but kept her smiling eyes upon her discomforted husband.

That night he was undressing for bed when she moved over in the bunk and pushed the covers aside for him expectantly. He gave the inviting space a sidelong regard then finally looked away.

"I'd better not sleep in the bunk anymore," he said. He glanced at her, saw her confused frown and cleared his throat. "It's warmer weather now and we need not share the heat, and I—ah—I've been concerned that I— in my sleep—might roll upon you and injure you or the babe. There'll be more room for you without me."

And in clumsy haste, he swung into the hammock and settled himself to take the rest he sorely needed. With lower lip thrust out in a petulant pout, Heather fluffed the quilts, gave him a last sidelong glare, turned her back and pulled the cover close about her neck.

The days grew into weeks and after making their turn at Grand Banks the weather began to warm as they sailed further south with the strong northerly breezes behind them hastening their journey. Under the ever warming sun the natural color returned to Heather's cheeks and all signs of illness faded away. She bloomed more beautiful than any flower, and to look at her one could surmise motherhood definitely agreed with her. Whenever she was about on quarter-deck, close under Brandon's hand, every man's eyes were drawn to her at one time or another, and with the wind whipping her cloak about her and teasing a stray lock of hair she was something to behold. But never was there anything said nor done to suggest they thought of her as anything but the finest of ladies, and her delicate condition brought about many helping hands when she climbed to the quarter-deck.

The new sleeping arrangements seemed to agree with Brandon. His eyes dropped the signs of strain. His face no longer appeared gaunt, and the shadows faded from beneath his eyes. His skin darkened under the sun and wind and turned a deep coppery brown, and Heather, being very much a woman, found herself watching him more and more.

They were nearing Bermuda and soon would be expecting to make a landfall on the island when a rain storm drenched them, and Brandon came up to the quarter-deck to find that George had lashed an empty barrel in the corner of the rail and was rigging a large piece of sail to funnel water into it.

"George, might you be going mad, man?" Brandon quested, shouting over the pounding of the rain. "What the hell are you doing with that up here?"

The servant came to attention and squinted up at him through the pelting downpour. "Your lady, sir. I thought she would be liking a bath what she would enjoy. Fresh rain water will be a relief from the salt, cap'n."

Brandon looked at the barrel with a critical eye and George rubbed his feet together in agony as he waited, hoping his captain would not order it from the quarter-deck. Brandon turned his gaze on the servant, then moved it again to the rain barrel and slowly back to George. His cold scrutiny held his man for several seconds, then an eyebrow raised and a half smile softened his face.

"Sometimes, George, you amaze me," he said, and strode off the quarter-deck.

George heaved a sigh of relief and whistling to himself, rechecked the lashing.

Heather eased herself into the warm water, taking great delight as the delicious heat crept up her body. Brandon sat at his desk, completely distracted by her hurried disrobing upon discovering the steaming tub. George had discreetly prepared it while she was on deck taking a breath of the refreshing evening air. On seeing it she had squealed with delight and kissed the old man upon his pate, and the servant had fled from the cabin, blushing in pleased embarrassment.

She breathed a great sigh and lay her head back against the rim of the tub. She dipped her arms into the water then lifted them up, letting the sweet fluid cascade over her shoulders. Brandon swore beneath his breath as he totaled a column of figures incorrectly for the eighth time. His wife was completely engrossed in her delightful interlude and missed his silently mouthed curse. He thrust the quill into its well as if this might relieve his agitation and closed the ledger. He rose from the desk to pace about the room and gaze out the windows upon the moonlit sea in an effort to redirect his attention to something less frustrating. He failed abjectedly, and found himself gazing down upon his wife, watching her breasts tease the water as she bathed. He ran his finger lightly around her ear and brushed the nape of her neck with his knuckles. She turned liquid eyes up to him and smiled and rubbed her cheek against his hand. Brandon groaned and gritted his teeth and withdrew to a safer sector of the cabin. And having grown accustomed to his unreliable moods, Heather ignored his plight and continued with her bath, unconcerned.

"Brandon," she sweetly plied to his ignoring back. "Will you pass that bucket of water from the stove?"

He turned eagerly, relieved to have some task to occupy his mind. He poured the water into the foot of the tub and stood clumsily holding the pail as he watched her luxuriate in this new warmth. She sank her shoulders beneath the water then rose again with rosy breasts agleam as if with a morning dew. Brandon turned abruptly, mumbled something about fetching more water, and retreated from this torture chamber.

Heather lay relaxing in the tub, almost purring with her contentment. She dribbled water from the sponge across her knees and splashed it on her face. The water seemed as satin against her skin, and she luxuriated in the feel of it, having long grown tired of sea-water baths.

A persistent sound from above drew her attention and for a long while she listened to the footfalls pacing back and forth across the quarter-deck. She recognized them as Brandon's and each time his shadow fell upon the small skylight above as he passed in front of a lantern hung alight on the quarter-deck, she wondered if he was impatient to be off the ship and at his home.

Her bath concluded and the water emptied from the tub, she sat now before the stove in a nightgown, the quilt she had wrapped about her having fallen away as she brushed her hair. She was still at this task when her husband returned, and she smiled warmly at him as he entered.

Seeing her thus Brandon paused at the door in indecision. The dainty night garment was like a hazy cloud over her body, holding little from his regard. Her round breasts swelled generously over the top of the gown, and seeing their softly veiled peaks, he was again at odds with himself, not knowing how to keep himself from staring at her. He began to pace about the cabin, finding its small space even more confining than usual. He ceased his agitated pacing by her sea chest and noticed her robe lying across it. He stared for a moment at its deep red hue and touched the soft velvet fabric, his fingers casually caressing it as if it held her within its folds. Suddenly he realized what he was doing, and stopped, muttering an oath. He took up the garment and went to her and spread it about her shoulders. She smiled up at him again, murmuring her thanks, but made no move to put her arms through the sleeves or pull it closed. He waited, chafing at her delay at doing so, and finally bent and drew it together himself.

"Heather, for God's sake," he groaned, "I'm not a

suckling babe to think nothing of your scanty attire. I'm a man and I cannot bear to see you so displayed.''

Obediently she slid into her wrapper and fastened it snuggly about her neck, keeping all emotion from her face, but inwardly she smiled.

As they neared Bermuda, Brandon grew restive and constantly rechecked his navigation. He and MacTavish compared notes and knew approximately when they would arrive, but neither would say a word for fear of being wrong. It was a week into December and the men discussed whether they would make port before Christmas. The two ships that had departed before them were due to dock around the New Year. If the *Fleetwood* could make Charleston before they did, she'd be the first ship from England in several months and her cargo would bring a high profit. The crew knew that Bermuda was not more than twelve days out, thus the islands would bring the end of the voyage in sight. It was nearly noon the next day, the eighth of December, when a lookout's voice rang from the top of the main mast.

''Land ho! Off the port bow.''

From the deck nothing could be seen. Brandon glanced at his timepiece and made an entry in the log but held course until the islands were firmly in sight, then gave the long awaited order to bring the ship about on the last leg home.

The *Fleetwood* bucked and heaved to the new course and seemed to strain forward as the men leaped into the rigging and spread her last inch of sail to catch the gentle southern breezes.

One week before Christmas, after more than a month and a half at sea, they entered Charleston Bay. At sight of land they had hoisted signals, giving the word that the *Fleetwood* was coming into port, and Heather wrapped a cloak about herself and came up to have her first glimpse of this new land. Her first sight of the continent was a blue haze on the horizon and she had to squint to identify it as land at all. As they drew closer and could finally

pick out features of the coast, it was apparent that they
had made landfall some miles north of Charleston Bay
and Brandon brought the ship several points aport to correct. This brought them angling down the coastline to the
main channel and Heather viewed a vast panorama of
what was to be her new homeland. From the books she
had read and the people she had listened to she had
formed a mental picture of a rather dingy settlement
squatting in the midst of a steaming coastal swamp. She
stood amazed at the clear blue water curling beneath the
bow of the ship and the white sandy beaches stretching
for miles. Beyond them stood great forests of mangrove
and cypress, cottonwood and live oak, marching for endless leagues into the distance. When they finally rounded
the point and entered the bay, she gasped at the sultry
beauty of the whitewashed city sprawling before her like
a handful of white pearls on the sunlit beach. A log fort
on a small sand island swept by the port beam and sails
were taken in and other preparations made to warp the
ship into her berth.

As the *Fleetwood* dashed the last mile home, Heather
saw that a large crowd had formed on the dock, and
almost with a start she realized that in that throng were
Brandon's brother, his friends, and—his fiancée. Her
heart froze in her throat at the thought of facing them all,
and she fled below to make herself as presentable as she
thought fitting for a captain's wife. She dressed carefully,
donning a pink wool gown and a highwaisted coat of the
same hue, cut on the fashion of the Hussars and trimmed
with silk braid and frogs. Her apprehension grew as she
worried with her hair and finally coiled it about her head
and stuffed it beneath a dark mink hat. At last she was
ready, and with nothing else to do she sat in the familiar
chair by the now cold stove and stared into the gloom of
the cabin, her hands gripped tightly in her fur muff. Fear
ran with spiked hooves across her nerves, and her composure became a matter of sheer will. She felt the ship
grind against the dock and some moments later started

when Brandon opened the door and entered the cabin. His eyes passed over her, and with face set he crossed to his desk. He removed the ledgers and tied them with a ribbon and then reaching back into the drawer, withdrew a bottle of brandy. Chewing her lip nervously, she rose and went to stand beside him as he tossed off a healthy portion. He glanced at her, frowning, poured himself another and gulped it down before setting the glass upon the desk. Feeling in need herself of something to barricade her wits against the scene so close at hand, she took the glass and raised it to him. His eyebrow lifted doubtingly, but she stared up at him until he finally poured a dainty draught into the tumbler. Aping his casual manner, Heather raised the glass to her lips and downed it all in a single swallow. Her eyes flew open in surprise, and she wheezed in air, trying to catch her breath against the searing, choking fire that burned its way into her stomach. She gasped and coughed and thought she would never be the same. But at last she was able to draw a deep breath as the fire died into a warming glow. She raised watery eyes to Brandon's amused expression and nodded bravely, ready now to venture forth and face the crowd that waited on the quay

Brandon tucked the ledgers beneath his arm, replaced the bottle and riding his hand on the small of her back, guided her through the door and out across the deck to where the gangplank awaited. He handed her over the small step onto the plank and stepped up beside her. Their eyes met briefly before he presented his arm, and Heather, taking it and a deep breath, let him lead her down the gangplank. As they descended, a couple separated themselves from the crowd and hurried to meet them. The man was as tall as Brandon but of a slighter build. There was no mistaking him. He bore a great resemblance to his brother. And the woman, tall, buxom, beautifully blond, was undoubtedly the fiancée. Her warm brown eyes were filled with happiness, and as the couples drew near she rushed forward to fling herself upon Brandon and kiss him long and more lovingly than seemed proper for even engaged couples. He bore her affections with arms spread, determined to make no concession to her advances, and cast a glance awry at Heather who observed the whole thing rather brittlely. As her greeting subsided, Louisa looked into his face for a moment, somewhat taken aback by his coolness, then seizing his arm, hugged it close to her bosom. Finally she turned and her cold appraisal swept Heather.

The two women regarded each other for a moment with mutual and immediate hostility. Heather saw before her the well rounded, experienced woman of the world, at ease with men and determined in her goals, while Louisa viewed a young, exquisitely beautiful girl, barely attaining that full blossom of youth that she herself would soon be yielding. Each woman saw in the other the things she feared most, and in this first moment of meeting they became enemies.

Louisa completed her calculated assessments and turned again to Brandon. "And what's this you've brought back, my darling?" she questioned. "Some poor thing from the streets of London?" Her tone of voice carried the implications home.

With discerning eye, Jeff had drawn his own accurate conclusion and smothered a chuckle when Brandon made his reply.

"No, Louisa," he said rigidly. "This is my wife, Heather."

Louisa gasped as her eyes flew open and would have crumpled had she not still held Brandon's arm. The color drained from her face, and she stared at him, open mouthed.

Brandon hurried on, hoping to bypass the storm. "Heather, this is my brother, Jeffrey. Jeff, my wife."

"*Your wife!*" Louisa shrieked, regaining her tongue in a fury. "Do you mean to say you married this little bitch?"

Ignoring her outburst, Jeff smiled broadly and took

Heather's hand into his. He bowed low over it and straightening, spoke. "I am most pleasured to meet you, Mrs. Birmingham."

Heather returned his smile, accepting him as a future ally. "I've looked forward to meeting you, Jeff," she murmured demurely. "Brandon has spoken of you."

Jeff cast a doubting eye to his brother. "Well, knowing him, I—"

"You roving bastard!" Louisa choked, glaring at Brandon. "You left me to twiddle my thumbs around your empty promises while you, the great hunting stud, strolled about the streets of London!" Her clenched fist flashed a large stoned ring in front of his eyes. "You bade me wait and cool my heels until you sailed this one last time, then you return and gift me with your wife! You present this common slut to take my place after you've played the round with my affections! Damn you, you crusty bull! You've pleased your brother fine. He stands there and drools and smirks as if he planned this underhanded act himself!"

She took a step toward Heather and eyed her coldly. Her voice became a feline mew. "You conniving wench, what brothel did he find you in? Indeed, what cradle? You took the promised of another!" She advanced another step as Heather stared at her. "And look, so young, so gentle, so very talented you are. You must have spread yourself upon his bed with glee, you high-flown whore!"

Louisa drew her arm back to strike but found it seized in Brandon's hand. He spun her about and caught her by the shoulders, almost lifting her clear of the dock.

"Be warned, Louisa," he stated slowly. "She is my wife and carries my child. I wronged you, true, so wreak your vengeance upon my frame, but *never—ever* lay one hand upon her head!"

Louisa's pallor increased and fear was evident within her eyes. Brandon released her and moved between the two women, but there was no need. Louisa now stood cowed.

"Your child?" she wheezed. Her eyes slid past him to Heather and down to the rounded belly as if noticing it for the first time. She turned away, silently making a vow to revenge herself upon her rival.

"Now that we've become the center of attention here at the dock," Jeff grinned, "shall we go to the carriage?" He glanced toward the fair-haired woman. "Louie, old girl, will you be journeying with us to Harthaven or shall I tell James to let you off at Oakley?"

She turned and gave him an ugly look, then whirled to Brandon again and smiled sweetly. "You must stop at Oakley, darling. I had planned a nice tea for us." She lifted sultry eyes to his. "Of course you will not disappoint me. I do insist."

Jeff glanced between them and saw Brandon raise an eyebrow at the woman. Smiling devilishly, the younger brother reached out and pulled Heather from behind Brandon's back and winked at her as he spoke to Louisa.

"Tell me, Louie, does that invitation include the rest of the Birminghams, or is it a private affair? I'm sure my sister-in-law is not anxious to be parted long from her husband."

Louisa's glance at him shot daggers. "But, of course, darling," she cooed sweetly. "You're all invited. I'm sure the child would enjoy some nice warm milk in her condition."

Jeff's grin deepened as he reached up to tease the fur of Heather's hat with a finger. "Do you like warm milk, Mrs. Birmingham?"

"Yes," she replied softly, smiling up at him. His charm had already won her. "But I really do prefer tea."

Jeff turned to Louisa and his eyes gleamed. "I do believe tea would be more fitting after this long voyage, don't you, my dear?"

Louisa fixed him with a venomous glare. "Yes, of course, darling. We must do everything to please your new house guest," she returned, emphasizing what she considered to be a temporary arrangement. "The child may have anything she desires."

Jeff laughed softly. "Why, dear Louie, it would seem to me that she already has everything she could desire," he quipped.

Louisa spun from him in a huff, and Brandon cast a warning glance to Jeff who grinned with glee and turned his back and gallantly presented his arm to Heather.

"Come, Mrs. Birmingham," he said. "We must be careful of your condition, and I'm sure you'll be much more comfortable in the carriage."

As he cleared the way for her through the crowd he plied her with questions, using again and again the form of address that seemed to irk Louisa so.

"Mrs. Birmingham, did you have a good voyage over? The north sea can be quite boisterous this time of year, wouldn't you agree, Mrs. Birmingham?"

Louisa trailed them, hanging on Brandon's arm. Her eyes were narrowed and her anger seethed anew for by the time they cleared the mass of people the air was buzzing with whispered conjectures, and she knew that word would spread like wildfire of Brandon's marriage and her thereby broken engagement.

Brandon, who had once strutted with Louisa through this city's streets, now found the woman's clinging nearness burdensome and he took exception to Jeff's open courting of his wife. But he knew his brother had heartily disapproved of Louisa as a possible sister-in-law and would play this charade to its end. He concentrated on the small, slender figure of his wife, watching her skirts swing jauntily ahead of him, and his eyes glowed.

With great aplomb Jeff handed Heather into the carriage, and as he pointedly sat beside her, he met his brother's aggravated gaze with a calm and deliberate stare. Brandon assisted Louisa into her seat and took the only place remaining, beside her. She immediately slid close to lean against him and rested her forearm casually on his thigh as if declaring her intimacy with this man.

With lips grim in vexation, Brandon crossed his arms and sat stiffly, glancing back and forth at the pair opposite him, wishing for mercy from his brother.

Heather looked askance to her husband's lap and the possessive hand that had claimed it and finally raised her eyes to his face to see his reaction. Her regard was caught by Louisa and a bland smile twisted the woman's lips.

"Tell me, darling," she asked coyly. "Did Brandon tell you anything about us?"

"Yes, he did," Heather murmured, and before she could enlarge upon the statement Louisa interrupted, raising an eyebrow mockingly.

"But of course he didn't tell you everything about us." She turned to Brandon, smiling coquettishly and blinking her lashes. "Surely you didn't tell her everything, darling. I do hope you didn't go that far."

No slap on the face could have hurt so much. A sudden weight fell on Heather's heart at this crude revelation, leaving her stunned. Her eyes dropped in bewilderment, and a thousand thoughts raced across her brain and crashed together in confusion. She had not thought of this at all—that Brandon and the woman had been lovers. No wonder he was so resentful of their marriage. And though she carried his name and his child, she was the outsider, not Louisa. Hadn't he said before that she was just a servant in his eyes?

She bit a trembling lip and smoothed the fur of her muff with a hand that shook, and her dejection was caught by both men. The muscles worked in Brandon's cheek as his jaw tightened. Jeff leaned forward with a somewhat forced smile and anger showing in his eyes.

"Regardless of what you say, my darling Louie, our Heather bears the proof of Brandon's devotion."

He stared hard into the woman's eyes, and she withdrew a bit from Brandon, slightly miffed at being so put down. Brandon remained silent, content that his brother could keep Louisa in her place.

Laying his hand upon Heather's, Jeff gave it a small squeeze in gentle consolation, but she looked away in perplexity to the carriage window, fighting the tears that threatened to come. She saw George approaching the carriage and somehow she managed a tremulous smile for him when he came to the door. He snatched his wool cap from his head and returned her smile.

"Why, lordy, mum, you look grand in all your finery. You seem to make the very sun shine brighter."

She nodded her thanks and blessed him with a sweet look. Louisa sat back and watched them half sneeringly. She could not mistake the respect within the servant's gaze as he looked up at his mistress, and she felt a twang of bitter jealousy that this man, so trusted and valued by Brandon, showed to Heather what he had never given to her. Now he even ignored her completely as he turned to Jeff.

"And you, sir. You're looking fit to fight a brace o' wildcats."

Jeff grinned and gave him word for word. "Why you barnacle bottomed old sea dog, I declare you blind me with your shining head."

He clasped the old man's hand heartily and with the pleasantries exchanged, the servant spoke to Brandon.

"We have the trunks loaded on the wagon, cap'n, and Luke and Ethan want to get those mules moving before they fall asleep. With your permission, cap'n, we'd like to start."

Brandon nodded. "Tell James to come and we'll be under way. We'll be dropping Miss Wells at Oakley and possibly spending a few moments there. If you miss us continue on home."

"Aye, cap'n," George replied. He gave Louisa a single passive look before stepping away.

An elderly Negro came running back a moment later to lift the tether stone into the footboards. He mounted the seat and, clicking his tongue, roused the horses from their dozing in the warm sun and shook them into a lively trot away from the docks.

The group within the carriage was silent. Occasional comments were made as an interesting item here and there was pointed out to Heather, and she, trying not to think at all, kept her mind occupied with studying the city as they passed through it. She was astounded by the elegance of the iron work and masonry and by the secluded estates that seemed to abound behind tall walls.

The journey progressed to Oakley with no further bickering among the passengers, and as the carriage drew up before the plantation house, Jeff made to rise in continuation of his solicitude of Heather and met a sturdy elbow which jarred him back into the seat. Brandon rose and, taking his wife's hand, climbed down and assisted her from the carriage. Their gaze met briefly before she glanced away, and still holding her hand, he placed it firmly within his arm and led her into the house, leaving Jeff to grudgingly help Louisa down and most reluctantly hold her elbow as they followed.

Upon entering they found that the butler already had Heather's coat and muff and she was being guided into the drawing room by her husband, who had placed a possessive hand upon her waist. With a grin Jeff joined them, leaving Louisa to be assisted by her manservant. Glaring at his back, the woman gave orders for tea and some small hors d'oeuvres to be served, then followed. Brandon had seated Heather in a corner of the settee and was close beside her with his arm behind her on the back of the sofa, leaving no room for his brother to further intervene. Jeff was anything but displeased with the situation, having succeeded in goading Brandon into providing his wife's protection, and he stood before them exchanging idle chatter about the sea voyage.

As she went to the bar Louisa directed a question to Brandon. "The usual, darling? I know just how you like it," she said smugly.

Heather folded her hands in her lap and looked down

at them, not feeling particularly witty at the moment.

Louisa sought to set the spur deeper as she prepared the drink. "You have much to learn about your husband, my dear. He's most touchy in his tastes." She looked pointedly at Heather. "He prefers his drinks to be blended smoothly and this takes some experience. I could teach you much about his dislikes." She smiled knowingly. "And his pleasures."

Jeff joined the conversation, uninvited. "You do have much to teach, Louie darling, but nothing I would think appropriate to a young wife."

She glowered at him and went to give Brandon his drink, standing behind the seated couple where she could stare down at Heather without having to meet her eyes. Jeffrey replaced her at the bar and poured himself a liberal drink of bourbon from her stock.

"It will take a great deal of experience to make your husband happy," Louisa purred. "I know that well. Such a pity you're so young and unknowing."

Brandon's hand moved to Heather's shoulder, and with his thumb he lightly traced her jawline and gently caressed her ear. Rather bewildered by his attentiveness to her in front of the woman, Heather lifted her eyes to his face. The soft fur of her hat brushed his hand, and he fingered it lightly. From Louisa's viewpoint it seemed a very loving exchange. She scowled down at them, stricken with jealousy, and she longed to pull them apart. She raised her eyes to find Jeff's gaze fixed upon her. He smiled mockingly and nodded briefly, lifting his glass as if in toast, then sipped it slowly.

A young Negress entered whom Brandon greeted as Lulu. She served the refreshments. Louisa seated herself before them in a chair to continue her badgering and raised an eyebrow at Heather as the younger girl stirred her tea.

"Tell me, darling, how long have you known Brandon?"

The cup rattled on the saucer, betraying her discomposure, and Heather quickly put them down on the table beside her and folded her trembling hands in her lap. Brandon slid a large hand over hers and squeezed them reassuringly. She raised her eyes to the woman.

"I met him the first night he was in London, Miss Wells," she murmured.

Louisa studied her, letting her eyelids fall lazily over her brown eyes. Her lips twisted in a shallow smile. "So soon? But of course, it must have been. How else could you be so far along with child? How long have you been married?"

Brandon smiled slightly at his former fiancée as he moved his hand on Heather's shoulder, drawing her closer. "Long enough, Louisa."

The woman glanced from one to the other and thought Heather looked a little pale. She went on, directing her questions to her.

"But however did you meet him, darling? I would have thought it extremely difficult for a well bred English girl to meet a Yankee sea captain." She raised an eyebrow, stressing the words "well bred" as if she really doubted the fact.

Brandon regarded Louisa somewhat coldly for a moment, then again a small, one-sided smile appeared and he answered calmly. "Heather and I came together through the efforts of Lord Hampton, Louisa, a very good friend of my wife's. He wanted us to meet and threatened me with dire consequences if I refused him. He is what you would call a matchmaker of sorts. Very willful old gentleman."

Heather turned toward Brandon. He told no lie yet made it all seem so completely proper, saving her the pain of having them know the more embarrassing facts. She smiled at him, pleased with his answer, and as if the baby realized her pleasure, it moved strongly and abruptly. Her eye widened in surprise, and she knew Brandon had felt it also when his smile broadened into a grin. He bent over her, and his lips brushed her ear, causing every nerve in her body to tingle.

"Hearty little rascal, isn't he, sweet?" he murmured softly.

Louisa was upset over Brandon's display toward his wife. "What did you say, Brandon?" she questioned in a rather demanding tone.

"It appears, Louie," Jeff grinned, "that it is none of our business. But I think their child approves of the match."

The remark was lost upon Louisa. She looked in confusion between the two men who exchanged amused glances in brotherly communication. It was not the first time their wit had flown over her head, and it maddened her to be left out, especially now when that intruding chit of a girl seemed to know what her brother-in-law meant. But she could handle her.

"Brandon, darling, would you care for another drink?" Louisa asked.

He declined and the woman now looked to Heather. "I hope you don't mind if I call your husband by his given name, my dear. After all, I've known him so long it doesn't seem right to call him anything else, and we *were* to be married—remember."

Heather turned her smile on Louisa, feeling some confidence now. "I see no reason why you should not remain on friendly terms with the family, Miss Wells," she replied softly. "And please feel free to call upon us anytime you desire."

Jeff chuckled with delight. "Well, Louie, I do believe the girl can teach you something of the good grace of a sincere hostess. Too bad you can't appreciate the lessons."

Louisa jerked upright and glared at him. "Will you please keep your dirty mouth shut and refrain from showing what a clod you are!" she spat.

Brandon laughed softly as he caressed his wife's shoulder. "My dear brother, you'll be fighting for your life if you continue with this madness. Have you forgotten Louisa's temper?''

"No, Brandon," Jeff grinned. "But apparently you have. If you continue fondling your wife in front of Louie, you'll find that you're the one clawed.''

The older brother chuckled good naturedly and almost sorrowfully withdrew his arm from around Heather, then rose. "We really must be going, Louisa. The voyage was most tiresome for Heather, and she's anxious to get settled. I too am eager to get home.''

He thanked her for the refreshments and then, giving Heather his hand, assisted her from the settee as Jeff drained his glass. In the hall he helped his wife on with her coat and held her muff as she fastened the garment. Louisa watched his attentions with a sick feeling, knowing she had been preempted in this affair of the heart. She followed them out, at a loss for words to further torment the young wife.

Brandon handed Heather into the waiting carriage and said a polite farewell as Jeff climbed in and took a seat opposite his sister-in-law, leaving the space at her side for Brandon. As the carriage rolled away Louisa stood alone upon the veranda in the lengthening shadows of the late afternoon and watched them go.

Once upon the road, Jeff and Brandon conversed with an easy camaraderie, and it soon became apparent that these two brothers understood each other with a clarity not found in normal friendships. As the matched pair of horses clip-clopped along through the quiet afternoon, they renewed the companionship of a lifetime. Brandon pointed out to Heather a large squared stone that marked the boundary of his property, and she strained to catch some sight of the house from the carriage windows. Seeing nothing but endless forests, she drew her bewildered gaze within to find Jeff wearing an amused smile.

"It will be some time yet before we arrive," he informed her. "We have nearly two miles to go.''

She turned to Brandon with blue eyes wide. "Do you

mean you own all of this?'' she asked, gesturing outside.

Brandon nodded slowly and Jeff grinned.

''You just didn't realize what you were letting yourself in for when you married a Birmingham, little sister.''

Suddenly Brandon pointed. ''That's Harthaven.''

She followed his finger, leaning against him to see, but could glimpse only a slight haze of smoke rising above the treetops some distance from the road. Above the clatter of wheels and hooves she could hear the sound of happy voices. They approached a lane lined with huge live oaks from which gray streamers of Spanish moss hung swaying. The carriage turned into the lane and she gasped, for at its far end stood a house the likes of which she had never seen before. Huge doric columns held a roof level with the tops of the oaks and supported a wide veranda for the second floor. From the center of this veranda hung the huge antlers of some great buck of the forests. Both brothers sat smiling at her astonishment, and she realized that here was the place she would raise the child she had within her and, with great hopes—many more. She leaned back, now filled with a calm contentment and a new trust in the future.

Chapter 7

*T*wo small Negro children were playing in the dust in front of the house as the carriage jolted to a halt. At the first sight of Brandon's face they scurried away, leaving a few moments of dead silence. Only an occasional sound of a voice in the distance broke the quiet. A child's giggle was heard from the corner of the house and another came from the other end of the porch. There was a loud *shhh* and then a whole chorus of giggles. From the back of the house sounded a youngster's strident voice.

"Mister Brandon's here! He done come home!"

Then from an older female throat, "Lordy me! That boy's finally got home."

Footsteps pounded through the house coming toward the front. Children began to filter out from every crack and from behind every bush until more than a score stood goggling at the carriage. The front door flew open and a more than ample Negress strolled onto the porch, wiping her hands on her apron. She squinted into the carriage.

"Lordy me, Mister Jeff. What you bother bringing that waterfront trash home with you for?"

Brandon swung open the carriage door and jumped down, grinning broadly, "Hatti, you old hounddog, one of these days I'm going to twist your tail proper."

The woman cackled gleefully and rushed to meet him, arms held wide, and Brandon swept her into a hearty embrace, squeezing her tightly as he laughed. When he released her she let out her breath with a whoof.

"Oooeee, Mister Bran, you ain't getting no weaker. You gonna crack my ribs for sure one of these days." She peered past him into the carriage. "Who that in there with you, Mister Jeff? You trying to hide somebody from old Hatti? You just bring her out here and let me look at her so I can see what Mister Bran done gone and got for himself this time. Last time he brought that big old bull Bartholomew home with him. But it sure don't look like no bull this time and I can see it ain't Miss Louisa."

As she spoke Jeff rose and got out of the carriage and turned to help Heather down. With hardly a pause Hatti continued her chatter.

"Hurry up, Mister Jeff," she directed impatiently. "Get her down here so I can see her. And get out of the way, boy. You always was a clumsy one for your age."

Jeff moved aside, a merry twinkle lighting his eyes, and let the old Negress have her first look at Heather. Hatti's eyes roamed across Heather's face and she smiled with satisfaction.

"Why, she ain't hardly more'n a child. Where'd you find something this sweet, Mister Bran?"

She grew serious as her gaze fell to Heather's stomach, and she turned to Brandon with eyes deep and troubled, having no doubt that he was to blame. Dropping his given name, she inquired with a raised eyebrow:

"Mister Birmingham, you gonna marry this child? She needs you more'n Miss Louisa. Your poor mother would turn over in her grave you didn't do right by this girl."

Brandon grinned at the old woman. "I took care of that in London, Hatti. This is my wife, Heather."

Her big, broad, toothy smile reappeared, and her eyes lit up. "Oh, Lordy me, Mister Bran," she cried happily. "You done stopped your tomfoolery and got us a new Mrs. Birmingham for Harthaven, and now we gonna have babies in this house, lots and lots of babies. It's about time. Yassah, you sure took your time and scared us plenty with that other woman, giving my old heart a hard time. I almost gave this family up.''

She turned to Heather, beaming brightly, and put her hands on broad hips. ''Mrs. Birmingham,'' she grinned. ''The name sure fits. Ain't nobody what got the good looks like the Birminghams. You is pretty as a peach, child, and such a little slip of a flower.''

She gave no time for replies and took her smiling mistress by the hand. ''Come with me, you little sweet honey. Don't let these menfolk keep you standing out here in the dust no longer and in your condition.'' She cast a shaming eye to Brandon. ''Traveling all that way on a little boat with nothing but men to take care of you, you must be plumb tuckered. But don't you worry none, Miss Heather. You is here with old Hatti now and you is gonna be took care of proper. We get you out of them traveling clothes and get you nice and comfortable. That's a long ride from Charleston for you and the baby. You gonna need your rest before supper is ready.''

Heather looked over her shoulder at Brandon in complete helplessness as the woman drew her past him and laughed gaily.

Hatti gave rapid orders to two young girls they passed. ''You get yourself out back and get some water for the Missus' bath, and don't dillydally, you hear?''

Jeff guffawed, leaning against the carriage in his glee. Brandon shook his head and chuckled.

''That old woman,'' he muttered. ''She hasn't changed one bit.''

''You tell George and Luke to get the Missus' trunks upstairs fast when they get here,'' Hatti ordered back over her shoulder. ''Those mules sure take their time.''

The front door slammed behind her and Heather found herself in an enormous hall that smelled nicely of beeswax where the floors shone with a soft velvety sheen under her feet and not one speck of dust could be seen.

A large curving stairway led to the second floor and some pieces of furniture occupied the room, elegant in the rococo manner and bright and fresh in color. Yellow and royal blue velvets and multi-colored brocades were used in upholstering, and the light blue walls were clean and spotless.

Heather gazed around her with wide eyes, and Hatti, seeing her interest in the house, made a detour through double doors into the drawing room, never ceasing her chatter. She pointed to a portrait over the fireplace of a man looking a great deal like Brandon and Jeff but with dark eyes and a much sterner line of face.

"That's the old Master. He and the Missus built this house."

In this room the walls were covered with a mustard flocking with a cream background, and velvet of the darker hue was draped over windows with soft silk draperies criss-crossed beneath. French doors led onto the porch and the woodwork was a warm gray magnolia wood. Fresh green silk covered the settee and there were Louis XV chairs of light blue and of mustard. A luxurious cream and pale gold Aubusson carpet covered the floor, and a bombe Louis XV commode took its place of honor between a pair of cane-backed chairs of the same era with a gilt Chippendale mirror above the piece, complimenting the beauty of the commode. A tall, elegant French secretary stood by double doors leading into the dining room through which they passed. As in the rooms before, this was decorated in the rococo manner. A long dining table dominated the room and a crystal chandelier sparkled brilliantly above it.

Heather stared agog at the splendid furnishings and Hatti chuckled with pride as she pulled her along again into the central hall and up the stairs.

"Where you from, Miss Heather?" the woman continued, but she gave her mistress no chance to reply. "You must be from that place London. Did Mister Bran meet you there? He sure do get around, that boy. We got a nice fire in his room to take the chill off it, and your bath will be up here shortly. We'll have you nice and comfortable in just a little while.''

The Negress turned at the top of the stairs and led the way to the master bedroom, a large room occupied by a huge four-poster canopied bed, with the family crest carved into the headboard and yards of mosquito netting tied to the posters. It was a warm and cheery room, and Heather immediately felt content. It seemed a place where she belonged, and as she went to stand beside the bed, her heart pounded a little faster as she thought of the coming night when her husband and she would again share a bed. Then a thought flashed through her mind that this was where she would give birth to their child when the time came—and where others would be created—if there were to be others.

The bath was readied and as Hatti helped her undress, Heather's eyes fell on a gilt framed miniature portrait of a woman on the dressing table. She picked it up in curiosity and stared at it. The green eyes unmistakably declared her heritage to Brandon and the smile carried a hint of Jeff's perpetual gaiety. Neither the light brown hair nor the small face resembled anyone she had ever seen before. But the eyes—oh, the eyes!

''That's Miss Catherine,'' Hatti beamed proudly, ''the Master's mama. She was a little sweet thing like you, but Lordy, she sure run this house. She had a way with her that made those two young bucks she bore and their pa bend over backward to do for her. And if those boys did something they not suppose to, she just speak soft to them and they'd go crawling under the front porch. But they don't know she run this house and them. Leastwise if they did, they liked it that way, 'cause there never was no complaining. She was soft and all honey. And she love the old Master and her boys like there wasn't no others in the world like them. Now the Master, he was something else. He was so contrary and ornery, he could have fought the war alone and won. Mister Bran's just like him. He's so contrary he'd spite himself. And proud, Lordy! Ain't nobody like him. I done thought that Miss Louisa caught Mister Bran for sure. But that would have been bad trouble. He'd a killed her before too long."

Heather glanced up at the woman in surprise. "Why do you say that, Hatti?"

The Negress pursed her lips. "Master says I talk too much," she replied, rolling her eyes, and she hurried off to find bath oil for the water.

Heather sat perplexed. Her curiosity was aroused now, but the Negress seemed, for the moment at least, to have run out of words.

A shout and an angry whinny from outside caught her attention and she went to the window to see Brandon astride a black horse which pranced and snorted and wasn't at all pleased to be mounted. Jeff stood aside watching his brother battle the horse for control, and Hatti joined Heather at the window to view the scene below. Angry under the bridle and spurs, the animal reared and lunged, throwing up great clods of dirt with his hooves, but Brandon carried a heavy riding crop with the butt forward, and each time the animal tried to rear he struck him smartly between the ears with the heavy end. Finally the raging beast began to run in frustration. Brandon shortened the reins and even then forced his commands upon the horse. He ran him around the pasture until the steaming, sweating beast condescended to stand shivering and subdued by the gate.

Hatti shook her head. "That old horse, there ain't but Master Bran can ride him. And he's sure feeling this cool weather and all that corn he's been eating. The Master has to break him all over again every time he comes back."

As Jeff opened the gate to let the horse and rider out, Heather stepped closer to the window, pushing the curtain aside so she could watch them ride away. Man and beast faced the house for a moment and Brandon looked up to see her standing there in her shift gazing down at him. The mount pawed the dirt and champed at the reins, impatient now to be gone, but his master held him tight, distracted with the view at the window. When Brandon made no move to go through the gate, Jeff turned and followed his gaze upward. Heather drew back for modesty's sake and dropped the curtain, and Brandon's attention returned once more to the horse. In a flurry of hooves, the animal charged through the open gate and took off in full stride, stretching his powerful muscles in magnificent anger. Brandon shook out the reins and let him run, enjoying again the rhythmic surge of the great steed beneath him.

"Come on, honey child," Hatti urged. "Your bath is ready and it's gonna get cold if we stand here much longer. The Master knows how to ride old Leopold, so there ain't no use fretting."

Heather soaked in the bath while Hatti hustled George and Luke up the stairs and into the room next door with the trunks and began unpacking them, putting the clothes away in the master bedroom. From the assortment of gowns she selected one of mauve velvet for her mistress to wear and spread it carefully upon the huge bed.

"Is this dress all right, Miss Heather? It sure is pretty. Master Bran will like it. Did he buy all them clothes for you? He sure takes care of his own, that man."

Heather smiled and let the woman ramble. She had already realized that Hatti continued on and with conjectures, in most cases, answered her own questions with amazing accuracy.

The Negress came to the tub with a huge towel spread to encompass her young mistress. "Stand your little self up here and let old Hatti dry you off, child," she directed. "Then I'll give you a good rubbing with some rose oil and you can rest a little before supper. Master Bran'll be wanting his bath when he gets back."

Some moments later Hatti closed the door quietly behind her and left a drowsy Heather lying across the bed, a soft, downy quilt spread over her. It was deep dusk when she woke and stirred, and the Negress, somehow sensing her awakening, came to help her dress for dinner.

"You sure got pretty hair, child," she said, smiling broadly as she brushed its lustrous length slowly. "I suspect the Master's strutting proud of it." And under her breath she added, "Humph, that Miss Louisa don't hold no candle to this at all."

A moment later Heather heard Brandon's footsteps in the hall and Hatti's hands flew in frenzied haste to finish the task of combing her hair.

"Lordy me, Master Bran's home and I ain't got you near ready."

The door opened and Brandon walked in, carrying his coat slung over his shoulder. His face was still red from the ride and he was slightly breathless.

"Yassah. Yassah. I's gonna have her ready in just a minute," Hatti hurriedly assured him.

He laughed softly as his eyes fixed on Heather sitting before the mirror in her shift. "Don't let yourself fly to pieces, Hatti. You're going to drive yourself into a fit."

"Yassah, Yassah. There's no rest for the wicked," she grinned.

Brandon dropped his coat in a chair and began unbuttoning his waistcoat as the old Negress piled Heather's hair on top of her head and tied it loosely in place with a ribbon. He watched with a warm, appreciative gaze as she helped Heather into the gown, but when the Negress reached up to fasten the back he moved to them.

"Here, Hatti, I'll do that. You go see about my bath."

"Yassah, Master Bran," she chuckled and shuffled out.

He took the back of the dress in hand and slowly and deliberately fastened it, taking exceptional care that each hook was secured. With his nearness Heather was aware of the masculine smell of horses and sweaty leather. At the top of her gown his hands seemed to linger and he lowered his head until his face brushed her hair and he inhaled its sweet fragrance. Heather stood with eyes half closed, hearing him, smelling him, feeling him, afraid to move lest she break the spell of the moment, but Hatti's voice came from the stairwell.

"Now get that water up there. Master Brandon is waiting for his bath."

Heather turned to face her husband but he had already stepped back and was unbuttoning his shirt. Hatti opened the door to allow several boys in with buckets of steaming water. They filled the tub and were quickly ushered out by the anxious old woman. The Negress paused at the door and turned to inquire:

"Is that all you'll be wanting right now?"

"Aye," he replied, beginning to peel his breeches off, and Hatti fled, closing the door behind her.

Heather readied his towel and clothes and with a discreet gaze watched him as he finished undressing, admiring with smoky eyes the long, sinewy muscles of his body, the narrow hips and the broad shoulders. She was suddenly filled with a possessive pride, knowing that he was hers and no other woman had a right to claim him, not even Louisa.

She went to the bed and sat on its edge to put on her stockings and shoes as he got into the tub. When she lifted her skirts above her knees, Brandon turned his attention on her and lathered soap idly over his chest as he admired her slender legs.

"Has Hatti shown you the house yet?" he inquired, watching her fasten a frilly garter around her thigh.

She shook her head. "No," she replied happily. "Only the drawing room and dining room. But I'm anxious to see the rest. I never thought the house would be so grand nor half so beautiful." And with a delightful giggle, she added, "I imagined we'd be living in a cottage. You didn't tell me we'd be living in a mansion."

Brandon grinned as she stood up and dropped her skirts, smoothing them down. "You didn't ask, sweet."

She laughed, passing the tub, and reached out and flicked her fingers through the water, splashing it on his chest. "Hurry up, please, Brandon. I'm starving."

Brandon was shrugging into a waistcoat when a giggling in the next room caught their attention.

"Lordy me! What's this?" Hatti's voice came through the door. "I ain't never seen nothing like this before!"

Brandon opened the door and Heather came to his side to peer into the other room at Hatti who stood holding up a pair of the quilted pantalets. She glanced at Brandon as they came into the room and raised her eyebrow.

"Master Bran, these things yours?" she questioned. "They sure got pretty lace on them."

Heather threw a hand over her mouth and tried to suppress a burst of giggles.

"They're way too little for you, Master. What you buy these for?" Her eyes grew wide suddenly as she shifted the pantalets around before Heather. "These yours, Miss Heather?" she asked incredulously.

"I'll have you know, Hatti, I had those made especially for my wife to keep her warm," Brandon informed her with a grin. "The North Atlantic during the winter is no place for a woman to be sashaying around with nothing beneath her skirts."

"Yassah, Yassah," the Negress agreed with a snigger.

Brandon chuckled and shook his head. "Hatti, get out of here. Go see how close supper is to being ready. Your mistress is about to collapse from hunger."

The woman grinned broadly. "Yassah, Master Bran."

She hurried out and Heather roamed into the room and wandered about, touching the bed curiously and lightly running her fingers over a chair. Brandon watched her intently as he buttoned his waistcoat.

"This was a sitting room, but my mother had the bed put in here after I was born. She didn't like disturbing my father the few times Jeff and I were ill, so she stayed in here when we needed her. The nursery is next door."

His eyes followed her slender form about the room as she familiarized herself with each item in it, and within him an urge began to grow, an urge to take her to him, to caress those shining locks. Her attention was drawn to the bed and its hand-sewn coverlet, and he moved to stand close behind her, almost taking her into his arms then, but he paused.

What if here again she would resist him, fight him? If met with violence he might conceivably injure the child or her.

His mind reeled with the nearness of her, the smell of her, the soft curling tresses before him. He could not force her again. He would not fight her or make her bend to him. She must come willingly.

"A choice," he thought. "This room or mine. This lonely bed or sharing my attentions. I'll let her make the choice."

He cleared his throat. "This bed—" he began. "This room—it is yours if you want it so, Heather."

He paused, fumbling for words in his own inept confusion, and Heather froze. A pain seized her chest as if a dagger had been driven between her shoulder blades.

"My God," she thought. "He stands so close and hates me so. He cannot bear to let me share his bed. Now that he is home and can take up his life with Louisa again, he will put me aside and forget that I even exist."

Tears came to her eyes as she thought of her hopes for a happy, normal life with him. She leaned forward in dismay and smoothed the coverlet.

"It's a nice bed," she murmured. "And the room is handy to the nursery. I suppose it would be the best place for me."

Brandon's shoulders slumped wearily. "I'll tell Hatti to move your clothes back," he sighed and turned and went back into his room. He closed the door and leaned against it in weak frustration, now angry with himself for having brought the subject up. He cursed himself beneath his breath.

"You fool! You gibbering baboon! You blithering idiot! You could have introduced her to your house and to

your bed and pressed the issue home without ever opening your mouth!''

He strode angrily to the table which held a bottle of
brandy and poured himself a more than hearty drop, then
stood staring at the glass in his hand.

''You *would* have to play the gallant and let her
choose!'' He downed the fiery brandy in a gulp, not tast-
ing its mellow age. ''So bear the winter's cold alone, you
simpleton.''

He slammed down the glass and snatching up his coat,
fled angrily from the room. He met Hatti in the hallway
and growled at her.

''Mrs. Birmingham has decided she prefers the other
room. See that her clothes are taken out of my room
before I return.''

Amazed at his extreme change of mood, the Negress
stared at him with her mouth open. She muttered an obedient answer as he stormed past her and watched him
descend the stairs. Shaking her head at his foul temper,
she opened the sitting room door and found Heather
perched on the edge of the bed with tears streaming down
her face. The girl quickly turned her back and brushed
at her cheeks as she came in.

''You sure do look pretty, honey child,'' Hatti softly
assured her mistress. ''Master Jeff is chomping at the bit
waiting for you to come down. He declares if his brother
don't be careful he's gonna swipe you right from under
his nose.''

Managing a tremulous smile, Heather straightened her
back and turned to the old woman. Hatti's brown eyes
searched her young mistress's face for a moment and
reflected the pain she saw, but she hurried on in cheerful
tone, seeking to allay the sorrow.

''Now you get that pretty face freshened and go get
something to eat. That baby is gonna starve before long
if you don't.''

Hatti's chatter dispelled Heather's gloom to some degree, and she felt her spirits respond to the servant's end-

less gift of gab. A few moments later she entered the drawing room, and Jeff quickly rose from his chair and greeted her with a bouquet of compliments. As he took her hand in his she glanced uncertainly at Brandon, but he had his back turned and looked sternly unapproachable. Jeff bowed low over her hand as if she bore the royal crown, and she dragged her eyes from her husband and smiled, determined to appear gay. She would not give her husband the pleasure of seeing her disturbed by being set from his room.

"Ahhh, my Lady Heather, your beauty bursts upon this soul as does the open tide of spring upon the forests," Jeff sighed, flamboyant in his praise, having had several bourbons during his somewhat lengthy wait. "You are as tender to my sight and taste as the first plump berry of the summer."

She curtsied and answered his inane prattle. "Why, sir, your appetite is showing. Perhaps this late supper has done you ill. Of course you seek the food and would cover my ugliness with your gentle words."

He started back as if sorely insulted. "Oh, most precious sister, you do me deepest hurt, for in this boorish bachelor wilderness the very sight of you dispels all thought of nourishment from me."

"Most gallant knight," she sighed, as if consoling him. "Your simple words of kindness are most dear to hear." She turned a hand toward Brandon. "But yonder stands the darkest dragon of them all, and I fear that he would gobble you all for a morsel. Oh nay, kind sir." She put up a hand as if to stop him. "I fear more staple goods we must soon dine upon or face that cruel beast that would digest us both."

She laughed gaily at their idiotic playing, and Jeff chortled, then prancing like a jester, poured a glass of light wine at the bar and brought it to her.

"Begging join us, m'lady. We've both progressed too far for sober pleasure."

Brandon turned, his temper little improved at having

been made the butt of their game and commented caustically to the room in general. "It's not enough that I'm beset by worries of my own, but I am gifted with an idiot brother who would be better playing the buffoon in a traveling troop and a simple-minded wife whose temerity is exceeded only by her ability to mock me. At any time you two have had your fill of childish games I would appreciate it if we could get on with the meal. My hunger aggravates me more than my need for such witty entertainment."

Jeff chuckled as he offered Heather his arm. "Methinks my surly brother is sorely vexed with us, m'lady. He needs be humored, wouldn't you say?"

Heather glanced over her shoulder at her husband who stood staring at her and lifted her nose into the air. "Oh indeed, dear brother. He needs be humored much. You see, the gay bachelor he is nevermore but is burdened instead with wife and she with child. It would vex many a man to find himself thus tethered."

Brandon scowled at her but she turned back to Jeff with a bright, beguiling smile and tossed her head coquettishly, making her loose ringlets dance. "Now we must, sweet brother, find a wife for thee, so you may be as grave as he and sit and mope without a hint of glee. Wouldn't it test your good humor to find yourself so?"

Jeff threw back his head and laughed heartily. "With anyone but thee, dear sister, I would be so," he grinned. "Therefore I must wait until they make a replica and thus might keep my charming nature."

They laughed together and Jeff swept her through the French doors into the dining room. There the long table was formally set, Brandon's place at the head, Heather's at the foot, two crystal candelabras between them, and Jeff's place at the middle. The light-hearted brother seated Heather at her place then stood beside her frowning at the distance between their services. Brandon waited at his chair for his brother to assume his place, but Jeff still stood and frowned and stroked his chin.

"Dear brother, you may have some penchant for lone-liness, but I for one am most friendly and cannot bear to see my tender sister dine alone."

Smiling happily, he seized his service, plate and goblet and moved them close to Heather's left. Brandon glared at him a moment, then sighed heavily and, relenting to their gaiety, joined the group. The meal progressed more informally and their gay and constant chatter lightened his mood somewhat. The servants swept the last dishes away and poured a cordial glass for each now sated diner. Heather sat back and sighed, having done some noble justice to the food, and now felt the weight of it upon her stomach. A drowsiness began to dull her senses and she had a need to stretch and exercise a bit. Brandon rose and came to slide her chair back from the table, and they went to the drawing room where he and Jeff began to trim long, green cigars, but she grew uncomfortable on the settee and felt the need for fresh air.

"Brandon," she murmured. "I fear that wonderful food has made it seem stuffy in here. If it is permissible, I'd like to walk outside."

He replied with an affirmative answer, glancing down at her rounded belly, then stepped to the door to call for a servant and bade him fetch a wrap for the mistress. When the young boy returned, Brandon placed the shawl snugly about her shoulders and accompanied her to the front door. He opened it and made as if to follow her out but she turned and placed a hand lightly upon his chest.

"No," she murmured. "I know that you and Jeff have much to talk about. I won't be long, only a few breaths of fresh air."

He seemed reluctant to let her go without him, but finally consented. "Don't venture too far from the house."

With a nod she turned and walked to the edge of the porch as he closed the door and went back to the drawing room.

It was a beautiful evening, cool and brisk, with small,

white fluffs of clouds drifting across a brilliant starry sky. Under the full moon the great live oaks with their hanging moss seemed to stand like gray sentinels. The air hung still and quiet, no breeze stirring, and small night sounds drifted from the forest. A few lights shone from the servant's quarters and an occasional voice drifted up. She descended the steps and put her foot upon the cool, damp grass and strolled slowly out beneath the great trees, watching their branches stalk across the moon.

"My first night here and yet I feel an odd, delicious oneness with this land. It's so immense, so vast beyond my wildest dreams, a great wide space to let my heart run free and never know again the mean toil of a drudge."

She turned and looked back toward the house. It seemed to be silently watching her, contemplating her, not menacingly, but as if to see what sort of mistress she might prove. Its countenance seemed to soften and in her thoughts it became—"A home to raise my children in, a haven, a comforting place."

"Oh, great white house," she murmured. "Please let me find happiness here. Let me bring my children into life within your walls. Make my husband proud of me and may I bring no shadows to fall before your doors."

A great relief came over her, as if a burden had been lifted, and she began to hurry back to its warmth, feeling now its kin and a strange companionship. She entered the house again, opening and closing the door behind her quietly, not wishing to disturb the men. As she removed the shawl she heard Jeff's voice from the drawing room, raised in anger at his brother.

"Why, pray, did you go back there this afternoon? Dammit, you saw how the bitch treated Heather. She wasted no time in letting her know how it was between you two before you left. She was out for blood, Heather's blood, and she sank her claws in as deep as she could."

"Is it so unreasonable for you, dear brother," Brandon growled, "to believe that Louisa might have suffered a considerable shock this afternoon when, expecting to meet me as her returning fiancé, she was introduced to my wife? She did not have it easy and we were not the most gallant of gentlemen. The news of my marriage could have been broken a little gentler to her. I'm not too pleased with myself for having done her that way. I did treat her rather badly.''

Heather stood in indecision, not knowing whether to turn and flee outside once again or hasten across the foyer to the stairs. She felt some sinking of her heart as she thought of Brandon alone with Louisa.

''Ah, hell, Bran, do you think she played the pure virgin while you were gone? She made the rounds as if it were her last days on earth and your friends can vouch for that.''

Silence answered him and Jeff laughed shortly.

''Don't look so surprised, Bran. Did you think she'd go that long without a man? Sure, she considers you the best stud around, but while the stallion is away, do you think that mare is going to go without her pleasures? And you might as well know now since you're going to have to pay them anyway. She ran up quite a few debts in town in the name of the future Mrs. Birmingham. The merchants came to me with their bills to verify that you were marrying her, and you'll find she spent more than five hundred pounds in your name.''

''Five hundred pounds!'' Brandon cried. ''What the hell did she do?''

Jeff laughed as if amused. ''She purchased jewelry, clothes, everything you can imagine, then had Oakley refurbished on top of it. I'll wager she's the most expensive piece of tart you've come across in your lifetime. She's not the least bit frugal, as you know. If she were, she'd have had a life of ease with the money her father left her. But she ran that through in less time than it takes to skin a rabbit and let her plantation run into the ground while she went into debt. She was licking her lips in anticipation of your money.''

As he finished talking Jeff strode across the room to refill his glass and in passing the doorway saw Heather standing without, now sheepishly holding the shawl. He stopped and looked at her, and her cheeks pinkened at having been caught eavesdropping. She shrugged her shoulders nervously.

"I'm—I'm sorry," she stuttered. "It was chilly outside and I—just wanted to go to my bedroom."

Brandon came to the door beside his brother and she blushed even deeper, and now in complete confusion, she clutched the shawl to her, hurried across the foyer and fled up the stairs. Brandon stepped into the hallway and watched her hasty ascent. When he turned there was a scowl upon his face and Jeff raised an eyebrow in wonder at his turn of mood. Brandon gulped the remainder of his drink and stalked to the bar to pour himself another and treated it the same. Jeff observed his mounting agitation with a quizzical gaze, amazed to see him so abuse fine brandy. Brandon splashed more liquor into the snifter and seizing it with something of a vengeance, turned, and Jeff watched him with growing concern. Usually his brother had the good grace to enjoy his drink, but he seemed now completely out of sorts, and treated the brandy as some strong balm to ward off evil spirits.

"Offhand, I would say married life doesn't agree with you, Bran," he commented slowly. "I've seen you less upset with a reluctant whore, and I fail to see your problem. You watch your wife like a stud who smells a mare in heat and dote upon her every move. Yet when she turns to face you, you act the husband scorned or greatly wronged. You seem afraid to touch her, and still I've seen you maul the best. And hell, what's this I hear of separate bedrooms?" He saw his brother wince and send this drink to join the rest. "Have you lost your wits? She's pleasing to the eye, damned beautiful in fact, soft spoken, gentle, everything a man could hope for and you own it all. But for some strange reason which I can't understand, you've set her from you as if she had the pox. Why do you go so far to abuse yourself? Relax. Enjoy her. She's yours.''

"Leave me be, Jeff," Brandon snapped. "It's none of your affair."

Jeff shook his head as if exasperated. "Brandon, with some amazing stroke of fate you've been bestowed a woman worth keeping. Just how you found such tender fruit quite puzzles me, though I doubt that any great talent of yours for choosing feminine companionship was responsible. Your tastes always ran toward prostitutes and loose women, not sweet innocents like Heather. But I'll tell you this, Bran. If you somehow manage to lose her, you'll lose far more than you could recognize."

Brandon whirled and growled at him. "Brother, you sorely stretch my temper. I beseech you, close your mouth. I know full well the extent of my fortune and do not need your mothering instincts to remind me."

Jeff shrugged. "From my point of view you need someone to tell you what to do because you're doing your best to ruin your damn fool life."

Brandon flung up a hand impatiently. "Well, forget it. It's mine to ruin."

The younger brother finished his bourbon and set the glass down and met the other's gaze. "I'll be around to see just how you solve your problems. Now good night, brother, and I wish you pleasant dreams in your lonely bed."

Brandon glared at him, but Jeff had already turned his back and was walking from the room. The older brother was left standing alone, holding an empty glass in his hand. He stared down at it for a long time, already feeling the loneliness that would greet him in his room—and his bed, already missing her small presence beside him under the quilts. With an oath he sent the glass flying to the fireplace and he too quit the room.

The sun rose bright and clear the morning after and Hatti rapped gently on her mistress's door to usher in a young woman she introduced as Mary, her granddaughter. The girl was to be established in a post of honor as Heather's personal maid. The old Negress hastened to assure Heather that her granddaughter was well versed in the necessary skills.

"She been learnt the best, Miss Heather," she beamed proudly, "so's she could take care of the new Mrs. Birmingham proper when we got one. She know how to fix hair pretty and all the rest."

Heather smiled at the slender girl. "I'm sure if you say she is the best, Hatti, she is. Thank you very much."

The old woman grinned from ear to ear. "You sure is welcome, Miss Heather," she replied. "And Miss Heather, Master Bran say he gonna be in Charleston for a few days. He's got to tend to his boat."

Heather bent her head over a cup of tea as she thought of what she had overheard the night before. No doubt Louisa had welcomed Brandon with open and loving arms, and when he had come back he had set her, his wife, from her rightful place, shrugging her off as he might his cloak. Now he would come and go as he pleased, not even caring to bid her farewell when he went.

She sighed and spread a warm muffin with butter. At least she had been well received in his home and she could find contentment in being among kind and gracious people.

While she breakfasted, her bath was readied in the master bedroom and as she drank the last of her tea and set the cup down, Mary was there with brush and comb to quickly coil her hair in a large knot upon her head. Soon she was enjoying a steaming bath.

The grooming was completed and Hatti returned to inspect Mary's handiwork, which seemed without fault. She nodded as she viewed the coiffure.

"You did just fine, child," she said, yet she picked up the comb and lightly touched the hair and smoothed a curl. "But for Miss Heather it's got to be perfect," she added, lightly admonishing the girl.

The routine of the day began with Hatti's invitation to look over the menu for that day. Heather followed the woman downstairs and out to the cookhouse to meet Aunt Ruth, who reigned supreme over the building and the preparation of the food for Harthaven. The interior was spacious and spotless, dominated by a large slab table which stood in its center and two huge fireplaces which bracketed it. Four young Negresses with clean white smocks covering their dresses were chopping greens, preparing meat and tending various brews on the fires. Heather was awed by the cleanliness and flawless routine maintained by Hatti and Aunt Ruth. Both women were experts in their respective arts.

Hatti guided her back to the house amid a torrent of detail and explanation. As they passed each bush or tree or structure there was some comment to be made about it. They entered the house and the old woman bustled about, painstakingly inspecting the immaculate neatness which the house staff had bestowed upon each room while her mistress struggled to stay beside her. It was some time later when they paused in the drawing room and Heather, with a laugh, sank into a chair.

"Oh, Hatti, I simply must rest. I'm afraid the long voyage did not prepare me for this activity."

Hatti gestured to Mary who had remained close at hand and the young girl left to return shortly with a tall, cool pitcher of lemonade. She poured her mistress a glass and it was gratefully accepted. Heather insisted the other women have some.

"And, Hatti, please do sit down."

Murmuring her thanks, the old woman accepted the glass from Mary and seated herself cautiously upon the edge of a chair. Heather leaned her head back and closed her eyes for a moment and sighed.

"Hatti, when I first met Brandon, I never dreamed that because of him I would be living in a house like this."

She opened her eyes and raised her head to look at the woman, a soft, thoughtful smile curving her lips. "And even when we were married I only knew him as a sea captain and thought I would spend the rest of my life in dingy waterfront rooms, but never this, never anything like this."

Hatti chuckled. "Yes, ma'm, that's Master Bran, he always likes to tease the people he loves the most."

Heather grew restless after lunch and decided to explore the house for herself. Intrigued by the beauty of the ballroom, she returned again to it and paced once more the glistening oak floor and caressed the white silk moire that covered the walls. She admired the gilt trim and stood beneath one of the crystal chandeliers, looking up at it, dazzled by the myriad twinkling rainbows. When she opened the crystal-paned doors to the garden, the winter breeze set the chandeliers tinkling with a soft and gentle music. She stood for a long while listening to it, lost in thought. Sighing softly, she closed the doors and left the sweetly chiming room behind her. Seeking Brandon's presence, she went to his study and found it in the heavy chair that sat before his massive walnut desk. Testing the chair, she found it hard and uncomfortable, as if it resented her imposing upon its masculine stature. She rose and gazed about the room and despite its lack of order, sensed that here was where the Birmingham men sought their ease. The room was neat and clean, yet the huge chairs seemed to stand where they had been last used and where they would again serve a manly mood. Books arrayed great shelves in no apparent order, simply replaced as they had been read. A tall rack held a score of guns whose well worn sheen spoke of common usage, and a great roebuck stared silently from above the fireplace. The only hint of a woman's touch in the room was a large portrait of Catherine Birmingham hanging where the sunlight fell upon it, seeming to set the gentle figure aglow.

Her reverie was broken by a child's voice shouting from the front. "The drummer's come! The drummer's come! He wants to speak to the mistress of the house."

Heather was undecided for a moment, not knowing whether she should welcome the peddler or not, but when Hatti came through the house from the back, she followed the woman out onto the porch. The drummer greeted the Negress with familiarity and she responded in kind before turning to present her mistress.

"And Mister Bates, this is the new Mistress of Harthaven, Master Bran's wife."

The man doffed his hat and bowed gallantly. "Ah, Madam Birmingham, it is my most honored pleasure. I had heard rumors of a new wife in the family and may I say, madam, you do most splendidly confirm those rumors."

She acknowledged his gracious comment with a smile.

"With your permission, Madam Birmingham, I should like to display for you my wares. I have a great many items of common need about the household and mayhaps you will find one or some of them to your liking." At her nod of approval he hastened to fold back the canvas side of the wagon and lower a shelf. "First of all, madam, I'd like to display utensils for the kitchen. And I have, of course, many spices."

As he said this he swung down a hinged cover with a bang, revealing a copious collection of the mentioned products. He hurried on, making a show of the sturdiness of his pots and pans and other wares. In these everyday items Heather showed little interest, but Hatti attended each display closely. He went through his hard wares and introduced them to scents purportedly from the Orient and fragrant soaps of which Hatti coyly selected several, asking her mistress if she desired any of these heady stuffs. Heather declined gently, not wishing to betray her lack of coin to the woman. Then Mr. Bates began displaying his materials and Hatti chose for herself a fine piece for Sunday wear while Heather watched, smiling.

It was when the man brought out a deep green velvet that
her interest grew, and she thought how handsome Brandon would look in the color. She gazed at it longingly
before a sudden thought came to her. She begged a moment's absence from them and hurried into the house and
up the stairs to her room where she began tearing through
her wardrobes for the gown she would barter. She found
it at last and pulled it out and for a moment stared at it,
remembering too well the history of this beige gown she
had worn the night she met her husband. Too many other
memories were associated with it for her to feel any dismay at trading it off. Pushing those discomforting
thoughts from her mind, she clutched the dress to her and
hastened from her room and down the stairs to the front
porch.

"Are you open to barter, Mr. Bates?" she asked the
drummer.

He nodded. "If the piece be worthy, madam, of
course."

She spread the gown before him and the man's eyes
widened and then gleamed in anticipation. She indicated
the green velvet and asked to see a display of threads,
braid and some light matching satin for the lining. As he
climbed into the wagon to search out the requested items,
Hatti sidled close and whispered softly.

"Miss Heather, don't go trading that pretty dress off,"
she pleaded. "The Master leaves money in the house for
these things. I'll show you where."

"Thank you, Hatti," Heather smiled. "But this is my
surprise to him, and I prefer not to use his money unless
he bids me so."

The Negress drew back with a disapproving frown but
gave no further objection. Heather turned again to the
man as he came to her with the items she requested.

"The green velvet is an expensive piece, madam," he
said shrewdly. "I've carried it carefully as if it were gold,
and as you can see, it is of the finest quality."

She nodded graciously and went on to praise her item

likewise. "The gown is worth far more, sir, than your materials." She put her hand inside the gown and displayed the handiwork about the bodice, making the beading glisten in the afternoon sun. "It's not everyday you should have the good fortune to come across a gown such as this in your trading. It is the latest fashion as you can see and many a woman would desire to have it."

He complimented his cloth again but Heather was not to be outdone, and soon the bartering was completed with both participants content. The drummer gave Heather her goods and took the gown from her carefully and folded and wrapped it ever so gently. He put it away tenderly, then turned and doffed his hat again, and being a trader of the first cloth, spoke ruefully.

"My foolishness and your skilled tongue, Madam Birmingham, have no doubt ruined my profits for the entire day."

Heather raised an eyebrow and chuckled as if in sympathy with his feigned injury. "Good sir, you know full well the value of such a delicate piece and have indeed rooked me into accepting these simple rags in exchange."

They both laughed in mutual regard, and he bowed low before her.

"Madam, your beauty hath such charm that I shall soon return again and allow you to deplete my wares for another simple token in return."

Hatti grunted sharply in abject displeasure, and Heather warned him gracefully.

"Should you, sir, I beg you sharpen your wits, for never again will I be so pliable in allowing my great treasures to so easily slip away."

He laughed and bid goodbye and she waved him off and began happily gathering the materials while Hatti shook her head and grumbled.

"I don't know what's got into you, Miss Heather, trading your pretty clothes off to that drummer. Master Brandon, he got money. He ain't no poor white trash."

"Hatti, don't you dare say a word about what I've done when he comes home," she warned softly. "I'm going to make him a Christmas gift out of this and I want it to be a surprise."

"Yas'm," Hatti mumbled and stomped along behind her into the house, thoroughly disgruntled.

Brandon returned from Charleston near midnight of the following night. The house was quiet and everyone asleep except for the butler, Joseph, who greeted him and George at the door. The three of them woke first Jeff, then Heather, carrying bags and chests upstairs to his room. Hearing voices from the other room and realizing her husband was home, Heather rose from bed and, donning robe and slippers, entered his bedroom to find the brothers and the two servants indulging in a midnight tipple. She smiled sleepily as Brandon came to her and leaned against him lightly as he gave her a husbandly peck upon the brow.

"We didn't mean to wake you, sweet," he murmured softly, slipping an arm around her.

"I'm," she sighed drowsily. "I would have waited up if I had known you were coming home tonight. Have you finished your business on the ship?"

"Until after Christmas, pet, then we must get the *Fleetwood* ready and in top condition for her buyers. I'll be taking her to New York when she's done and selling her there."

Heather lifted her head and met his gaze now with alert eyes. "You will be going to New York?" she asked slowly. "You will be gone a long time?"

He smiled down at her and smoothed her hair from her face. "Not too long, sweet. A month perhaps, a little less, a little more. I'm not certain. Now, you'd best go back to sleep. We'll be rising early to go to church in the morning."

He kissed her brow once more and watched her leave him and go to her room, and with a slight frown wrinkling his brow, he turned back to the other men and found both George and Jeff with their gazes fixed on him. The servant quickly averted his, but Jeff slowly shook his head as if in exasperation. Ignoring him, Brandon poured himself another brandy and drank it slowly.

Heather woke the next morning to find Mary poking up the fire in her room and she rose from bed shivering to go huddle before it. The wind whipped at the trees by her window and a chill possessed the room this December morning.

She dressed carefully for church, donning a gown of sapphire blue silk. It was the one Brandon had selected especially to compliment the color of her eyes, and when she stood arrayed in it before the mirror, the servant girl caught her breath.

"Oh Mrs. Birmin'ham, I ain't never seen no one as pretty as you. I sure ain't!"

Heather smiled at the girl then regarded her own reflection critically. She was exceedingly anxious to look her best this morning since she would be meeting many of Brandon's friends, and she wanted so very much to make a good impression. Afraid that she wouldn't, she chewed her lip nervously and left the room rather reluctantly, carrying a matching blue coat and silver fox muff. A hat of the same fur had been chosen and she worried with it as she hurried down the stairs and even thought of going back and changing it for a bonnet but time did not allow.

The men were waiting in the drawing room, a striking pair in their Sunday finery. As she entered their conversation stopped in mid sentence. They gazed at her in appreciation of her trim beauty until she grew uneasy under their stares. Sensing her discomfort, both brothers stepped forward at the same time and collided abruptly. With a chuckle, Jeff stood aside and allowed his brother to proceed.

"Am I suitably dressed?" she questioned Brandon worriedly, hoping that her appearance would do him credit with his friends and meet with his approval.

He smiled and helped her on with her coat. "My sweet, you needn't worry. I assure you that you'll be the loveliest to grace our church today." He bent his head near her ear as he stood behind her and let his hands rest lightly on her shoulders. "You will no doubt set the men agog and the women's tongues wagging."

She smiled with pleasure and did not fear now having to face his friends.

As the landau rumbled to a halt before the church, those persons still remaining outside turned to watch the Birminghams descend from their carriage. Jeff stepped down first, then Brandon, and as he turned to assist his young wife, all eyes were glued to the door in curiosity. Heather appeared and a murmur ran through the crowd. A few sneers and derogatory remarks came from the still-single maidens and their mothers, and from the men a complimentary silence. Bonneted heads came hurriedly together as the women whispered back and forth and grins broke wide on male faces.

Jeff smiled in amusement. "I do believe our lovely lady has drawn everyone's attention," he commented to his brother.

Brandon glanced around and noticed as he did so several people turn rapidly away in embarrassment at having been caught gaping. The corner of his mouth lifted as he offered Heather his arm and those persons he passed on the way into church he nodded a greeting to and touched his hat.

Just inside, a matronly woman stood rudely gawking as her daughter peered over her shoulder at the new arrivals. Their attention was centered upon Heather, as they looked her up and down with anything but a friendly interest. The mother possessed broad, heavy hips and narrow shoulders and in other than dress and length of hair, she bore no resemblance to the gentler sex whatsoever. Her daughter was taller than she and fairly well proportioned, but her heavy-boned face with slightly protruding teeth spoiled the effect. Her skin was pale with freckles spattering it and her mousy brown hair was almost hidden under a rather ridiculous bonnet. Weak, grayish blue eyes were framed by steel-rimmed spectacles and she stared at Heather from behind their lenses. Both women's gazes slid to her rounded stomach and in the daughter's it could be said an envious glint shown. Brandon doffed his hat and acknowledged first the older then the younger woman.

"Mrs. Scott. Miss Sybil. Rather chilly day, isn't it?"

The mother smiled stiffly and the daughter blushed and giggled and stuttered a reply.

"Yes. Yes, it surely is."

Brandon passed them by and escorted Heather down the aisle toward the family pew near the front. The people already seated turned to look and smile a greeting. He stood aside with Heather at their pew to allow Jeff to enter first, and then they too took their places. The two tall, broad shouldered men flanked her slight figure, and as Brandon helped her off with her coat, Jeff leaned near her and spoke in a hushed whisper.

"You just had the pleasure of seeing Mrs. Scott, the water buffalo and her shy calf, Sybil," he smiled. "The girl has been sweet on your husband for a long time and the mother, seeing the advantages of having a rich son-in-law, has done everything in her power to get them together. She has been disturbed because Bran has always ignored her darling. At the moment, I'd wager they're staring a hole through your back. There are several other young maidens doing the same thing. You'd best sharpen your claws for the ordeal of meeting the rejected after church. They're not a happy group, but quite numerous."

She smiled her thanks for his warning and turned to gaze up at Brandon. He bent his head near as she leaned toward him.

"You didn't tell me you had more than one fiancée," she murmured, finding it maddening to think there might have been other women besides Louisa. "Which of these fine ladies here should I steer clear of? Is Sybil likely to lose control of herself? She looks to be a strong girl. I'd hate to find myself under attack by her, or perhaps by some other young girl here.''

Brandon's narrowing eyes shifted to his brother but Jeff just grinned and shrugged.

''I assure you, madam,'' he whispered irritably. ''I have never crawled into bed with any of these ladies. They are not of my desiring. As for Sybil, you're hardly the one to be calling her a girl since she's ten years your senior.''

Sitting several pews behind them, Sybil and her mother watched the Birmingham couple together and were none too pleased when the young woman smiled at her husband and picked a small piece of lint from his otherwise immaculate coat and smoothed it familiarly. They seemed to all appearances to be a most loving couple.

When the services were over, the Birminghams passed through the doorway and greeting the minister, paused for a moment as Brandon introduced Heather to him, then continued down the steps. Jeff was hailed by a group of young couples who were apparently friends of his and excused himself to join them. Shortly afterward, several men approached Brandon as he made to give Heather his arm.

''You're a good judge of horseflesh, Brandon,'' one of them said with a grin. ''How about coming over here and settling an argument.''

Two men took an arm each and dragged him away and having no other choice, Brandon laughed over his shoulder.

''I'll be back in a moment, sweet.''

They took him to one side and when they were out of sight of the minister, Heather saw one of the men produce a small, brown jug from beneath his coattails. She smiled a little to herself as they passed it to Brandon and clapped him heartily upon the back. She was doubtful now that there were any great problems to be solved.

She stood undecided for a moment, watching groups

of women gather about the churchyard, feeling a little lost without a familiar face in sight. Her attention was drawn by a well dressed elderly lady seeking a warm, protected spot in the lee of the church. The woman carried a long parasol which she used more as a cane than as shade. The footman from her carriage placed a chair for her, and she eased herself into it. She saw Heather and gestured imperiously for the young girl to join her. When Heather drew near, the elderly woman tapped the ground directly in front of her with the tip of her parasol.

"Stand here, child, and let me have a look at you," she said sternly.

Heather nervously complied and was subjected to a lengthy scrutiny.

"Well, you are a very pretty young thing. I almost feel jealous," she chuckled. "And you certainly have given the sewing circles much to talk about for weeks to come. If you don't already know, I am Abegail Clark. And what is your name, my dear?"

The old woman's servant brought a blanket and tucked it about her knees as Heather answered.

"Heather, Madam Clark. Heather Birmingham."

The woman sniffed loudly. "I was a madam once, but since my husband died, I prefer to be called Abegail." She continued without giving the girl a chance to reply. "Of course you know that you've destroyed the hopes of all the eligible young ladies here. Brandon was the most pursued young man I know. But I am glad to see he made such a fine choice. He had me worried for a while."

A considerable group of ladies had gathered about them and were listening to the conversation. Jeff made his way through them to Heather's side and placing a comforting arm about her waist, grinned at the seated lady who continued her comments, ignoring his presence.

"And probably now Jeff will inherit the attentions of all these feather-headed girls."

She chuckled to herself over her own wit. Jeff smiled and glanced down at his sister-in-law.

"You'll have to watch out for this old dowager, Heather. She has a tongue as sharp as a saber and the temper of an old bull alligator. In fact, I think she's been known to take off a leg here and there."

"You young dandy. If I were two score younger, you'd be on your knees at my stoop begging for a kind word," Mrs. Clark declared.

Jeff laughed. "Why, Abagail, love, I beg for a kind word now."

The old woman waved his charming words away. "I need no prattling young fop to sweet talk me."

He grinned. "It's plain to see, Abagail, that this bright sun has not warmed your love for me nor dulled your wits."

"Ha!" the old lady chortled. "It's that bright, young thing that stands beside you that has made my day. Your brother has done well for himself and been busy besides." She looked at Heather. "When are you expecting Brandon's child, my dear?"

Feeling every lady's acute interest turned to her now, Heather replied softly, "Around the last of March, Mrs. Clark."

"Humph!" The snort came from Mrs. Scott who had joined the group. "He didn't waste much time with her, that's for sure." She sneered at Heather. "Your husband is well known for his preference for young ladies' beds, but you hardly seem old enough to bear a child."

Mrs. Clark stamped her parasol on the ground. "Be careful, Maranda. Your spite is showing. Just because you couldn't trap him for your Sybil, don't abuse this innocent."

"Of course, it was just a matter of time before someone caught him," Mrs. Scott smirked, glancing around her smugly at the other ladies. "The way he made his rounds, it's a wonder some girl didn't trap him sooner."

Heather felt herself blush but Jeff replied easily with a grin.

"But that was all before he met his wife, Mrs. Scott."

A sly look came in the woman's eyes as she spoke to the younger girl in a loud, clear voice, heavy with insinuation. "Just when did you get married, my dear?"

Mrs. Clark's umbrella chewed up the turf by her feet. "That's no concern of yours, Maranda," she interrupted testily. "And I detest this badgering."

Mrs. Scott ignored the elder and continued in a mincing tone. "But however did you manage to entice him into your bed, my dear? It must have been some simple lure you used. He's certainly shown no hesitancy around here."

"Maranda, have you taken leave of your senses?" Abegail screeched, gripping her umbrella as if it were a club. "Where are your manners?"

Brandon had come around the corner of the church in time to catch this last exchange, and now with angry strides he came to Heather's side and turned an icy stare upon her tormentor. Mrs. Scott's waspish composure became more cautious and she retreated a step.

"There are some young ladies I show great hesitancy toward, madam, as you yourself are well aware," Brandon said coldly.

Mrs. Scott drew herself up stiffly as a titter ran through the group of ladies, but Brandon turned his back, dismissing her, and smiled to Mrs. Clark as he took Heather's hand into the bend of his arm.

"Well, Abegail, you're in the center of the fray as usual."

She chuckled. "You've quite upset the town bringing in an outsider as your wife, Brandon. But you've restored my faith in your common sense. I never did abide your other choice." Her eyes moved to Heather. "But this one—this one I think your mother would have been proud of."

He smiled and gently replied. "Thank you, Abegail. I was afraid you might be jealous."

"Will you sit a while and chat with an old woman?" she asked of him, then grinned a little wickedly. "I'd like to hear how you captured this charming creature."

"Perhaps another time, Abegail," he declined. "The ride home is long and we really must get started."

She smiled and nodded her head as she glanced toward Mrs. Scott. "I quite understand, Brandon. It has been a trifle cold today."

"You haven't graced Harthaven with your presence for quite some time, Abegail," Jeff commented.

She chuckled. "What? And ruin my reputation, too? But now that you two have a woman about to keep you in check," she continued more softly, "I'll feel better about coming."

He bent over her hand and brushed a kiss upon it. "Come out and visit us soon, love. It's quite a different place since Brandon brought her home. Even Hatti approves of this change."

After the Birminghams bade their farewells, Brandon steered Heather through the crowd with Jeff following. As they passed, Mrs. Scott raised her nose disdainfully.

"With all the lovely young ladies here he had to go to England and bring back a Tory as a wife," she sneered.

Jeff grinned and tipped his hat. "Prettiest damned bit of Irish Tory I've ever seen," he said and moved on past her.

As the three neared their carriage, Heather glanced up and saw Sybil Scott seated in that family's carriage, watching them forlornly as they made ready to depart. She looked so dejected, Heather could not help pitying her and even her mother who stood glaring after them, having lost the futile game she had waged. She had gained little and lost face with many. If she had intended to strike revenge by informing her of Brandon's past, it had been a wasted effort because she knew considerably more about her husband than the woman ever hoped to know. From their first meeting she had known he was no saint, so the woman's words had had little effect.

Brandon handed her into the carriage as the two Scott women continued to stare. She sank down in the rear seat and unfolded a lap robe over her knees, holding half up invitingly as her husband climbed in beside her. He glanced up into her eyes in question to her mood, but she smiled gently and slid close against him for warmth. He stared thoughtfully at her gloved hand upon his arm before his gaze lifted to some distant spot outside the window.

A cold north wind played a mournful tune in the tops of the tall Carolina pines and brought a chill in upon the occupants as the carriage rattled along the dry, dusty road beyond the outskirts of the city. Heather snuggled against Brandon under the blanket while Jeff did his best to stay warm alone opposite them. She watched with some amusement as he tried to get some blanket on the cold seat under him, some across his long legs and some to keep his feet warm. He huddled in the corner with his greatcoat pulled about his shoulders and at every bump some corner came loose and had to be readjusted. Finally she slid even more tightly against Brandon, leaving space for Jeff to sit beside her.

"They say three's a crowd, Jeff," she smiled. "Would you care to sit beside me and make it a warm crowd?"

He complied with no delay and spread his blanket across their knees. Heather wiggled back between the two men, under Brandon's arm, and Jeff smiled down at her with amusement.

"Fie upon thee, madam." He feigned injury. " 'Twas not my comfort that concerned you. You only sought to be warm on this side too."

Heather glanced up at him and giggled. Brandon smiled.

"Be careful, Jeffrey. This little Tory can charm the very warmth from your body." He turned a contemplative scrutiny down upon her. "I can't for the life of me imagine just whose side she would have fought on, being half Irish, half Tory, and married to a Yankee."

Jeff joined with a teasing banter in his voice. "It's her English accent I'm afraid that makes people wonder about her. Why, with speech like that she'll soon have the whole country in arms against us. Poor father would turn over in his grave to know we harbored a Tory in our midst." He grinned down at her and affected a simpering tone. "My dear Tory, you simply must learn to drawl like a Yankee."

She acknowledged his comment with a nod of her head and mimicked the best drawl she knew. "Why, yassah, Misser Jeff."

The two brothers roared with laughter and she glanced between them, a bit confused at this response. Then she realized she had used a servant's drawl, one quite different from those smooth, lazy voices of the women she had heard this morning, and she joined their hilarity, laughing at herself.

The servants had received their presents the night before when all of them had gathered in the Christmas spirit and enjoyed their master's generosity with food and drink and celebrated the holiday in their own happy way. Heather had kept her gift for Brandon until this Christmas morning to give to him in private. She had awakened early to await the sounds from his bedroom of his rising and finally heard him move about, a splash of water as he washed and then the slam of the wardrobe doors. It was then that she rose and took the gaily wrapped present and gently pushed open the intervening door. He did not note her entry into the room. He was busy digging through his wardrobe for a shirt and was only partially dressed, wearing a pair of breeches and standing in his stocking feet. She placed the gift upon the bed and crept to a chair by the fireplace, sitting in it and drawing her feet up under her. Brandon found his shirt and turned, putting it on, and noticed the open door. His eyes went about the room and found his wife curled up in the chair with a wide, impish grin sparkling upon her face.

"Good morning, Brandon," she said brightly. "Merry Christmas."

Her attitude was so much that of some puckish sprite, Brandon could not resist a smile. "Good morning, sweet, and may yours be merry too."

"I brought a present for you," she said, pointing to the bed. "Aren't you going to open it?"

He chuckled as he tucked the shirttail into the waistband of his breeches and did as she requested. With some surprise, he held the robe up and admired it, noting especially the family crest she had embroidered upon the left breast.

"Do you like it, Brandon?" she asked quickly. "Put it on and let me see."

He slipped it on to find the fit perfect. Smiling with pleasure over the gift, he tied the belt and examined the handiwork in the crest more closely.

"It's quite a handsome garment, Heather. You didn't tell me you were so talented." He glanced up with a devilish gleam in his green eyes. "And now that I know, you'll have to make all my shirts. I'm not an easy man to please. Even my mother found me a tiresome burden when it came to making my shirts." His voice became gentle and his eyes held something very strange as his look consumed her. "I'm glad to find my wife clever enough to please me."

Heather laughed happily and jumped up from the chair to circle him and admire both robe and man. "It does fit rather well," she admitted proudly, smoothing the fabric across his broad shoulders. "And you do look handsome in it." She stepped back and smiled brightly. "But then, I knew you would."

He chuckled as he went to his sea chest and obtained from it a small, black box which he brought back to her. "I fear my simple gift to you will be outshone by your radiant face and seem dull in comparison.''

He stood beside her as she opened the gift. The large emerald stone and surrounding diamonds sparkled brilliantly in the morning light as she lifted the lid, and Heather stared at the brooch in wonder and disbelief, then slowly raised her eyes to his in amazement.

''This is for me?'' she questioned.

He laughed softly and took it from her and removing the pin, tossed the box on the bed. ''And who, madam, would I purchase such a gift for if not for you? I assure you, it is yours.''

He slid his fingers under her wrapper and pinned the jeweled brooch to the burgundy velvet over her breast though his fingers trembled at the warmth of her soft flesh and it took him longer than seemed normal.

''Can you fasten it?'' she questioned, watching his lean, brown hands at their task. The impish gleam in her eyes was gone, leaving behind a soft, warm glow which his touch had kindled. An old trembling possessed her.

''Yes,'' he replied, finally securing the catch.

She leaned against him, not wanting him to move away, and caressed the brooch. ''Thank you, Brandon,'' she murmured. ''I've never had anything so lovely.''

His arm slid around her, and her heart pounded as he lifted her chin, but from the door came a knock and in frustration Brandon moved away. He pulled a chair from the breakfast table for her as Hatti came in with a tray of food, and Heather slid into the seat as he teased the old Negress.

''Where is that parasol I gave you, Hatti? I thought you'd be pounding it about the floors this morning to get everyone's attention. Mrs. Clark is bound to be jealous.''

''Yassah, Master Bran,'' the woman grinned. ''She sure is. She ain't never had one that pretty before. And that's a mighty fine coat you're wearing too.'' She glanced at Heather and rolled her eyes as she served them.

"Thank you, Hatti," he said, smiling to Heather. "My wife made it for me."

The old Negress served them with lips pursed and took her large shape to the door, but before leaving she turned and eyed his coat again.

"Yassah, that sure is a mighty fine coat." She paused, then continued with a bit of ire in her tone. "But it's too bad the missus got to trade her clothes off for the makings."

Brandon laid down his fork abruptly and looked at her, but she turned away with a self-satisfied grin and left the room. Brandon slowly turned his attention to his wife, leaning his elbows on the table, and clasped his hands before him. Heather had turned her gaze out the window and seemed to be staring thoughtfully at some distant object. He propped his chin upon his hands and spoke with deliberate slowness.

"Trading clothes off for gifts, Heather? What's this all about?"

She turned an innocent expression to him and shrugged her shoulders. "I had no money, and I wanted to surprise you with a gift. And it was just an old gown."

He frowned at her. "You had no old gowns."

She smiled brightly and quickly replied. "Yes I did."

He stared at her blankly for a moment, raking his memory, but could not remember her having an old gown. Except for her bridal dress, she had come to him virtually naked. He raised an eyebrow at her.

"And which gown did you consider old, my love?"

She met his stare and leaned back, smoothing her hand over her rounded stomach. "The one you met me in, remember?"

"Oh," he grunted. He raised his fork and took a bit of his breakfast and chewed rather irritably upon a piece of ham for a moment then swallowed it. There was disapproval in his tone when he spoke. "I wish you hadn't, Heather. I dislike the idea of my wife trading clothes with peddlers." A few more bites of pancakes downed and now stern admonishment in his voice. "There's usually money in the desk downstairs. I'll show you where later. It's there to be used when you need it."

She sipped her tea daintily and lifted her nose with a slightly injured air. "Sir, I understood quite well," she needled, "that your money was not mine to spend."

He dropped his fork and gripped the table and glared at her. "You traded off an object that was mine, madam, mine!" he ground out through clenched teeth. "Before we were married you took some money from me and left that piece in payment. To me, it was a trophy of a battle, so to speak, a keepsake of a comely wench I met, and I retained it for the memories I had of her and of a night gone by."

Heather frowned in confusion and regarded him. Tears came to her eyes as she thought of his displeasure with her. "I am sorry, Brandon," she murmured softly. "I didn't know you treasured the garment."

Her gaze dropped to her lap, and unconsciously she fingered the brooch, completely dejected now. Brandon looked at her and realizing it was Christmas day, softened and felt chagrined at having meanly snatched the joy from her gift. He hastened to set aright her spirits and rose and went to kneel beside her chair.

"My sweet," he murmured and tenderly took her hand. "I do like the robe and shall wear it with pride in your skill at joining the fabric so neatly, but I am not a niggardly man and would not have my wife trading clothes with peddlers like some farmer's hag. I have money and it is yours to use. Now come." Rising, he drew her to her feet and slipping his arms around her, held her close for a moment. "Let's have a gay Christmas and no more tears. You'll ruin your pretty face."

The day was rainy and the house was quiet and few servants about. Jeff had gone to Charleston to make his rounds with presents and wouldn't return until evening to join them for Christmas dinner. Brandon built a fire in the drawing room and sat on the floor beside her chair, leaning back against it with his legs outstretched before him, his arm resting across her knees, reading to her from Shakespeare's *A Midsummer Night's Dream*. She listened contentedly, sewing on a garment for the baby, and laughed lightly as he brought the characters to life. In front of the fireplace rested a huge birch Yule Log which Jeff and Ethan had wrestled in the evening before. It was gaily decorated with pine boughs, mistletoe and holly all twined about with red ribbons and two huge candles burned at either end.

The story at its end, he brought out a chess set and set about teaching her the game, though she grew a bit confused with the moves of the pieces as he continued to explain. She laughed over her many errors and drew chuckles from him with her ineptitude. Evening approached and she excused herself to change her gown and came downstairs wearing a deep green velvet to compliment the brooch. Her bosom swelled daringly above the décolletage, and as she curtsied, Brandon kissed her hand and devoured her with his gaze.

"The brooch is not one tenth so lovely as the one who wears it, madam," he murmured with a grin.

He poured her a glass of Madeira and she took it with a smile.

"I fear you are just being kind with me after I lost so badly at chess."

He laughed softly. "You're very suspicious, my dear. How can you distrust me when I only try to praise your beauty."

She smiled as she went to the window and looked out upon the stormy night. The wind howled about the corner of the house and drove the rain down between the trees and against the great mansion with a vengeance. But within the drawing room, a cheery fire burned and hearts were warm. It had been a most delightful day for Heather and one she would always treasure. As she stood there daydreaming, Brandon came to stand behind her and gaze out over her shoulder into the darkness.

"I love the rain," she murmured. "Especially when it's like this, stormy and with everything cozy inside. My father always stayed with me when the winds blew hard. I suppose that's why I like it so. I was never afraid of the rain."

"You must have loved him a great deal."

She nodded her head slowly. "I did. He was a good father and I loved him very much, but it always frightened me when he went away and left me alone." She laughed a little. "I'm not very brave. Papa always told me I wasn't. I was such a cowardly child."

He smiled softly and gently took her hand. "Little girls are not supposed to be brave, sweet. They are to be cuddled and protected and always kept safe from their fears."

She stared up at him in wonder at his reply, then finally dropped her eyes and laughed awkwardly as her face pinkened. "I've been boring you with my life's story again. I'm sorry. I didn't mean to."

"I never said I was bored, sweet," he murmured.

He drew her with him to the settee, and they were there when footsteps pounded across the porch, and Jeff burst through the front door, accompanied by a gust of wind and a shower of rain. Joseph hurried from the back of the house to take his sodden hat and cape and produce a pair of low shoes as Jeff stepped to the boot jack beside the door and wrestled his tall boots from his feet. He slipped the shoes on and brushing droplets from his face, joined the couple in the drawing room.

"Good Lord, but it's a rotten day," he commented, pouring himself a healthy bourbon from the bar. He went to warm his backside before the fire and removed a long, slim case from his coat and presented it to Heather. "My most gracious little Tory, I've brought you a gift, though I declare its usefulness might be questioned on this day."

"Oh, Jeff, you shouldn't have," she murmured, but she smiled happily anyway. "You make me seem the fool for I have nothing for you in return."

He grinned. "Enjoy the gift, Heather. I'll choose mine later."

She hastened to open the box and withdrew a beautiful fan with an elaborately carved ivory hilt and a wealth of delicate, white Spanish lace. She spread the fan and fluttered her long lashes coyly above it.

"Why, Mister Jeff," she drawled, successfully imitating those genteel ladies of quality. "Y'all sure do know a lady's heart."

He chuckled. "True, Heather, but I fear my brother's present makes mine seem a pauper's gift."

"It is beautiful, isn't it?" she murmured, touching the pin proudly. She raised her eyes and smiled to her husband who regarded her with a warm gaze.

Jeff cast a knowing glance toward Brandon. "My brother chooses well in all things. In that I've been reassured."

Hatti swung open the double doors to the dining room and announced dinner. "You all best come and get it while it's hot."

Heather rose from the settee and smoothed her gown, her bosom swelling precariously from the bodice. Her movement caught Jeff with his mouth open, and his eyes widened at her unknowing display. Brandon came to his feet and placing his forefinger beneath his brother's chin, gently closed his mouth and quipped:

"Relax, Jeffrey. She's taken. But don't despair. Mayhaps someday you will find a girl of your own to drool over."

He turned and placing a hand at the small of Heather's back, guided her to her seat at the table. The chairs now were grouped together, and Brandon stood beside his at the head of the table and waited for Jeff to join them. As he came to his chair, the younger brother shrugged his shoulders, almost in apology.

"Well, Louisa never looked like that."

Brandon raised an eyebrow to his brother, and Heather glanced quizzically between them both, wondering what

exchange she had missed, but with no further comment
the two brothers seated themselves, and the first course
of the Christmas feast was placed before them.

The meal was a masterpiece of culinary artistry, complimenting Aunt Ruth's delicate ways with food, and
over it, the men's conversation turned to business. His
brow knitted thoughtfully, Brandon sliced off a piece of
roast goose for his wife and placed it upon her plate.

"Did you find out any more about the mill or Bartlett?" he asked the younger brother.

"Not much really," Jeff replied. "I know he uses
slave labor to work his mill and prices his goods very
high. At present, they're losing money."

"It could be made into a relatively sound venture
then," Brandon commented, half to himself. He looked
at his brother. "If the slaves were taken out and wages
given for good workers, we could make it pay. There's
an excellent market for ship timber in Delaware and the
way things are building in Charleston, there should be no
trouble selling finished lumber right here. We can look
into it and discuss it after we've checked things over. I'll
be leaving in about two or three weeks to take the *Fleetwood* to New York. We'll have to make a decision about
the mill and get it settled before I leave."

"What about Louisa?" Jeff inquired, not looking up
from his plate. "She was in town today and she cornered
me and wanted to know if you had had a chance to look
over her debts and decide about them. I told her I didn't
know a thing about it."

Heather had been listening to their discussion with
only half an ear until she heard Louisa's name mentioned. Brandon noticed her renewed attention and replied easily.

"She came to the *Fleetwood* the other day to see me
about her financial situation. I made an offer to settle her
debts and give her a goodly sum besides in exchange for
the land, but she's being ornery as usual, so out of de-
cency I'll pay the smaller bills she acquired while ex-

pecting to be my bride. The larger ones she ran up without such hopes I'll not touch unless assured that the land will be mine. She would like to have me free her of her obligations so she can still bargain with the land, but I'm in no such mood. I'll tell her of my decision and settle with those debtors who gave her credit because of me before I leave. So it would seem that I'll be busy from now until then, especially if the mill looks tempting. By the way, would you be interested in investing a small sum if it proves worthy?''

Jeff grinned. ''I thought you'd never ask.''

The conversation covered a myriad of topics and when the meal was concluded, Jeff hurried around the table to help Heather from her chair before Brandon could rise. He guided her into the drawing room despite his brother's frown and stopped her beneath the chandelier where he looked up and murmured thoughtfully:

''Poor little thing. It's been up there all day and doesn't look as if it's been used at all.''

Her eyes followed his upward and there from the center of the chandelier hung a small, lonesome sprig of mistletoe. Jeff cleared his throat and smiled.

''And now, madam, about that gift you mentioned earlier.''

He took her into his arms and ignoring her startled expression, bent over her and kissed her long and in anything but a brotherly fashion. She was passive to his amorous embrace, but Brandon's displeasure with his brother's free manner plainly showed in his face, and he glowered at the two of them. Jeff drew back, yet left an arm about Heather's waist and seeing his brother's scowl, grinned.

''Relax, Brandon. I never did get to kiss the bride.''

''You give me cause to wonder if it's safe to leave her alone with you while I'm gone,'' Brandon retorted. ''If she weren't well along, I'd have second thoughts.''

Jeff laughed and raised a mocking eyebrow. ''Why, Brandon, is it that great, green monster I see upon your back? I thought you had long ago declared yourself safe from the demon, jealousy.''

The weeks had passed swiftly, and it was only a brace of days before Brandon was to leave. He had been busy during those weeks, seeing to his ship, Louisa's debts and the mill, which they had decided to buy, and he spent very little time at home. Several times he remained on the *Fleetwood* and did not return for three or four days. When he was at home, the study was where he could be found most any hour, working over books and ledgers, papers and receipts. The Sabbath was their only time together. They usually went to church where Heather was greeted now with considerable respect and friendliness.

This day, shortly after lunch, Brandon had taken Leopold out for a last good ride before he sailed. It was late in the afternoon when the horse returned and caused considerable concern for he came back without his rider. Heather was nearly frantic when one of the servants drew her attention and pointed across the pasture, and there from the edge of the forest came Brandon. As he drew near, they could see he was covered with dust, and sweat made streaks down his grimy face. He limped slightly and swung his riding crop with vicious intent as he saw the group awaiting him. Leopold peered at Brandon and seemed in light spirits as he shook his head and snorted as if degrading his master's equestrian abilities. Brandon swore, throwing his crop against the stable, and sank to a bench in exhaustion.

Hatti chuckled merrily and inquired, ''That old horse got the best of you again, Master Bran?''

He cursed again and sailed his hat at the old woman, but she ducked, heehawed in full glee, and beat a hasty retreat.

Jeff laughed heartily. ''One thing sure, Brandon, at this rate you'll wear out the back of your jacket before the seat of your pants.''

George turned his face away and coughed loudly as if

seized with a choking fit, and then struggled to keep a straight face under his master's angry glare.

Heather still wore her worried frown. "What happened, Brandon? You were limping!"

"That damned fool beast caught me unaware and ran under a low branch," he snapped gruffly. "And as for the limp, it's a blister. These boots weren't made for walking."

With that, he presented his muddied back and stomped off toward the house. As he left, the black horse tossed his head again with a snicker and then whinnied and pranced about. Brandon turned and clenched his hand several times and shouted:

"One of these days I'm going to kill you, you mangy, black-hearted mule!"

He turned his back once more and stormed into the house, and George spoke with laughter still in his voice.

"I'd best go fix his bath. He looks as if he'll be needing one."

The meal that night was starkly silent as Brandon's curt replies did not lend to light conversation. It was not hard to determine that his pride hurt more than the bruises and blisters. His disposition was little improved the next day, and as Heather knocked on his study door, she did so quite timidly. When he bade entry, she found him sitting at his desk, going over ledgers and statements.

"Do you have a moment, Brandon?" she asked uncertainly. She had never bothered him before when he was working, and she was more than hesitant to do so now.

He nodded his head. "I believe so."

He lounged back in his chair, watching her walk across the room, and motioned for her to take a chair beside his desk. He waited while she poised herself nervously upon the edge of the chair. She fidgeted as she sat, trying to work up courage to open the conversation and almost jumped up and ran when he asked:

"You had something to discuss, madam?"

"Yes—ah—how long do you plan to be gone? I mean—will you be back before the baby comes?"

He frowned slightly. "Yes, I don't plan to be gone longer than a month," he replied, a trifle brusquely, piqued at being interrupted for such trivialities. "I thought I had told you this before." He turned back to his work.

"Brandon," she started. "Ah—while you're gone I was wondering if I could have the nursery redone."

"Of course," he replied curtly. "Have Ethan arrange for the men and whatever else you need."

Thinking her done, he turned again to his work and again she interrupted.

"There would also be work to be done in—the sitting room."

He looked at her. "My dear wife, you may have this whole house rebuilt if you want," he retorted sarcastically.

Heather dropped her eyes to her hands folded primly on her knees. Brandon glowered at her for a moment and once more returned to his work. The room grew silent, yet Heather made no move to leave. After some time, Brandon glanced up at her. He stabbed the quill into the inkwell and sat back.

"There was something else you wished, madam?" he questioned gruffly.

Clear blue eyes met angry green. She tilted her chin upward and when she spoke it was rapidly.

"Yes, sir. While the sitting room is being redone, I should like permission to use your bedroom since you'll be away."

He slammed his hand upon the desk and rose to stride about the room in anger, finding it ridiculous that his own wife should have to ask his consent to use a bed that was meant for both of them.

"Dammit, woman, you need not nag me in asking my permission to use anything in this house while I'm gone. I've had enough of this silly game you play. What is in this house is yours to use, and I have neither the time nor the temper to approve your every whim. I pray you exercise your scatterbrain and begin to be the mistress of this home. You do not seek to share my bed, but I gladly give you leave to share whatever else you might. Now I have work to do, madam, as you can plainly see. I seek peace some moments of the day and in this quest, I beg you leave this room."

The last word was almost shouted. Heather's face was pale and drawn when he finished his tirade. She rose and almost ran from the room but stopped short outside the door for Jeff and George stood just inside the front entrance and Hatti was frozen by the stairs. Wide eyes on all spoke clearly that they had heard his every word. Tears flooded down her cheeks and with a sob, she fled up the stairs to her room and flung herself upon the bed, crying in complete misery.

Brandon strode from the study, now wanting to follow her and comfort her and set aside the agony of his outburst. Instead, he met the angry gaze of Jeff and stood feeling the condemnation of the three. Hatti let out a derisive snort and spoke as if to Jeff.

"Some men ain't got no sense at all." And with that she turned her back abruptly and left.

George stepped before his captain for the first time in anger. He opened his mouth several times, trying to speak, then jammed his cap upon his head and left as if he could no longer bear to stay in the room.

Jeff stood and stared into Brandon's reddening face with a half sneer upon his lips. "There are occasions, brother, when you disgrace our common sire. If you want to play the fool then do not abuse others in your idiocy."

Then he too turned and left.

Now Brandon stood alone, feeling the full weight of his own rash tongue. It was bad enough that his two trusted servants, nay, trusted friends, should turn upon him so and that he should feel chagrin at having sorely berated Heather and could now hear her sobs in the si-

lence of the house, but that his own brother had joined
them and rejected him so completely!

He returned to the study and sat in deep thought at his
desk. Even the house seemed to press down upon him as
if in frowning displeasure with his manners. He felt indeed an outcast in his own home, and he could find no
way to ease his pain.

The evening meal was passed in embarrassed silence.
Heather's chair remained conspicuously empty throughout. Hatti served the two men and seemed to take pleasure in setting Brandon's food as far away from him as
she dared. Jeff finished the meal and slammed his knife
and fork down angrily, then rose and left without so
much as a glance at his brother. As he paused in the
hallway, Hatti approached him and spoke loudly enough
for Brandon to hear.

"Master Jeff, Miss Heather—she's sitting up there by
the window, and she won't eat nothing at all. What
should I do to get her to eat, Master Jeff? She and that
baby gonna starve!"

He replied in low concern, "It's all right, Hatti. I think
the best thing we can do is leave her alone for a while.
She'll be all right, and he'll be gone tomorrow."

Hatti left, shaking her head and mumbling to herself,
and Jeff, not feeling like retiring yet, went outside and
sat on the steps for a while, staring down the lane in deep
thought, wondering how big a fool his brother could be.
Sighing heavily, he rose and strolled through the cool,
quiet night toward the stables. As he leaned against the
stable door, he heard Leopold stamp and snort within. He
entered and went to stroke the steed's silky nose, making
him snicker in contentment. A mumbling voice drew his
attention from the horse and he saw a dim light coming
from the tack room where George slept. Wondering
whom the old man would be talking to at this hour, he
drew closer. The upper half of the door stood ajar and
he could see George sitting at the head of his cot with
his legs folded before him. A half-empty bottle rested

between the man's legs and a sleepy cat, dozing on the foot of the bed, seemed to be the object of his monologue.

"Oooh Webby, I done the little mum wrong giving her to him, I did. Look how he treats her now when she's burdened with his child!" He shrugged his shoulders slowly. "But how was we to know she were just a poor scared girl, Webby? Most any lass what roams the streets o' London 'lone at night be a strumpet, and the cap'n, he had his sheets to the wind that first night in port. He wanted a woman to warm his bed. But why, Lordy, did we have to pick her for him—she a poor girl, lost from her family and having no ideas where she was? He must of treated her bad that night, and she a virgin, too. That's the worst of it, Webby! She a little innocent girl being taken like that. Oh, the shame of it! Oh, Webby the shame—"

He tipped the bottle to his lips and drank deeply, then laughed as he wiped his sleeve across his mouth.

"But that Lord Hampton, he fix the cap'n. He made him come and marry the mum when they found her carrying his wee one." He chortled and peered glassy-eyed at the cat. "The cap'n sure were mad, Webby. Ain't many people what can force that man to do a deed again his will."

The old servant grew silent and slumped back, staring thoughtfully at his bottle.

"Still," he mumbled after a moment, "the cap'n must of took a fancy to her the way he tore old London apart when she run off after spending that night with him, and I've never seen him in such a rage afore when he found her gone. We'd 'ave still been there yet, looking for her, if it hadn't been for that old gentleman bringing her back for him to wed."

He roused himself and took another long pull from the bottle, then jabbed his thumb against his chest. "But it were me what first got her for him, Webby. Me! I done the blasted deed. I put her in his hands! And oh, what she's had to put up with being his. The poor sweet mum. . . ."

His voice dwindled off and his head slumped wearily upon his shoulder. Almost immediately his drunken snores filled the tack room. Deep in thought, Jeff walked back to the stable door and leaned against it. A small smile broke his face.

"So that's how he found her," he mumbled to himself. He chuckled suddenly. "Poor Bran, he's got it cut out for him this time. Hell, what am I saying? Poor Tory!"

He left the stables whistling, his good humor restored, and made his way to the house. The study door was closed and as he passed it, he saluted it casually and grinned.

The next morning he came downstairs in the same jovial mood, and though Heather's place at the breakfast table remained unoccupied, he spared not his brother. He waited until Brandon had his mouth full and then casually spoke.

"You know, Brandon, it takes about two hundred seventy days for a woman to have a baby. It will be interesting to see how long this one takes. It might seem odd if you had to marry Tory while still at sea. Of course, being a ship's captain, that would have posed a problem, wouldn't it? Marrying yourself? Tsk! Tsk! Tsk!"

He continued his breakfast thoughtfully as if contemplating this circumstance while Brandon eyed him quizzically. Jeff finished his meal and wiped his lips with a napkin and sitting back, spoke as if to himself.

"I'll have to keep track."

And before Brandon could comment, he rose and left, leaving his brother sitting in puzzled solitude.

The bags were loaded on the carriage and George sat beside James on the driver's seat, painfully squinting bloodshot eyes against the bright morning sun. The two brothers were standing beside the carriage door when Heather came out on the porch. She stood watching them, solemnly holding a shawl about her shoulders.

"I hope you have a good journey, Brandon," she said softly. "Try to come home as soon as you can."

He took a couple of steps toward her, his face grim, then stopped and stared up at her. With a mumbled curse, he turned and got into the carriage.

Jeff watched the landau rattle down the lane and then mounted the porch to stand beside Heather.

"Have patience, Tory," he murmured. "He's not as stupid as he sometimes seems."

She gave him a quick smile for his understanding, turned with a heavy heart and went into the house.

In the days that followed she gave herself no time for thought. She busied herself with menial and major chores, making arrangements for repairs to be done to both nursery and sitting room, selecting material for new drapes and curtains and wallpaper to compliment the rooms. When she sat, her fingers were usually busy with making baby's clothes and small blankets for the child. It was only at night, when she lay in Brandon's bed and lightly ran her fingers over the carved headboard, that she thought of how lonely Harthaven seemed without him.

Chapter 8

*B*randon entered the inn and doffed his greatcoat and hat and placed them in a chair at the table he took, failing to notice George sitting near the bar, tending a mug of ale. He ordered food and wine and was sipping the Madeira absently, distracted by his own thoughts, when the door of the inn opened and admitted a family of great number, all painfully thin and scantily dressed for the cold weather. Brandon watched the procession of tow-headed youngsters and their mother shuffle to the fireplace and sit down on the raised hearth to warm themselves before the fire while the man went off to talk with the innkeeper. Brandon guessed the woman's age to be no more than his own, but her face was deeply lined and shallow, and her red, gnarled hands gave signs of a hard life. The dress she wore was patched and frayed, and only one button held it in place over her sagging breasts, but like the children she was clean and had a well-scrubbed look. She held a baby, not more than eight months old in her lap, and a timid toddler had a firm grip on her threadbare skirts. A boy who seemed to be the eldest of the ten children at an age of twelve, stood stiffly beside his mother, holding a younger sister's hand while the other children sat very quietly watching a serving maid bustle about with a well filled tray, their round blue eyes as large as moons at this display of so much food.

Their father approached Brandon's table, holding a weather-beaten hat clutched in his hands, and Brandon turned his attention to him.

"Begging yer pardon, sir," the fellow said. "Would you be Cap'n Birmin'ham? The innkeeper said you were the one I was looking for."

Brandon gave him a slow nod. "Yes. I am Captain Birmingham. What can I do for you?"

The stranger gripped his hat tightly. "I'm Jeremiah Webster, sir. The word is that you're looking for a good timber hand. I'd like to have the job, sir."

Brandon gestured to a chair. "Have a seat, Mr. Webster." When the man complied, he inquired. "Just what are your qualifications for this work, Mr. Webster?"

"Well, sir," the man started nervously, shuffling his hat in his hands. "I've worked in big timber since I was little more than a lad, some twenty-five years now. The last eight years I was a foreman and the last two a straw boss. I know the working end of the business inside out, sir."

Brandon started to speak but was interrupted by the serving maid with his food. "Do you mind if I eat while we talk, Mr. Webster?" he inquired. "I hate to waste good food."

"No, sir," the man quickly replied. "Go right ahead."

Brandon nodded his thanks and returned to business while he ate. "Why aren't you employed now, Mr. Webster?"

The man swallowed hard and answered. "I was until last summer, sir. I was caught in a log jam and had my left shoulder and arm smashed. I was laid up until early winter and since then have only been able to get occasional jobs as common timber hand. All the better positions were taken, and the cold and wet up north sets an ache in my bones. It's a bit of a tiff keeping a family going on a millhand's pay."

Brandon nodded, chewing his food. He sat back and

folded his hands, looking squarely at the man. "Actually, Mr. Webster, I'm looking for a manager for my mill." He paused and the poor fellow seemed to slump in his chair. "Your name is not unknown to me," he continued. "In fact you were recommended to me by Mr. Brisban who purchased my ship. He said you were a good hand and had as much experience as anyone around. I'm starting a mill and I need someone who knows the ins and outs. I think you fit the bill, and if you'll accept the position, it's yours."

Mr. Webster sat as if stunned for a moment, then smiled broadly. "Why, thank you, sir. You'll not be sorry for one moment, sir, I promise. Might I tell the missus the good news?"

"Of course, Mr. Webster. Please do so. There are a few more matters that need to be discussed."

The man departed and as he talked to his wife, Brandon watched the children who were much more interested with the food around them than their father's news. He remembered the man's eyes constantly dropping to his plate as he ate, and looking over the family now, he realized they were very low on their luck indeed. The father returned to the table and Brandon frowned slightly.

"My most humble apologies, Mr. Webster, but have you eaten?"

The man laughed nervously and was quick to assure him. "No, sir, we came directly here, but we have some vittles in the wagon and we'll eat later."

A smile touched Brandon's lips. "Now, Mr. Webster, you have just been employed by me to a very responsible position, and I believe that deserves a bit of a celebration. Would you please invite your family to be my guests for dinner. I would deem it an honor."

Flabbergasted, the man bobbed his head. "Why—yes, sir, thank you, sir."

He hurried to his brood as Brandon motioned for a serving maid and gave the appropriate order. She hastened to set ample chairs around a large table nearby and with quiet manners the Webster family gathered around it and took their places. Brandon rose as Mr. Webster led his wife to a chair at his table.

"Cap'n Birmingham, this is my missus, Leah."

Brandon made a shallow bow and graciously commented. "It's my pleasure to know you, madam. I hope you both and your children will find our country to your liking."

The woman smiled quite shyly and cast eyes downward as the baby she held hid his face against her bosom. Brandon resumed his seat and waited until the meal was served and the initial hunger satisfied before he again took up business.

"We hadn't discussed wages, Mr. Webster," he began, "but my proposal is this: The wage will be twenty pounds a month and quarters near the mill. If it proves a success you will be in for a share of the venture."

Again the man seemed speechless and could only nod his agreement.

Brandon continued, withdrawing a paper from his jacket. "Here is a letter of credit drawn on my bank in Charleston. This will pay your fares, and if you know of any good men who would like a job at the mill, you may bring them with you on this letter. Do you have any debts that need settling before you leave?"

Mr. Webster shook his head and smiled as if in amusement. "No, sir, they don't let a poor man have credit."

"Very well then," Brandon replied and reached into a vest pocket for his purse and counted out ten coins.

"Here is a hundred pounds for traveling money. I shall expect you within a week of my arrival. Do you have any questions?"

The man looked a little hesitant to speak but then ventured, "There is one thing, sir. I don't like to work with slaves or convicts."

Brandon smiled. "You are a man of my own beliefs, Mr. Webster. For good factory labor, paid men are best."

The dishes were cleared away and the older children

whispered among themselves while the younger ones sat drowsily blinking back sleep. Watching the quiet group, Brandon wondered about his own child.

"You have a most wonderful family, Mrs. Webster," he commented. "My own wife is carrying our first. He'll be due some time in March so I'm anxious to be home."

The woman smiled timidly, too shy to even answer.

The business was concluded and the two men rose and clasped hands. Brandon stood thoughtfully as he watched the family depart, then sank again to his chair and poured himself another glass of Madeira.

A rather attractive woman with a daringly low gown, flaming red hair and heavily rouged lips got up from her chair where she had sat eyeing Brandon for some time with bold appraisal. The sight of his bulging money purse had not dampened her spirits, and she moved forward now with a sensuous gait and stood pointedly by an empty chair at his table, letting the sleeve of her gown fall over her shoulder.

"Hello, guv'na," she purred. "Care to buy a lonesome lady a drink?"

Brandon raised a cold expression to her gaze. "I'm afraid I'm occupied elsewhere this evening, madam," he replied. "Please excuse me."

He gestured her away abruptly and she turned in a huff and stalked off, and George, having seen the woman's interest earlier, smiled to himself and gave a sigh of relief. Since disembarking from the *Fleetwood* a month ago, he had watched his captain turn away one strumpet after another and retire to his room alone. Tomorrow they would be leaving for home and he would be returning to a wife too far along with child to ease his manly discomfort, yet not one woman had he taken to bed nor touched since arriving here. Having discovered a new respect for his captain, George nodded his head.

"Aye, the cap'n's been stung, and deeply too. The little mum has wiggled into his heart without his knowin' and there he sits adreaming of her while willing wenches parade before him. Aye, poor cap'n. He'll never be the same again.''

George lifted his mug toward his captain as if in toast and set it to his lips in a long draught. Brandon rose from his table, unmindful of his presence, and the last the servant saw of him, he was mounting the stairs to his room.

Brandon closed the door of his room behind him and slowly began to undress for bed, his thoughts now centered on only one thing. He took off his shirt and dropped it over the back of a chair and gazed at himself in a long mirror which stood in a corner of the room. He saw a rather handsome man return the perusal and flex rugged muscles. The image inhaled deeply and Brandon looked with some satisfaction at the tall, broad shouldered, slim waisted figure before him, but he turned away in exasperation.

''Damn,'' he thought. ''I'm not so ugly that even a pretty wench would lightly refuse my bed. How can I approach that vixen when she so despises the very image of my face that she cannot accept the small thought of me slumbering by her side?''

He strolled thoughtfully across the room.

''I've known wenches here and abroad. Why does this simple one strike wisdom from my skull and make of me a bumbling fool? I've bade the most haughty spread their thighs and gladly they complied as if the greatest favor of the world I did them. But when I'm before Heather, phrases flee my tongue and leave me groveling as in a gutter for my words.''

He strode to the window and stood gazing out, knowing that within the block many a warm bed waited, and his hunger grew, but it was not for them out there. It was for in part a memory and in part a gentle dream he carried within him. His thoughts grew tender as he remembered golden candlelight upon creamy, silken flesh still moist from an evening's bath and dark, softly curling hair flowing across a pillow as she slept, and his thoughts brought dreams to mind of how those sweet and gentle arms might feel about his neck and of how those full, pink lips might press against his and how her warm, young body might curve to him and small, white teeth would nibble at his ear to rouse his passions.

He turned away from the window and struck his fist into his hand in mute frustration.

"My Lord!" he thought. "That quiet virgin denies me and my very soul crumbles. What affliction besets me that I should tremble so?"

He seized a glass and poured himself a drink and sank into a chair to consider further his problem.

"I have not bedded another woman since that night they dragged her through my cabin door. This Heather, this tiny purple flower from the moors, has dined upon my heart and now it grows within her and I have no more a heart to share. But my heart, thou hast betrayed me deep. You have closed all doors but one and that I slammed in anger. My God, that I should love her so! I thought that simple emotion was below me. I thought that I had transcended that which other men declare. I drew myself the worldly gentleman, above those simple words of men, that I could casually accept a wife of well-experienced joys. But now I find myself so stricken with the innocence of that one, that I cannot rouse myself to seek relief in someone else's bed."

He leaned forward with his elbows on his knees and hung his head.

"And even when I forced her maidenhood, she served my pleasure well, more than any woman ever. She took my seed within her and betrayed me not with another man and from that first moment I clutched her to me, has held my every thought so tightly that even in my sleep I dream of nothing else but her and that her good favors might turn to me."

He raised his head and sat back. He sipped his drink slowly and formed a new resolve.

"Her time grows near," he mused. "I'll bide my moment carefully. I'll play the suitor and court her tenderly and then perhaps she'll come to me."

He finished his drink and rose and went to bed, and with the realization of his love and new resolve, for the first time in many months sank quickly into slumber.

The rain pounded down upon Harthaven and clouds hung low above the trees. The night was black and silent as if the rest of the world had already withdrawn and curled itself in some cozy nest against the storm.

Heather gazed about the room and saw that she had removed all traces of her presence here. She had spent these many nights in this great chamber and had grown to know it and feel a part of it. She stood looking down at the huge bed which seemed to welcome her and felt a pang that she must leave it now and return to the smaller bed in the sitting room. She sighed pensively and slowly made her way into the other room. The door of the nursery was open and taking a candle, she went to inspect it once again. She ran her finger lightly over a rocking horse that had been Brandon's as a child and went to stand beside the crib and smooth the blanket in it.

"Strange, we all assume that the child will be a boy." She fluffed the lace on the canopy. "Of course my husband has declared it so, and who will deny his right to wish a son?" She smiled to herself, thinking how she had once prayed for a girl. "Poor daughter, if you grow within my belly; seek your finer pleasures now for blue will be your maiden's color."

She turned and with a last slow look about, wandered from the nursery, through the sitting room and returned once more to the master bedroom where a fire glowed cheerfully on the hearth. She relaxed before its warmth in a large overstuffed chair and stared with pensive mood into the flames. She sighed and thought of Brandon's return in the next few days. His brief letter to her some weeks ago had been curt and mentioned only his approximate day of homecoming.

What would his manner be? Would he be more gentle or perhaps more temperamental? Had he found some northern wench to ease himself upon? He'd given her, his wife, that other bed and other room. . . .

"He could not stand the sight of me before," she thought sadly. "Now I'm plump with child, ill-shaped and so clumsy in my moves I must waddle more like the goose than a feminine woman. I will not blame him for his distant mood when he sees my swollen shape."

She leaned her head back and closed her eyes.

"Oh Brandon, would that I had been more tender when I had the chance, perhaps I'd share your bed and would soon feel your warmth again beside me. I would be sure no other bed you'd share."

She looked again into the fire and felt a flare of anger within her.

"What sultry trollop has he chosen to pass the time with? Was it a sweet, simpering thing he cajoled to keep him warm in the north?"

Her temper softened some.

"I would have never seen this land, this house, these kind and gentle souls I've met, had not the fates decreed my maidenhood should be the price! I've but to make the best of it and when this child has come and I regain my former worth, then I shall ply my woman's wiles to gain my husband."

She wrapped her arms about her and grew warm in memories. That moment at the inn when he had seemed so tender, almost loving, and on the ship, his careful tending of her person. And even with Louisa he did deflect the more cruel blows and played the lover dear.

"Is it possible," she wondered, "that somewhere beneath that scowling brow he does harbor some loving thoughts of me? If I would be the gentle, devoted wife, could he some time begin to love me? Oh, dearest love, and I do love thee, could you be in truth my husband, loving me above all others? Would you take me in your arms and caress me as a lover would? Oh Lord, I tremble

at the thought that he would find me all that he should
ever want.''

The fire had burned low. She rose and by its softened
glow stood beside the great and tempting bed once more.

''And you, oh lovely resting place, will soon feel my
weight again, I vow. You'll not seem so lonely long for
I will tempt him to my ends which are the same as yours,
to be shared, to be loved, to be gently courted as if a
maiden still. Oh, he will bend and time will be my friend.
I'll let my patience mend the bleeding wounds we share
until they are no more and he will seek my comfort, my
love forever more.''

She sighed and returned to the sitting room. She
thought of it as the sitting room now, only temporarily
hers until she took her rightful place. She sought her bed
and bravely courted sleep.

Leopold and a wagon and team had been taken into town
several days before to be left with friends against Brandon's return. The day was one of the few sunny ones
they had had so far, and Heather had taken the opportunity to go to the cookhouse and chat with Aunt Ruth
and learn more of the strange Yankee foods and those
dishes which were Brandon's favorite. She sat on the
stool, sipping tea that the old woman had prepared for
her and listened intently as the Negress described some
of her methods of preparing foods, impressed by the fact
that with Aunt Ruth it was more a matter of talent and
artistry than of actual knowledge. She seemed to know
instinctively how foods and herbs would taste when
blended and could make even a simple dish a true adventure of flavor.

The pleasant moment was interrupted by shouts from
afar and soon Hatti bustled in breathlessly exclaiming:

''Master Bran—Master Bran's coming lickety split
down the back road! He-he,'' she giggled. ''He's in such
a hurry he's gonna run that black horse into the ground.''

Heather's eyes widened and she gasped as she slid

from the stool. Her hands flew to her hair and then to her gown and she seemed horrified.

"Oh, I must look a fright!" she cried. "I've got to. . . ."

She turned without finishing and fled to the house and as she labored up the stairs, she called for Mary. The girl came running and was there when she flung open the door to the sitting room. Breathlessly Heather bade the servant lay out a fresh gown and hurried to press a cold, wet cloth to her face and pinch her cheeks to bring the color forth. She yanked her dress off, and as Mary hastened to fasten the selected gown of yellow muslin, she urged her on.

"Hurry, Mary! Hurry! Brandon is coming! He'll be here shortly!"

She smoothed her hair, dressed and hurried down the stairs and outside to stand casually on the porch and see her husband slowly walk Leopold down the lane. The heaving sides of the horse and heavy froth upon his glistening coat belied the leisurely gait, for Brandon had pushed the mighty steed to the limit in his eagerness to regain his young bride. Now he approached the porch and dismounted with deliberate slowness. He handed the reins to a boy with instructions to walk the horse well and rub him down and be careful of the water. All this done, he turned to his wife and a slow smile grew upon his face. His eyes moved over her as he mounted the steps, taking in every detail, and slipping an arm about her waist, he greeted her and placed a somewhat fatherly kiss upon her lips. She smiled sweetly in reply and leaned against him lightly as they went into the house.

"Did you have a good trip?" she questioned softly as he passed his hat to Joseph. "The weather was so bad here I was quite worried about you."

His arm tightened about her. "No need to have fretted, sweet. We beat the worst of it into New York and had no problems coming back. How have things been here? Did you get the nursery finished?"

She nodded quickly, her eyes shining. "Would you care to see it?"

"I would indeed, sweet," he replied.

Smiling brightly, she took his arm and let him assist her up the stairs. He contemplated her stomach as she climbed.

"Have you been well?" he inquired.

"Oh yes," she hurried to assure him. "I've been in the best of health. Hatti says she's never seen a mother-to-be more fit, and I do feel wonderful." She looked down rather ruefully at her belly as they reached the landing and laughed a little in apology. "Though I'm afraid I'm a bit of a sight and not very light upon my feet."

He chuckled and put his arm around her again as he brought her chin up for their gaze to meet. "I hardly expected you to look like a prim little virgin while you carried my son, sweet. But even so burdened, you'd make many a slimmer maid turn green with envy over your glowing beauty."

She smiled softly and pressed her cheek against his chest, more than content with his answer. In the nursery, he strode about the room as she stood with her hands behind her back, anxiously awaiting his reaction. Brushing aside the new mosquito netting, Brandon bent to inspect the crib under its ruffled canopy. Next he rocked a nearby cradle gently with his boot as a smile played about his lips, then slowly gazed about at the light blue walls and the snowy white curtains. He carefully stepped around the vividly hued rugs which lay about the shiny oak floor and opened a bureau drawer in curiosity, finding it full of neatly folded baby clothes, some of which he had seen his wife sewing before he left.

Heather went to stand beside the wooden horse with its painted red saddle and pushed it lightly with her fingers, setting it into motion.

"We found this in the attic," she said, drawing his attention. "Hatti said it was yours so I bade Ethan fetch it down. When our son is old enough to go astride it, I can tell him his father once sat upon it.''

He grinned and came closer to look at it. ''Sure hope it doesn't run under a branch with him.''

A giggle escaped her before she turned hurriedly and pointed to a rocking chair of some expense. ''Jeff gave me that. Isn't it lovely?''

He nodded his approval and quipped, ''Leave it to him. He always did like to be rocked to sleep.''

Heather started to point out another item of interest, but she stopped as if horrified. ''Oh my goodness, Brandon! You haven't eaten! You must be starving, and here I've been chattering on.''

She quickly called Mary and gave orders for a tray of food to be sent up and water heated for his bath. Brandon had gone into his bedroom and removed his jacket and stock and was pulling off his boots when she joined him.

''I'm no longer a captain of a ship, pet,'' he commented, giving her a sidelong look as she picked up his coat and put it away. ''I sold the *Fleetwood* for a tidy sum, and now you may expect to see me about the house every day.''

Heather smiled to herself, deciding she approved whole-heartedly of this situation.

A servant brought food, and Heather sat across from Brandon, watching him as he ate. She was pleasantly pleased by the intimacy of the moment and warmed by her new found love for him. The water was hustled in while the tray was taken away, and she tested its warmth before nodding her dismissal to the servants then busied herself putting out fresh linens as her husband disrobed.

Brandon eased himself into the hot water and lay back for some moments relaxing in it. When he finally sat up and began to scrub, Heather came and reached for the sponge. She dipped it into the water and held it up expectantly but waited for his approval. He gazed up at her for a long time contemplating this, then leaned forward, presenting his back to her.

"Scrub it hard, will you, sweet? I feel like I'm covered with a thick coat of grime."

She bent happily to her task, lathering the soap up well with her hands over his well muscled shoulders and down his back. Impishly she initialed a large "B" through the white suds across his back and giggled lightly as she placed an "H" before it. He peered over his shoulder at her with a raised eyebrow and a one-sided grin.

"What are you doing, miss?" he questioned.

She laughed and wrung out the sponge over his head. "I'm branding you, m'lord."

He shook his head vigorously, flinging water on her, and she laughed with glee. Stepping back to a safe distance, she threw the sponge at him and then gasped with surprise when he stood up and stepped over the rim of the tub and came after her, still soapy and wet.

"Oh Brandon, what are you doing?" she shrieked in merriment. "Get back in the tub."

She turned as if to flee, but he flung out both arms and lifting her up, swung her up over the tub. She was laughing with him, enjoying the play until he gave her a little dip as if to drop her into the tub, then she squealed and clasped her arms tightly about his neck.

"Brandon, don't you dare! I'll never forgive you."

He smiled into her eyes. "But, sweet, you seemed so interested in my bath, I thought you might like one."

"Put me down," she demanded, then her mouth curved sweetly. "Please."

His eyes sparkled. "Ah, the truth will out, madam. It's only that you have a fetish for scrubbing men's backs, is that it?"

He set her down gently on her feet and grinned as she lifted her arm and twisted to see her wet dress.

"Oh, Brandon, you're impossible! Look what you've done to me!"

He laughed heartily and pulled her back against him, encompassing her in his wet embrace again. Her giggles joined his merriment as he hugged her, his arms about her just above the rounded belly, pressing into her soft bosom. He spread his hand over her abdomen.

"I don't deny a thing, sweet. But must you still be so outraged over my misdeed?" he teased. "That was eight months ago."

"I was talking about my dress!" she corrected indignantly. "You got me all wet and now I'll have to change. Now do be good and unfasten me. I shouldn't want to ask Mary to help me change again."

"Again?" he repeated.

"Never mind," Heather said quickly. "Just unfasten me please."

He complied and resumed his place in the tub before she turned to him, holding the gown up over her shoulders.

"Thank you," she smiled and bent to press a kiss upon his cheek, then swept around and into her room.

The spot her lips had touched burned as Brandon leaned back, but he found it impossible to relax and enjoy the warmth of the bath. A movement caught his eye, and he could see her reflected in his tall, dressing mirror as she stepped out of her dress. A sudden, powerful urge struck him to ask her here and now if she would share this great room with him, to lie beside him in his bed tonight and let him hold her, not with passion's intent, but gently and with love, as a husband should when a wife is nearing her time. But caution brought second thoughts. She had acted sweet and willing before and yet not cared to share his bed. She seemed so content and happy with present arrangements. Yes, later, he thought. When she will have no excuse and will not be able to plead motherly shyness. Then he would approach her and that bed would feel both their weights.

He closed his eyes, thinking of his homecoming. He would never like leaving her, but coming home to her— well, that was an entirely different matter. He relaxed, resting his head on the back of the tub, and the heat of the water was just beginning to take the aches from his tired body when there was a quick thump on the door and it was pushed ajar to reveal Jeff's beaming face.

"Are you decent, eldest son?" he asked with belated concern.

"More so than you," Brandon grunted, chafed at the interruption. "Now close the door. Preferably from the outside."

Unruffled, Jeff pushed within, catching the door with his heel and slamming it shut behind him.

"Why, dearest Brandon," he mimed. "I sought only to bring you some fine diversions, and," this overly loud and directed to the other room, "to rescue my sister-in-law from your unusually brutish temper."

There was a sound of soft laughter from the sitting room, and Jeff, chuckling over his own jest, placed a full glass of brandy and a fresh box of cigars on the stand by the bath.

Brandon nodded his appreciation and sipped the brandy and rolled a cigar between his fingertips. With a raised eyebrow he addressed his brother.

"I think I'll keep you around. There seems to be some hope for you after all."

Heather entered the room, smiling brightly, and greeted Jeff, paying only small attention to their conversation while she gave wifely attention to the laying out of fresh clothes for her husband. It was only when Brandon began to relate his meeting with the Websters that she moved to stand behind him and listen to his story. Brandon half consciously took her hand from where it rested on the high back of the tub and gently rubbed it against his ear as he spoke to Jeff. The movement was not completely lost on the younger brother, but it was not until later that he would wonder about this strange shift of manners between his brother and sister-in-law.

As Brandon finished his tale, Heather realized how little she really knew her husband. She was touched by the plight of the Websters, and yet she felt a strange pride with his own compassion for them. Her eyes were warm and moist as she looked up for a moment and found Jeff's gaze full upon her. He smiled and returned his attention to his brother as Brandon spoke.

"Well, anyway they should be arriving on next week's packet."

Jeff helped himself to one of the cigars he had brought and lit it as he commented. "We'll have to find a house for them."

"There are plenty of houses at the mill," Brandon replied. "They can stay in that big old house Mr. Bartlett used for his office."

Jeff let out a derisive snort. "I thought it was your intention to have them stay. They'll take one look at that house and head north again. Bartlett was a damned gutter rat, not mincing words, and that place is worse than a pigsty. He made use of his female slaves in those beds there, and the poor souls were covered with vermin. It's not fit for swine, and you want to put the Websters in it? It would make your stomach turn to see the filth inside."

"I have seen it," Brandon replied with a slow smile. "That's why we're going tomorrow with some help and see to its cleaning."

"I should have kept my mouth shut," grumbled Jeff good naturedly.

Brandon chuckled. "If that moment ever comes, I'll have to send for the reverend."

Ignoring the jest, Heather stated a demand with a firm voice. "I'm going too. I wouldn't trust the two of you to put a house aright for a family." She looked at them and saw great hesitancy in their manner and hastened to add in a softer tone, "I'll try to keep out of everyone's way and not be too much trouble."

The men's gazes lowered to her oversize belly, and the common doubt in their glances was far from belied by their nods of approval.

The group that drew up in front of the overgrown and ill-kept house dismounted and stood looking at the structure with some apprehension.

Hatti snorted contemptuously. "Humph! No wonder that man got to sell. I ain't never seen a house let go to such wreck and ruin in all my born days. I think they let the pigs loose in there."

Jeff chuckled as he took off his jacket and laid it in the carriage. "It looks like we've got our work cut out for us, doesn't it, Hatti?"

Brandon's coat joined his brother's and with a rueful grin, he muttered, "Well, let's get to work. There's no need to waste any more time."

He set two boys to cleaning up the yard and went inside to see what was needed. Hatti and Heather trailed behind him, making their own feminine estimates, and Heather wrinkled her nose in disgust at the sight that greeted her. Rotting food was strewn about the floors and furniture. Dirt and trash were thick beneath the feet and a foul odor permeated the place.

"I do believe you're right, Hatti. Swine have definitely nested here."

Servants were soon carrying any and all movable objects outside for a thorough cleaning. Jeff set off to search through the other quarters for usable furniture. Hatti gave orders to the women and they were soon about the task of cleaning the house from top to bottom. Hatti's husband and grandson, Ethan and Luke, took charge of the grounds and repainting the house. Brandon left the women to their work and went with George to check the outdoor facilities, which they found in poor state of repair. No hand lay idle.

In the bustle of the moment Heather had been ignored and left to her own ends. She tied a large kerchief about her hair, rolled up her sleeves, and with a long handled brush, set about cleaning the parlor fireplace. She was seated on the hearth and intent upon her labor when she was rudely startled by a voice behind her.

"Miss Heather! Lordy me, child! You gonna ruin yourself and that baby!" Hatti hustled to her mistress's side and taking her arm, helped her to her feet. "Miss

Heather, you ain't supposed to be working, child. You just come along to give advice. Master Bran see you doing work and he'll have a fit. You let these young girls do that what ain't got no baby in their belly. You just sit yourself down and take it easy!''

Heather looked about the empty room and laughed.

''Just where am I supposed to sit, Hatti? They've taken all the chairs out.''

''Well, we'll just find you one, and you make yourself comfortable.''

Heather was soon seated in a well-worn rocker before the dingy front windows with a book in her lap. Hatti bustled off and she was once more alone. She tried to read for a while in the dim light filtering through the grime and the filthy drapes, then out of curiosity wet her finger and brushing the drapery aside, ran it across a pane, leaving a clear streak in the dirt. She closed the book and rose in determination and soon had torn down the dirt-rotted drapes, and equipped with bucket and rag, was busily scrubbing away at the windows. She had climbed on a straight chair which she had brought in and was washing the upper panes when Brandon came through the front door. He took one look at her on the chair and didn't waste time with words. He strode up behind her and swooped her up in his arms, startling her so she cried out in alarm.

''And just what did you think you were doing?'' he demanded.

''Oh, Brandon, you gave me such a fright!''

He set her down on her feet. ''If I see you up on a chair again, miss, you'll have cause to be frightened. You're not here to work,'' he admonished. ''We just brought you along for company.''

She shook her head in exasperation. ''But Brandon I . . .''

''No argument, Heather. Just sit yourself down and take care of my son.''

She sighed in surrender and sank into the rocking chair

again, trailing her hands over the arms in resignation.

"Companionship, huh! You're all working while I sit here alone."

He smoothed a stray lock of her hair and kissed her lightly on the brow. "You're much more important to me sitting still than this whole damned house."

She thrust out her lower lip in a pout, picked up her book and began to rock. "I'm treated like an old woman already."

Brandon laughed softly. "Never, my love. Only when I'm an old, old man."

He left her to her reading, but it wasn't long before she rose and began to wander through the house. She passed a room upstairs where the young girls were busy mopping and scrubbing and another where two young men were putting up new wallpaper, then went downstairs again to the cookroom. Here the filth had not yet been disturbed, and she shuddered at the sight of it. Locating a straw broom, she began to sweep up the trash and dirt and discarded bones of many a meal. She coughed and choked at the dust she stirred up while she cast occasional glances to the door and listened for footsteps, but to no avail. The old woman came on silent feet.

"Miss Heather!" Hatti yelled.

She jumped and dropped the broom and stood shamefacedly with her hands behind her back. Hatti blocked the doorway with arms akimbo, her mouth screwed into a scowl.

"That ain't good for you, breathing in all that dust! And you gonna have that baby right here in this filthy old place if you don't set yourself down!" she scolded. "I's gonna fetch Master Brandon right now. He'll make you set."

And with that she turned and left. Heather pursed her lips, mumbling something about it being more unhealthy for a person to be startled out of their wits, and gazed downward as she scuffed a small foot at the dirt on the floor. The two came back and stood silently frowning at her.

"You, madam," Brandon sighed, "are the most will-ful woman I've ever known. It's plain to see we'll have to find some light task to keep you busy."

He was at a loss for what until Jeff hailed him from the back yard. The three strode outside as some boys were setting down several large barrels. Jeff threw the tops off to show them packed full of a weird assortment of dishes, pots, and kettles and other utensils.

"I've an idea Mrs. Bartlett sent these out for the slaves to use," Jeff surmised. "They were stored up at the mill so I doubt if Mr. Bartlett even let the poor devils see this stuff."

"Mr. Bartlett is married?" Heather questioned her husband, remembering Jeff's words from the day before.

Brandon nodded. "A very nice lady too, so I hear. She must be blind to his ways though. It seems everyone in Charleston knows what kind of man he is."

"White trash, that's what he is!" Hatti grunted. She pursed her lips and went back into the house, mumbling to herself. "That man ought to have been strung up long time ago."

Brandon examined a few of the items in the barrels and then cocked his eye to Heather, thinking he had found just the chore for her. "Well, my busy little mouse, perhaps you can stay out of trouble with these. You can sort out the best and set them aside for the Websters. It wouldn't do to give them back to Mrs. Bartlett and give her any ideas about her husband."

As he helped her descend the rickety steps she smiled at him brightly, a little flirting grin that melted within his heart and ran through his veins like wine, leaving him a bit intoxicated. He had difficulty concentrating on what Jeff was saying as he watched her poke about the barrels and finally had to turn his back upon her so he could give his brother his full attention. After a moment Jeff looked past him and stopped in mid sentence, grinning, and Brandon turned to find Heather head first in a large barrel, struggling to raise a large kettle from its bottom.

"Dammit!" his voice rang out.

The kettle thumped and Heather stood up, brushing her hair from her eyes. Her kerchief was askew and there was a large greasy smudge across her chin. Jeff melted into laughter as Brandon shook his head in exasperation.

"Jeff, have your boys unpack all these things and set them up on the porch," he said, and seizing a white porcelain dish from a barrel, held it up before Heather so she might see her reflection. "And you, Miss Black Face, will not lift anything heavier than this. Do you understand?"

She nodded vigorously and made an effort to wipe her face on her apron.

Brandon sighed. "Here, you're making it worse. Let me." He took the hem of her apron and gently wiped the grease from her chin. "Now be good," he cajoled. "Or I'll have to send you home to keep you out of trouble."

"Yes, sir," she murmured meekly, and Brandon's eyes caressed her gently.

Now that Heather had something to occupy her mind, she kept out of everyone else's hair. Brandon and George spent the rest of the morning cleaning out and repairing the well. Jeff continued his search of the cabins and found a fairly good selection of furniture. The front yard was jammed with the fruits of his search. Just before lunch Hatti pronounced the upstairs clean and fit for habitation, and the front of the house gleamed with a fresh coat of whitewash. They stopped and brought huge baskets from the wagon, and a gay, lighthearted repast was enjoyed by all. The meal was finished and everyone relaxed, sprawling about in a bit of sun or shade as each taste dictated. A feather tick had been placed beneath a lofty pine for Heather, and Brandon joined her on it while Jeff sat nearby with his back propped against an ancient chest and regarded them with smiling eyes.

"I was beginning to wonder if you two had an aver-

sion to sharing one of those things," he grinned.
"Though for the life of me, I couldn't figure out how
Heather got in her present condition without you doing
so. Of course, it could only take one night for the deed
to be done, couldn't it? And then she's caught."

A silence prevailed as Heather exchanged glances with
her husband. Brandon shrugged his shoulders slightly in
answer to her questioning gaze then raised an eyebrow
at his brother and contemplated him, but Jeff just smiled
and leaned back against the tree and closed his eyes.

The afternoon was as busy as the morning. The downstairs was put in spic-and-span shape, though it had
seemed at first to be an impossible goal. A smell of pine
soap now pervaded the rooms and everything shone and
sparkled in a mantle of impeccable cleanliness.

Heather was relieved that the labors of the day were
drawing to a close. She was bone tired, grimy, sticky with
sweat and hardly looking like the mistress of a great mansion. Long tendrils of black hair tumbled down her back
from beneath the kerchief around her head, and little
beads of moisture could be seen in the deep cleft between
her breasts where she had opened her bodice to allow the
cooling breeze to touch her skin.

No man except Brandon had been within the house
since the furniture was brought in, for all the chores remaining there required only a woman's hand for com-
pletion. Sheets were smoothed across new feather ticks
and dishes were washed and placed within cupboards. So
as Heather stood with Hatti before the now clean hearth,
discussing the things yet to be done to make the place a
bit more comfortable for the Websters, and gathering
from the old woman's knowledge a list of items packed
away at Harthaven that could be used, she was not conscious of any male presence. Her back was to the hall
door and Hatti was half turned away, following attentively her every word. With her gown soiled with dirt
and an apron tied beneath her bosom, she looked no different from the rest of the servants. A stranger coming

up from behind might think her a small, trim Negress.

That was Mr. Bartlett's folly when he saw her beside Hatti, and he entered the room with noiseless stride to force his presence upon the two women. Heather became aware of him only when she felt a hand crudely clapped between her buttocks and heard a voice boom in her ear.

"Ho! What a tidy piece I've found me. Old woman, go tell your master Mr. Bartlett's here to see him, but don't hurry. I've a mind to taste this tempting morsel while you're gone."

Heather spun about, choked with outrage as Hatti swung round with a gasp of surprise and stared horrified at the intruder. Bartlett showed only mild surprise at the color of the smaller woman's skin and eyes. His initial thought was that she was a bondwoman; he never dreamed he had just insulted a Birmingham. His tongue flicked over his lips as he viewed the cleavage between her breasts, and his grin thickened into a leer as he took hold of her arm.

"Well, honey girl, it looks as if someone climbed on you ahead o' me. Your master, perhaps? He sure's got taste, I'll give him that." He gestured Hatti out with his thumb. "Get, old woman. This is white folk's business. Your master is going to do a little sharing whether he wants to or not." His eyes narrowed at the Negress. "And don't go blabbing or I'll cut that tongue outa that black head."

Hatti and Heather found their voices at the same time. Heather let loose a screech of indignation as she tried to snatch free.

"How dare you! How dare you!"

Hatti gripped a rag mop nearby, waving it menacingly as she screamed. "You let her go! Get out of here, white trash. Master Bran'll make hash of you."

Mr. Bartlett took a step forward and lifted his arm to backhand the Negress but found himself under attack instead by Heather who struck him hard across the face.

"Leave her be!" she demanded.

His hand flew to his cheek, and he turned his shocked attention upon her.

"Why, you little hellcat!"

She glared at him, her bosom heaving, and pointed to the door. "You get out of here," she hissed. "And don't ever come back."

He snatched her to him. "You're talking mighty big for being just a servant girl, honey."

Angrily she pummeled his chest and face with her fists, demanding her release. He only laughed in uproarious glee and locked an arm roughly about her shoulders, smothering her blows in a sweaty embrace.

"You're sure anxious to save this old woman's skin, lil' gal," he chuckled. "But you're going about it in the wrong way. All you have to do is be nice to me. What's your master got that I ain't?"

Hatti swung her mop at the same time Heather's sharp heel fell crunchingly on his instep. Bartlett's pained howl was abruptly choked in a tangle of wet mop and both wounded and thrown off balance, he stumbled backward into the hall. Now faced by the huge Negress with blood in her eye, brandishing her mop, and a tiny wildcat gripping a bar of soap as if it were a dagger, he turned and fled from the vengeful pair. As his foot lit on the top step of the porch the huge bar of soap struck the back of his head with a meaty *chunk* and sailed off into the yard to be followed shortly by Mr. Bartlett who did a beautiful somersault in midair and landed the full length of his backside in the dust. He rose, gasping for breath, enraged at being so sorely abused by two common servants, and women at that. The small one faced him from the porch with a feral gleam in her eye.

"Now take your filthy, slimy person from these premises and make haste doing so," she sneered. She raised an eyebrow contemptuously. "Or *my master* will make you wish you had."

"Why, you little bitch!" he choked. "I'll teach you to set upon your betters."

He stepped forward threateningly and the huge mop whistled within inches from his face, leaving small trails of dirty water dripping down it. Hatti pulled Heather behind her and her voice rumbled with rage as she spoke slow but painfully clear.

"Now, Mr. Bartlett. If you ever lay a hand on this Birmingham again I'll wrap that mop so hard around your head they'll have to shave you like a sheep."

The man's next retort was startled from him as he heard a rapid thud of feet behind him, and he turned to see the master of Harthaven coming toward him with an angry grimace distorting his reddened face. In that brief moment Bartlett realized what it was like to face death. He had insulted the wife of a Birmingham, and not only a Birmingham, but Brandon Birmingham, the one known for his foul temper.

Whitening considerably under his swarthy skin, he stood rooted to the spot, unable to move, with fear oozing from every pore. Brandon had heard enough to set his mind afire and now saw only the man before him, all else blotted out by a reddish haze. He yearned only to feel that same one's bones break beneath his hand and as he neared he swung his fist with blood-thirsty vengeance. His knuckles caught the man across the cheek and right eyebrow, laying skin open and spinning Bartlett around. Brandon drew back, with his fist ready to fly again, but Bartlett fled toward his carriage with an agility amazing for his age and size. Brandon was hardly in the mood to let him go and was just reaching forward to seize the man when Jeff entered the fray. Realizing his brother's blood lust rage, he flung his body full length into Brandon's, sending them both tumbling into the dust. He sought to hold him down but Brandon flung him off, and Jeff looked up to find his brother standing legs spraddled in a cloud of dirt, swearing at the rapidly dwindling carriage. Mr. Bartlett raised once from his seat to shake a hurried fist and then settled again to the task of full flight.

Brandon quieted as he stared down the now empty

lane. He shook himself and ran his fingers through his hair and turning, gave Jeff a hand up. He looked toward the house, his wild rage being rapidly replaced by concern for Heather. A worried frown wrinkled his brow by the time he reached the first step, and he paused before his wife who fell into his arms, laughing with almost hysterical relief as she spread tearful kisses on his throat and chest and dabbed with the end of her apron at the dirt on him and the tears in her eyes. Thinking her truly overwrought and unable to find another explanation for her behavior, Brandon guided her tenderly to a chair to try to soothe her.

Brandon questioned Hatti a moment later, and Jeff found himself again on the verge of using force to restrain him as the story unfolded. Brandon rose to his feet, his cheek flexing tensely, vowing to kill Bartlett, and Heather's heart jumped into her throat.

"Please," she gasped, catching his hand. She drew him down again before her and pressed the palm of his hand against her abdomen. He felt his baby moving vigorously within her. She gazed into his eyes and smiled gently as she reached up to caress his cheek. "I've had enough excitement for the day. Let's finish here and go home."

When Jeremiah Webster first glimpsed the house prepared for him and his family, he thought it to be the Birmingham house and remarked what a fine place it was. The three Birminghams looked at him in some surprise, and Brandon hastened to correct him. The man's jaw dropped in astonishment, and it was several moments before he regained his wits and turned to his wife.

"Did you hear, Leah? Did you hear? This here is to be our house."

For the first time since they had met, the woman spoke with tears brimming her eyes, her shyness forgotten for the moment.

"It's too good to be true." She turned to Heather as

if to reaffirm what her husband had said. "We're to live here? In a real house?" she half questioned, still uncertain.

Heather nodded to assure her and flashed a soft, warm smile to her husband for his kindness to these people as she took the woman's arm.

"Come," she murmured gently. "I'll show you around inside."

As the two women entered the house with Mr. Webster following close behind, Jeff gently nudged Brandon who stared after his wife.

"A few more good deeds, Brandon, and you'll be her knight in shining armor."

As the month of March grew middle-aged, the days waxed warm and sunny. Brandon found that preparing the mill for production demanded most of his time, and he saw little of his wife or home. Both he and Webster made many trips between the mill and the logging camps upriver. Great rafts of logs were floated down to rest in the backwaters behind the mill and await the first greedy screams of hungry saws. Most of the old stock of lumber in the millyard went to repair and rebuild the tumbledown shanties that had housed the slaves. Two families and some half-dozen single men had come from New York on Webster's urging to add their experience to the crews.

The hot, dusty days and the cool, damp nights formed a dreary pattern for Heather with both Brandon and Jeff absent from the house. She fought the lassitude of monotony and found brief moments of relief in small things. A spring shower broke the month's drought and paved the way for a night of pounding rain. The next few days brought a pleasant metamorphosis to the land, and Heather was amazed at the sudden change caused by the rains. Almost overnight the burnt, dry browns of winter were replaced by the verdant, blushing greens of spring. Magnolia trees sent their rich scents across the countryside and purple cascades of wisteria fell from the trees where it clung. Azaleas, oleanders and assorted lilies threw their riotous colors across the woodland and pungent dogwood delicately graced the glens. Ducks and geese ranged overhead and the forest came alive with abundant animal life.

In the midst of this grandeur Heather felt her time approach. Her burden lowered in her belly, and when she walked her stomach cleared the way. Despite the beauty of the land she ventured out but rarely. She felt herself clumsy and slow, but whenever she sought to move, she always found a hand ready to assist her. When Brandon was gone, either to the mill or the logging camps upstream, it was Jeff, or Hatti, or Mary, but someone was always near.

A score of family friends came out to pay their respects to her and welcome Brandon home. It was on a Friday afternoon when they ventured forth. The pits had been readied for roasting early that morning, and young boys set to turning sides of beef and pork. Kegs of ale were cooled in the chilly waters of the creek, and food prepared in abundance.

Reverend Fairchild and his wife and brood of seven were among the first to arrive, and soon after, Abegall Clark's huge, black landau came smartly up the lane without pausing to halt before the big house. The party grew light as the day grew long, and Reverend Fairchild was sorely set to keep some men from imbibing too much and with routing the young couples from behind the bushes where they were wont to lie and exchange poetic phrases. Brandon ordered several kegs of ale set out beneath the trees and Jeff in kind brought out a hogshead of his own aged bourbon. Spirits grew high and private kegs were brought out and tapped, ostensibly for comparison with the Birmingham wares. Children ran and played across the great lawns and consumed many pitchers of lemonade. The women collected in groups and stitched samplers while the men admired the horses and the women and seemed unable to decide just whose keg bore the sweetest brew.

It was Sybil Scott who drew most everyone's attention at some time during the afternoon. She wore a daringly low gown of some considerable cost and was pursued consistently by a paunchy, middle-aged merchant whose intentions were clear to everyone but her. She evaded his pawing lunges with shrill giggles, somewhat overwhelmed by this unusual attention from a man and the absence of her mother's restrictive hand.

Heather's eyes widened as she saw the formerly reticent girl now giggling and flirting with her suitor and meeting his roving hands with only token resistance. Seated beside her, Mrs. Clark showed her anger by sniffing loudly and stamping her umbrella on the ground.

"Maranda Scott will rue the day she gave her daughter freedom. That poor young girl will end up broken hearted. He buys her wealthy clothes and gifts and makes no further promises, and she's been too long protected to deal with a man and that one especially. Poor girl, she needs a guiding hand."

"I thought she seemed like such a shy young girl," Heather murmured, rather confused at the change.

"Sybil, my dear, is not young," Mrs. Fairchild commented. "And most certainly seems to have lost her shyness."

Mrs. Clark shook her head sadly. "It's obvious since she failed to catch a Birmingham, Maranda has given up on her."

She glanced at Heather, who for all her roundness was startlingly beautiful in that mysterious way expectant mothers are. She wore a gown of light blue organdy with frothy ruffles at the throat and wrists, and her hair was caught in a mass of soft ringlets with narrow blue ribbons falling over the cascading curls. Even so obviously pregnant, she was the envy of many.

The grand dame continued, now speaking directly to Heather. "You must know by now that Sybil had her eye set for your husband, though I can't see where she, poor child, ever thought she had a chance with him. He rarely gave any of even the prettiest girls of our church a second glance, and then, of course, there was Louisa, who we must admit is a beautiful woman. Even then Sybil held some hope for herself, but that day she saw you I believe she finally realized her dreams were ended. It was a shame the way Maranda encouraged her to believe Brandon would notice her. He hardly knew the poor girl was alive.'' Nodding toward Sybil she stated flatly, ''This is Maranda's fault, what is happening now, but she sits in her house and damns Brandon and will not think of her daughter.''

The woman's voice ended full of ire and she stamped her parasol on the ground as if to emphasize it. Down the lane Brandon and Jeff were walking toward them when Sybil, trying to avoid her heavy handed suitor, darted around a tree and almost collided with them. Brandon stepped aside and nodded a greeting and continued on his way without so much as a second glance. The poor girl's eyes widened as she recognized him and the blood left her face. She stood staring at his back dejectedly, all the gaiety driven from her day by his mere presence, and she watched him take a chair beside his wife.

Sybil's view was obscured when a barouche came up the lane and stopped in front of the seated group. As the richly dressed Louisa descended from the carriage leaving her beau looking rather surprised at her hasty departure, Heather put her needlework down in her lap and waited for her to approach. Louisa smiled brightly as she strode forward and warbled a gay greeting. Her new beau climbed down and followed her but she ignored him, bestowing her full attention upon her former fiancée. She frowned when Brandon rose to stand behind his wife's chair, and then she turned to consider Heather.

''My goodness, child,'' she smirked, her eyes dropping to the round belly. ''This will probably ruin your figure for the rest of your life.''

''What would you know of it, Louie?'' Jeff asked sarcastically.

She disregarded him and spun around, showing off her attire as well as her voluptuous figure. "How do you like my new gown? I found the most talented couturier. He does such wonders with a bolt of cloth and a bit of thread." She wrinkled her nose as if in distaste. "But he's such an odd little man. You really must see him. It would almost make you laugh." She looked pointedly at the younger girl. "But then he's one of your countrymen, darling."

She flitted away to talk to a group of young couples nearby as her beau turned to greet Brandon.

"Heard tell you got married, Brand," Matthew Bishop drawled.

Brandon slipped his hands to Heather's shoulders as he introduced her to the man.

"Matt and Jeff went to school together," he explained to his wife.

"It's a pleasure to make your acquaintance, Mr. Bishop," she murmured, smiling.

The man glanced first to her stomach and grinned, then his eyes rose to her face and he seemed surprised at what he saw.

"This is your wife?" he questioned, almost incredulously. "Why, Louisa said . . ."

He stopped, realizing what he had almost let slip. He had thought it odd when Louisa ranted and raved to him about the homely little beggar who had used witchery to snatch Brandon from her. He had found it hard to believe Brandon that anxious to be caught or the type to take an unappetizing wench to bed much less to wife. He should have known the man would have found the prettiest to warm his bed.

"I believe the jest is on me," he smiled. "You have a most lovely wife, Brand."

Louisa hurried back in time to hear his last comments and scowled at him as she took his arm, but she turned to smile at Brandon.

"Darling, you give the most fabulous parties," she simpered. "Even when there were just the two of us, your parties were never boring."

Brandon seemed oblivious to her as he bent to ask his wife of her comfort, but Abegail was not so silent.

"You seem to dote upon parties, Louisa. As to men— it's not often that you've displayed the taste to limit your affections to just one."

Jeff gave a hearty chuckle and winked at the old woman. Louisa glared at them both. She turned her attention to Heather in time to see the girl rub her cheek lovingly against her husband's hand and murmur a reply to him as he bent over her. Jealousy raged within her. Her eyes fell to the handkerchief Heather was monograming for her husband and her eyes narrowed slyly.

"Whatever do you have there, darling? Do you waste your time with trivial sewing? I thought you would have more important things to attend to, married to Brandon." She cast a glance toward him. "But then, I suppose there are few real pleasures you can indulge in when you're that far along with child. As for myself, I . . ."

"Sewing is a gentle art, Louisa," Mrs. Fairchild interrupted, paying close attention to her own needlework. "One which you might do well to learn. It occupies the hand and keeps the mind from less desirable pursuits."

Deciding she could not successfully ruin Heather's fun without someone barging in to protect the little mouse, Louisa strolled away, bested for the moment but never beaten. There'd be another opportunity to shred the girl's confidence to ribbons, and she was patient. She smiled up at her new beau and rubbed her breast against his arm to tease him. He was not as handsome as Brandon nor half so rich, but he would do until she connived to get that arrogant and talented stud in her bed again.

Forever the bachelor on the make, Matt pulled Louisa behind a large bush and into his passionate embrace. He taunted her in turn with his own body, and his parted lips sought hers as his hand slid inside her bodice to caress her warm, abundant flesh.

"Not here," she murmured, pulling away slightly. "I know a place in the stables."

Hatti came out the front door with a tray of lemonade for the ladies, and Mrs. Clark greeted her warmly as she served them.

"Aren't you ready to leave this den of iniquity and come live with me, Hatti?" she iniquired. "We older folks must stick together, you know."

"No'm," Hatti declined with a chuckle. "I'm gonna have a new Birmingham to bring up shortly and Master will have to kick me out before I leave this place and Miss Heather. A team of Master Bran's mules couldn't pull me from here."

She drew a laugh from all present, and with a questioning look at Heather, she turned her attention to her mistress' comfort.

"How you feeling, honey child? Don't tire yourself out sitting too long. That baby gonna come soon enough without nobody rushing it. Master Bran, don't you let her do too much, you hear?"

"I hear, Hatti," he chuckled.

It was well after dark when the meat was pronounced ready and torches were brought out to provide light. Savory dishes from different families were brought together on a long table, and the guests avidly devoted themselves to the food. The beef and pork were sliced right over the pits and heaped on eagerly presented plates as everyone formed in lines. Heather and Brandon moved around the table with their own plates and selected those foods which tempted them most. He pointed out the dishes unfamiliar to her but which he thought she might enjoy. As they walked from the table to the pits she looked down rather amazed at her plate.

"I am so fat that my eyes cannot see my feet and yet I burden my plate like this." She lifted a corn pone from her plate and giggled happily as she fed him a bite.

"You'll just have to help me eat it, Brandon. That's all there is to be done."

He chuckled and pressed a warm kiss upon her lips as she gazed up at him with her smile bright. "Anything to please you, sweet. Anything at all."

When they returned to their chairs, Heather watched her husband place his plate upon his knees and slice off a juicy bit of rare beef with the greatest of ease, while she sat in indecision, not knowing where to put her plate. She contemplated his long legs, then her own loss of lap. Brandon glanced up at her as she gazed doubtfully at her belly and chuckled with amusement. Getting up, he handed her his plate and went to fetch a small table for them.

"I believe you'll be able to manage here, madam," he grinned when he set it before them.

As they sat together Brandon caught sight of a disgruntled George sitting at the far end of the porch, whittling on a twig with vicious intent. Puzzled by this display of temper from the old man, he beckoned him over.

"What ails you?" he questioned when the manservant stood by his side.

George glanced hesitantly at Heather and was slow to answer. "There were some varmints in the stables, cap'n."

Brandon raised an eyebrow at him. "Varmints?"

The servant shuffled his feet and peered at Heather again. "Aye, cap'n. Varmints."

Brandon thought this over for a moment and then nodded in understanding. "All right, George. Take yourself a plate and settle your thoughts on some of this beef and forget what you may have seen or heard."

"Aye, cap'n," the man replied.

When he had gone, Heather looked at Brandon with a puzzled expression. "Did George find rats in the stables?"

Brandon laughed heartily. "You might say that, sweet."

The party continued into the night. Brandon took Heather for a stroll among their guests and then once again settled her in the midst of the ladies. He was drawn away by a group of men and it was a late hour before he could free himself from their hold and return to her. She sat quietly, listening to several middle-aged women talk of their current illnesses and womanly upsets. Mrs. Clark was no longer present but had retired some time earlier to one of the bedrooms upstairs. Mrs. Fairchild had left for home with her husband and their brood. Brandon took Heather's hand and drew her from the chair.

"Ladies, I must beg that you excuse my wife now. She's had a long, tiring day and needs her rest. I hope you don't mind."

They hurried to assure him that they did not mind, and smiled among themselves as they watched him so considerately help his young wife up the steps and into the house. Inside, Heather released a tired sigh.

"Thank you for rescuing me," she murmured. "I'm afraid they thought me quite dull. I couldn't think of anything to say that would impress them with my intelligence, and besides, that chair was most uncomfortable."

"I'm sorry, sweet. I would have come sooner, had I known."

She dropped her head against his arm and smiled. "I fear you'll have to drag me upstairs. I'm so tired I don't believe I can manage them alone."

He stopped and lifted her into his arms amid her protests.

"Put me down, Brandon," she pleaded. "I'm so heavy. You'll hurt yourself."

He chuckled. "Hardly, madam. You still weigh no more than a mite."

"Well, well, well. What can this be?" a woman questioned from behind them and there was no mistaking Louisa's soft, purring voice.

Brandon turned slowly with his wife in his arms and met the woman's mocking eyes as she came toward them.

"Do you do this every night, Brandon?" she inquired jeeringly, with a raised eyebrow. "It surely must put a strain on your back, darling. You know you should take better care of yourself. Whatever would you do if you broke your back? You would certainly be no good to her anymore."

His face was expressionless as he made his reply. "I've lifted heavier women in my life, Louisa, including you. I'd say my wife has yet to gain before she matches your weight."

The mocking smile was replaced by a tightly-set mouth, and she glared at him, but he turned away and without a backward glance spoke again.

"By the way, Louisa, you should go comb your hair. You have straw in it."

Over his shoulder Heather permitted a small, triumphant smile to appear on her lips as she looked at the other woman, and she tightened her arms about her husband's neck.

Instead of going directly into the sitting room, for Louisa still stared up at them, Brandon carried her through his room. In her room he lounged in a chair while Mary helped her undress behind a screen. While she was so misshapen, Heather preferred her nakedness concealed from him. She would wait until she was again slim and could tempt him with a trimmer waist, then she would gladly yield her body to his gaze—and to whatever might follow.

When a gentle breeze ruffled the draperies by her bed the next morning, Heather stirred from sleep. The dull ache in her back still was with her, and she felt strangely tired, though she had rested some eight hours or more.

As she rose from bed she felt the heavy weight of the child within her pressing downward.

The day was slow to pass. She saw the last of the overnight guests leave by late afternoon, with the exception of Mrs. Clark, who would be staying a few more days. Night came and dinner was served. Family and guest enjoyed a delectable bouillabaisse of Aunt Ruth's artistry, and as the last dishes were taken from the table the group settled in the drawing room, but Heather soon found there was little more comfort to be had in the chairs here than in the dining room. She sought her bed early and when Brandon escorted her upstairs and left her in the sitting room, she dismissed Mary and undressed herself.

Time was forgotten as she lay in the darkness. She heard Brandon come upstairs again and move about his room, then silence returned once more as he retired to bed. Sleep came finally for her but it was not long. She woke slowly as the drawing within her belly became painfully real and no longer a dream. It left her wide awake as it passed, and she slid her hand to her stomach knowing her time had come.

The pains gripped her until it seemed every muscle in her body ached with the strain. She struggled from the bed finally, intent upon sending Mary for Hatti, and lit a candle by her bedside. By its glow she saw that her gown had been stained and seeking another, carefully moved toward the bureau. She was half way there when her eyes widened in surprise and she gasped. The discharge left her gown soaking, and the fetal water ran from between her legs without stopping. Standing in helpless confusion, she looked around as the door from Brandon's room opened. He walked in naked, just shrugging into his robe.

"Heather, are you all right?" he questioned. "I thought I heard . . ."

He stopped abruptly, his eyes falling to her stained and clinging gown, then he came to her in a rush.

"My God, it's the baby!"

"Brandon," she said in an amazed tone. "I'm all wet. It happened so suddenly. I didn't know it was coming."

She stared up at him as if her soaked condition was the only thing that concerned her, then she began unfastening the garment.

"Please get me another. I can't go back to bed in a wet gown."

He hurried to her bureau and threw open the drawers, scrambling through them like a madman and leaving them gaping and lingerie hanging over the sides. He finally located the gowns, neatly stacked in the bottom drawer, and ran back to her with the top garment, but Heather declined it.

"But, Brandon, that's pink. I'm having a boy, and boys don't wear pink. Go get a blue one, please."

He stared at her for a moment in astonishment and finally regained his wits.

"Madam, God's truth, I don't care whether it's a girl or boy," he exclaimed. "Just put this on and let me get you back into bed."

"No," she said stubbornly, "I'm going to have a boy, and I shan't wear that."

"But, madam, *he* won't be wearing anything when he gets here so it doesn't matter," he cried. "Now will you get this on?"

She met his stare and pursing her lips, slowly shook her head in negative motion.

Brandon threw up his hands in exasperation and the nightgown floated to the floor as he ran back to the bureau and began tossing gowns this way and that in a frenzy. Finally he found a blue one and rushed to her with it. She looked up at him expectantly as she took it, but he was most confused and just stared down at her dumbfoundedly.

"Will you turn your back, please?" she requested, seeing his bewilderment.

"What?" he asked stupidly.

"Will you turn your back, please?" she repeated.

"But, madam, I've seen you without clothes be . . ."

He stopped and spun about, realizing it would do him no good to argue with her for she was hell bent to have her way and he would only delay things by trying to explain anything to her.

Heather threw the blue gown over his shoulder, finding no other place to put it, standing in the middle of the room as they were.

"Madam, will you hurry," he urged. "You're going to whelp right there if you don't and our child will be the only one ever born on his head."

Heather giggled lightly and let the wet gown fall to the floor as she reached up for the clean one. "I doubt that, my dearest."

"Heather, for God's sakes," he pleaded. "Will you stop chattering and get that gown on!"

"But, Brandon, I wasn't chattering. I just answered you." She drew the gown in place and began tying the ribbon. "You may turn around now if you want."

He whirled and bent to pick her up.

"But, Brandon," she protested. "I must wipe up the floor."

"To hell with the floor!" he exclaimed and gathered her into his arms. He stood holding her for a moment in indecision, glancing from her bed to his door and made up his mind quickly. He hurried from her room into his.

"Where are you taking me?" she questioned. "Hatti will never find me. She'll have to go all over the house looking for me."

He placed her carefully in the middle of his huge bed. "There. Does that answer your question, chatterbox? It's where I'd like my son—or perhaps my daughter born."

"I'm not having a girl. I'm having . . ."

She was again wrenched with pain as another contraction seized her and she bit her bottom lip in agony.

"I'll awaken Hatti," he muttered and fled the room quickly.

But the old Negress, having seen from her cabin

Heather's room alight, had sensed the situation and was already in the hallway when he came flying out.

"She's having the baby!" he cried when he saw her. "Hurry."

She shook her head as she speeded with him into the master bedroom. "It'll be a long while yet before she has that baby, Master Bran. It's the first and they takes their good natured time. It'll be hours yet."

"Well, she's in pain now. Do something for her."

"Master Bran, I's sorry, but there ain't nothing I can do for her pain," she replied. With a concerned frown creasing her black brow, she bent over the writhing Heather and smoothed her hair from her face. "Don't fight it, child. Just pant while you're having them, then relax when they go. You'll need your strength for later."

With Hatti directing, Heather panted. The pain eased soon and she was able to smile at Brandon as he came to stand near her. He sat down on the bed's edge and his hand moved to hers, and she saw that his face was grim and seemed suddenly lined.

"I'm told every mother has to go through this," she murmured consolingly. "It's part of being a woman."

Hatti roused the household and banked fires were stirred up and great kettles of water set to boil. Fresh linens were brought and with Brandon's help some of these were placed beneath Heather. The blue gown was pulled up out of the way and a clean sheet spread to cover her nakedness, and the time went slowly for some, swiftly for others. Hatti rocked in a chair by the bedside when she was not tending her mistress, and Brandon with each contraction became more distraught.

"Hatti, how much longer do you think it'll be," he questioned anxiously, wiping his brow.

"No one knows that, Master Bran," the woman replied. "But it sure looks like Miss Heather is holding up a darn sight better 'n you. Why don't you go have a nice big drink of that stuff you like to drink. It sure couldn't hurt nothing, and it might help a lot."

Brandon felt in strong need of a brandy but declined, wanting to stay and comfort his wife in any way he could. She clung to his hand tightly, seeming to want him there by her side, and he could not leave her when she was so tortured with giving his child birth.

Again the agony came and again it went. Brandon wiped Heather's face with a cool, wet cloth and brushed her hair up from her neck and looked a little paler than he did before. Hatti moved to the bedside and taking his arm, urged him from it.

"Master Bran, you best let Master Jeff fix you something strong. You don't look so good." She guided him to the door and opening it, gently pushed him out. "You go get drunk, Master Bran. Go get drunk and don't come back until I calls you. I don't want you fainting while I got to tend the missus."

The door closed and Brandon was left staring at it, feeling lost and out of sorts. He glanced around him, and finally went downstairs and into the study where George and his brother waited. Jeff took one look at him and pressed a stiff drink into his hand.

"Here, you look as if you need this."

Brandon tossed the drink down without hardly noticing the two who regarded him, and Jeff motioned to George and the servant quickly took his captain's glass and poured a small draught of brandy in it and an ample supply of water. Brandon didn't realize the difference as he paced the floor.

Between the two of them, Jeff and George managed to keep Brandon's drinks pretty well watered. Jeff watched his brother light up one expensive cigar after another then crush them out after taking only a puff or two. He moved in a sort of daze around the study, inattentive and unconcerned with what went on around him, ignoring them and paying no heed to what he did. He strode into the hallway many times and gazed upward toward the second floor, then he would turn again and reach for another drink. A maid scurrying up or down the stairs now and then would send him rushing to the door, but for no reason. When he poured himself a bourbon and swallowed a good third of the contents without noticing the difference, Jeff knew he was in another world entirely.

"Brandon, you're getting too old for this sort of thing or else that little girl up there matters more to you than you admit. I've seen you go after a wounded boar without fear, knowing exactly what you were doing. Now you're so addled, you're drinking my bourbon and you can't stand the stuff."

Brandon thrust the glass at him. "Well, why the hell did you give it to me then if you knew I disliked it?"

Jeff turned a bemused expression to George, and the man smiled in return and shrugged his shoulders. The younger brother went to the desk, shaking his head, and relaxed back in the chair. After a moment he took up quill and paper and began to scratch out a few figures. When he turned to Brandon again, he wore a grin broader than a barn door. It couldn't have worked out better if he had possessed a hand in fate.

"You know, Brandon, according to my calculations, you'd have had to marry Tory the first day you were in London port."

George spewed a mouthful of ale out in surprise and coughed and choked as some went down the wrong way, while Brandon lowered his head between his shoulders and scowled at his brother.

In the master bedroom Heather writhed in silent agony as she bore down in an effort to force the child from her. She breathed in deeply as the pain eased, but her relief was short and she was again tortured. She clung to the servant's hand and gritted her teeth while Hatti encouraged her.

"The head is about to come, Miss Heather. It won't be long now. Push down. That's it. Scream if you want. You been silent too long, child."

A whimper escaped Heather as her body was consumed in pain. She fought the urge to cry out, but as the child's head emerged, a scream did come, and down below in the study Brandon slid weakly into a chair as he heard it. He stared unseeing across the room, and George caught his glass as it tipped. Both the servant and the younger brother glanced at each other in nervous indecision, realizing that Heather's cry had affected them too.

Some time later, with a broad grin upon her black face, Hatti opened the door of the study, holding the wee Birmingham close. She went to Brandon first as the two other men stared at the bundle, drawing back the blanket for him to see his child.

"It's a boy, Master. A strong, fine, healthy boy. He was asqualling before he left the hatch."

"My God," Brandon uttered as he came from his daze to see the wrinkled, red face of his son before him. He grabbed up his drink and tossed it down and looked around as if he needed another badly.

Jeff and George sidled closer to view the child and beamed proudly as if they were the ones responsible for his being there, forgetting Brandon entirely. Jeff poked a gentle finger at the small hand.

"He doesn't look much like Brandon," he commented.

George quickly glanced from father to son, but Hatti spoke up in disagreement.

"Master Brandon looked just like this when he was born. He was just about as long too. This baby's gonna be as tall as his pa, that's for sure. He's already got a good start."

Brandon stood up and peeked leerily over George's shoulder at his son again. He moved from the group as they continued to admire the baby and hurried out of the room and up the stairs to the master bedroom. Heather smiled drowsily as he came to the bedside and took her hand.

"Have you seen him?" she questioned as he sat beside her. "Isn't he beautiful?"

He nodded to the first inquiry and reserved opinion on the second. "How do you feel?" he asked softly.

"Sleepy," she sighed. "But wonderful."

He pressed his lips to her brow. "Thank you for the son," he murmured.

She smiled and closed her eyes, holding his hand clutched to her breast.

"We'll have your daughter next time," he whispered.

But Heather had already drifted to sleep.

Brandon gently eased his hand from her grasp and tip-toed out of the room to the sitting room, leaving Mary to sit with his wife. He paused by a window and saw that dawn was breaking. He smiled to himself, feeling fit enough to wrestle a bear and quite good despite the fact that he had been up all night. He brought a chair to the window which he opened and sat down, propping his feet on the sill. A moment later when Hatti came through the room she found his head slumped on his chest and his eyes closed in sleep.

She shook her head slowly and smiled, "Poor Master, he sure had a hard night."

The sun was streaming down in bright rays over Hart-haven when Brandon woke to the sound of angry squalls and realized his son was making his demands. He rose and washed the foul taste from his mouth left from the night of drinking, then pushed open the door to the nurs-ery to find Hatti bending over the wee one. She was clucking to him and cooing and talking in a soothing tone, but he raged on.

"We gonna have you fed in just a minute, lil' Bir-mingham. It ain't the end of the world."

Feeling now a fatherly interest and pride in his son, Brandon drew closer and stood with hands behind his back as he watched the old Negress struggling to remove the wet clothes. The baby drew up his knees and wailed the louder, turning red with his anger.

"Whooee, that boy sure is mad. He's a wanting something to eat and he's letting everybody know it.''

As soon as he was dry, the young Birmingham's manner calmed some. He smacked his lips, opening his mouth like a little bird everytime his fist brushed his cheek, and released whimpering little gurgles, now and then letting out a disgruntled yelp.

Hatti chuckled at him. ''Look there, master, he's trying to sweet talk me into giving him something to eat.''

Brandon smiled and the baby gurgled pleadingly.

''You sure is an impatient lil' fella,'' Hatti cooed, picking him up and cuddling him to her big bosom. ''But your mammy is awake, and we're gonna take you in there right now.''

Running his fingers through his tousled hair, Brandon followed the servant into the master bedroom. There he saw Heather sitting up in bed, hair combed and ribboned, fresh and frilly gown donned, and looking irresistibly beautiful. When she saw him she hurriedly motioned Mary away, giving her a hand mirror, and then turned to give him a radiant smile and hold eager arms out for her son. He followed Hatti to the bed, sitting beside Heather as she took the babe gently into her arms. He saw a light blush spread across her features when she undid her gown and pushed it aside, and sensed her unease with this new, unfamiliar task of motherhood, yet she cooed to the baby softly and tried to direct him as he rooted about eagerly. The nipple brushed his cheek and he turned his head hurriedly in that direction and latched onto it with the ferocity of a starving pig, causing Heather to jump in painful surprise as his mouth clamped down on her. Brandon smiled, and Hatti chuckled as she viewed the babe sucking at his mother's breast.

''Lordy me. The young master is hollow from the feet up. Most likely, we'll be having to fix that boy a sugar tit to tide him over until his mammy gets milk.''

The tiny, tugging mouth sent strange rivers of delight pulsating through Heather's body as she gazed lovingly at her son. Already she thought he looked a great deal like his father. Soft, black hair covered the small head and magnificent little brows were already shaped with his sire's curve and not his mother's slant. With a maternal pride, she thought him a most handsome baby.

"He is beautiful, isn't he, Brandon?" she murmured, lifting warm eyes to his, and Hatti prodded Mary out the door, closing it behind them as Brandon replied.

"He is indeed, madam." He reached and thrust a gentle finger into the tiny fist that pressed against her breast. It was readily accepted and firmly held, and Brandon smiled in pleasure.

He returned his gaze to his wife's face and lost himself in the soft liquid eyes that beheld him. He was barely conscious of his actions as he leaned forward, almost mesmerized by the deep pools of blue. His free hand slipped through her hair to the nape of her neck and still she stared, and then his mouth found hers and eyelids lowered. He felt her lips slacken and begin to tremble and then open as his mouth moved upon hers. He tasted response, sweet, warm and clinging and was aware of the rapid beat of her heart beneath the fingers resting on her breast.

Heather struggled for breath under his flaming kiss, all too aware of his hands upon her, of his searing mouth taking hers. Feeling faint, she tore free and laughed shakily.

"You make me forget the baby." She sighed as his lips slid to her throat and tried to stop the spinning of her head. "What shall we name him?"

He drew back and looked at her. After a moment he murmured, "If you have no objections, I'd like to name him after a friend of mine, now dead. He was killed a few years back fighting a fire that burned his church. I admired the man very much, but you might be warned that he was a Frenchman—a French Huguenot. I will understand if your English ancestry disapproves of naming our son after him."

"You forget, m'lord," she smiled, "that in all actuality, you are more English than I. What was your friend's name?''

''Beauregard—Beauregard Grant,'' he answered readily.

She tested the name on her tongue, then nodded her head. ''It's a nice name. I like it. Beauregard Grant Birmingham is what he shall be called.''

Freeing his finger from his son's grip, Brandon opened a drawer in the bedside commode and removed a long box which he presented to her.

''With gratitude, madam, for giving me a son.''

He lifted the lid for her and she stared at the necklace within. Two long strands of large, carefully matched pearls were clasped together by a generous ruby set in gold filagree.

''Oh, Brandon, it's lovely,'' she breathed.

His eyes fell to her throat and bosom and his voice was hoarse when he spoke. ''Somehow I thought pearls would compliment the beauty of your skin better than diamonds.''

She could almost feel his stare caressing her. A warm feeling again swept her, and her pulse throbbed in her throat, then he glanced away.

''I'll get dressed,'' he said huskily as he rose from the bed. ''I imagine Abegail is anxious to see the baby.''

He selected clothes from his wardrobe and turning again, gave her a long appraisal before he went into the sitting room to dress.

Some time later, Abegail came in with Jeff to view the baby who now lay asleep on the bed beside his mother. She lifted a lorgnette and peered at the new born, then raised an eyebrow as she smiled at Brandon.

''Well, I see there'll be another generation of girls set upon by a Birmingham. But I do hope you plan to have enough to make a lot of those frilly-skirted things happy. They shan't like it if there's only himself there.''

Jeff smiled slowly. ''They'll probably have at least a dozen, but I doubt if their children will be all boys.''

The old woman looked in obvious glee to Brandon. "Well, now that would be justice indeed, to have one of you two defending a maiden's honor." She chuckled merrily at the thought. "It would stir your blood more than a mite if you had to force a gay bachelor to wed your daughter."

Heather cast a quick glance to Brandon and was amazed to see for the first time a dark blush on his face. Jeff smiled to himself, seeing his brother's discomfort, but Mrs. Clark was gazing again at the babe and missed the exchange, having no idea how close she had brought everything home to him.

"You have given the world a most magnificent child, my dear," she commented to Heather. "You must be quite proud of him."

Heather smiled at the woman and raised warm eyes to her husband. "Thank you, Mrs. Clark. I am."

With the birth of his son past, Brandon once more devoted his time and energies to readying the mill for operation. Heather remained in the large bedroom and had set her mind to the fact that she would stay there. It would take physical force to move her out again, and each day her presence was more firmly established. Brandon first noticed her brush and comb upon the dressing table, then her powder and perfumes resided there. More and more of her clothes hung beside his in the wardrobe as her lingerie found its way into the bureau with his items of apparel. It became so he had to search through her soft and lacy chemises and nightgowns to locate his stockings and stocks, and more than once pulled out one of her dainty handkerchiefs when he thought he had one of his.

In deference to her tender condition, he had taken up what he hoped was a temporary residence in the sitting room, but many a longing glance he cast at the huge bed, for the small one in the sitting room was not made for a tall frame. Either he banged his head or his feet stuck out, and he cursed the damned thing often and heartily.

Yet he could never quite find the right moment to tactfully assert his rights and take a place there in his bed beside his wife, and watching her slow movements about the house, he knew it would be some time yet before he could find relief for his baser needs with her, though he found her newly regained slimness most distracting. But she made no offer either to move out of his bed nor for him to join her. So with many a long sigh, he doubled up his knees and made the best of the small comfort he had.

Though most of his time was consumed at the mill what spare moments he had he spent with his wife and son. He rose early in the mornings, yet found Heather up and tending the babe, either bathing him or giving him his morning nourishment. Enjoying both sights it became part of the rote for him to join her there before his day's work began. A new, stronger yet unspoken bond began to build between them in those quite morning moments they spent together with their son.

Chapter 9

The month of May brought the summer in earnest and after the rain ceased each day seemed hotter than the one before. Cotton had been planted and the spring's work done. The mill was now operating at nearly full capacity and the lumber yard was beginning to fill. As soon as the newly sawed boards and timber had seasoned for a few weeks in the sun the first shipments would be made. Orders had already been placed for several month's worth of the mill's products Mr. Webster's able talents had proven themselves and he kept the saws humming and the pond full of ready timber. All indications were that this first season would turn a handsome profit, and Brandon was well pleased with the progress.

Now as the long, hot days bore heavy on the minds the gay life of the planters began. The first party of the summer's social whirl was set at Harthaven the weekend following. A great deal of Heather's attention was directed toward the preparations for this gay event. Invitations were sent out, champagne purchased, foods planned. She conversed with Hatti about new uniforms for the house staff and the mansion's overall appearance while the gardeners strove to meet her approval by manicuring the grounds to perfection.

While Heather's time was taken up planning the party

and tending Beau, Brandon found himself more and more the extra man at the mill. He now had time to spend with his wife and son and set into motion his own strategy of winning a place beside her in the huge bed. So it was with considerable malice aforethought that he chose this day to gently bribe her. He had purchased earlier in the week a small, fine chestnut mare with flashing white stockings aforefoot and a startling blaze across her face. She was a spirited but gentle filly and one he thought his wife could easily take to. He smiled to himself as he put the sidesaddle astride the animal and caressed the leather where his wife would sit, thinking what the gift might lead to. He would be most gentle with her as he taught her how to handle the beast, and he might even gain a soft kiss or two this very day.

Smiling at his thoughts, he led Leopold and the mare to the front of the house and tying them there, mounted the steps to the porch. Heather was in the drawing room, carefully stitching a shirt for him, and she was so intent upon her task that she failed to notice his entry into the house. He leaned against the door sill and watched her for a long moment as she sat unaware of his presence. Their son indulged in an afternoon nap in a wicker crib near her, having been fed just a short time earlier, and that too worked to his advantage. He smiled as her brows drew together over a difficult stitch.

"Don't frown so, my love," he teased. "Or you'll be looking like that prune-faced Mrs. Scott."

Heather jumped at his first word. "Brandon, you gave me a fright!"

He grinned in a roguish way. "Did I now?" he questioned softly. "Well, I'm sorry, sweet. I didn't mean to."

Heather laughed and put her sewing aside as he came forward, more handsome than any man she had ever seen. The sun had darkened his skin to a deep tan and his green eyes seemed to shine that much brighter. He looked quite manly and masculine in casual riding attire, and her heart beat a little faster with his presence.

He stopped before her and reaching out for her hand, pulled her to her feet, noticing as he did so the soft, sweet scent of her perfume. As he led her into the hall he told Joseph to fetch Mary to sit with the baby, then turned again to his wife who looked up at him quite perplexed.

"Where are we going?" she inquired.

He smiled as he put his hand behind her back and urged her forward.

"Just outside," he replied, noncommittal.

Heather walked out onto the porch and glanced around to see the two horses tied to the hitching post, both awaiting riders and the smaller one bearing a sidesaddle. She lifted a questioning gaze to her husband and he flashed her a grin.

"Don't you like her? I never asked if you were fond of horses or could ride, but it will be an easy matter for me to teach you—your health permitting, madam."

She laughed brightly as she hurried down the steps to the mare. "I'm in perfect health," she said over her shoulder.

Brandon's grin broadened and he quickly followed.

Quite taken with the trim and shapely filly, Heather caressed the silky nose and smoothed the chestnut mane and could not contain her excitement.

"Oh, Brandon, she's lovely. What's her name?"

"Lady Fair," he replied.

"Oh, it's most fitting. She is a fair lady." She whirled to him and smiled. "Will you lift me up?"

He raised an eyebrow and pointedly gazed at the light and low cut summer dress she wore.

"Don't you think you'd better change, my sweet? That dress is not the most . . ."

"No," she interrupted, thrusting out a lower lip in a feigned pout. "I want to ride her now and it would take too long to change." Her mouth curved in a cajoling smile as she ran a finger down the buttons of his waistcoat. "Please, Brandon. Please."

He chuckled at her coquettish pleading and could do

nothing but give in to her. He bent and clasped his hand to receive her dainty foot, then raised her up. After seating herself and placing a knee about the horn, Heather bent low to set her foot firmly in the stirrup. The low cut gown she wore fell away from her bosom and presented to Brandon every detail of those lovely, round breasts it sought to cover. He stood frozen, his hands holding the reins, his eyes fastened on her display. He swallowed with difficulty and a sound much like a groan escaped him. Heather lifted her eyes to his face and her lips curved softly upward as she met his gaze in warm communication. Brandon's heart thudded heavily within his chest, and his hand was half raised to her when she straightened, leaving him somewhat bewildered. But one could hardly fondle his wife on the front steps of his home. Regretfully he handed her up the reins.

Heather took them in a practiced grip, much to his surprise, and wheeling the mare away from him, with well-placed heel, she sent the horse dashing down the lane to the fields. Brandon leaped astride Leopold and with great concern riding his mind, sent the huge black thundering after her. A race ensued and Heather, with lighthearted abandon, turned the mare from the lane and sent her dodging through the trees. Leopold's huge hooves sent clods of earth flying as he strove to follow the twisting path, but was forced to slow his pace much to Brandon's consternation. Thus the mare held her lead until they reached an open field and the laboring black could stretch his mighty tendons to their advantage. He rapidly overtook Lady Fair, and Heather pulled her horse back to a walk as Brandon drew up beside and laughed at the worried frown upon his face.

"You laid me false, madam," he finally chuckled when he could see the humor of her play. "But your skill is exceeded only by your lack of common sense."

"Ha!" she returned impertinently. "I've ridden to the hounds, and given a deeper grove you'd still be panting at my heels."

She laughed again and urged her mount into an easy lope across the fields. Leopold, warmed by the sprint and sensing the mare, lifted his feet high in a jolting prance, fought the reins and continually sidled close upon her heels. The ride continued until they topped a grassy, windswept knoll, and Heather stopped to let Lady Fair blow and cool in the gentle breeze.

Giving Leopold a damning glare as he finished tying the reins to a bush, Brandon came around to lift Heather down. Reaching up he gently grasped her beneath the bosom, and she laughed gaily as she dropped her hands upon his broad shoulders, having thoroughly enjoyed his gift and the ride. He stood close beside the horse, and as she slid to the ground her thigh brushed hard against his loin, the contact catching them both unaware. Heather moved quickly away, her leg burning with the touch. Behind her Brandon put his hand on the mare and closed his eyes, intense desire for his wife torturing him and making him tremble. The unexpected contact had made him acutely conscious of the celibate life he had led since first he caressed and wooed that sweet, young body months before. His flesh betrayed his need, rising up against his will. He was hungry for her and could hardly restrain himself from gathering her up into his arms and finding the softest, sweetest grass on which to lay her. He imagined his haste to free her from her garments, possibly even tearing them if they resisted his fingers, and he thought of the eyebrows that would raise. He cursed the lack of privacy they had, recalling the many frustrating times he had been interrupted just when he thought he was gaining ground. But he was not planning for just one roll in the grass, rather a lifetime of pleasure-filled moments. He must think first of his goal and of gently courting her and not of fulfilling his momentary desires.

He struggled for control, finding it with an effort, and finally moved to stand behind her and to gaze out over the hazy, wooded hills. He slid his arms around her, fold-ing them before her as she leaned back against him and touched his lips to her hair, breathing in the sweet fragrance that was a part of her. As they stood bathing in this new found togetherness and each other's nearness, Heather turned soft blue eyes up to him and smiled slowly, her lips moist and parted. Brandon needed no other invitation to taste their honey sweetness. He lowered his head and his mouth moved over hers hungrily, and seemingly by magic Heather turned in his arms and melted more closely to him, slipping her hands behind his back. His arm tightened about her waist and his other encircled her shoulders, crushing her to him, and she clung to him, wanting the moment to go on forever. His kiss filled her with desire, leaving every muscle in her body weak and pliable. She felt his thighs hard pressed against her own and realized his passion matched hers. Her lips parted under his mounting fervor and she rose on her toes to fit herself more intimately with his body.

With a gust, the wind changed and whipped the grass about their feet, and the first large drops of a summer thunderstorm struck their heads. They drew apart and looked up to see that the storm was upon them. Brandon then knew frustration so thorough he almost raised a fist toward the blackened sky, but Heather was already running toward the horses. He followed and swung her up on Lady Fair and quickly mounted his own steed. The gale struck in full force, and long before they reached the shelter of Harthaven they were drenched to the skin and their clothes and hair lay plastered to them. From the edge of the pine forest they raced across the lawn to the porch with Leopold arriving several lengths ahead. In the drenching downpour Brandon lifted Heather from the saddle and carried her to the porch and then ran back to tie the horses. As he did Heather gazed downward to find her garments only a transparent film over her body, clinging closely to every curve. With the chill of the wet clothes her nipples rose taut and stood in small peaks against her bodice. She picked at the fabric, pulling it away from her skin, not wanting to face Jeff or Joseph in this condition. Brandon hurried up the steps out of the downpour and seeing her, understood her predicament. He quickly shed his waistcoat and wrapped it around her, then hugged her close as he whispered in her ear.

"I wouldn't want to fight anyone over you today."

She giggled and they staggered together into the house, laughing in carefree glee. Their mirth ended as they came face to face with Hatti's disgruntled frown. She stood with hands on hips and shook her head at them and pursed her mouth at her master.

"Master Bran, I swear sometimes I think you ain't got a lick of sense. What you wanna take that child out riding in the rain for and her just barely over having Master Beau. Lordy me, she's gonna catch her death of the ague." She grunted disapprovingly. "Now, Miss Heather, you get yourself right upstairs and out of them wet clothes."

She grasped Heather's elbow and gave her no choice in the matter, and Brandon chuckled as his wife was towed up the stairs like a child by the worried old Negress. At the landing, Hatti turned and shook her finger at him.

"You just stand there and laugh and you gonna have Master Beau without his mammy one of these days."

She turned and stomped angrily toward the bedroom, dragging her much bemused mistress in her wake. Heather smiled over her shoulder at her husband and blew him a kiss before she was pulled out of sight. Brandon stared upward for a moment, reflecting upon her parting gesture. He smiled to himself, feeling quite satisfied with the day after all. He shucked his boots then ran in stocking feet up the stairs to the sitting room where he found dry clothes and a towel laid out for him upon the bed. He stripped and was toweling himself dry when he heard a splash of water from the next room and the door close and Hatti's footsteps going down the stairs. He moved quietly to the door between the rooms and eased it carefully open to find Heather sitting in the tub with her back to him. As he watched she leaned back and raised a water-laden sponge above her and squeezed it, letting a streaming torrent gush down her arms and full, ripe breasts. She began to hum a vaguely familiar air and soon the words broke from her lips.

> *Black is the color of my true love's hair*
> *His looks are something wondrous fair*
> *The purest eyes and the firmest hands*
> *I love the ground on where he stands.*

He stood and watched her lather her silken skin, lifting a slender leg to soap it well, then the other as he listened to the happy, lilting sound of her voice. After a few moments the strain upon him began to tell and he gently eased the door shut. Turning, he leaned his back against the sill and mentally rubbed his hands together, overjoyed at the unfounded success of his plans.

He remembered with clarity the sultry smiles, the startling display of her breasts, the fiery kiss and the moment just before the storm broke when she had molded her body to his in the most provocative way.

"It had to be love and willingness I saw within her eyes and felt against me this afternoon," he thought. "And with but a simple urging she'll most surely yield to me tonight."

He laughed softly to himself. "With our play we'll make that old bed tremble like it's never done before. Oh, tonight—tonight I will take her again and my monkish ways will end, for I will play a lusty song between her thighs and know the sweetness of being born again within her."

With renewed vigor, he dressed and found himself humming snatches of the song she had been singing. He left the room with light-hearted step and kept himself busy with simple tasks until the evening's feasting hour was near.

*   *   *

Heather woke from a nap, feeling greatly refreshed, and lay still for a moment, listening to the sound of the house in the quickening dusk. When she thought of the afternoon, she could still feel Brandon's arms around her and his warm lips upon hers and the full length of their bodies pressed tightly together. Her pulse quickened and she knew they would soon be sharing this great bed.

She stretched upon it and almost cried out in pain, for it seemed every muscle in her body was stiff and unbearably sore and aching. She hadn't realized the unaccustomed exercise of the ride would affect her so. She could hardly move. Carefully she eased herself to the edge of the bed and stood up, rubbing her misused buttocks in misery. Her slow movements about the room brought Mary with Beau. When the babe was again asleep in his crib the young girl attended her mistress, rubbing a soothing balm over her aching muscles and the abused posterior. She helped her dress for dinner, selecting a cool, white gown and the pearl necklace that Heather wore quite often now. Narrow red ribbons dangled over the mass of soft ringlets, and despite the way Heather felt, she looked most ravishing and quite tempting as the pearls dipped coyly between her breasts which swelled generously above the gown's décolletage.

With slow, careful step Heather managed to descend the stairs and enter the drawing room. Jeff stopped in mid sentence as he saw her painfully making her way, and Brandon turned quickly with a smile to welcome her. His gay expression faded as she stood undecided before him and returned his greeting with an apologetic murmur.

"I fear I overdid this afternoon, Brandon."

He laughed softly and offered his sympathy, not yet aware of the full import of her statement. As the evening wore on, his disappointment was drawn out to its extremes. He studied her slow, agonized movements and saw her wince now and again. She lowered herself into a chair at the table and grimaced, squirming uncomfortably until Hatti brought her a small pillow to sit upon. After sitting through the meal she had stiffened and was almost unable to rise. Brandon took her arm and helped her out of the chair, and as he did so the luminescent pearls, drooping between those swelling breasts, aggravated his sorely depressed disposition further.

The evening was but a foundling youth when she drew the brothers' attention with a brief struggle to rise from the settee. She turned an almost tearful face to her brother-in-law.

"Jeff, you simply must forgive me," she implored. "I'm afraid I haven't been very good company this evening, and I must now beg your leave to retire."

He bowed slightly, clicking his heels. "Your beauty is always refreshing company, madam, and I regret that you will leave me now, but I quite understand. Until tomorrow then, sweet sister."

She nodded and raised her hand and her eyes to Brandon, silently begging his assistance. He helped her up and holding her arm tightly, aided her progress to the foot of the stairs. She mounted the first several steps and her movements were so painful and awkward that Brandon bent down and took her up into his arms. She slid her arms about his neck as he carried her up and sighing, dropped her head against his shoulder.

Below, Mary made to follow to assist her mistress but found her arm seized by her grandmother.

"Let them alone, child," Hatti directed wisely. "The missus don't need your help tonight."

Brandon pushed open the door to the master bedroom and carried his wife in. He sat her gently on the edge of the bed and knelt to remove her stockings and slippers, his hands hesitating a brief moment at the frilly garters. He swallowed hard and touched the warm flesh of her thigh with unsteady fingers and slid the garter down her leg. He stood undecided with her stocking in his hands as she pushed herself slowly from the bed and stood up. She turned her back to him.

"Will you unfasten me?" she requested. "Mary doesn't seem to be coming."

He obeyed and when she let the gown fall to the floor, he bent and picked it up as she rubbed her buttocks in agony.

"I'm afraid my softer parts have been abused. I should have been wiser and not tried so much. I regret that I was not."

Brandon bit off an agreeing reply and went to get her a nightgown from where he had last seen them in his search for his own clothes. He selected one and turned to bring it to her but stopped short when he saw her standing in the candlelight, her chemise at her feet, her young, graceful body bare and glowing golden in the soft light. His eyes went over her slowly in a longing caress. Childbirth had not depreciated her figure nor marred the silken flesh. In fact, she now bore a mature fullness of womanhood which he found terribly disconcerting at the moment. His mouth was dry and his hands shook and all his senses were completely occupied with her. He swallowed hard and brought the gown to her and helplessly feasted his eyes as she donned it. As she bent slightly, pulling it over her head, he saw black and blue marks and angry red welts upon the otherwise flawless buttocks. He sighed softly and mentally committed himself to several more chaste nights alone.

Hearing his sigh, Heather finished tying the bow beneath her bosom and turned to him. She slid her arms behind his neck.

"I beg your forgiveness, Brandon," she murmured. "It seems that common sense is indeed among my less notable virtues."

She pulled his head down to her and placed a fleeting kiss upon his lips, then turned and painfully crawled into the depths of the huge bed.

Brandon stood grinding his teeth, telling himself over and over that it simply wasn't gentlemanly to take a woman in this condition, especially one's own wife. His better instincts won the argument, much to the disappointment of his alter ego. He blew out the candles then went into the sitting room where he removed his coat and waistcoat and stared at the tiny bed, thinking many ill thoughts about it. He had an aversion to entering it for another night, and he cursed it beneath his breath. In exasperation he snatched up a towel and fled the room and down the stairs. Jeff was coming from the study when he passed, and the brother stopped and gestured toward the towel.

"Where the devil are you bound for?"

"I'm going to take a bath in the creek," Brandon said shortly.

"It's freezing cold!" Jeff warned.

"I know!" Brandon growled and went about his way with his brother's laughter ringing in his ears.

The next day was a flurry of activity in preparation for the ball. Several house guests, among them Abegail Clark, arrived in the late afternoon. Although Hatti's balm had done wonders for her, Heather played the hostess with a stiffness that was neither manner nor mien. She suffered another massage before bed and by morning was feeling as bright and gay as ever. She spent the day in fevered activity, assuring that all necessary preparations were complete.

Brandon had departed for Charleston early to attend business. The first shipments of lumbers had been made and payments received and there were finances to be settled now that money had begun to roll in. The morning had been spent taking care of a multitude of items from one end of the city to the other, and a break in the busy schedule had been taken at the noon hour. Brandon was just returning to his affairs when he passed a small sewing shop and was nearly flattened by a heavily laden Miss Scott.

As usual Sybil became flustered and uncertain at the mere sight of Brandon, and she struggled mightily with this affliction as he helped her gather up her packages again. She was decked out in her expensive finery and felt very irresistible. She possessed an overconfidence her gentlemen friends had brought into being since she had come out of her shy cocoon and found them panting on her doorstep, seeking her charms. She was so taken with their flattering compliments she did not guess they were all after only one thing.

"Imagine running into you when I most need a strong, handsome man to come to my aid, Mister Birmingham," she flirted, fluttering eyelids heavily drawn with kohl. Even under many layers of cosmetics, poorly though amply applied, her plainness was evident. She straightened her eyeglasses as he tipped his hat courteously and pushed the bundles into his arms, missing the raised eyebrow he cast her way as she continued on.

"These things are just too heavy for poor little me. Now if you'll just follow me I'll show you to my buggy."

Brandon obeyed as he listened politely to her endless chatter.

"I'm just so excited about the ball tonight. I've had such a lovely gown made, but I'm afraid I just simply blush every time I put it on. I've never owned anything so daring before. The dressmaker does say I do wonders for it though. He knows so much about women's clothes, you know. He came from England and tells me some of the most beautiful women in the world have worn his gowns. But you'd never be able to guess it, the way he looks. He's terribly, terribly ugly. Why, I'd almost feel sorry for him if it wasn't for the way he looks at me. I had to slap his hands this morning, you know, and he looked so shocked afterward that I couldn't help but laugh at him. Imagine, a man like that thinking I might favor his attention!"

She stopped in crossing the street to wait for a carriage and looked up at him shyly.

"He's not the sort of man I fancy at all."

Brandon coughed uncomfortably and looked around for a sign of her buggy.

"You know, Mr. Birming . . . Brandon," she managed, sounding a little nervous. "I—I have so many gentlemen callers now I simply lose count when I try to think of them all." Her eyes lifted to his. "I don't call any of them my true love though. There's only one man I consider that and he doesn't come calling."

"Is your buggy near here?" Brandon questioned uneasily.

"Do you find me attractive, Brandon?" she asked suddenly.

"Why—yes, yes, Miss Sybil," he lied kindly.

She giggled and caught her breath and looked at him again. "As attractive as your wife?"

He glanced around for the carriage again, thinking of Heather, soft and lovely, and he wondered how Sybil could even ask such a question.

"Oh, that was unfair of me, wasn't it?" she warbled. "Naturally being married to her, you'd have to say she was prettier or be thought a cad, wouldn't you?"

"I think my wife is a very beautiful woman, Miss Sybil," he said, trying to hide his annoyance.

"Oh yes, and she is too," Sybil replied readily. She giggled again. "I've been told I'm beautiful too. Why, just the other day Mr. Bartlett told me so."

Brandon glanced at her with a start. The hair on the back of his neck bristled at the mere mention of the man's name. "Mr. Bartlett is one of your callers?"

"Why, yes," she smiled. "Do you know him?"

"Yes," Brandon muttered. "I know him." He sighed heavily and eyed her. "Tell me, Miss Sybil, what does your mother say about your gentlemen friends?"

Her brow knitted in confusion. "She won't speak of them. I don't know why. She always wanted me to have lots of beaus and now when I do, she won't even set foot in the parlor when one of them is there."

"Perhaps she doesn't think they're fit company for you, Miss Sybil."

She giggled happily and fluttered her thin lashes. "Why, Brandon. I do believe you're jealous."

He sighed in exasperation and was greatly relieved when she stopped at a buggy. He placed the bundles on the seat for her, and as he turned to tip his hat in farewell Sybil smiled and reached out to pick an imaginary bit of lint from his coat just as she had seen Heather do in church.

"I'll be looking forward to having a dance with you tonight, Brandon," she murmured. "I hope you won't disappoint me."

"Why, Miss Sybil, you'll probably be so occupied with beaus, I won't be able to get near you," he replied, taking his hurried leave. He turned and found a group of ladies gawking at them, and he touched his hat in greeting and continued on his way.

Brandon searched through the wardrobes and bureaus in the master bedroom for his clothes and cast an occasional sidelong glance at Heather who sat before the mirror in a light shift while Mary arranged her hair into an elegant coiffure, twining narrow turquoise ribbons in and out through the lustrous strands. He brought out a box he had tucked away in a bottom drawer and set it before his wife.

"My mother loved jewelry," he said, rather hoarsely, finding her barely concealed bosom unnerving. "She left part of it to me and part to Jeff for our wives when we married. This is my share. You might find something in here you wish to wear."

He lifted the lid and Heather gasped at the contents. It contained a vast assortment of jewelry abounding with different types of precious stones.

"Oh, Brandon, I never, ever, dreamed I'd own even one piece of jewelry, and here you gift me with so much at once. What can I say? You spoil me so."

He laughed and placed a warm kiss upon her shoulder, his beard tickling her soft flesh, and met her gaze in the mirror.

"No longer the cad, my sweet?" he questioned softly against her ear.

She shook her head and her eyes deepened in color as a pleasant sensation ran through her body. "No, never, my love."

Brandon left her to her primping, feeling reassured. He bathed and began to dress, thinking of how her eyes had darkened when he kissed her. He straightened his lace-edged stock and slid the emerald green coat over the white waistvest. Except for his silk coat and his black gold-buckled shoes, he was attired in flawless white and his tanned skin seemed that much darker against the lightness of his shirt. When he was done, he regarded himself critically in the mirror, wondering if she would find him handsome.

As Heather came down the stairs, the long pleats of her vivid turquoise gown swished about her and seemed to open and close in a strange undulating pattern as she walked. The gown clung closely to her slender body and about her long limbs, and the shallow bodice pressed her bosom upward until she was precariously close to over-flowing its bounds. When men first saw her, they seemed to hold their breaths in anticipation of that event. Brandon was the first to display this unique reaction to her dress. She was standing by the front windows, looking out, when he came down the stairs, whistling gaily, extremely light of spirit. She glanced around at him and greatly admired the splendid masculine figure he presented. When he saw her, he smiled broadly and came to stand near. He reached out to tease one of the diamond earrings that dangled prettily from her ears. It was the only jewelry she wore.

"Are you nervous, sweet?"

"Only a little," she replied.

She turned to face him and watched his eyes drop to

her bosom and widen with surprise. His breath seemed caught in his throat. Knowing Louisa would be coming, she had worn the gown for the purpose of keeping his attention on herself and not allowing it to wander to the other woman. Finally Brandon coughed lightly and regained his tongue.

"Perhaps you should wear something a little less revealing, madam."

Materializing from somewhere behind them, Jeff laughed and came to stand beside his brother. Heather was very conscious of both men's eyes upon her.

"Let her wear it, Brandon. You never let the rest of us have any fun," he said and smiled. "Of course, I can understand how you feel. If she were mine, I'd keep her under lock and key." He half turned to his brother and loudly whispered. "You know she looks a hell of a lot better than Louisa."

Heather threw her arms akimbo and stamped her tiny foot as if in anger, and Brandon blanched, expecting to see her come out of her gown.

"Now, Jeff, if you want to ruin my evening, just mention that woman's name again!" she declared.

Jeff chuckled and clasped his brother's shoulder. "Come on, Bran. Don't play the Quaker tonight. Let her wear it. She looks too damned beautiful. Don't make her change, and I promise I'll try not to look at her too hard this evening."

Brandon scowled blackly at his brother and started to say something but changed his mind. Instead he turned back to Heather.

"Wear what pleases you, madam," he said, none too happily.

Jeff laughed and rubbed his hands together. "Oh, I think this is going to be one hell of a party." He took Heather's hand and placed it into the bend of his arm. "Come, sweet sister, I must show you off to the house guests."

Heather smiled over her shoulder at Brandon as she

let her brother-in-law led her away, but he frowned and looked around as if he didn't know what to do with himself. As she entered the drawing room, she glanced back to see him going into the study and some moments later he joined them, carrying a liberally filled brandy snifter.

Brandon stood first at the door to greet his guests and made certain that all the bachelors were passed quickly onto Jeff and given minimum opportunity to leer at his wife. Louisa swept in with a wide smile on the arm of a new beau. Her eyes rested briefly on Heather's décolletage before she spoke a greeting, and the smile faded somewhat. Her own gown of yellow silk was just as low and slightly transparent, but her self-assurance was rather shaken to see visible proof that Heather needed no stuffing for her gown.

"Why, my dear Heather, you look quite charming this evening," she said, recovering slightly from the shock. "Motherhood seems to agree with you."

"You're very kind, Louisa," Heather replied smoothly. "But I'm sure I must seem quite dowdy beside you. That is a lovely gown you're wearing."

Louisa smiled slowly as her eyelids drooped a little over her brown eyes. She lightly ran a hand across her bosom as if wanting to bring attention to the transparency of her dress.

"Yes, isn't it. Thomas designed it especially for me. He is quite clever with the needle, don't you think?"

Heather had only a chance to smile a reply before the woman went on.

"Did you have your gown made here, darling? I never see you in any of the shops in Charleston. Don't tell me Brandon has become a penny pincher since he married you. He was always so generous before."

"He had this gown made for me in London," Heather replied rather brittlely.

"Yes, of course," Louisa smiled. "It must have been that same shop where he bought some gowns for me."

Heather chose to ignore the woman's crude barbs. It was Brandon who felt the irritation and anger because his former mistress couldn't acknowledge his marriage and treat his wife with at least a nominal respect.

"Did you also get those earrings in London?" Louisa inquired. "For some reason they seem familiar."

"They belonged to Brandon's mother," Heather answered.

Louisa stiffened. "Yes, I recognize them now," she said and without another word strode haughtily away.

Jeff chuckled as he bent near Heather's ear. "You've cut her to the quick, Tory. She had already laid claim to everything that was Brandon's."

It was some moments later when Matthew Bishop arrived by himself, free by choice to direct his attention to any young woman who happened to catch his fancy. His raiment was composed of the finest of pinkish gray silk with a light plum jacket to accentuate the hue. His stock rose so high it seemed about to swallow his chin as great billows of lace tumbled down his chest and hung from his cuffs to nearly cover his hands. He doffed his plumed hat and ignoring his host, stepped to take Heather's hand. Brandon mumbled a hasty introduction and tried to urge him on, but the man held his place and spoke in reply.

"Brandon, I always admired your taste in horses but I never dreamt you could extend it to the realms of feminine pulchritude with such an amazing degree of success." He turned to Heather with a confident smile. "Madam, you are most enchanting." And lowering his gaze to her bosom he continued. "Your beauty makes my poor heart flutter and your charms almost bring a stutter to my tongue."

He bent low over her hand for what seemed to her husband an unduly long time. Brandon reddened slightly and clenched his fist. When Matt rose again, it was Jeff who took his arm and ushered him quickly into the ballroom, out of harm's way.

The music was quick as another dance began, and

Brandon took his wife by the hand and presented her to the ballroom. Two lines were formed by gay couples, one of the belles, the other their escorts, and Heather found herself swept along in the happy group. A minuet followed and Brandon bowed to her as it began, where in turn she smiled and sank into a deep curtsy before him. They grapevined, toepointed and crossed to the music while he, quite frequently, cast anxious glances toward her bosom. When the dances were done, he drew her aside and spoke low.

"Madam, you're ruining my evening with that gown. I beg for some consideration."

She raised innocent eyes to him. "But, Brandon, Louisa's gown is much more immodest and there are others."

"I don't give a damn what anybody else is wearing," he ground out. "It's your attire that concerns me. I expect you to come out of it any moment—and it makes me nervous."

"I'm quite safe, Brandon," she replied sweetly. "I don't think there's anything for you to worry . . ."

"Brandon, good fellow," interrupted a man's voice, and Matt joined them. "Would you allow me to dance with your charming wife? I shan't keep her for long."

Brandon could see no out and handed her over grudgingly and watched unhappily to say the least, as the other man led her onto the floor.

As they danced Heather felt the man's devouring gaze upon her, and he took advantage of the steps of the minuet. His eyes as she curtsied were on her bosom, his hands held hers possessively as they crossed, and through the entire dance she was aware of being leered at.

Now, as Matt had earlier requested, the music swept into a rhythm called a waltz, and he pulled a reluctant Heather into his eager grasp to teach her the steps.

"It's really quite simple, Heather, dear sweet. Just relax and follow my lead."

It was not possible to relax with his arms around her

so familiarly, and she fought him to keep his hands where they should be. He was bound to make Brandon furious with this dance, and she was about to beg her leave of him when she glanced to where her husband stood and found him in Louisa's clutches. The blonde was laughing and leaning against him, giving him every opportunity to take advantage of her gaping neckline which Heather was sure bared her to the floor. He made no move to pull away, and Heather's back stiffened as unreasonable jealousy possessed her. She missed the step Matt was trying to teach her and ended up on his foot. Her face flamed scarlet.

"Oh, I'm terribly sorry, Mr. Bishop. I fear I'm far too clumsy for this dance."

Matt laughed. "On the contrary, Heather, you're very graceful. Yet you must relax more." His hand squeezed her waist. "Come, don't be so nervous. I won't bite you."

She tried again to follow him but she couldn't keep her eyes away from her husband and as a result, Matt's foot suffered again.

He laughed. "Perhaps if we have some wine," he said, gazing down at her apologetic face.

"Yes, perhaps," she whispered, mortified, and let him pull her along to the refreshment tables.

It was a determination born of jealousy that made her laugh gaily as they spun about into another waltz. The champagne had little to do with it. She learned the dance quickly and after a few sweeping whirls about the floor, found it rather delightful.

Though he was not the best of dancers, Matt was persistent and when Jeff came to claim her after several more waltzes, he gave her up almost as reluctantly as Brandon had.

"It appears that you have captured another male heart, Tory," Jeff grinned, when they were into the dance.

Only half listening, she shrugged her shoulders as she searched the room for Brandon. She found him standing with a group of men and Louisa nowhere in sight. But where had he been when she had looked for him several moments before? She had not been able to find him or Louisa, and their disappearance disturbed her. What if he had found the sight of Louisa's bountiful bosom more than he could bear and had taken her outside for a few fevered caresses? She bit her lip as she thought of Brandon fondling Louisa and a dull ache crept into her heart.

"What's troubling you, Tory?" Jeff inquired softly. "You don't appear to be enjoying yourself."

She managed a smile for him. "I'm afraid I've been bitten by that friend of yours, the green monster. I find I really can't ignore Louisa as I thought I could."

He laughed softly as his eyes shone. "So you love him then?"

"Of course," she replied. "Was there any doubt?"

"Oh, some," he smiled. "I would have guessed that once you hated him."

Her head snapped up in surprise. "Whatever made you think that?"

His mouth twitched with amusement. "Oh, I don't know. Just a passing thought, I suppose."

When the last strains of the melody were fading from the hall Jeff led her back to Brandon who scowled blackly at her as his brother went to find a partner for the next dance. His jaw was set firmly and a muscle twitched in his cheek.

"Did you enjoy learning the waltz, madam?" he inquired sarcastically. "I'm sure you had a most adept instructor. I could not have taught you half so well."

She lifted her nose into the air. "I wasn't aware that you knew how to waltz, Brandon," she replied saucily, though she was not feeling that way.

"Oh? And would you have allowed me to teach you if you had known?" He laughed sharply. "Surely being in your husband's arms isn't half so exciting as being fondled by a strange man."

Heather bit off a sharp retort about Louisa and stood stubbornly silent.

"Perhaps you would care to demonstrate what you have learned." He motioned for the musicians to begin another waltz. "Come, let us see what he has taught you."

He took her by the arm, none too gently, and guided her onto the floor as the strains of the waltz filled the room. They began to dance, slowly at first, almost haltingly, until the rhythm of the music eased their angry tensions and they began to unbend. The haunting chords seemed to entrance them until each was filled with the other's presence, forgetting everything else. They moved with the music and swept and swirled around the hall as the enchanting refrain became a part of them. Heather knew only that his arm was around her and his dark, handsome face above her. He was conscious only of her softness within his embrace, her deep blue eyes before him and the fantastic rhythm that seemed to lead them around the floor as if they were nothing more than puppets on a string.

Gradually the two of them became aware that the hall was silent but for the music and that they danced alone. They stopped and gazed about as if newly awakened and were met with a long round of applause from their guests who had retreated to the edge of the dance floor and had watched their blissful flight in silent awe.

With a laugh Brandon bowed and Heather stepped deep into a curtsy, acknowledging the gracious appreciation of their guests, then Brandon nodded to the musicians and they picked up another waltz. He took Heather into his arms once again and they began to dance as other couples joined them. From the sideline Louisa glared at Heather's back over her glass of champagne.

Having reestablished the tempo of the party, Brandon and Heather left the dance floor and made their way to the refreshment table. Heather accepted the glass of champagne he proffered and saw that for himself he chose a stronger brew. They made their rounds together among their guests and conversed lightly and gaily with them. But as a rigadoon began, an elderly gentleman snatched Heather away. Then one man after another and among them that gay blade Matthew, found his way again to trying his skill on the ballroom floor with her. But Brandon favored few women with that invitation and spent most of his time drinking.

Heather finally pleaded for a rest from her eager partners and found Brandon contemplating the amber liquid in his glass as Louisa hung about his neck, whispering to him how he was being ignored and seeking to console him while she pointed out that his wife spent her time dancing with other men. Heather slowly burned when Louisa raised a triumphant eyebrow and smiled tauntingly at her. Brandon slowly lifted his gaze to his wife's face and his agony was successfully concealed behind a dark scowl. Matt took that inopportune moment to come up behind Heather and place a drunken kiss upon her shoulder. Brandon's eyes filled with rage and excusing himself and Heather, he took her by the arm and escorted her out of the ballroom, through the hall and into the study where he closed the door behind him and sneered at her.

"You seem to be having a gay time, madam. Apparently you enjoy being pawed and petted."

Heather stiffened and her eyes flashed with anger. "How dare you!" she gasped. "How dare you say that to me!"

Setting his drink down, Brandon strode forward, but she stood her ground and returned him glare for glare.

"Your sodden mind deceives you, sir," she spat. "I did but play the gentle hostess and entertained *your* guests while you portrayed a trembling stud to stand in rut as that fair-haired cow twisted her tail and bared her udders and lowed so sweetly in your ear."

"Oh hell!" he cried and threw up his hands. "You turn on me when all this night I've had to stand and

watch you pulled and petted and rubbed against that simpering fop who seeks to prove himself a man by bedding
every simple-minded wench who falls his way!''

"Simple minded—Oh!'' She could not find the words
to reply and spun about angrily, turning her back upon
him.

Brandon's whiskey laden reasoning betrayed him and
self-satisfaction rode his voice. "So, you cannot face me.
You know I speak the truth.''

He stepped close behind her and the heady smell of
her set his sodden senses reeling and turned his countenance to one of self-pity.

"Why do you do this to me? Why do you turn from
me and seek another's caresses? I sit in calm exile, always wanting but never touching, and you let that simpering dandy whom you hardly know console your body
with his nearness.''

His raging desire overcame his common sense and he
grasped her roughly from behind, one hand crushing a
tempting breast while the other slid downward over her
belly to rest between her thighs, his lips hungrily seeking
the bare white shoulder. She gasped in equal parts of
anger and surprise at the swiftness of his passion, then
whirled and with all her strength, pushed him away,
stumbling backward to lean breathless against the desk.
Her face burned in embarrassed resentment at the callow
crudeness of his ploy.

Brandon stood with his arms spread in amazement at
her reaction. Almost pleadingly he spoke.

"What do you have against me? God above, tell me
why I must live this monkish existence and then stand
aside and watch you whet some other's appetite.''

"You fool!'' she choked. "You utter raving fool!''
She thrust a trembling finger at the door. "Do you think
I want—Oh!''

She could go no further and in dejected frustration,
flew past him to that portal, but before opening it, she
turned and spoke in withering contempt.

"Go on. Go find your mewling bedmate and share your drunken wits with her. You deserve each other."

With that she fled the room, leaving Bandon standing in painful confusion, and hurried toward the ballroom door. Suddenly realizing her flustered state, she paused outside a moment to regain her composure. Nearby Jeff stood conversing with two young ladies and when he glanced up to see her expression and hesitation, realized something was wrong. He excused himself immediately and came to her side.

"What's the matter, Tory? You look as if you've just bitten the devil's tail."

"My vision of the devil is a blonde whore," she said derisively. "How can one man be so blind?"

Looking beyond her to the study door, he laughed softly. "I can guess my brother is being his usual charming, idiotic self again. But come on, princess, don't be sad tonight." He took her hand. "Would you care for some refreshment?"

She nodded and soon found herself with a glass of champagne of which she took a deep sip, raising the glass to her lips with trembling hands.

"You always seem to be near when I need someone to comfort me, Jeff," she murmured when the heady drink seemed to have calmed her.

He laughed. "Yes, around here they call me Saint Jeffrey behind my back."

She smiled, feeling her spirits lighten a trifle with his jest, and he led her by the hand to a quiet corner.

"There are a few things I should explain about Brandon," he said. "Perhaps you will be able to understand him better then. You see, my father couldn't bear to see another man's hands upon Mother, however innocently, and Brandon is realizing he has the same problem where you are concerned. Before he met you, he believed he could control his emotions and felt very self-assured. Having never sampled honest love, he obviously finds himself now at a loss and cannot cope with the emotions you inspire. Believe it or not, Heather, he's a man of strong convictions, and with you he finds he betrays some of these old convictions. You lay bare his soul before him, and he finds himself an entirely different man from what he had supposed. It's a little frightening for a man his age to come awake and find that a mere girl can disrupt his thoughts so completely.''

"Is that what I do, Jeff?" she questioned softly.

He grinned. "Honey, you can bet he never troubled himself with a second glance when Louisa danced with other men.''

Before he could go on to reassure her, Matt joined them and was in a festive, ebullient mood considerably enhanced by a liberal intake of alcoholic spirits.

"Oh come now, you two. You're looking much too serious for such a gay evening," he admonished. "Heather, my dear, it's apparent your spirits need reviving.''

He made a monocle of his forefinger and thumb and peered at her through it, allowing his observing gaze to move from her face to her dainty silk shoes and then back again, pausing a very brief but pleasurable moment on her breasts.

"And Doctor Bishop prescribes more exercise for your condition. And to that end, a brief tour of the dance floor is in order." Presenting his arm in a stiff decorous manner, he smiled charmingly. "Will you accompany me, my most lovely Madam Birmingham.''

Out of the corner of her eye, Heather saw Louisa approaching and not wishing to bear the brunt of her jealous jibes, accepted his arm.

Jeff also caught sight of Louisa and understood Heather's decision to dance. The woman stopped to watch the couple whirl away, and he contemplated her narrowing eyes and her tightening mouth as her gaze followed them around the floor. Obviously she didn't take kindly to finding herself no longer the center of attention and almost completely ignored while Heather was nearly fought over for dances by enthusiastic males smitten with her beauty.

From her Jeff's eyes wandered to his sister-in-law. Matt was busily making petting attempts while Heather's hands constantly moved to keep his from making any serious contact. He watched the two of them for a while wondering if he should cut in, then glanced toward the door and saw Brandon standing there, a completely blank look upon his face as he watched his wife in Matt's arms. Jeff realized what an effort his brother was making to appear calm and that he was precariously treading the fine brink of violence.

He wasted not one moment more in making his way to Heather's side. She looked up in relief as he approached but Matt was not grateful at all for the interruption.

"Oh really, Jeffrey, old chap, not again. It's become a dreadful bore not being able to complete a dance with her. Someone's always breaking us apart."

With arms akimbo, the exasperated bachelor watched as Jeff swung his partner away and round the floor. When they were near the open garden doors, Heather looked up pleadingly at her brother-in-law.

"The fresh air does smell inviting, Jeff. Would you think ill of me if I begged for a walk in the garden. I fear I'm rather exhausted from all this dancing."

He laughed. "Your smallest wish is my command, princess."

They escaped to the rose garden outside and strolled along a path away from the house past a tall hedge and to a spot where sweet shrubs scented the air and a large oak spread its limbs to cover the night sky. They were out of sight from the house and only the strains of a waltz drifted softly to their ears. She sat beneath the tree on a wrought-iron settee and brushed her skirts aside in an invitation for him to join her.

"I may stay out here all night," she threatened. "It's definitely more peaceful here than inside."

He chuckled. "What you need, Tory, is another drink, and I believe I fancy another myself. Will you be all right here while I go back and get us some champagne?"

"Of course," she replied with a laugh. "I'm a big girl now. I'm not afraid of the dark."

"You should by now know, Tory," he grinned, "that big girls have more reasons to be cautious of the dark than little ones."

"Oh, Jeff, and here I was beginning to trust you too," she teased.

"Baby, if you weren't Brandon's," he retorted with a gleam in his eye, "you'd be busier right now than you were with Matt."

His laughter floated back to her as his tall, darkly clad figure disappeared into the night. She smiled and leaned back with a sigh, idly opening and closing the lace fan that dangled from her wrist. She stopped to listen as she heard a rustling sound nearby and wondered what he might be coming back for. She glanced up as a dark shadow came through the hedge and realized it wasn't Jeff at all but a shorter man who wore lighter colored garments. The man came closer and she recognized Matt. Immediately she rose and backed around the settee.

"Jeff just left, Mr. Bishop, if you wanted to see him," she said nervously.

He laughed softly and followed her around the garden bench. "Now whatever would I want to see him for, my lovely Heather, when here you are and the sight of you puts my mind to confusion. There's no one here to interrupt our dance so might you care to finish our waltz now? I vow it will be the only way we will."

"Thank you, but no, Mr. Bishop. I'm a trifle spent I fear."

She backed against the trunk of the tree as he continued to advance, and he leaned forward as he came up close and braced both hands behind her.

"Perhaps then," he breathed against her ear, "you'd care to sit this one out."

He pressed his lips against her throat as he leaned his weight upon her, and Heather did her best to squirm away.

"Mr. Bishop, please!" she protested indignantly. "Brandon will . . ."

"He doesn't have to know," he whispered, kissing her shoulder. "You won't tell him, will you? He's got such an ugly temper."

She struggled with him, trying to push him away, but he was not to be discouraged.

"Don't fight me, Heather," he murmured. "I've got to have you. I can't help myself. You place me in a fit of madness."

"Let me go!" she demanded. "Let me go or I'll scream, and my husband will kill you."

"Shhh," he shushed. "Don't fight me."

He covered her lips with his in a hungry kiss as he moved his hands upward from her waist, intent upon cupping her sweet, young breasts within them. She squirmed and squealed under his lips and pushed against his chest only to have him increase his weight upon her. Suddenly he was seized from behind by two strong, very capable hands and torn from her, yelping in fright. Brandon's face was distorted with rage as he threw the man into the bushes and as Matt struggled fearfully to rise, Brandon firmly planted a foot upon his buttocks and sent him sprawling through the shrubs. Matt scrambled to his feet and fled the scene with coattails flying behind him, and Heather leaned against the tree for support, noting with satisfaction how fast the man ran. As her husband swung around to her she managed a shaky, rewarding smile, but it quickly faded when he grasped her and pinned her to that same tree.

"That mincing fop has trouble finding his way out of his britches, madam, but as you should remember, I have no such problems."

His mouth swooped down hard upon hers, forcing her lips apart savagely as he thrust his tongue between them.

Her lips were bruised as he kissed her hungrily, passionately, no longer with restraint. Heather gave him no resistance. Though she had thought herself saved from rape, she now feared she was headed for that same fate again. She had no will power to keep Brandon from taking what he wanted and what he had every right to, and whereas she had been coldly unmoved by Matt's unwanted attentions, she found herself growing deliciously giddy and suddenly weak in her husband's embrace. His hands moved over her breasts, his fingers meeting together in the deep valley between and lingering there for a pleasurable moment before sliding under her gown. Heather moaned softly and began to tremble as though she stood braced against a fierce wind that whipped at her skirts and tore her hair loose from its mooring. She had never known how deeply she could be aroused by passion's fires and a lover's caress, and the sensation mounted within her, never to be fulfilled until put to some strange end she was ignorant of. Brandon muttered unintelligible words as his lips moved to the corner of her mouth, pressing fevered kisses there and along her throat, her perfumed warmth adding fuel to the flame within him. His hands freed those sensuous breasts from her gown, and their pale roundness gleamed tantalizingly in the night. He embraced them with greedy kisses, his breath hot and heavy upon her flesh, and Heather closed her eyes in ecstasy and leaned her head back against the tree, reveling in this new experience. His hand, sliding along her thigh, found its way under her gown over her bare buttock as his knee urged her legs apart. He pulled her hard against him. Then his face was above hers again in the night and his voice husky as he muttered against her parted lips, their breath warm in each other's mouth.

"You are mine, Heather. No one will have you but me. Only I shall taste your body's joys. And when I snap my fingers, you will come."

His arms slid from her and Heather watched, disbelieving, as he turned and strode away, leaving her limp and trembling, her body hungrily yearning for his kisses and his touch. She shuddered in painful frustration, wanting him back and almost crying out for him, but she heard Jeff call her name in worried tone and she quickly turned her back to repair her garments and cover her breasts.

Jeff came through the bushes, carrying now half-filled glasses, the champagne sloshed over his hands, and looking back over his shoulder.

"What's been going on here? I saw Matt hitailing it away and now Brandon almost knocked me down." He glanced around then to see her disheveled appearance and his eyes widened. "Tory, are you all right? My God, if Matt . . . if either of them have hurt you . . ."

She shook her head as she took a glass of champagne from him, clutching it in both hands as she tried not to spill it in her shaky grasp, and raised it to her lips to drain it without a pause.

"You were right, Jeff," she commented unsteadily. "Big girls do have much more to worry about in the dark."

"Did Matt come out here and bother you? So help me God, I'll wring that bastard's neck!"

"He was out here," she breathed. "But Brandon sent him on his way."

He released a chuckle. "That must have been something to see. Bran was madder than an old hornet as he watched you two dance together. I could almost wring Louisa's neck for cornering me in the ballroom, making me miss all the fun. But if I know her she probably knew what was going on and didn't want me to interfere, thinking Bran might blame you." He looked at her and sobered. "He didn't, did he?"

Heather laughed, a bit hysterically, and shrugged her shoulders. "I have no idea what he thought."

He contemplated her a moment. "Heather, are you sure you're all right? You don't act yourself."

"Oh, Jeff," she half choked. "I'm not sure about anything right now, least of all myself. I really must try to collect my wits about me, mustn't I? How can I face anyone in this condition? I think I'd best retire to my room for a spell."

He pulled her hand into the bend of his arm. "Come on then, honey. I'll take you back."

"Not through the ballroom," she pleaded. "I'm afraid I would draw too much attention."

He chuckled. "All right. I'll take you around to the front."

She let him lead her to the door and took her leave of him as they entered. Hoping no one would notice her disheveled appearance, she hurried to pass the study door which was open. Inside the room some of the men had gathered and were laughing and talking in a jovial manner as they enjoyed their host's liquor. She recognized her husband's voice among them and heard his deep chuckle, the first of the evening, and the amiable retort he made to some jest. Her heart beat a little harder as she hastened past the door.

From where he stood, Brandon observed his wife's flight across the hall, and with a smile, excused himself from his guests and went to stand just outside the study door. He drew leisurely upon his cigar, squinting through the smoke as his eyes followed her ascent up the stairs, watching the graceful swing of her slender hips and the way the gown clung to her.

At the head of the stairs, Heather paused uncertainly, feeling eyes upon her and gazed back over her shoulder to find him staring up at her, an unreadable expression occupying his handsome, bearded face. She blushed, remembering what had passed between them and was about to turn to flee to her room when Mary came out of the nursery, trying to quiet Beau. Heather held out her arms for him, and Brandon watched his wife take their son into her arms and cuddle him close to her as she cast one last glance at him and then turned and hurried to her room, and he pulled out his timepiece and noted the hour.

Thirty minutes had flown when Mary came down the stairs after putting Beau to bed again. Brandon strode out of the study where he had been waiting near the door talking idly with a few men as he kept an eye upon the stairs. He stopped the servant and told her she wouldn't be needed any more that night. A confused frown passed briefly across the girl's brow but she nodded obediently and disappeared toward the back.

Brandon mounted the stairs with slow and measured tread. He glanced briefly over his shoulder to find the hall empty and the guests enjoying themselves in the ballroom and study. Without knocking he opened the door to the master bedroom and entered, closing it behind him, and leaned against the wall to gaze at Heather. Seated at her dressing table, she had been busy restoring her coiffure and now watched him warily out of the corner of her eye as she continued to do so. She was wearing only the light shift he had seen her in earlier and her full, ripe breasts could not have been more alluring had they been bare. Her body glowed softly in the warm candlelight and her dark hair shone with a rich luster. His eyes moved slowly over her, resting for a time on her soft white shoulders and the pink hued nipples that strained against that sheer cloth and finally returned to her face. He seemed completely at ease, once more self-assured, the self-confident Brandon. He smiled most leisurely as he came forward to the dressing table and put out his cigar in the ashtray there.

"I've come to some conclusions this night, Heather, and I have several things I wish to tell you."

He strode behind her to the bed and leaned his shoulder against the massive post at the foot and met her gaze in the mirror.

"One point I should like to clear first of all. You know me well enough by now that you might guess what would have happened had I been completely opposed to marrying you. If you really think that any man on this earth could have forced me entirely against my will, then let me assure you, madam, you are mistaken. I would have rotted in prison had it been anyone but you.''

Heather's eyes widened a trifle and she sat now listening quietly but very alert.

''Once, a long time ago,'' he continued, ''I spoke in anger to you and denied myself what I desired most. Call it my damnable pride, for it was in truth that beast which sought to hurt you and cast upon you my revenge for many things that were a mystery to even me. But it was I who suffered, I who beat my breast in frustration while you frolicked gaily upon my heart and vowed your hate for me in simple language. The revenge was not mine after all, my sweet, but yours. So now, I am through playing games in which I am the loser. I am tired of being the outsider in my own home, my own bed. I've reached a point where I have a choice to make. I can either bed you or I can leave and find relief with another woman. But I seek no other, Heather. I yearn for no other. I want *you*.''

He began to loosen his stock as a half smile played about his lips.

''So the games are over and the act is done and I am a man and I will have my due. For almost a year I've been without a woman to ease my needs. No other have I had since I touched your virgin body that night, many nights ago. I'll tell you true it hasn't been easy keeping my hands off you. But no more will I play the monk. It was not my intention to take you again by force. I do not choose that relationship. But if I must I will, for I cannot go on living under the same roof with you and never finding my pleasure within your body. So my mind is made. I'm going to have you and not only tonight. You may resign yourself to the fact that we will be sharing a bed from now on and that our relationship will be very . . . intimate.''

He removed his coat and slung it over his arm.

''I'll leave you alone for a few moments. When I return, you be in this bed, whether willingly or grudgingly.

And remember, my dearest, this is not Lord Hampton's house now, but mine, as you are mine, and no one will dare come through that door to save you.''

Heather sat stunned and as the door closed behind him a fiery rage flared within her. With a swipe of her arm, she sent the ashtray flying.

"What thinks he that he may come in here while the house is overflowing with his friends and among them that blonde bitch and command me to spread my thighs for him? Does he think there need not be words spoken of love nor soft caresses to soothe my body? Am I truly then to him a possession and not a wife, a whore who's met his fancy? Oh, once he played himself upon a frightened girl. Well, no longer am I frightened nor just a girl. I am a woman and he will truly know my vengeance for I will fight and claw and scratch and keep my thighs closed tightly until my strength has been exhausted. Only then will I submit and lie unresisting. He has no right. . . .''

She sat silently for a moment deep in thought.

"But he does,'' her gentler self argued. "He is my husband and father of my child. He owns me and I am the one without right to hold myself from him.''

Her eyes lifted slowly to regard the face reflected in the mirror, and her body quivered as she remembered his lips upon her breasts, his hand upon her naked flesh.

"Why do I delay?'' she asked herself suddenly. "This is what I've wanted and yearned for. This is what I've planned for, worked to have. Must my pride tear us apart like this?''

She rose from her chair as a denial burst from her lips and she began to yank open bureau drawers until she found what she sought, the blue gown of her wedding night. She lifted it from the drawer with loving hands and smoothed it gently upon the bed, then with fevered haste she flew back to the dressing table to prepare herself for her husband's coming.

Brandon closed the door behind him and stood a mo-

ment, his mind filled with racing thoughts of the minutes
behind him and those ahead. He heard the ashtray thud
upon the floor and it was like having the wind knocked
out of him, and he slumped wearily against the wall.

"So that's the way it will be. She really has her wind
up this time."

He threw his jacket upon the bed in sore aggravation
and moved toward that hated resting place, shrugging out
of his waistcoat.

"Damn, it's come to rape. There have been a dozen
times I could have had her, had I kept my mouth shut or
played the lady's man. Even in the garden tonight I could
have taken her right then. But hell, what's the good of
looking back. I've made my stand and regardless of what
passes tonight, at least this damnable waiting is over.
She'll fight me again, that's sure now, and I must take
her contrary or gentle, holding myself in restraint as
much as my body will allow and treating her kindly,
though to touch that silken flesh I swear will drive me
out of my mind." He sighed heavily. "I had such
thoughts of tender tidings sweetly exchanged between us.
But now I must lie upon my bed of thorns or none at all
and to have nothing of her frightens me more than the
battle yet to come. But perhaps this moment yet to be
will lead to more fertile ground between us and we might
sometime hence share tender passion more bent of love."

He stood now naked before the mirror.

"So, of time she's had enough and of me, well, we'll
soon see."

He glanced to the door and in second thought picked
up his robe and donned it so the sudden sight of his
nakedness would not disturb her further.

"Hell," he thought, "I've dallied long enough. I've
set a task and now it must be done."

He strode to the door and paused before it. With all
his self-control, his breath came quickly and his heart
beat high in his throat. He swallowed and squared his
shoulders, taking a deep breath, and pushed open the

door. The canopy curtains were half drawn about the bed and Heather was nowhere in sight.

"Oh God, I've pushed too hard," he thought fearfully. "She's gone. She's flown from me."

He took two large paces into the room and some slight movement from the bed drew his attention. He slowly turned in relief and closed the door, draping his robe across a chair beside it, then moved softly toward the foot of the bed and around it to the parted curtains.

The breath caught in his throat as he saw her and his blood surged through his veins in a violent rush as his senses were filled with her presence. His eyes swept her body in one long passionate caress. Her hair fell freely about her shoulders as she lay half reclining on her side among the pillows with the covers drawn out of the way to the foot of the bed. The gown teased him with its cloud of sheer blue, leaving one lovely hip and leg bare as it fell open from her narrow waist to be caught coyly between her thighs. Her breasts pressed against its transparency and lured him with their eagerness to be out, causing his breathing to become labored and hard. She smiled softly and her eyes held a seductive promise as she raised an arm to him. Almost fearing that he was in a dream, he bent over the edge of the bed, and she slipped her hand behind his neck and drew him down to her. Her skin was warm and silky smooth against him, and her intoxicating fragrance encircled him as her arms did. His hands slid to the ribbons on her gown, and her breath whispered in his ear.

"It took you long enough, my darling."

Brandon's world reeled and he grasped her tightly to him, murmuring soft words as his lips sought the tempting flesh of her throat.

"Heather . . . Oh, Heather," he rasped. "I've wanted you for so long, hungered for you. I couldn't bear it a moment longer."

His mouth eagerly took hers and their bodies strained together hungrily, Brandon's nearly famished for the full draught of love, Heather's just beginning to taste it. She moaned softly under his exploring, practiced hands, his fierce, fevered kisses and clung to him as she gave herself wholly to his passion, becoming so enmeshed in its intensity that she found herself returning it with a wild and free abandon that amazed herself as well as him. She felt his manhood against her, gently searching as he tried not to be rough in his eagerness, and reached down a hand to give assistance. When first she touched him, she almost recoiled with surprise at the warmth and passion he displayed, but at his hoarsely muttered encouragement led him on to his nest and felt that heat and pride press deep within her. Her eyes widened at the sensation inspired and in the soft light she saw her husband's face above her, his features sharp and hardened with his excitement. He seemed to luxuriate in the moment, so intimate, so tender between them. To her he appeared as some splendid, godlike being. Murmuring her love to him, she slid her arms about his neck, pressing her soft breasts into the mat of hair that covered his chest, and pulled his head down to hers. Her kiss was full and inviting, without reserve, flaming under his lips as her small tongue penetrated between. Brandon trembled above her, holding her close, and began to move, gently at first, taking care, but the violence of their passion consumed them both and they forgot themselves in its mounting storm. A startled murmur broke from her lips as she at last found what awaited her.

"Brandon!"

And he gloried in his triumph as they were dissolved in a mutual fire which died slowly, leaving them cinders on the hearth of love.

The candle flame flickered in the gentle breeze that stirred the curtains at the windows and bounced eerie shadows across the ceiling as it illuminated the figures within the bed. Heather lay back against the pillows, wrapped in Brandon's arms, her limbs entwined with his, feeling strangely disembodied as if she floated on a cloud somewhere detached from the world around. Her eyes were closed and a dreamy, contented smile shaped her lips as Brandon lightly traced his finger over her face, caressing her mouth, her eyes and the slanted brows.

"Always before I assumed a great degree of experience was needed for love's play to be at its richest, and now I find in that too I was wrong. I have never tasted joy so sweet before."

"Oh, my darling, you are not alone," she smiled, opening her eyes to gaze at him with love. "Had I known before what it was like I would have demanded my rights." She laughed a little and looped her arms around his neck. "It's a shame we wasted so much time to know each other."

His lips replaced his fingers and he murmured against her mouth as he pressed soft kisses upon it.

"You hated me, remember?"

"Hmm, in the very beginning perhaps I did," she replied, returning his kisses. "Then perhaps I didn't. I just know you frightened me more than I could stand."

He laughed and rolled over with her and sank his lips against the warm flesh of her throat, enjoying the feel of her unclad softness against·him.

"I frightened myself too. I was afraid I'd lose you completely."

She rose up on his chest and thrust out her bottom lip sullenly. "You were as mean as a rutting boar, Brandon Birmingham, and you know it."

He half smiled as he idly ran a finger from her shoulder downward across a breast and around the pink peak thrusting forward impudently.

"Being forced into marriage went against my grain," he murmured. "And having your aunt treat me like a boorish clod from the colonies did not help my disposition. Then having to spend my wedding night under the scrutiny of Lord Hampton tested my temper more. But when you said you hated me, my anger found full bloom and since you were the only one there I could lash out against, my anger sought you. Beware, my pretty. Revenge is not a double-edged sword at all. It is purely single-edged. I found myself astraddle the sharp edge and whenever you rocked it I felt the bite.''

Her eyes grew innocently round. ''Whatever did I do to injure you?''

He dropped his head back against the pillow and putting his hand across his brow, closed his eyes and laughed with a sigh. ''Oh, tell me what you didn't do, my love. That would indeed be simpler. You played the woman as if you created the part, and I had to stand by, the helpless male, and watch you feast upon my heart. You bared your breasts before me and swung your full ripe cheeks to tease the very eyeballs from my head, and were so damned tempting I nearly took you by force at least a thousand different times.''

She giggled and laid her cheek against his shoulder and ran her fingers idly through the hair on his chest as she fell into deep thought. ''Do you know, Brandon, I almost feel sorry for Aunt Fanny. She never knew what it was to be loved or to even have a friend.''

He smiled and opened his eyes. ''Don't feel too badly about her, pet. She's probably living quite contentedly on the money I gave her.''

Heather sprang up with a start and searched his face. ''You gave Aunt Fanny money?''

He nodded. ''A handsome amount it was too. It went to pay a debt she said I owed her for taking care of you the two years you lived with them.''

''And you paid her!'' she cried indignantly. ''Oh, Brandon, she was well paid in advance when she sold all my belongings. And besides, I worked for my living those two years. She had no right to claim that debt to you. I feel so ashamed. You must have thought we were all money grabbers.''

He laughed with amusement, drawing her close again. ''I gave it to her for more than that one reason, my love.

She might have tried to make a claim upon you and my child, guessing that I had the wealth to care for her in a luxurious fashion, and I had no wish for her constant presence around me nor around you. It's one thing to have a reluctant wife but quite another to have an offensive in-law complicating matters. The next time she would have laid a hand on you I probably would have killed the hag anyway. So not wishing to commit mayhem upon that bovine beast I gave her the money without an argument. In fact, I gave it to her so quickly I fear she was shocked.''

''Oh, Brandon,'' she laughed gaily. ''You are so wonderfully impossible.''

He chuckled as his hand swept her body. ''Well, we are rid of her, aren't we, sweet?''

Heather's smile faded swiftly as she suddenly remembered the lifeless form of William Court sprawled upon the floor, and she threw her arms about her husband and clung to him tightly.

''I hope we are rid of her, Brandon. I hope we are.''

Brandon smoothed her hair from her face, and when he spoke it was most gently. ''Will you tell me why you are afraid, my love? Will you let me help you?''

She rolled away and closed her eyes, frightened of what might happen to them if he found out that she had slain a man. She shook her head, managing a laugh.

''It's nothing, my darling. Truly, there's nothing.''

She opened her eyes to find him above her, waiting, his eyes searching, trying to see within her mind. Then he bent slowly toward her mouth, pressing her back into the pillows.

''I love you, Heather. I love you more than my life, and my love is strong. Trust me, my darling.''

His mouth moved over hers and again Heather melted within his arms. A long time later her breath was warm against his ear.

''And I love you, Brandon, my very dearest husband.''

*　　*　　*

Brandon was aroused from sleep by Hatti's voice in the hallway, and as her footsteps neared, he sat up in sudden realization of where he was. His movement roused Heather, and she rolled closer, her eyes unopened, a sleepy smile curving her lips. She reached out a hand to caress his lean, muscular ribs, and he lay back, reluctantly pulling the sheet over them as Hatti flung open the door. The old Negress stopped dead in mid stride as she saw the two of them together in the huge bed, then a broad grin made tiny wrinkles about her eyes and she bustled on into the room as if it were an everyday occurrence. Ignoring Brandon's frown, she went to the windows, throwing aside the heavy drapes to let the brilliant sunlight fill the room. She stood with arms akimbo, chuckling to herself.

"Yassah, it sure is a mighty fine day. Why, I don't think I've seen so much sun in one day in the last twenty years, not since your mammy was in this house, Master Bran."

Heather fluffed the pillows and leaned back against them half sitting, drawing the sheet up over her bosom, and Brandon joined her there, dropping a hand over her thigh as he scowled from under his brows at the Negress. Heather's eyes sparkled with suppressed merriment as she watched Hatti sweep about the room, throwing clothes over her arm and straightening things here and there.

"I suppose you all be wanting your breakfast soon," the old woman rambled on. "I ain't never known you to be a late riser before, Master Bran. I suppose Master Jeff is eating his heart out wondering where you is. Hee-hee-hee."

She chuckled, unable to contain her happiness and then grew serious as she picked up Heather's blue gown from the floor beside the bed and spread it carefully on a chair close at hand. She continued onto the wardrobe where she found a robe for her mistress and laid it beside the gown.

"I suspect he's gonna be up here soon. He was eating some time ago and said he wanted to see you." The wide grin came again as she looked at the two in bed. "That Master Beau gonna be wanting to come in here pretty soon, too. I ain't never known him to sleep this late before either. You sure got him trained, Miss Heather."

"He's just better mannered than some people I know," Brandon gruffly retorted, drawing a chuckle from the old woman.

She shuffled to the door and opening it, turned to give Brandon a last wicked gaze before she left. "Yassah, it sure is a mighty fine day."

Before she could leave, Jeff's voice sounded from the other room. "Where is he, the lazy dolt? Leaves the party early, forgets his guests and lies abed until midday."

His head poked through the doorway, and with a gasp Heather quickly slid down in bed, snatching the sheet up close under her chin. There was a moment's silence as his gaze took in the scene.

"Well, you're not exactly decent, but I'll come in anyway," he grinned.

He slipped past Hatti as the old woman left and entered the room, coming to stand at the foot of the bed where he regarded the two within. His lips twisted into a one-sided grin as his gaze rested mostly on his brother while that hearty squirmed under the thoughtful eye. Then he strolled to the window, eyeing Heather's blue gown as he passed the chair. Resting one hand upon the sill and with the other drawing his jacket aside, he stared musingly out upon the sunlit grounds.

"Yes, sir," he murmured, deep in thought. "It's going to be a right beautiful day."

With that he threw back his head and laughed heartily at some private joke. Brandon groaned and rolled his eyes upward, gritting his teeth.

"Well, it's a damned sorry day when a man's own bedroom gets as public as a sale house on auction day. I'm going to have Ethan see about locks for these doors."

Jeff turned and with an amused smile, bowed. "Your pardon, sir. Had I been aware of your change of venue, I would have been more discreet. However, I would remind you, dear brother, that we have guests about and they grow worried about your absence. Shall I tell them you are ill?" At Brandon's answering growl he laughed and continued. "Very well, I'll simply tell them you're lazy and will be down shortly."

He turned as if to go but faced them again. "I must remember to congratulate George. He'll be happy to know he's not a complete failure as a matchmaker."

He watched them in amused silence until the full impact of his words were brought home and they looked up almost in unison to stare at him in stunned surprise.

"It's quite all right. I've known the details for some time now, but don't blame George too much. He was well into his cups and thought himself completely alone." With another deep laugh he went to the door and there eyed Heather's gown again and then grinned at Brandon. "You had a hell of a lot more willpower than I would have had, sweet brother."

He winked at Heather and chuckling to himself, turned and left, closing the door behind him

Brandon muttered something disagreeable about not being able to have any secrets or privacy and swung his long legs over the edge of the bed and sat up. Heather laughed gaily and springing up, embraced him fiercely from behind.

"Oh, it is a beautiful day, isn't it, Brandon?"

He smiled as he closed his eyes and rubbed his back against her bare breasts, delighting in the feel of them against him.

"Indeed it is, sweet," he breathed. "Indeed it is."

He got up suddenly and laughing, swung her off the bed and gave her a lustful pat on the naked buttocks.

"If you don't see about our son pretty soon, madam, he'll have to wait just that much longer for his breakfast."

She giggled and came into his arms and stood up on her toes to kiss his lips, looping her arms about his neck.

"Don't go away. I plan to keep you within my sight most of the day."

He gave her a deep kiss, holding her tightly to him, and then sighed against her ear.

"You'll have trouble getting rid of me, m'lady."

Beau, seeming to sense his parent's good spirits, was in the mood to play after his stomach had been adequately filled. He kicked his legs happily in his bath, splashing his mother, and chuckled merrily when his father spoke to him of his bad manners. When Heather carried him into the drawing room, he was more than content with the attention he received there from the guests who cooed and fussed over him.

Mrs. Clark regarded the gleam in his father's eyes and sat back, bracing her hand on her cane, and nodded slowly. "Well, Brandon, you look a great deal better tempered today than you did last night. Your night's rest must indeed have done wonders for your disposition."

Jeff smothered a chuckle and received a warning glance from Brandon who turned and spoke to the woman in good humor.

"Thank you, Abigail. It did. I do feel considerably better this morning."

He met Heather's smiling eyes over his son's head and his own were warm and bright.

Daylight had almost flown when the last of the guests climbed into their carriages. A light repast had been served and hearty farewells made around. Most of the men had a last sample of Jeff's whiskey warming their bellies, the women a last drink of cool water or a sip of chilled wine to shorten their trip some small whit.

When the house was once more left to the Birminghams, they gathered in the drawing room to pass the evening leisurely. Heather sat with Beau on a quilt spread upon the rug where he waved his arms excitedly and cooed and with bright eyes watched the dust motes that swam in a nearby shaft of sunlight. The babe drew chuckles from the men who sat nearby, Brandon on the settee within hands' reach of his wife, and Jeff stretched out across from them in a comfortable chair, each sampling an evening libation of his choice.

A rattle of a carriage and a thunder of hooves broke the quiet moment, and Louisa's landau careened to a halt before the stoop. The woman stepped down with an eagerness and lightness of foot that belied the solemnity of her face. She bounced up the steps and flounced past Joseph to force her presence upon the small family without preamble. Before she spoke a word, she took the glass from Brandon's hand and nearly drained it, abusing the fine brandy, then wrinkling her nose as if in distaste. He set the glass on the table when she handed it back, and Jeff smiled slightly at the subtle insult that went completely by her.

"Well, Brandon," she blurted out. "Once more you've given the gossips of Charleston something to talk about."

He raised an eyebrow in query at her statement and she explained breathlessly.

"Sybil was found murdered this morning." She half smiled at Heather's gasp of surprise. "And you were seen with her yesterday on Meeting Street. In fact, you were apparently the last person to speak with her."

Something cold and dreadful began to grow deep inside Heather. She reached a hand to Brandon's thigh and his slid over hers and gripped it reassuringly. A dead silence filled the room and everyone seemed to hold their breath. Louisa stiffened and almost frowned as she gazed at the clasped hands and then she continued on unchecked.

"They found her in the woods outside the city with her neck broken. She was quite brutally abused. Poor girl, no one even missed her at the ball last night, did they?

Her clothes were torn from her, and the surgeon says she was raped." She raised a meaningful eyebrow to Heather then smiled at Brandon. "Of course I know you'd never treat a woman so, darling, but the sheriff has some doubts. In fact, he should be here soon. It seemed that Mrs. Scott had some definite ideas as to whom the beast might be."

Jeff laughed coldly in the silence. "Maranda Scott's tongue usually outdoes her brain in its activity."

Louisa almost sneered as she smiled at him. "There are several other strange occurrences that have come to light which I'm sure the sheriff will ask about. But of course," she simpered and glared at Heather, "Brandon can explain them all." She turned to him and asked, "Just where *did* you disappear to last night, darling?"

Heather could stand no more and came fiercely to her husband's defense. "He was with me all night, Louisa, and all of today and that I can vouch for."

"Oh!" Louisa's eyes widened and then narrowed as she stared down at Beau. "And I suppose you'll be having another brat to prove it. But then . . ." She turned to Brandon. "I suppose keeping her pregnant is the best way of being sure, isn't it, darling?"

Heather gasped at the snide insult and both Jeff and Brandon shot up from their seats. Brandon's eyes grew dark and his cheek twitched angrily. He stepped forward with his hands half raised as if to throttle her, and Louisa's eyes showed fear. Then he checked himself and she smiled tritely.

"Tsk! Tsk! You must watch that violent temper of yours, darling. What will the sheriff say?"

She half turned with a swirl of her skirts. "I really must be going anyway. He won't appreciate my giving you a warning." As she strode out, she sweetly laughed over her shoulder. "I'll go home the back way so he won't know I was here. Ta ta, darling."

A moment later her carriage swept around the house and down the back lane. Heather held her whimpering son in her arms, and the three adults gazed at each other in wonder and consternation.

"Anybody's mad to believe you had anything to do with Sybil's death, Bran," Jeff raged suddenly, slamming his glass down on a table. He muttered an oath and began to pace the room. "The silly girl—she had every lascivious reprobate in town knocking at her door. It could have been any one of them. But what good reason could anybody give for blaming you? My God, you hardly looked at her. And I'm damned certain if you would have, she'd have raped you."

Heather gazed up at her husband worriedly and made an effort to quiet Beau who rooted at her breast and when he could not find what he sought through her gown, fussed impatiently, now and then letting out angry squalls.

It was Brandon who spoke calmly.

"Mrs. Scott is naturally upset, and it's Townsend's job as sheriff to investigate every possibility, even an hysterical woman's rantings. I did help Sybil to her buggy with her bundles yesterday, and I'm sure more than a few people saw us together. But I shouldn't think that proves me her murderer. Townsend is not shallow witted. He'll listen to reason."

Heather made to rise to attend her son, and Brandon bent to help her to her feet. As he drew her up his eyes held hers and if there were any doubts in Heather's mind, they fled swiftly. It was not possible that he could look at her with so much gentleness and love and be guilty of such a horrible act. Her eyes mirrored that tender emotion, and she lifted her face to his that their lips could meet in a soft, unhurried kiss.

"I won't be long," she breathed when they drew apart, then she turned to hurry from the room and up the stairs, holding her son close.

When Heather came downstairs after nursing Beau and putting him to bed, she heard a man speaking whose voice was unfamiliar to her. Her husband's angry reply made her pause in her step.

"Dammit, Townsend, that's a fool question to ask. No, I've never made love to her. I found her totally unattractive and undesirable, and it would have been physically impossible for me to get aroused with her."

"Mrs. Scott says differently, Bran. She states that you carried on a secret affair with Sybil for years—that when she started seeing other gentlemen after your marriage you became jealous and enraged and in a fit of temper forced yourself upon her and then killed her."

"Bald-faced lies!" Brandon declared angrily. "Maranda is undoubtedly thinking she will get some sort of compensation for her wagging tongue. For years she sought to force her daughter upon me, but I swear, Townsend, upon my mother's grave, I never touched that girl."

"I hear you gave a fancy ball here last night," the sheriff drawled. "And I also hear from some of your guests that you were in a foul mood."

"Our most helpful Louie, no doubt," Jeff muttered contemptuously.

"I assure you, Townsend," Brandon ground out, "my actions last night had nothing to do with Sybil. I didn't even realize she hadn't come until a few minutes ago when Louisa gave us the news."

"Then what was the reason for your behavior?"

Jeff chuckled. "He was trying to keep all the men from ogling his wife."

"Then you are possessed of jealous fits?" the sheriff quested.

"As far as my wife goes, yes," Brandon admitted.

"Why only her? You could have felt the same about Sybil if you possessed that temperament."

Now Brandon laughed. "Undoubtedly, Townsend, you've never seen my wife or you'd see the truth of the matter. Besides Mrs. Birmingham, Sybil was put to shame."

Townsend cleared his throat and spoke as if reluctant

to do so. "There's been a rumor among your friends that you don't sleep with your wife, Bran. Is that true?"

Her blood stirring, Heather swept into the drawing room to find the three men standing and faced the stranger who stared at her for a moment in surprise then blushed profusely and hung his head. Townsend was as tall as the Birmingham men but a great deal heavier. Whereas Brandon's weight was double hers, this man's was triple, and it seemed strange to see so large a man squirm in embarrassed silence. She went to her husband and sliding an arm about his waist, spoke in measured tone.

"You have heard falsely, sir. It is true that while I carried our son we took separate rooms, but I see nothing strange in this if a woman has a husband as considerate as mine. He was afraid that he might in his sleep do injury to the babe or myself." She raised an inquisitive eyebrow. "Are you so thoughtful of your wife, sir?"

Ill at ease, Townsend muttered a negative answer then coughed and corrected his reply, turning that much redder. "I'm not married, m'am."

Jeff snickered and Heather lifted her head a little higher.

"Ah-h," she sighed. "Then you know little of women having babies. But as to your question. Do we sleep together? Yes, sir, we do." Her eyes flashed with anger. "And I am such a demanding wife, sir, I can't possibly see how my husband could have the desire to look at another woman, much less attack her."

She ended on a furious note, and Jeff laughed lightly and clapped Townsend on the back.

"You'd best be warned, Townsend. Our lady has a bit of an Irish temper, and when the matter warrants she comes out with claws bared."

The man glanced around him uncomfortably and coughed again and shuffled his hat in his hands. "Well, I can rightly see what you said is true, Brandon, but I hope you understand that I have to check out every detail in something as bad as this.''

He turned hesitantly to go then stumbled through another apology and made his exit. They heard his horse charging away from the house as if pursued by demons and the three Birminghams breathed a sigh of relief.

Jeff chuckled. ''I've never seen Townsend so ashamed of himself before. I believe as far as he's concerned, Bran, you're as innocent as a new-born babe.''

Brandon's mouth twitched with amusement. ''Thanks to my demanding wife.''

Heather swept away from him to turn and face him with chin raised.

''He was much too personal to please me,'' she said. ''He needed to be set back upon his heels.''

Her brother-in-law smiled. ''Honey, you did that the minute you walked through that door.''

A short time later Brandon closed the bedroom door and went to stand behind his wife where she sat at the dressing table and began loosening the back of her gown. She smiled up at him in the mirror and rubbed her cheek against his hand when he caressed her shoulder.

''Oh, Brandon, I love you so much. I'd die if you ever tired of me and sought another.''

He knelt and slid his arms around her and pulled her back against him tightly, pressing his lips to her fragrant hair.

''I've never done anything half measure, and my love for you is no exception, Heather. When I say a person is my friend I commit myself wholly to his behalf, thus when I say you are my love, you own me body and soul.''

She smiled softly and sighed. ''It must be obvious that I'm frightened of Louisa and I suppose I was of Sybil. The poor girl wanted you so badly that even a moment with you pleased her. I am more selfish. I must have you all the time, without having to share you."

"Do you think I feel any differently about you, my sweet?" he breathed. "Lord, I'd kill any man who tried to take you from me. And no woman can lure me from you. As for Sybil—she was a simple, addled girl who would have bargained for the world and found an end to hers."

"Do you have any idea who might have murdered her, Brandon?"

He sighed and stepped away and began to remove his own clothes. "I don't know, sweet. There were many men who courted her—even a few married ones."

"Married!" Heather said in amazement. She stood up and slid out of her gown, dropping it to the floor. "Surely, Brandon, her mother . . ."

He grunted. "That addlepated bitch! As long as Sybil failed to catch a rich husband, Mrs. Scott didn't care what her daughter did. Sam Bartlett was one of Sybil's beaus."

"Sam Bartlett!" Heather gasped. She remembered vividly her experience with him.

"The one and only," Brandon returned gruffly.

Anger possessed Heather. "And Sheriff Townsend came here to question you when that man was left walking around without a care? Oh, to think of it!"

Brandon laughed and came to her. "Easy, sweet. He might be a salacious old rooster, but there's nothing to prove him a murderer."

"Any man who would force himself upon his female slaves . . ."

"Sh-h," Brandon said, kissing her shoulder. His hands cupped her breasts inside her shift. "Let's not talk of him. There are too many much more interesting things I'd prefer to discuss—like how beautiful you are without your clothes."

His hands locked into the soft fabric of her chemise and separated it down the front with a rending tear.

"That's better," he grinned. He bent and lifted her up

in his arms. "You'll just have to learn to undress faster if you want to save your shifts, madam."

Before his lips covered hers, she was heard to murmur, "Who cares about a silly old shift."

Chapter 10

*T*he long summer days slipped by into weeks and July grew into an elderly month as Heather's nineteenth birthday came and went. Sybil's murder ceased to be topic of conversation as the search for her assailant brought no results. Her known suitors all seemed to have had adequate alibis, and the affair sank into the background, though most women remained unduly cautious of alleyways, dark doorways and wooded copses at night.

With the passage of time, Heather found her life changing as she settled securely into her place as Brandon's wife, performing the intimate duties of that position with an abandon that left her radiant. She enjoyed sharing a bedroom with him and having his presence beside her in the huge bed at night. She delighted in the feel of his hands upon her. He knew her body better than she did herself, and he used that knowledge to heighten her pleasure. He treated lovemaking as an art and was a master in his own right. His technique was as unpredictable as it was sophisticated. There were times when he wooed her, cajoled her, seduced her as if there were no marriage bonds between them, as if she were a maiden still, sweet-talking, teasing, nibbling until shivers of delight shattered every nerve in her body. Then other nights when she innocently did something to arouse him, he would rip her clothes from her with a lusty laugh, fling her on the bed and take her with a violence that nearly drove her insane with pleasure and left them both panting and exhausted but fulfilled to the ultimate. He played with her, he pampered her, he teased and tormented her, and she loved every moment of it. He taught her how to purr as he once claimed he could. He encouraged her to be not only a wife but a mistress, giving of herself freely and provoking his desires as well as satisfying them, though that proved a very simple task indeed.

"Are other men so romantic?" she inquired one night as he pressed her back into the pillows. "Are all wives blessed with such loving husbands?"

He smiled and smoothed her hair from her face.

"Are all husbands blessed with seductive vixens for wives?" he counterpointed her question with his own. "Are other women so beautiful and yet so willing to please their men?"

August made its debut with a bright, hot sun, sending most families scurrying to the city to cool themselves in the ocean's breeze. The Birminghams spent several days as guests of Mrs. Clark in her mansion near the beach, and the old woman took great pleasure in letting it be known to her acquaintances that Brandon and his young wife did indeed share a bed and were in fact a most loving couple.

Shortly thereafter, Brandon had to go to the mill to bring the books up to date, and the Websters extended an invitation to Heather to come with her husband and bring their son and have dinner with them. When she first glimpsed Leah, Heather found herself amazed by the change in the woman, for Leah Webster now was a woman of some beauty. She had gained some slight weight, and her skin shone bronze with her hair bleached flaxen by the sun. Her bright blue eyes had lost their hollow look, and she appeared years younger than she had before.

"How marvelous she looks, Brandon," Heather commented as he helped her from the barouche. "She seems a different woman."

He nodded as Jeremiah hastened down the steps of the big white house to bid them welcome. Leah helped their youngest child in his descent, following close behind as the baby toddled along after his father. The woman gave Brandon a friendly greeting, having grown accustomed to his presence about the mill, and smiled shyly at Heather who could not contain a comment on her hostess' appearance.

"Oh Leah, there's no doubt the Carolinas have agreed with you," she said gaily. "You've grown so beautiful."

The woman blushed with pleasure, and Jeremiah put his arm around his wife's shoulder and gave her a gentle hug.

"I've tried to tell the missus how she looks but she thinks I talk just to hear myself."

"I've never felt so wonderful before," Leah admitted shyly. "And with another baby on the way I hardly know I'm carrying."

Heather and Brandon both smiled at the surprise announcement and gave their congratulations.

"It'll take my wife a few more years to catch up, Leah," Brandon chuckled. "But I have reasons to suspect she will. I did little more than look at her and she got caught with this one."

From the security of his father's arms, Beau contemplated the strangers warily and didn't care in the least that he was being discussed. Heather cast a shaming eye to her husband, making him laugh, and pinkened a little.

"No one can deny who he belongs to, Mr. Birmingham," Leah smiled. "He's like your very image and with those green eyes of his there's no mistaking it."

Brandon grinned proudly and murmured softly to his son, bringing a smile from the little fellow. With their faces close together there was no question they were father and son. The baby's eyes were a mirror of Brandon's, emerald green and darkly lashed. Heather now knew that if she had never seen Brandon again after her escape from the *Fleetwood*, she'd have always been reminded of him in their son.

"Will he come to me?" Leah inquired, holding her hands up to receive him.

Beau definitely declined, giving a little grunt of rejection as he turned away to lay his head against his father's shoulder.

"Don't feel badly, Leah," Heather apologized. "He won't go to many people from his father. He's formed quite an attachment for him." She turned her head to one side as if carefully studying her husband and then continued with a gleam in her eye. "It must be the beard."

Her remark brought a chuckle from all as the children meandered from the porch to get a closer look at the Birmingham offspring. Soon the oldest girl had managed to entice Beau from his father and strolled proudly about the grounds with him. Jeremiah excused himself some time later to attend to duties at the mill and Brandon went with him. The women were left to relax on the shaded porch in rocking chairs, Mrs. Webster now and then rising to see about her meal.

"I feel more excited about this baby coming than I believe I've ever felt about any one of my others," Leah timidly confessed. "Always before we faced doubt and dread with our lack of coin. Sometimes we had good luck but mostly it was bad. Now, it seems as if we're in Eden, and we give thanks for your husband in our prayers. He took us away from nothing and gave us everything."

Heather paused sipping her tea, and her eyes grew suddenly misty. "It's strange, Leah, but that's exactly what he did to me. He snatched me away from a nightmare and gave me joy. My life was nothing until he came into it."

Leah regarded her for a moment. "You love him very much, don't you?" she questioned softly.

"Yes," Heather readily admitted, then she sighed. "I love him so much that sometimes I'm afraid. Our life seems so perfect I become frightened that something will happen to interrupt it, and if I lost him or his love I would die.''

Leah smiled. ''When I first saw your husband, Mrs. Birmingham, he sat alone in an inn up north. There were painted women admiring him from afar, but he gave not one a glance. He just stared thoughtfully into his glass of wine, and there was no mistaking the look he had for he seemed sad. Later he spoke a few brief words about you waiting here and bearing his child, and his expression changed, and I thought then that he must love you very much. Since that time I've gotten to know him and find my first impressions to be true. I've never seen a man love his wife as he does you.''

Heather brushed a tear from her cheek and laughed in apology. ''I seem to be in a mood today, crying over nothing. You mustn't think unkindly of me, Leah. I don't make a habit of doing this.''

Leah smiled gently. ''On the contrary, Mrs. Birmingham, if anything I think more of you. A woman who sheds a tear or two for the love of her man is very sensitive to life.''

Later Leah made lemonade to serve the guests, children and the mill-workers and asked Heather if she might care to take the men each a glass of the refreshing drink. As she bore the tray carefully down to the mill, Heather caught her first glimpse of it in operation. Tall pines towered above the buildings, and the smell of pitch from the large boiling vat in the yard was heavy in the air. The logs lay thick in the millpond and beyond, the giant water wheel blurred as it spun. The busy saws hummed and snarled and set the key for a chaos of sound as a team of mules labored to pull the logs to its hungry maw. There were several men standing on a framework around the boiling vat, skimming pulp from the top of the six-foot-wide kettle.

She found Mr. Webster outside the mill, discussing a problem with a few of the hands. He gave her a friendly smile when he saw her and offered to help with the tray, but she declined and served the men herself as he introduced her around as Mr. Birmingham's wife. They nodded and acknowledged her greeting respectfully with a great deal of awe at her beauty and watched after her as she strolled toward one of the smaller buildings where Jeremiah had said her husband could be found. Then the foreman gave a brisk command for them to close their mouths, and they continued on with their work, casting a last furtive glance at her over their shoulders.

Heather stood for a moment in the open doorway of the dingy office. The room held the barest essentials of furniture, and rough wood walls had never seen signs of wallpaper or whitewash. Her husband sat upon a high stool at his desk with his back toward her. The day was warm and he had removed his shirt to catch every breath of breeze that now and then drifted in through the open windows. She watched with pleasure the play of muscles across his back and smiled as she thought of them beneath her fingertips, hard as oak. She shifted her weight and a board creaked under her foot. Brandon turned and seeing her silhouetted in the doorway, rose with visible relief at his rescue from the tedium of bookkeeping and came forward. Smiling, he drew her in, closing the door behind her, then took the tray to set it down on a rough table and raised the glass of lemonade to his lips to drain it without a pause.

"Ah-h," he sighed. "Just what I needed to ease my boredom, a thirst quenching drink." He reached out an arm to pull her into his embrace. "And a pretty wench to feast my eyes upon."

She laughed and nuzzled her nose against his hairy chest. "I can remember once when you stormed at me for keeping you from your work. Have your labors grown less desirable or have I become more so?" she teased.

He dropped a kiss on the top of her head and grew serious. "Forgive me for that, my love. I was at my cruelest that day. Your refusal to share my bed taunted me into proving how big a jackass I can be."

"My refusal!" she protested. "But, Brandon, I never did anything to deny you your rights. You were the one who refused to sleep with me on the *Fleetwood* after I was ill and rejected me the first night at Harthaven. Each time I would have gladly complied with your husbandly ways, but you turned from me to sleep in your solitary bed."

"I see our marriage was full of misunderstandings," he murmured. "You had the mistaken idea that because of our marriage my desire for you had lessened since that summer's night I first took you, and I was sure you couldn't bear my touch, that you'd fight me if I tried to have you. Strange, how our minds played against us. We should have followed our instincts." He bent and pressed his lips against her white throat. "We'd have found love that much sooner."

Heather tingled with delight and knew as long as she had breath in her body she would thrill to his touch. She could summon no resistance when he caressed her. Her very soul seemed to be his, and her body responded more to his will than her own. He had the power to make her life seem an enchanted dream or, as in the past, make hell appear a pleasant garden in comparison. She was his without reservation.

His lips traveled down her neck until they hovered above the hollow at the base of her throat where a froth of white ruffles hampered further descent. His hand went to the tiny buttons of her gown and toyed casually with them as he murmured softly in her ear, sliding to the second button, the third, the seventh and the last. A smile brushed his lips and with a simple unhurried motion that left her gasping, he raised both hands to spread the front of her gown and chemise and bare her breasts. He kissed the soft flesh that was now revealed to him, and she trembled under the fiery heat of each kiss.

"Someone might come in, Brandon," she whispered breathlessly.

"I'll kill the first soul who dares touch that door," he returned casually without pausing in his caresses.

"But what if someone should just barge in?" she protested weakly, finding it hard to resist.

His hands slid under her garments to her back and pulled her against him until her breasts teased his chest with their peaks.

"There needs be a lock on that door," he murmured huskily, kissing her brow. "And a bed in here would suit my mood. These chairs are not very accommodating." He sighed and in some exasperation pulled away. "Very well, madam. I yield to your pleas."

Still distraught, Heather pulled her chemise together. She sought to fasten it but found her fingers were like so many thumbs and proceeded slowly to disguise her clumsiness with the fasteners. Brandon had returned to his desk and now watched her intently yet with a gaze that was soft and loving. She looked up to find the green eyes holding her and blushed deeply, now fumbling in confusion with the many bows and buttons. Brandon laughed and came to her, brushing aside her hands.

"My love, you tempt the very saints. So before I take you here and now let's get thee clothed again."

When she left the building there was still a deep rosy glow to her cheeks, and she was so unaware of what she was doing that she almost stumbled over Alice, one of the Webster's younger girls, who was down on all fours inspecting a toadstool.

"Oh, Mrs. Birmingham, look what I've found."

Heather bent down beside the little girl. "Do you think it belongs to some elf who lives in the woods?" she inquired, smiling.

The girl looked up, wide-eyed and eager. "Do you really suppose so? Maybe he left it behind."

"It's very likely," Heather replied, enjoying the little girl's excitement.

"Can we go in the woods and look for him?"

"Of course. Perhaps we'll find a whole fairy circle."

"Oh, yes, let's," Alice cried, tugging at her arm.

Laughing, Heather let the girl lead her into the forest. It was so dense only an occasional ray of sunlight penetrated the lush green foliage. Soon they entered a small glade when a bird somewhere up above them called to its mate, and a squirrel sat scolding them from the limb of a tree. A live oak tree towered majestically over the clearing, and a few wild flowers peeped out of the earth where the mulch was not so forbidding. The pines gave off a scent as sweet as the brightly colored blossoms.

"This here is where I'd live if I was an elf," Alice said as she spread her short arms wide and turned round and round.

Heather smiled. "Have you been here before, Alice?"

"Yes'm. Plenty of times."

"It's an enchanted place. I like it."

"Oh, Mrs. Birmingham, I knew you would," Alice cried happily.

Heather laughed and smoothed back the flaxen hair that had fallen into the little girl's eyes, then gazed around.

"I don't see any sign of elves though, do you?"

The girl frowned. "No'm," she said, then she grinned again. "But I think one is watching me. I can feel it."

Heather smiled, enjoying herself as much as the child. "That's even better than finding where they live, isn't it? Not everyone is fortunate enough to have an elf watch them. Perhaps we should pretend we don't notice."

The girl dimpled and her eyes gleamed. "What should we do?"

"We'll pick flowers and make believe we don't even know he's around. Perhaps he'll show himself then."

"Oh, yes, let's."

Heather watched Alice walk away and knew the girl

was trying for all she was worth to act nonchalant, as if she were more interested in the flowers than in the elf she was sure was observing her. With not so much interest in the unseen as the seen, Heather began to gather flowers to make a bouquet for Mrs. Webster's table. Alice soon forgot both elf and flowers and ventured off to chase after a butterfly and finally wandered back toward the mill, but Heather remained, picking as many of the daisies and lilies as she could.

Busy with her task in the small clearing, it was a long time before she too began to have an odd feeling that she was being watched. The short hair on the nape of her neck rose on ends and her spine tingled coldly. As she began to turn slowly to see if her suspicions were correct, she was half expecting to see Alice's imagined elf, for she was sure now that the girl had not been mistaken about being watched. Her eyes strained through the darkness of the trees and then she saw him. It was no elf but a man on horseback, not more than seventy-five yards from her. His shape was dark and sinister, for despite the warmth of the day he wore a black cloak that draped his entire body. The garment's stiff, high collar covered half his face, and the black tricorn he wore came down so low that barely a slit for his eyes remained. He started moving forward slowly, menacingly, with his head slunk in the collar of his cape and Heather froze for a second, unable to turn and flee, then she began to back away cautiously. He urged his horse to quicken its pace, and she whirled with a frightened cry and raced across the glade to the weaving path that led back to the mill. The horse and rider gained ground and were almost upon her; the hoof beats seemed to pound like iron against metal in her ears. She screamed, dropping the flowers, and dodged through the trees. She glanced fearfully over her shoulder, but all she could see was the large, black gruesome shape of horse and rider that seemed inseparable. A hand was reached toward her, branching from the blackness of the man's cape. Then from somewhere in front of her she heard her husband cry out her name. The horseman stopped, apparently to listen. A sound of thrashing came from ahead, and Heather fled in that direction sobbing Brandon's name. Glancing back, she saw the horse rear straight up as the man pulled tight upon the reins and turned the animal back into the forest. She had a brief glimpse of his back before he disappeared into the dark shadows. There was something strangely familiar about the figure that she couldn't quite put into words.

Brandon came racing through the trees, and she fell into his arms, sobbing.

"Oh, Brandon, he was horrible!" she cried. "Horrible!"

"My God, what happened! I was coming to get you for dinner, and I heard you scream." His arms tightened around her. "You're shaking like a leaf."

"There was a man—on horseback," she choked through tears. "He came after me. He almost caught me."

Brandon held her away from him and looked into her face. "Who was he? Had you ever seen him before?"

She shook her head. "No. No. He wore a tricorn and a cloak, and I wasn't able to see him clearly. I was gathering flowers and felt someone watching me. When I saw him, he started coming toward me and when I ran, he chased me." A shudder ran through her. "He looked so evil, Brandon."

He pulled her close again and held her tightly, soothing her fears as best he could. "It's over now, sweet," he murmured. "You're safe here in my arms and I won't let any harm come to you."

"But who could it have been, Brandon? What was he doing here?"

"I have no idea, my love, but Sybil's murderer has yet to be caught. It's best that you don't wander off alone anymore. We must warn the Websters too. If the man comes back, I wouldn't want any of the women or children in his path. I'll have a few lookouts posted. That should keep him from doing any harm.''

''He made me drop my flowers,'' she sniffled tearfully, as if just realizing it. ''I picked an armful for Leah's table, and he frightened me so I dropped them.''

Brandon chuckled. ''All right, sweet. We'll go back and get them.'' He lifted the hem of her gown and dried her tears with it. ''Now stop your crying before you get your nose all red.'' He gave her a kiss. ''You're not frightened anymore, are you?''

She leaned against him. ''Not with you here.''

Heather's fears rose anew at the front door of Harthaven when Joseph announced that Miss Louisa Wells had come to call and was waiting in the drawing room. She glanced up to her husband and saw his face take on a black scowl and the muscle begin to twitch in his cheek. She followed as he entered the drawing room, carrying their sleeping son in her arms.

Louisa reposed prettily in Brandon's favorite chair, wearing a muslin gown of considerable beauty, and took a sip of the drink which she had prepared with Jeff's bourbon and a sprig of mint. She smiled slowly over her glass at Brandon and leaned her head back against the chair.

''You're looking well,'' she commented in a lazy voice. ''But then, darling, you always do.'' Her eyes devoured him before she turned to Heather. ''Poor dear, you must find Carolina's heat a dreadful bother after your England. The little flower seems a little wilted.''

Self-consciously Heather sank into a chair and gave her hair a quick, nervous smoothing with her hand. Stone faced, Brandon went to the bar to fix himself a drink.

''To what do we owe this unexpected . . . pleasure, Louisa?'' he inquired with a bit of sarcasm. He came to stand behind Heather's chair with his drink. ''We haven't seen you since you brought us news of Sybil's murder, and I'm wondering what you may have to report now. Not another murder, I hope."

She laughed easily. "Of course not, darling. I've been away visiting my aunt in Wilmington, and I just returned and wanted to pay my respects to everyone. I'm disappointed that you didn't miss me." She sighed and rose from her chair. "But I'm sure you haven't been allowed too much time to yourself." She gave Heather a quick glance from behind lowered eyelids, and then handed her a gaily wrapped package. "This is for Beau, dear, a little something I picked up in Wilmington. I, ah-h," she smiled smugly, "never donated to the cause before."

Heather lowered her gaze and murmured her thanks, stumbling over the words. Her confidence was lagging badly. The scare she had had that afternoon had worn her nerves thin and now before Louisa she was tense and unsure. She unwrapped the present and a small silver cup emerged from the paper. *Beau* and the year *1800* had been engraved on the metal.

"Thank you, Louisa," she said softly. "It's very lovely."

Louisa sensed her advantage over the moment and did not let it slip by.

"I wouldn't have felt right not giving Brandon's son a gift." She looked down at Beau as he stirred in his mother's arms, finally opening his eyes. "After all, as close as we are—were," she smiled. "It would have been in poor taste to ignore his son. Aren't you glad though, Heather, that the boy looks so much like his father? I mean—it would have been a pity if he had taken after you, say, though I expected as much. I just knew the little darling would be the very image of his mother. Perhaps it's because she looks so much like a baby herself."

Words failed Heather. It was hard to sit calmly while the woman deliberately tried to antagonize her. Brandon was not so gracious.

"What in the hell do you want, Louisa?"

The woman ignored him and bent over Beau, displaying every measure of her bountiful bosom to both Heather and Brandon. She clucked the baby under his chin, but Beau was not in favor of being touched by strangers the minute he woke up. His bottom lip quivered and he began to squall as he strained away, pulling on the neck of Heather's gown.

Louisa stiffened and her expression for a moment was full of venom as she stared down at Heather trying to quiet her son. A brief smile crossed Brandon's face as he regarded Louisa over his glass. But Beau would not be hushed, and Heather, glaring at Louisa from under her lashes, finally undid her gown and put Beau to her breast. The baby quieted immediately but kept a wary eye upon Louisa. Brandon chuckled and gave his son a pat on the rump before moving into a chair beside his wife's.

Glancing up from Beau, Heather saw an uncertain frown flicker across Louisa's brow. It was such a brief expression she wondered if she could have imagined it. Was the woman at last realizing what it meant to be the mother of Brandon's child? Here was a bond that would not be easily broken. Brandon loved his son. It was plain to see. No one could believe that he would discard the child's mother very readily for another.

Louisa felt herself losing ground and tried to regain it, but ineptly, in the wrong way.

"I think it's perfectly adorable the way you take care of the business of feeding him yourself, Heather, instead of hiring a wet nurse. Most women would, you know. But I can see you're the domestic type and enjoy doing things like that. Of course, it does demand a lot of a woman. I'm afraid I couldn't be tied down like that."

"No, I suppose you couldn't," Brandon returned. "That's why we'd have never gotten along, Louisa."

The woman took a step backward as if struck and then sought to turn her words around.

"What I mean is—I couldn't give all my attention to a baby and ignore my husband."

Brandon laughed sharply. "Do you think I'm ignored, Louisa? If you do, let me assure you I am not. Heather has a marvelous ability to make both her son and her husband feel loved."

Louisa whirled and went back to her chair yet made no move to sit down. She spoke over her shoulder to Brandon.

"I've come here to discuss business. You might be interested in the fact that I've decided to sell my land. I thought I should come here first to you to see what price you'll be willing to pay to have it."

"Oh, I see."

"Well, it would have been rather unseemly of me to sell it to anyone else, knowing you wanted it. You've been after me for a long time to sell it to you."

"Yes," Brandon replied, still not appearing anxious.

"Well, damn it, if you're not interested I'll sell it to someone who is!" she stormed, spinning around.

Brandon gazed at her mockingly with an eyebrow raised. "Who?"

"Why, there—there are plenty of people just waiting to buy it. I could sell it in a moment."

She didn't sound so sure of herself despite her words.

"Louisa," he sighed. "Let's stop this pretense. I'm the only one interested in buying your land. Perhaps some poor dirt farmer would like to have it, but I don't think he could afford your price."

"That isn't true! I could sell it to anyone!" she declared.

"Oh simmer down, Louisa. I know exactly what you're trying to do but it won't work. Now I'll give you a couple of reasons why I'm the only one interested. No one of any wealth would have any use for your piddling acres. Our plantations are rather deserted out here and no one is going to ride all this way to bother with your little bit of land, especially when you have no intention of selling Oakley. I am the only one who can afford to be a little generous. But don't come around here with your schemes and expect me to panic and double my offer. I'm not that kind of fool. Now, we'll discuss the details in a few moments, but first I'm going to sit here and relax and finish my drink."

"Brandon, you big tease," Louisa laughed. "Why do you like to worry me so? You had every intention of buying the land when I said I would sell."

"I bargain in business, Louisa, never tease," he commented dryly.

When Louisa swept into the study, leaving her heavily perfumed scent trailing behind her, Brandon bent over Heather and breathed in her soft, delicate fragrance.

"I'll try not to be too long, my love. If you wish to go to bed when you finish with Beau, I'll make some excuse to Louisa after we get our business settled and send her straight home."

"Please do," Heather murmured. "I'm afraid I'm not entirely over this afternoon. I'd rather not see her again tonight." She bit into her bottom lip. "Oh, Brandon, she's so determined to break us apart. I hate her." She looked down at Beau, who kneaded her breasts with his small hand, and laughed a little nervously. "What I need is a good soak in the bath to forget my problems with her."

He chuckled. "I'll tell the boys to heat up some water. Anything else, sweet?"

"Yes," she replied softly. "Kiss me so I'll know that woman doesn't stand a chance with you."

He smiled and accommodated her and there were few doubts that remained afterward.

Now the land was his, Brandon mused as he climbed the stairs, and he was infinitely glad he had spared Heather from that dickering which had settled the matter.

He sighed heavily.

One thing he could always credit Louisa with was boldness and a great deal of nerve. She had started off with a blatant proposal that they renew their relationship, making unworthy and vulgar advances upon him that had stirred no other emotion but disgust. Finally she had offered the land at an exorbitant price and getting her down to a reasonable settlement had taken a great deal of wearisome arguing. She had pleaded with no thought of pride, threatened not to sell, propositioned him like any harlot. The meeting had left him feeling unclean to say the least and wondering how low she would stoop in her search for a fortune. It was common knowledge that she was in a poor state of finance and needed the money, but Heather had once been in even more dire straits and had not succumbed to selling herself or openly pleading for sustenance.

Heather—his beloved. Just the thought of her washed away the sour mood Louisa had left with him. He remembered the moment at the mill when she had stood half clothed against him, and his pulse quickened. He'd have to see about inside bolts for those doors so she wouldn't be so nervous next time. He chuckled to himself. He was worse than any rutting stag in her company, always thinking of her in his arms, of her soft, warm body curving to his, of her lovely limbs entwining him. The hot blood surged within him, and his thoughts raced to several days before when while out riding with her he had induced her to take a swim with him in the creek. She had been timid about shedding her clothes in broad daylight, fearing someone might come upon them, but after he assured her that it was a most private place, gesturing to the abundance of trees and shrubs, she had even been willing to concede it might be fun. Casually watching her disrobe and standing in the buff, as he was, his desires had grown quite evident, and seeing him, she had known how that swim would end. Playfully she had eluded him and dashed into the water, gasping at the coolness of it, and then tried to outdistance him with rapid strokes. He had chuckled at her efforts while he easily overtook her, coming to her side and then diving underwater to catch her ankle and pull her down into his embrace. He smiled as he remembered back. It had been a most pleasurable afternoon.

He opened the door to the bedroom and paused, taking in the scene. Heather sat in the tub, looking much as she had in London, sweet, desirable, irresistibly beautiful with the candlelight shining on wet, glistening skin, her hair piled on her head, a few loose curls dangling. She smiled as he closed the door and came forward to rest his hands on the tub to lean down to her.

"Good evening, sweet," he murmured.

She ran a wet finger over his lips. "Good evening, m'lord," she returned softly and slid her hand behind his head as he pulled her up to him.

September's harvest began and as the crops were taken to market, the streets of Charleston knew a milling throng. There were buyers and sellers and a great multitude of neither who yet sought to trim some small profit from the great sums of money that changed hands during the day. There were rich and poor, beggar and thief, ship's captain and slave. A great number of people came simply to sit in carriages, coffee houses and inns and watch the bustling mob and exchange comments on the endless streams of characters that met their eye. During the day the city was a bustling trading center, at night the activities changed and it became a fermenting caldron with entertainment for every whim.

When Brandon presented Heather tickets to a new play being featured at the Dock Street Theatre, she almost choked him in her excitement, spreading her thanks across his face with enthusiastic kisses. When her glee had subsided and she sat in his lap studying the tickets, she confessed that she had never been to such a place before.

Whenever they presented themselves to the public, the couple always drew attention. Brandon's tall, lean handsomeness and Heather's petite beauty made them unique and tonight as they entered the foyer of Dock Street Theatre they were especially so. Brandon wore white breeches and a waistcoat of the same color. A bit of lace fell over his brown hands and ruffled down the front of his shirt, and his coat of scarlet was artistically embroidered with gold thread over the lapels and board stiff collar. Heather was bewitching in a gown of black French lace, embellished liberally with tiny jets that shimmered in the candlelight. An ostrich plume had been woven into her coiffure and at her ears swung Catherine Birmingham's diamond earrings.

There were the usual envious stares to greet them and warm greetings from friends. Brandon watched over his wife possessively as the men bent over her hand. Many young bucks beat their way through the throng in hopes the ravishing beauty was some unattached Birmingham kin. They came to stand and posture before Heather and they found at close range she was even more delectable than from afar. Their faces fell and they turned away in disappointment as Brandon, with some humor, presented his wife.

Matthew Bishop was seen from a distance and seemed to prefer it that way. He kept his gaze from dwelling long on Heather and entertained some other regal wench with carefully zealous consideration.

Mrs. Clark greeted them with a critical but approving eye. "Heather, my lovely child, you're looking delightfully wicked this evening. You'll put these other girls to shame in their virgin pinks and whites." She turned to Brandon with an amused look as she leaned forward on her cane. "And I see you're watching over her as carefully as ever, sir."

He grinned. "After knowing my father, Abegail, is it possible for you to believe that I am worse than he?"

Mrs. Clark chuckled and tapped him affectionately with her fan. "It took a long time and a little slip of a girl to make you realize that, sir. You were too carefree in your bachelor days. I remember when you couldn't have cared less if some lady's affection was taken from you." She chuckled again. "But you looked at quite a few of the ladies in those days and I imagine tasted a goodly number. But now look at you, so stricken with this filly you're like a stag in rut." She turned back to Heather and smiled slowly. "I'm glad you happened along, child. The Birminghams are some of my favorite people and I like to see them get the best."

Heather brushed her lips against the old woman's cheek. "Thank you, Abegail. From you that is truly a compliment."

"Oh poppycosh!" Abegail protested. "I state plain fact and there's no need for you to be filling this poor old head with your Irish nonsense. I'm not so simply charmed as that." She smiled to soften her gruff reprimand and patted the younger woman's hand. "Don't waste those pretty words on me, child. Your man is more susceptible."

Later, in their private box, Brandon had his eyes more on Heather than on the stage. Her obvious excitement over the production delighted him. As the actors played their parts, she sat as still as a mouse, catching every word. She was more than enchanting and he found it nearly impossible to drag his eyes from her. When they stood again in the lobby, sipping a little wine, he listened with amusement as she warbled on gaily about the play.

"I shan't forget it ever, Brandon. Papa never took me to anything like this. It's so wonderfully beautiful, like a fairy tale come to life."

He bent over her and laughed softly in her ear. "Perhaps I'm being a bad influence over you, my pet."

Her eyes shone warmly as they met his. "If that be so, it is far too late to speak of it, for I'd have it no other way. I am doomed, for I can no longer be satisfied with just existing. I must love and be loved. I must possess and be possessed. I must be yours, my darling, as you must be mine. So you see, you've taught me too well. Everything you set out to do in the beginning you have accomplished and more so. I must live with you and be a part of you, and if we weren't tied with marriage bonds and you still sailed the sea, I'd follow you around the world as your mistress, and to me our love would be our sacred vows. And if confessing this makes of me a wanton woman, then I am truly a very happy one.''

Still holding her gaze, Brandon lifted her hand and pressed it to his lips. ''If you were my mistress I'd have to keep you under lock and key so no other man would be able to whisk you away from me. You too are an excellent tutor. The gay bachelor now prefers the security of marriage. I enjoy every moment of being married to you, especially that part where I can say that you're mine and mine alone.''

She smiled softly and her eyes were full of love.

''You shouldn't look at me that way,'' he murmured, returning her gaze.

''What way?'' she breathed, continuing to do so.

''The same way you do when we've just made love, as if all the world could pass us by and you wouldn't care.''

''I wouldn't,'' she returned in the same soft tone.

He grinned. ''I'll be hard put to stay and finish viewing the play if you continue, madam. You are a very fetching sight for even this old married man and you do test my manly control.''

She laughed with a light heart but her gaiety ceased when she saw Brandon stop and stare over her shoulder with an amazed expression on his face. She turned to see what had startled him and found Louisa coming toward them. She wondered at Brandon's reaction until her eyes fell on the beige gown the woman wore. It was exactly like the one she had given the peddler, the very same she had worn when she first met Brandon. Louisa, not to be outdone by anyone, had chosen to change it some slight degree in the style of the Parisians. The transparency of the gown would have been shocking to a more modest woman, but Louisa, never bothering about such a trivial thing as modesty, had very definitely rouged her nipples.

"Hello, Brandon," she purred in her silky voice when she stood before them, and she laughed softly as she felt his eyes as well as Heather's on her attire. "I see you've noticed my gown. It is lovely, isn't it? Thomas made it especially for me after I saw the original in his shop, and just for little old me, he put the other one away so no other woman would have a gown like mine."

Brandon cleared his throat and spoke inquiringly. "Was there some fault with the original that he had to make a second for you?"

Louisa reveled in the interest Brandon was showing in her dress. "No, there was nothing wrong with it, darling, but it was so dreadfully small no one could have worn it. Why, even Heather with her skinny little girl's figure would have failed to squeeze into it. It would have been much, much too tiny for her."

Brandon exchanged a glance with Heather. "It must indeed have been small."

"Well, I knew I had to have one just like it the moment I laid eyes upon it," the woman continued gaily. "And I'm so glad I insisted that Thomas make me this one. I do so like to please you, darling, and I see that I have." She feigned embarrassment. "Of course, you've been staring at me so hard I'm wondering if it's the gown at all—and in front of your wife too, darling."

Brandon looked at her passively. "The gown reminds me of one Heather wore when I first met her, Louisa," he returned dryly. "It was a gown worth treasuring for the memories associated with it."

Louisa's face turned to stone and she looked menacingly at Heather, then smiled tritely. "However did you get the money to purchase such a gown as this? You must have worked very hard to obtain it. But then if your husband is so interested in having you displayed in a garment such as this, my dear, you should meet my couturier. He's here tonight. He could do wonders for your skin and bones. You'd be pleased with him, I'm sure."

Heather felt Brandon stiffen beside her.

"I'm afraid the man wouldn't please me, Louisa," he replied. "I prefer that women sew Heather's gowns."

Louisa laughed a bit harshly. "Why, Brandon, you're becoming very strait-laced in your dotage."

Brandon dropped a hand on the bare flesh of his wife's shoulder and caressed it leisurely. "As far as Heather is concerned, Louisa, I've always been a bit strait-laced."

Louisa felt a quick, quivery spasm of jealousy grip her as she watched his fingers move gently over Heather's skin, remembering the feel of them against her own flesh, arousing sensual feelings that had never been matched before or since by any other man. She gave the smaller woman an evil glare.

"You really must meet Thomas anyway, my dear. Perhaps he can give you a few suggestions on what to wear to make it appear as if you had a little flesh on your bones. I've seen him do such wonders with a childish figure. Wait here, darling, and I'll find him for you."

Heather glanced up uncertainly at her husband as the woman walked away, having recognized the longing in Louisa's eyes, knowing well that tormenting emotion from her own experiences. She found an amused smile upon his face.

"If she only knew about that gown, she'd wring that poor fellow's neck," he laughed. "There's no doubt the one he has is yours."

"She looks very lovely in it, doesn't she?" Heather murmured.

Brandon grinned down at her and moved his hand to her waist to squeeze it fondly. "Not half so lovely as my vision of you in it or as you are every day, all day long."

Heather smiled, reassured, and watched Louisa disappear into the crowd of theatre goers. She forgot the woman for a few moments as Brandon brought her attention back to more pleasant things. But later, a feeling of uneasiness crept over her—the same strange, eerie sensation that had come upon her not very long ago at the mill. She was being stared at but with an intenseness that was anything but normal. She turned very slowly and saw him. The color drained from her face. The man stood beside Louisa, but his eyes rested upon her. He seemed not at all surprised to see her. He even nodded his head slightly in acknowledgment of her and grinned. It was he. The grin was too horrible. She was positive there was no other in the whole world with a one-sided smirk like Mr. Thomas Hint.

She swayed against Brandon, feeling faint, and the hand she put to her face was shaking uncontrollably. She tugged on her husband's coat to make him bend to her, for she doubted she could make her voice carry even that distance.

Brandon frowned with concern. "What's wrong?"

Louisa and Mr. Hint were walking toward them now. She couldn't stand there, trying to make words come from her mouth. She had to speak.

"Brandon," she wheezed. "I don't feel well. It must be the crowd. Please take me back to our box."

Then she heard Louisa's voice. "Here he is, Heather. I would like for you to meet my dressmaker, Mr. Thomas Hint."

Too late! Panic was gripping her. She had a great desire to flee from the room as fast as her legs would carry her, but they would not move. She was frozen, paralyzed with fear.

Brandon didn't waste time with unnecessary words or politeness. "Please excuse us, Louisa. I'm afraid Heather has had a sudden attack of the vapors. It's a pleasure to make your acquaintance, Mr. Hint. Goodnight."

It wasn't long before he had her in a chair in their private box. He took both her trembling hands into his.

"Do you wish to go home? You're shaking and you look as if you'd seen a ghost."

She almost laughed out loud in hysteria. He was right. She had seen a ghost or something out of her past that was as frightening as one. She was possessed with fear that she would see him again or have him talk to Brandon. He was such a horrible man—or was he a monster?

She clung tightly to her husband as he sat beside her and tried to soothe her. The curtains went up again but neither watched the stage now. A few moments later he leaned over her.

"Let's go. I don't want you fainting here."

He led her from their box to the lobby and from the theatre where he motioned for James to get the barouche and pull it around. When it drew up before them, he lifted her in and held her small, quivering form close as they rode home.

Heather was frightened now, more than she had ever been before. She had something now that she loved too dearly to part with—her husband, her child. If she were accused of murder, they would be snatched from her arms without mercy and she would rot away her life in prison. It would matter little that she had been attacked. They would not believe her, not with Mr. Hint to say that she had gone with William Court willingly. And Brandon would be so hurt. Oh, sweet Lord, be merciful, she prayed.

When they arrived home, Brandon carried her up to their bedroom and put her on the bed. He rolled her over to unfasten her gown and stripped it from her with her other garments. When she lay naked beneath the sheet, he poured a small bit of brandy in a glass and sat down on the bed beside her.

"Drink this, sweet. It will put some color into your cheeks."

Obediently she sat up and taking the glass from him, drank a big gulp of it, for which she was instantly sorry. She choked on the fiery liquid and coughed as she tried to catch her breath.

He laughed softly and took the glass, setting it on the bedside commode. "I should have warned you about the drink, but I thought you'd remember."

He began pulling pins from her hair, and soon the silky

curls were cascading loosely over her shoulder. He smoothed them under his hand.

"Before, when we were in London and on the *Fleetwood*, I used to watch you tend your hair. I could hardly keep my hands from it, it tempted me so. Do you remember when you were ill, Heather?"

She nodded, watching him as he played with a curl.

"You were very ill, my darling, but I took care of you. No one touched you but myself and when your fever raged, I was the one by your side. Not for an instant did I leave the cabin. You were mine and I needed you. I let no harm come to you."

Her brows drew together as she wondered why he was speaking so slow and deliberate.

"Do you think that now, when I know you are my very life, that I would let anything happen to you. I'd fight man and beast for you, Heather. So would you trust me enough to let me help you as I want to do. I know you are frightened, sweet, and I believe I can help if you'll only trust me." He bent over her. "I am very strong, *ma petite*."

Heather's eyes were opened wide. He knew something! Somehow he had found out! But how—and what? What did he know and who had told him?

Fear set her hands atremble and she clutched them together to keep them from transmitting their weakness to the rest of her body. She sank further down in the bed, the brandy lending her no false courage. What could she say? What could she tell him? If she hurt him she'd never forgive herself and if he walked away in shock at her deed and never returned to her arms, she would die.

Brandon smiled tenderly and drew the sheet up under her chin. "When you wish to tell me, my sweet, I'll always be near." He undressed and slid into bed beside her. Pulling her close, he kissed her troubled brow. "Go to sleep, my love."

In the security of his arms, she found comfort at last and she was able to sleep, but there was no peace in her

dreams. She saw Mr. Hint, his misshapened body standing over her, his clawlike hands holding Beau. Then she
was running—running after Mr. Hint—after Beau. She
had to save Beau from him! She rose from sleep screaming and struggling in Brandon's arms as he tried to wake
her.

"He has Beau! He has Beau! He'll hurt my baby!"
she sobbed.

"Heather, wake up. It's only a bad dream, sweet.
Beau's safe."

Her eyes lost some of their wildness as they focused
upon the face above her, the dark, handsome face of her
husband. It was a stable rock in a sea of swirling sand.
With a cry of relief, she flung her arms about his neck.

"Oh, Brandon, it was horrible! He took Beau and I
couldn't reach him and I ran and ran. It was horrible!"

She shuddered in the arms that held her. He was kissing her hair, her wet cheeks and the long lashes that were
salty with tears. She quieted in his embrace and felt secure again, knowing Brandon was there. When several
moments later his lips traveled down her throat to her
breasts, she became possessed by a different sort of emotion. She groaned with pleasure as his hands moved over
her body, slipping over her limbs as softly as a butterfly's
touch and sliding between as smoothly as the flight of
those winged wraiths. He was slow and deliberate in his
caresses, making her forget everything but the two of
them, until she writhed within his arms and pleaded with
him to take her without delay. But he proceeded at a
studiedly measured pace, sending her emotions, inflamed
and thrilling, spiraling upward. Her passion mounted until she became like a wild thing, quivering, biting, clawing at him. Yet he only laughed, the sound swirling above
their heads and mingling with her purring sighs, and nib-
bled with his teeth at her throat, the silky flesh beneath
her breasts, the smooth, flat belly and a shapely thigh.
She shivered with the passion he evoked as her hand
moved downward and closed over him. He shuddered

and took her fiercely, carrying her with him to frenzied, breathtaking heights that finally burst around them, shading them both in warm contentment.

The following afternoon Heather could be found in the drawing room helping Hatti polish furniture and looking every bit like a servant girl in kerchief and apron. George was seated upon the floor entertaining Beau who had crawled onto his lap and was chuckling at the old man's efforts. Brandon and Jeff had gone to Charleston on business and most of the household staff was busy with some task or another.

All day Heather had thought of nothing else but Thomas Hint and of what would happen to her if he spoke of her sins. When she heard a horse gallop up the drive, she knew without a doubt it was he, and fear mounted tenfold.

"Show him in, Joseph," she told the servant nervously when he told her a man wished to speak with the mistress of the house.

She rose from the floor where she had been kneeling at her task but left her apron and kerchief in place. A spark of surprise shown in Mr. Hint's eyes when he saw her so attired.

"You may go, George, Hatti," she managed.

They both frowned at the visitor and seemed reluctant to leave her with such an evil-looking man, but they did as they were told and left the room.

"What do you want?" Heather questioned when she was sure both were well out of hearing range.

"Done very well for yourself since we last met, haven't you? Though the apron, it gave me a start. I thought you ladies of wealth never dirtied your little white hands."

Heather straightened her spine. "I often help clean this home, sir. It is my husband's and I enjoy seeing it at its best for him."

"Ah-h, I see you've fallen in love with the bloke. Is

that his babe you have there or my dear departed employer's?''

Heather snatched up Beau from the floor and held him tightly to her. "He is my husband's child," she snapped. "William never touched me!"

"Aye, I can well believe that, I can. You killed Willy 'fore he could do harm to you. But the babe be a bit old for you to have waited too long to get caught with him." His eyes dropped to Beau. "But I can see now that the man you were with last night be the child's father. 'Tis no mistakin' the look of the gentry nor the handsomeness of your spouse. I figure you met him in London shortly after you did poor Willy in.''

"You've not come to discuss my baby nor my husband, Mr. Hint, so will you please tell me why you have come. My husband is not at all fond of me entertaining strange men in his absence."

The man made his grotesque substitute for a smile. "Do you think your man would be jealous of me, Mistress Birmingham? Nay, I wouldn't think it, but then he might 'come suspicious of why you're seeing such an ugly toad as me.'' He gave her a look askance. "Now I've known you to be the one what killed poor Willy but I've said naught to no man. 'Tis clear my holding my say has to make me a few shillings, eh, Mistress Birmingham?''

Heather trembled before his cold, calcuating look. "What do you want?"

"Just a few pounds now and then to keep myself cozy and content. I've a nice shop in Charleston now, but I'm a greedy man, liking what the rich do. A few of your jewels would do nicely or perhaps a nice sum of money. Your man is wealthy so I hear. He can afford it."

"My husband knows nothing of this," she snapped. "And I didn't kill William. He fell on the knife."

Mr. Hint shook his head sorrowfully, feigning sympathy. "I am sorry, Mistress Birmingham, but by any chance, did anyone see him fall 'sides you?"

"No, no one was there to see it but me. I have no proof."

He stepped closer to her and she became aware of a strong odor of cologne that seemed strangely familiar to her. She couldn't place when or where but it had left an impression associated with overwhelming fear that she remembered and felt now. She stepped back, clutching Beau to her tightly. The baby let out a squeal of protest at being squeezed so. Thomas Hint laughed and ran a clawlike hand over his mouth. It gave Heather quite a start to see his hands and realize they were no different from those of her dream.

"I have no money!" she whispered hoarsely. "I never have any need for it. My husband has always seen to my wants."

"Your man takes good care of you, eh? Would he pay to keep you from being hanged for murder?" he snarled.

Heather flinched. She could not let him tell Brandon whatever she did. "I have a few jewels. I can let you have them."

Mr. Hint sighed with pleasure. "Ah-h, that's more like it. What do you have? You wore some nice ones last night. Get them and what else you have, then I'll tell you whether they'll do or not."

"You want them now?" she asked uncertainly.

"Aye, I'll not be leaving without them."

She sidled around him cautiously and hurried from the room to quickly mount the stairs. She left Beau crying in disappointment in the nursery under Mary's care and ran to the master bedroom where she threw open her jewelry case and snatched up the emerald pin and pearl necklace Brandon had given her and the diamond earrings that had belonged to the former mistress of Harthaven. She left the bulk of the jewelry untouched, feeling guilty at having to take the earrings. She couldn't bring herself to give away any more of what had belonged to Brandon's mother, knowing how fond he had been of her. The pain of parting with her own gifts was deep. She remembered too well when Brandon had given the pieces to her. She was not likely to forget even when she no longer had them to remind her, and Brandon would surely notice when she no longer wore the pearls. They were her favorite and she had worn them often. She brushed the tears from her cheeks as she dropped the items in her apron pocket and releasing a deep sigh, opened the door.

Mr. Hint was waiting patiently for her, seeming at ease in his blackmailing schemes, and when she held out the pieces, he smiled and took them greedily.

"Aye, these will do nicely—for now. Are you sure they're all you have?"

She nodded.

"Not as much as I be thinkin' you wealthy people had."

"That's all I have," she cried, tears springing forth again.

"Nay, madam, do not upset yerself. And don't you worry that I should talk freely of your deeds. I'll be needing more trinkets."

"But I have nothing more!"

"You best be getting more before I need them," he threatened.

"Please go now," she pleaded tearfully, "before my husband returns. He's not a man I can hide things from, and if he sees you, he'll want to know why you've come."

"Aye, my face is not for the likes of a lady's parlor," he smiled bitterly.

He gave her a distorted bow, then left without a backward glance, and Heather sank wearily into a chair and in part misery, part relief, sobbed into her hands.

He would take all her possessions—except for the ones she valued above all—Brandon and Beau. But when she could no longer meet his demands, what would he do? Turn to Brandon then and tell him his tale? She shuddered as fear rose anew. She couldn't let that happen.

She must keep him satisfied above all so she could go on living—and loving.

Mr. Hint swung down from his horse and limped to tie the reins to the hitching post before his shop. He patted the jewel-filled pocket, feeling extremely pleased with himself. He had made a goodly sum this day with no work involved.

Wiping his drooling mouth on his coatsleeve, he opened the door to his shop, entered and turned to close it. He froze with a start as Brandon Birmingham removed his hat and greeted him from just outside the doorway of his shop.

"Mr. Hint, we had a brief meeting last night at the Dock Street Theatre, if you'll remember."

"Aye," Thomas Hint choked, nervously clutching the pocket of his coat.

"May I come in?" Brandon inquired. "There is a matter I wish to speak with you about."

"Speak with me, sir?"

Brandon strode past him into the shop, standing a good head and shoulders above the man. Mr. Hint swallowed hard and closed the door behind him.

"It has come to my attention that you possess the original of the gown Miss Wells wore last night. I'd like to see it, sir."

Mr. Hint almost breathed a sigh of relief. "Aye, sir. One moment," and he hobbled off toward the back of his shop. He was back shortly, placing the gown in Brandon's hands.

"I bought it from a bartering man some few months back, sir," he was careful to explain.

"I know," Brandon replied. "How much?"

"How much what, sir?" Mr. Hint started.

"How much are you asking for the gown? I desire to have it."

"But, guv'na . . ."

"Name your price," Brandon directed.

Mr. Hint dared not hesitate and spoke the first figure that came to his head. "Three pounds—ah, sixpence, sir."

Brandon raised an eyebrow questioningly as he fished into his pocket for the necessary coins. "I find it hard to believe you procured this so cheaply from the drummer, Mr. Hint."

The cripple realized his mistake and stuttered a reply. "It's your lady, guv'na. With her beauty she's the only one what can do justice to the garment. It's like a gift I'm giving her, a fellow countryman, sir."

Brandon gave the man a careful scrutiny. "You've not been here much longer than my wife, have you, Mr. Hint? A month longer, perhaps two? She . . ."

"Nearly four, sir," the cripple returned, then bit his lip.

Brandon paid close attention to the bead work on the gown's bodice. "Then you know when my wife arrived."

Mr. Hint wiped his perspiring brow. "Louisa, Miss Wells, mentioned it last night, sir."

"You must have left London about the time I met my wife," Brandon pondered.

"Could be, sir," Mr. Hint strangled out.

"Why did you leave London, Mr. Hint?"

The man went pale. "My employer died, sir, and I lost me work, so I took the few shillings I saved, sir, and come here."

"You seem to be very talented in your profession, Mr. Hint. Miss Louisa has commented to that effect."

"I try hard, sir."

"I'm sure that you do," Brandon replied, then handed the man the gown. "Would you mind wrapping this for me?"

Mr. Hint almost smiled. "Be happy to, guv'na."

Brandon strode into the drawing room of Harthaven and found Heather down on her knees polishing the legs of a table. On the floor beside her Beau played with a brightly colored ball, babbling sounds that only he could possibly know the meaning of. Brandon cleared his throat and Heather turned and with a glad cry leapt to her feet and flew into his arms. He laughed with pleasure as she embraced him fiercely and lifting her feet clear of the floor, swung her about in gay abandon. When he set her down again, she grinned up at him with bright eyes, straightening her kerchief and apron.

"My Lord," he swore, dropping his hands on his hips. "You don't look old enough to share my bed. Four and ten would be my guess. You couldn't be the same wench who threatened to wake the household last night while having her pleasure. Could it have been a witch who stole into my bed and clawed and bit at me?"

She blushed and looked at him uncertainly. "You don't think Jeff heard, do you? I'd never be able to face him if I thought he did."

The corner of Brandon's mouth curved upward devilishly. "If he did, I'm sure the sound was not unfamiliar to him, so he'll not speak of it, being the gentleman he is. But you have little to fear, my sweet. What escaped my kisses was hardly much more than purrs of contentment."

She laughed in relief and came into his arms again. "You make me forget myself, Brandon. And after a night like that I have trouble coming down to earth."

He kissed her brow and smiled. "Complaining, sweet?"

"Never," she sighed. After a moment she raised her head from his chest and caressed his beard with gentle fingers. "It's always an adventure going to bed with you."

He chuckled and stepped away from her into the hall. He returned with a package and placed it in her hands.

"This belongs to you and if you ever want to get rid of it again, burn it or cut it to ribbons, but don't barter it away so someone like Louisa, who has a damnable

way of irritating me beyond reason, can take it and make
a copy of it again. I remember too well the sight of you
in it, and I don't want another bitch ruining what was to
me a very sweet and glorious memory.''

The color drained from Heather's cheeks. ''You
bought my gown from Mr. Hint?''

''Aye,'' Brandon returned. ''I couldn't bear the
thought of another woman trying to wiggle into it.''

She smiled softly in relief. He had spoken with Mr.
Hint and the man had kept his word. Standing on her
toes, she gently kissed him.

''Thank you, my darling. I'll treasure it as much as I
do my wedding gown and on special evenings I'll wear
it for you.''

Almost a week had passed when Louisa came by one
evening unexpectedly. Jeff had gone to visit friends and
hadn't yet returned, and the remaining Birminghams
were spending a quiet evening together in the drawing
room. Heather was sitting on the floor at Brandon's feet
and had just finished nursing Beau who at the moment
was in his father's lap enjoying his parents' attention.
Heather's arm rested intimately between Brandon's
thighs as she played with her son, and she had not yet
taken the trouble to fasten her gown, feeling secure behind closed doors, but those portals did not stop Louisa's
entry when she swept past Joseph at the front door and
barged into the room.

Heather turned with a start, looking around, and Brandon glanced up. At sight of Louisa, he scowled blackly
and contemplated what pleasure he would gain from
wringing her neck. He would be damned before he'd
show her the common courtesy of rising when she entered.

''You seem to enjoy bursting in on people, Louisa,''
he muttered.

Louisa took in the scene with a snide smile and looked
pointedly at Heather's arm and the parted low-cut gown.

Brandon watched her perusal of his wife and remembered, thinking of one of the last times he watched Louisa stroll naked across a room, that she had begun to lose the firmness of figure which fades from every woman as she ripens with age. In Louisa it was becoming apparent in her slightly broadening hips and her less than firm breasts. If she had one whit of sense, she'd have blushed in embarrassment instead of looking at his wife with mockery.

Stubbornly, Heather refused to move her arm or fasten her gown under the woman's superior smile. Louisa's gloating expression infuriated her, and she found displeasure in the fact that the blonde was exceptionally well garmented in a yellow muslin gown that was no doubt one of Mr. Hint's creations. It seemed the man was a capable artisan, yet it was difficult to imagine one so hideous creating something so lovely to look upon. She wondered if the man had created those other gowns William Court had claimed as his own. It was something to think about.

Louisa paused for a moment, standing above them with her feet spread, arms akimbo. She smiled.

"Such a quaint little family circle. The more I see of you, Brandon, the more I think marriage does agree with you. *You* appear to be a perfect father and husband."

Brandon raised an eyebrow at her, but she turned away, removing her gloves and hat, carelessly tossing the dusty articles onto a polished table and took a seat facing him. With a casual hardness in her voice she spoke to Heather.

"Will you get me a drink, child? A little Madeira if it's cool."

Flushing angrily, Heather rose to her feet and went to the bar, jerking her bodice together and fastening it.

Louisa went on, speaking again to Brandon. "I acquired such a thirst on that dusty old ride from Charleston, and I do so enjoy your good wines, darling. It's so difficult to get them in town these days, and I've quite exhausted the supply you gave me.''

Brandon sat playing with Beau, who seemingly had lost the spirit of fun since Louisa's arrival, casting wary glances toward her; he wondered what had brought her this time. Heather returned and thrust a glass into Louisa's hand. Again the hard, impersonal tone was in the woman's voice as she spoke.

''Thank you. And would you leave us for a while. There's some business I wish to discuss with your husband.''

The last word seemed forced and Heather hurried to Brandon, biting a trembling lip, and reached to take Beau from his lap. Anger flared in her husband's face, and he caught her arm and looked past her to the other woman. His jaw tightened and he opened his mouth to retort, but tears flooded from Heather's eyes and she shook her head furiously, raised Beau and hiding her face against him, hurried from the room. She fled into the study to quiet her son, who had begun to whimper when he was taken from his father's arms, and wiped the tears from her face.

Brandon now looked at Louisa with a coldness in his eyes, knowing her crude manner had deeply injured his wife. ''Now, Louisa, what is your business?'' he ground out.

Her mouth curved into a slow, confident smile. ''I met an old friend of yours in Charleston this afternoon, Brandon.''

He raised a disinterested eyebrow. ''Who?''

''Well,'' she laughed, ''he's not really an old friend—just an old shiphand. I knew him right off as one of your men from the *Fleetwood* when my carriage passed him. Poor soul, he was completely out of his wits with drink, but he recognized me just the same as being a close friend of yours. He was very helpful.''

''Helpful? In what way?''

She threw back her head and laughed gaily. ''Really, Brandon, I never dreamed that you of all people would let yourself get caught like that—and by a conniving little prostitute, too. I swear I'd have tried that ages ago if I'd have thought it would have worked.''

"What in the hell are you talking about, Louisa?" Brandon demanded.

"Why—you know, darling. Heather, your sweet, innocent little Heather, a prostitute. Dickie told me everything—how he and George found her walking the streets selling her wares, how you were forced into marriage with her, everything.''

"Obviously not everything," Brandon growled. He got up and poured himself a stiff drink.

Louisa continued on happily. "I know you don't care about Heather, darling. There have been so many rumors about separate bedrooms. I didn't need anyone to tell me how you felt about her. I just couldn't understand why you had married her. But this afternoon—this afternoon when Dickie told me, I knew for sure your marriage was just a front. Now you can send Heather away, send her back to England. I can forgive you for that little escapade in London and take you back. We can be happy. I know we can. I'll take care of your son, for there is no doubt he is yours—luckily. I'll love him and be good to him. Everyone will understand when we tell them how you were forced to marry her.''

Brandon stared at her for a moment in amazement and then began to speak slowly but very carefully.

"Louisa, listen very carefully to what I say, for if you do not believe me, you are a fool. If you think that anyone could force me against my will into marriage or any other contract, you do not know me at all. Now believe this,'' and he spoke carefully, "as if your life depended upon it, for it does. My wife was no prostitute nor a streetwalker. She was a virgin the first night I took her and George will vouch for that. The child is mine. She is my wife by my consent and I will not again endure your rudeness to her in this house. From this moment on, you will treat her with all the respect due the mistress of

Harthaven. You have no further claim upon me, this house or my property.''

Louisa rose from her chair and poured herself another glass of wine. She stood before him and as she sipped, stared at him over the rim.

"So you choose that child over me," she half sneered.

Brandon smiled tolerantly. "The choice was made long ago, Louisa. I only reaffirm it now."

Her eyes grew narrow and she turned away for a moment to stare out the window. Suddenly she whirled to him again.

"Strange, Brandon, that you should be the one to speak of respect and property in the same breath." She sipped the wine and strolled across the room, placing the settee between them. She rested her free hand upon its back and half lifted the glass, almost as if in toast. "That is what I came to talk to you about, really. I've reconsidered and think my property is worth twice what you paid for it."

She paused and watched him narrowly, waiting for his reaction. His brow darkened somewhat, but he shrugged.

"We made a bargain, Louisa, and it's over—signed, sealed and delivered. You have no property but Oakley and the few acres it stands on. It's done with!"

"Done with, indeed!" she spat. "Then let's talk of respect. How much respect do you think you and your child bride will merit when I let it be known that you were trapped into marriage by a common whore off the streets?"

Brandon's voice rang through the house. "Shut your mouth, bitch! I will not have you slander my wife in her own house!" His voice lowered to a raging snarl. "I do not care what you do outside this house. Say what you will. No man or woman will dare stand up to me and repeat what trash you might spill. You are a bitch, Louisa, physically and mentally."

"Bitch is it now?" she screeched. With a backhanded motion she tossed the wine in his face and smashed the glass against the floor. "Bitch, indeed! I was a virgin when you took me, begging me to marry you and promising the world and all its trappings if I'd but give you that dearest treasure. Then you sailed off and wed the first driveling wench you could pick off the streets and then came dragging her back as your wife. You pledged your troth to me, took my maidenhood and then my lands for a tuppence. Well, I want more." She began to simper and her voice became wheedling and cajoling. "I must have more, Brandon. I had to pay my bills with the other and have only the house left and I can't sell it. Why, I'd starve but for the few pennies I manage to earn. No one will advance me credit since you've thrown me down."

Brandon raged and fought with himself to keep from striking her. He wiped his hand across his face.

"*Virgin!* Lord, all Mighty! You were no more a virgin than that ancient cow in the pasture out this window. Do you take me for a fool? Do you think me dumb and blind that I believed your half-witted play that night? I could not name in the next fortnight the men I know you bedded before and after that so called sacred engagement!" His voice made the walls tremble. "What simple idiocy makes you dream that I will stand and abide the slander of my own beloved?"

"You loved me once!" she screamed. "And you do not sleep with her. The very streets have whispered this fact. It's common knowledge. Why her and not me? I could share your bed and make you forget she ever lived. Try me. Take me. My God, you loved me once!"

"Loved you!" His laughter rang loud. "No! I only tolerated you and like a lad I thought I knew all my mind could want until I faced a truth and saw a beauty never seen before and then I knew what things I really wanted. Beauty? True. Passion? True." He bent close to her face and emphasized each word. "But also loving gentle kind devotion, unquestioning loyalty and a simple honest dignity for my name that lies well beyond your ability to give." His voice rose again. "I love her with every mo-

ment of my being. I give her my protection from the
street-born sluts that would tear her down and falsify her
virtue. With God's good grace we'll foster many sons
and daughters so do not hang your hopes upon that lie
and do not speak to me again of what you would do to
drag her down with you.'' He stepped to the table and
took up Louisa's hat and gloves and flung them in her
face. ''Now take your moldy presence from this home
and keep the stench of your disappointment from its door,
and never once let me hear a lie that I attribute to your
lips or I shall take great pleasure in wringing that dimpled
neck you prize so highly. Now get out of here, bitch.
You've abused the common courtesies and are no longer
welcome in this house.''

Louisa trembled before Brandon's flashing eyes and
found no further words to speak. Taking her hat and
gloves, she applied her energies to the indicated departure
and stalked out of the room, white lipped and with down
cast eyes, brushing hastily past Jeff who had stood for
some moments listening, awed at this rare display of violent temper directed at a woman by his brother.

She marched out onto the porch and down the steps,
and lifting her skirts high, climbed unceremoniously into
the carriage without assistance, failing to notice George
who leaned against a pillar and calmly spat in the dust
behind her.

As Louisa's carriage rumbled away, Heather came to
the study door and gazed across the hall to her husband.
He still stood with clenched fists and vibrating cheek, but
when he felt her eyes on him, his expression softened
and he turned to her, holding up an arm invitingly. Carrying Beau, she came quickly and was enfolded in his loving embrace.

Wiping her hands on her apron, Heather came from the
cookhouse, having had a delightful hour helping Cora
make bread. She glanced up as a horse came charging
through the gate and smiled as Jeff flung himself down

from the frothy, laboring beast and ran to her. The look on his face quickly squelched the greeting she was about to give and replaced it with cold apprehension.

"Where's Brandon?" he asked curtly.

"Why, I thought he was with you in the fields."

He jerked his finger and pointed near the stable where a boy was brushing Leopold down. The stallion was no better off than Jeff's buckskin. Both had been ridden hard.

"I didn't hear him come home," she tried to explain in her confusion but he was already running for the house. She caught up her skirts and started after him. "Jeff, what's wrong? What's the matter?"

He turned and a strange mixture of emotions crossed his face, upsetting her more than any words could. She grabbed at his arms.

"Jeff, will you tell me what's wrong?" she cried. In her frightened state she dug her nails into his arm but he took no notice, oblivious to pain, and she shook him as hard as she could shake a man who stood head and shoulders above her. "Jeff, tell me!" she screamed.

He seemed unable to speak for a moment, then he told her. "Louisa's dead, Heather. Someone murdered her."

She stepped back, pressing the back of her hand to her mouth. She shook her head disbelievingly.

"It's true. Someone strangled her, broke her neck."

"Why do you want to know where Brandon is?" she demanded.

He seemed reluctant to reply.

"Jeff!"

"I saw Brandon run out of Oakley. He didn't see me riding up and when I went in to see Louisa, I found her dead."

Heather almost strangled on a denial. "No!" She backed away, an accusing glare coming into her eyes. "He didn't do it. He couldn't have! He didn't, Jeff, he didn't! How can you even think it?"

"Do you think I want to believe it? I saw him,

Heather, and we both heard him threaten her yesterday.''

"But why was he there?''

He glanced away.

"Jeff, answer me,'' she demanded. "I have a right to know.''

He released a weary wigh. "Louisa sent him a note while we were out in the fields. It said that she knew something about you he should know. I tried to stop him, but he knocked me down and vowed to close her filthy mouth for good. Lulu brought him the note and he scared her plenty. She took off like a scalded dog, though I swear she was shaking like a leaf before she handed the damned thing to him. When I got to Louisa's, the damage was done. He came tearing out of that house like the devil was after him, and Louisa's stable hand, Jacob, saw him too and now that good man has gone to fetch the sheriff.''

Heather's mind whirled in confusion. A note? A note about her? What more could Louisa have told him?

She gasped audibly as she thought of Mr. Hint and his association with the woman. If he had told Louisa about William Court she would have tried to tell Brandon. Possibly in blind fury, he might have killed her. He had threatened her last night. . . .

No! She couldn't believe him capable of such a crime.

"No! He didn't do it! I just know he didn't!'' she said stubbornly, shaking her head furiously. "He is my husband! Wouldn't I know whether he was capable of that or not?''

"Lord, Heather,'' Jeff groaned, tormented that he should be the one to accuse his brother. He pulled her to him, crushing her against him. "Baby, don't you know I want to be wrong? I love him too. He's my own flesh and blood—my brother!''

Her firm resolve only tormented him more. Abruptly he whirled from her and ran toward the house and she followed. They went through it, Jeff frantically trying to convince himself that he was mistaken, Heather determined that he was, until he reached their bedroom door and flung it open. She came to his side when he made no move to enter and saw Brandon gazing out the open window overlooking the yard where they had just been. With a cry, she ran toward him and he turned and caught her tightly to him.

"Tell him, Brandon!" she commanded, clinging desperately to him. "Tell him you didn't do it!"

"My sweet," he murmured softly.

Jeff came forward, afraid to ask and have it confirmed. Brandon looked at him and smiled sadly.

"Do you think I killed her, Jeff?"

"Oh God, Bran," Jeff choked, shaking his head. His torment was deep. "I don't want to believe it, but I saw you leave her house and when I went in I found her dead. What am I supposed to believe?"

Brandon smoothed Heather's hair under his hand. "Would you believe me, Jeff, if I told you I had nothing to do with murdering her—that she was already dead when I got there?"

"Bran, you know I'll believe whatever you tell me. But if you didn't murder her, who did?"

The older brother sighed. "Why would anyone rape Louisa, Jeff?"

Heather gasped.

"Rape?" the younger brother started.

"You didn't notice?" Bandon smiled.

"She was raped!" Jeff asked incredulously. "But who would have raped her? She gave it away free."

"Exactly."

"My Lord, I really didn't think of that," Jeff admitted. He slid into a chair and stared at nothing in particular, reflecting upon what he had seen. After a long moment, he rose again and walked to the window near them to gaze out toward distant trees swaying in a strong breeze.

"It must have been as you say," he murmured thoughtfully. "When I first saw her—the room torn apart, her clothes ripped from her. I just thought that you had fought with her. Rape didn't enter my mind. You wouldn't have . . ." He blushed and glanced at Heather and found her listening calmly. "You wouldn't have bothered her that way," he continued, turning back. "And as I think back I agree with you that she had been forced into the act. The way she lay, she looked as if the man had just left her. Undoubtedly she was killed while they were still engaged. But who would she have refused so violently?"

Brandon's gaze shifted again to the window. "Jeff, I want to talk to Lulu. Can you get her for me?"

The younger brother nodded. "You know something then?"

Brandon shrugged. "I may. I'm not sure. I must talk to the girl before I can say."

Jeff smiled, no longer uncertain of his brother's innocence. "I'll go find her. You'd better have some facts before Townsend gets here."

When he was gone, Brandon lifted Heather's chin and looked into her eyes.

"Thank you for believing in me," he murmured.

"I wouldn't be much of a wife if I didn't believe in you," she returned softly, caressing his cheek.

He drew away from her and turned his back. "I'm not so sure I wouldn't have killed her, Heather, had I gotten to her first. I was in such a damnable temper I knocked Jeff down when he tried to stop me. I wanted to kill her when I read her note. When I saw her lying on the floor, the clothes ripped from that body she thought so highly of, I realized how close I had come to taking her life. It scared the hell out of me when I thought of what I almost did to us." He turned back to her. "You see, it didn't matter that she was dead. There was no grief in me for her loss of life. I just felt relief at being rid of her and not having to be hanged for the deed. But, Heather, I could have killed her if . . ."

"Oh, my darling," she choked, flinging her arms about his neck. "Perhaps you were angry, but nothing in this world can make me believe that you would have committed such an act. It's just not in you.''

He held her to him, his arms crushed about her slender waist, and found solace in her steadfast faith.

"Oh, Heather, Heather," he murmured. "I love you so much. I need you. I want you always."

Joyful tears brightened her eyes as she clung to him. It was so good to be loved by him.

Brandon breathed in the dewy fresh smell of her and the fragrance of her hair, and his eyes dropped to the hand he had clenched behind her back. His fingers relaxed slowly and there in his palm was one of Catherine Birmingham's diamond earrings.

Sheriff Townsend came and arrested Brandon that night. There was no talking to the man. He was convinced that he had his man and didn't waste time in discussing the matter with them. He told Brandon he was under arrest as soon as he entered the house and fifteen minutes later they were on their way to Charleston, accompanied by two deputies.

Heather was left fretting. Brandon had not been able to talk with Lulu. In fact, the girl could not be found. She had disappeared. No one could remember seeing her after she fled from the fields. The few slaves at Oakley were keeping well away from the big house and safe in their own cabins, preferring to know nothing of the comings and goings that went on there as Louisa's body was prepared for the journey to Charleston the following morning, thus they could not say if Lulu had returned at any time. Jeff sent several men to comb the countryside while he and George rode to the city, but they failed to find any trace of the girl in either place.

In the late hours, Heather paced the floor of their bedroom, feeling the loneliness of the room without Brandon there, and she wondered about his comfort. Sheriff Townsend had been so bullheadedly stubborn, not listening to her pleas or Brandon's reasoning, he might even be treating her husband now as if he were already condemned. She shuddered at the thought and went to the window where she pressed her face against the pane. It was pitch black without and the wind whistled around the corner of the house, leaving the trees astir. It had begun to rain but Heather found no comfort in it, only despair and misery. Wearily she dragged herself to bed and crept between the sheets and stared into the darkness at the white glow of the canopy above her, very much aware of the empty space beside her.

She rose in the morning to the sound of howling wind. Heavy gray clouds raced across the sky pushed by raging gusts and a yellowish light seemed to shroud the land. The rain was moderate but the drops beat hard against the window panes driven by the force of the gale. A storm was brewing.

The day wore on and the rain played havoc with Heather's nerves. Jeff came in once or twice from his search for Lulu, soaked to the bone, and when she gazed questioningly at him, he slowly shook his head. Though no one expressed it, they had begun to despair that something had happened to Lulu too.

It was late afternoon when Heather, no longer able to sit at Harthaven and not help her husband in some way, dressed in riding habit and heavy-hooded cloak and cautiously made her way from her bedroom and down the stairs. She feared that Hatti might see her. It was going to be difficult enough getting James to saddle Lady Fair without an argument, but to let Hatti see her going out in a storm certainly meant having her way blocked by the stubborn Negress.

Her escape was successful and she found James busy putting fresh hay down on the stable floor. He looked up with a start when she opened the door and stared for a moment in surprise as she struggled with the heavy panel, the wind threatening to send her flying if she held onto it for very long. Dropping the pitchfork, he came running to her aid.

"What is you doing out in weather like this, Mrs. Birmingham? You should be in the house, away from all this wind."

"I wish to take Lady Fair out, James. Will you saddle her for me? I've ridden before in the rain so there's no need to worry."

"But, Mrs. Birmingham, this is a bad storm brewing. When it gets like this, shutters fly off houses and trees fall down. It ain't safe. Master Birmingham would skin me alive if he heard I saddled a horse for you in this weather."

"He won't hear about it from me, James. If he finds out, I'll tell him I made you do it. Now hurry and saddle Lady Fair. Lulu must be found so she can tell Sheriff Townsend that Master Birmingham didn't murder Miss Louisa."

His dark, frightened eyes gazed at her as if he would say something more, but she frowned him down.

"If you don't saddle her, James, I will."

He shuffled off, shaking his head, and it seemed like hours before Lady Fair was saddled and ready to go. James checked the girth for the fifth time.

"Mrs. Birmingham, she may be skittish in this storm." His brow creased deeply, betraying his concern. "Ma'am—Mrs. Birmingham, you just can't!"

"Oh hush, James. I've got to go."

He yielded grudgingly and gave her a hand into the saddle. She settled herself and looked down at him. He stood holding her bridle, his eyes wide with fear. The same fear made his lips tremble, and she thought for a moment he might yet hold her there. Finally his hand dropped from the reins, and he turned to open the stable door. She put her heel to the horse and urged her out into the storm. It was as if she had entered a different world. The wind and rain and lightning blended into a fury of confusion. The chestnut paused and snorted, but her thumping heel drove the mare on. Sharp fingers of wind snatched her cloak and the rain soaked her through in a moment. Blinding bolts of brightness rent the heavens above and were quenched in belching peals of thunder.

Heather glanced over her shoulder and saw James braced against the storm, watching her as she rode away. For a brief second she was tempted to turn back and calm his fears—and hers. There was no denying that she was frightened. But the thought of going back passed quickly. If she didn't feel her going was necessary she'd have stayed, but Brandon's life depended upon Lulu being found and what better place to hide in a storm than in her mistress's now deserted house?

Horse and rider entered a forest gone wild. Once lazy branches lashed and stung and whipped and clawed. The trees bent and swayed in what seemed a frenzied determination to snatch her from the horse and failing, moaned their frustration to the wind. The mare slipped and stumbled from side to side on the muddy trail, now slashing her legs in the razor-sharp palmetto, now thrusting away from a thicket of brush. It took all Heather's concentration to cling to the slippery saddle. In desperation she twisted the reins about her fist and buried her face in Lady's mane. The ride became a tiring fight for both horse and rider as they battled the wind and rain, the forest and mud.

The wind seemed to abate and the rain no longer pounded her shoulders. Heather realized the horse now stood still, trembling with fatigue. She raised her face and found they stood in the shelter of the Oakley plantation house. The facade of the manor loomed above her in the storm, palely lit by the gloomy day. She slid from the horse's back and found her legs barely capable of support. She leaned against the steamy warmth of the animal and her strength gradually returned.

With her hopes and fears driving her on, she strode across the portico and entered the ominous structure. She closed the door against the storm and gazed about, doffing muddy boots and soaking cloak. The great house seemed to lean into the wind, of which small wisps crept through each crack in the shutters and stirred curtains and drapes and rattled panes of glass and seemed to set the house in motion. The floors squeaked and popped with the strain, the walls moaned and the shingles fluttered their fear on the roof. Shadows crept about each room and occasionally from somewhere deep in the bowels of the storm-battered house, a door creaked or slammed. The manor seemed to resent her intrusion and wailed its discontent, but her purpose overrode her apprehension. She must assure herself that Lulu was not cowering in some nook or cranny.

She called but received no answer. She searched through each room of the house with a thoroughness born of desperation. The rooms of the first floor were dark. Drapes were pulled over all the windows and there was little light from outside to filter in. Here and there she found a window left gaping. She went about her task, missing no space large enough to conceal a person. Drapes were snatched aside and no door left closed. Her labors warmed her and the chill from the journey left her bones.

She raced up the stairs in an unladylike manner, her skirts raised high above her knees, and pressed her search through the second floor. Here the storm seemed closer. The drafts were chilling and the rain battered with heavy hand upon the roof. Branches slammed against the shutters and set them banging. She flung each door wide and searched beneath each bed. She paused but a moment beside Louisa's bed and realized that here was where Brandon most likely had exercised his manhood on that woman's charms. In a quick, bitchy rage, she tore the satin covers from the bed and trod across them to continue her search.

The house was empty to her efforts. The attic entry was a small ceiling trap door, unattainable without steps or aid. She returned once more to the first level and realizing she had not looked here, entered the drawing room.

Heather drew a deep breath which seemed to freeze in her chest. Draperies were torn from the windows and a chair lay broken in the tangle of its pleats. A small table balanced precariously in front of the fireplace on three legs, the fourth leg missing. A writing desk stood with nothing on top of it; papers, pens and inkwell were scattered on the rug beneath. Several books lay tumbled from the bookcase and those remaining in it were in a sad state of disarray. The room bore evidence of a raging quest as if some object of great concern had gone astray. There was no reason to believe that the object had not been found, yet Heather began to probe the room as only a woman's query can. She had no idea for what she sought. She only knew something might lie here. Her eyes swept the rug and dusted the top of every level surface. Her hands rearranged bric-a-brac and knickknacks, straightened the hangings on the wall, and her fingers tested each crack for what it might contain. The fireplace screen stood slightly ajar and her woman's sense of neatness demanded it be righted. As she moved the screen, a twinkle at its base caught her eye. The object was lodged in a crack between two bricks on the fireplace floor. She bent and gasped.

It was one of Catherine Birmingham's diamond earrings, her own earring, one of the pair she had given Mr. Hint. Picking it up, she stared at it in disbelief.

In her note to Brandon, Louisa had stated her knowledge of some interesting information. And what other secret could the woman have learned except the one concerning William Court? There was no other. But why had Mr. Hint told her? Surely he realized that Brandon would not let her continue to pay blackmail to keep him silent, and if Louisa had knowledge of William's death she would do everything in her power to let Brandon know, for spite if not for another reason. So why had Mr. Hint told Louisa? Why had he given her the earrings? For what reason would he jeopardize a fortune by such a stupid act? Had he fallen in love with the woman and thought to bribe her with these trinkets? That ugly man? Louisa would have laughed in his face.

But was that it? Could he have killed her for laughing—or to insure her silence? Did he have the strength to break her neck with his bare hands? Brandon had such ability, she knew, but could a man almost half his size possess enough power for such a feat?

"Well, if it ain't my good friend, Mistress Birmingham."

Heather whirled in alarm. There was no denying who that high pitched, squeaky voice belonged to. Pure terror gripped her, paralyzed her. Mr. Hint smiled at her and showed a face clawed and bruised.

"Ah-h, I see you've found the earring."

She nodded once slightly, cautiously.

"In the hearth yet," he laughed. "I didn't think of that. Bless you for findin' it for me. I thought it be lost forever."

"Did . . ." She swallowed and began again. "Did you give my earrings to Louisa?"

"Well—not exactly. 'Twas like this, you see. I showed them to her and I promised her a life of ease with me." His mouth tightened hideously. "She seen them though and knowed them as being yours, she did. She would not rest 'til she found out why I had them. Then a queer shine come into her eyes when I told her about poor Willy and she grabbed the earrings in her fist and vowed to have her revenge. She went crazy. I had a hard time understandin' her. She was like a mad woman, one minute laughing, the next crying, all the time screaming what revenge she'd have on you. She vowed to see you hanged. I had to slap her face 'fore she come to her senses again. A cold look came in her eye and she told me what she was going to do. I tried to tell her she was being a fool, that she could have her revenge by the money we took from you. I knowed once your man found out about you there'd be no more jewels for me, you see, and he might kill me to hush my mouth. But she refused to listen. She was wantin' to see you hanged, but first she wanted to tell your man and watch him plead for your life. She sent Lulu to fetch him with that note. The girl seen I was mad and run off quick with the note while Louisa and me was arguing. I tried to reason with Louisa and tell her we could be rich, but she said she wanted to see you hanged. She was all set to tell your man about you and show him the earrings as proof, and she laughed at me and called me an ugly toad—said she'd been leading me on for what I could give her. I made every gown she ever wanted and give them to her without gettin' a farthing, and she called me a swine, a loathsome caricature of a man. I loved her, I did, and she called me that.'' Tears were streaming down his face and he began to sob. ''She hit me too when I told her it was your gown I copied for her and called me worse names that I ever even heard from a man, foul words what tore me insides to pieces. I couldn't help myself My hands reached for her neck without knowing what they were doing. She got panicky and jumped away from me into the drapes, but I caught her in them and dragged her down. I didn't know she had such strength. She kicked me and give me a wallop like a man would. Knocked me off her, she did. I never knowed a woman what was so strong. We had a regular fight as you can see by this room. I had my pleasure on her though, and she had hers. I could tell, her amoaning and moving under me. I be thinking we could still be happy together, but I sees her eyes go narrow when she was through with me. She spit in my face and called me a freak, said I'd be seeing what a real man was when your spouse come. My hands flew round her throat and they squeezed the life from her. I couldn't stop them. I'd just pulled my hands from her when your man come riding up. Furious, he was. Never even stopped to knock on the door. Hardly give me time to get off her and hide.''

''You mean you were here when my husband came?'' Heather choked out.

''Aye. He come a raging in here like the very devil, he did. He scared me good with him being so big and there I was hiding behind the door. Mayhaps it were the shock of seein' his work done that saved me from him. A man what looks the same as your man come in right after he left, and he didn't see me either.''

''Why are you telling me all this, Mr. Hint?'' she asked, already afraid of the answer.

''Why shouldn't I now? You knowed it were me what killed Louisa when you picked up that earring. I'll take it now 'fore it gets lost again.'' He snatched it from her hand and stared for a long time at the piece. ''Louisa told me when I made her gowns that I wasn't a cripple in her eyes. She called me her love and let me touch those white breasts and kiss them. I loved her, I did, and she called me a toad.''

Tears streaked down his ugly face. He looked up at her, his eyes narrowing dangerously.

''She weren't the first woman what I killed for laughing. That dress you wore when you ran from Willy's shop belonged to another what laughed. Willy, the bloke, he thought she never come back 'cause she couldn't afford the gown.'' He laughed wildly. ''She couldn't come back, you see, she was dead. I broke her bloody neck for her like I did Louisa's. I fixed Miss Scott too, for laughing.''

He moved toward Heather menacingly and she was again aware of that strong odor of cologne. She realized what he had just said, and with a start she remembered where she first had a whiff of the cologne. Her eyes flew open wide.

''You were there behind those curtains in William Court's shop! You saw me run out, wearing that gown!''

He smiled his horrible smirk. ''Aye. You never even

glanced back. I should be grateful to you. You made my work easy.''

''Your work?''

''Aye, my work. You really didn't think you killed Willy, did you, with only that little wound you give him? Nay. He only passed out, more from the wine he had than what you done to him.''

''You mean he lives?'' she gasped.

Thomas Hint chuckled as he shook his head negatively. ''Nay, madam. I slit his bloody throat for him, I did. It were easy. All those years I made his gowns for him and the bloke, he told everyone he made them. Why, he couldn't even thread a needle. It were very easy. Only thing—the cook she seen me kill him. She come back to clean up the dishes, and she seen me take me knife to him. I had to leave England 'cause of her. I couldn't get my hands on her neck. She took off like Lulu, scared enough for to die, and I couldn't find her.''

Heather backed to the fireplace, more than stunned. All this time she thought she had killed a man!

''It won't be so easy killin' you, madam. You never really done me no wrong. You never laughed at me like those other women. In a way, you were even kind to me. And you're such a lovely piece. I told Sybil once that some of the most beautiful women in the world had worn my clothes. I was speaking of you when I said it. You were really the only one what did me gowns justice. But now, you'll tell them I killed Louisa to save that man of yours.''

He was moving toward her now, blocking her escape. With her back to the fireplace he could go no further as he reached out for her throat. Seeing those clawlike hands of her dream coming toward her, Heather was possessed with the sudden courage to fight him, no matter what. In a quick eluding movement she darted past. He reached out, catching his hand into the back of her habit, but it ripped away as she leapt from him. He was quick despite his distorted shape and snatched at her skirt as she flew toward the door, closing his hand over a fold. The gown tore again but it held to imprison her. He jerked her back to him with frightening strength and spun her around. His eyes went to the white shoulder emerging from the tattered gown, and his tongue passed over his lips.

"Your skin is like satin. I've a fondness for the sweetness of a woman's flesh. Mayhaps we can delay your—departure—for a few moments," he muttered. With clawlike fingers he reached up and snatched the garment from her bosom. The habit fell away, leaving her clad only in a damp chemise. His eyes seemed to burn through the flimsy material, and his breathing deepened until he panted over her like a hungry dog over a bone. He tore at the garment until not a thread remained to cover her.

Heather screamed and strained against him, pushing at his chest, but he was strong despite his size and only laughed at her pitiful struggles.

"You've not half the strength Louisa had."

He crushed her to him, making her arch away in disgust, and covered her neck and breasts with loathsome kisses. Then, as viciously as if he were a mad dog, he sank his teeth into her shoulder. A scream tore itself from Heather's throat and her head rolled limply with the agony. Sobbing, she felt his mouth move downward toward her breast and realized he was going to bite her again. He had her bent so far backward she was sure she was the only thing bracing him. Suddenly she remembered when once before she had been bent against her will. She had sent William Court sprawling because she sank to the floor. She had no time to wonder if it might work again. Without giving him any warning, she picked up her feet. Immediately she felt both of them begin to fall. He let go of her in an effort to break his fall. She hit the floor first and rolled away from him and was on her feet in an instant and moving. He reached out a long arm and grabbed at her but his hand only brushed her thigh. She was running now, fiercely, toward the stairs, not looking back. She knew he was already on his feet, and she hoped the stairs would slow him down. Her breath came in quick gasps, and she forced every bit of strength she possessed into her legs to propel herself up the stairs. At the top, she glanced around. He was at the bottom steps, coming up fast, and now in each hand was a pistol.

With a cry, she turned and darted into the first room she came to. She ran through it to an adjoining bedroom, closing the doors noiselessly behind her. It was only when she reached the last room on that side of the hall that she stopped. She could go no further without entering the hall, and there his footsteps could be heard, soft and hesitant; he was wondering where she was.

Heather closed her eyes and tried to slow the fast beat of her heart. It was like a drum in her ears, making it almost impossible to hear the direction he took in his search for her. It was doubly hard over the noise of the storm outside. Quivering, she sank against the wall and touched her shoulder where the marks of his teeth branded her skin. If he caught her, he would not cease until he had torn her body to shreds with those cruel teeth, and she wondered if Sybil and Louisa had had to contend with that torture. He had raped both women and now was after her. A sudden flash of memory made a vision loom up before her of a dark, sinister figure on horseback, coming—coming toward her, swathed in a black cloak. But this time its face was visible. It was Mr. Hint's.

Heather threw her arm over her face to shut out the aberration. It was too horrible. He was too horrible. God grant her death before he used her for his pleasure!

She shivered as she stood huddled against the wall. Without her clothes, the drafts from the vibrating shutters seemed twice as chilling. She gazed down at her nakedness and bit into her lip. She longed to look for clothes in the wardrobe beside her but couldn't chance the slightest sound.

From somewhere in the bedrooms down the hall she heard him slamming wardrobe doors open and throwing furniture about. She would wait until he came into the room next to the one she was in before she made her move. If she could manage to slip by the door without being detected, she could make it to the stairs without much effort and slip away from him. Her cloak was in the hall. If she could snatch it up before he realized she was escaping. . . . But her life was more valuable than her modesty. Oh, pray, if she could just escape him!

With a start, she realized he had come into the adjoining room. Quietly, so as not to make a sound, she turned the knob on the hall door, keeping a wary eye on the door between the two rooms. Without glancing into the hall, she slipped out and pulled the door closed without a sound. She stepped backward a couple of paces, then spun around to run past the room he was in.

She screamed and died a thousand deaths as she felt a man's arms close about her.

"Heather!" Brandon cried, alarmed. His eyes went down her naked body.

With a half-choked sob, she fell against his chest, not even asking what miracle had brought him from jail to her side. He was soaking wet from the storm, but it was a nice, secure dampness. Then she heard footsteps running and knew Thomas Hint was after her again. Her heart in her throat, she tugged at her husband.

"Oh, Brandon, hurry! He has pistols."

Brandon's face was pale. "Has he hurt you, Heather?"

She had no time to reply. She knew his meaning, yet she could not pause to reassure him. She pulled him into a room across the hall and was just closing the door when Mr. Hint opened his and looked out. He saw her immediately and lifted the pistol. For a second she stood petrified and the shot exploded. The ball drove into the door by her ear, splintering the heavy wood, and shaken, she slammed it closed.

Brandon didn't stop to ask questions. The shot had been too close to his wife for comfort. He jerked Heather behind him as he pressed himself against the wall by the door. The knob turned as he stood tensed beside it. The door swung open and Mr. Hint barged through. Brandon raised his arm and brought it crashing down on the man's wrist, sending one pistol crashing to the floor. Mr. Hint jerked around, completely startled. It was apparent from the surprise on his face that he hadn't known of Brandon's presence before he entered the room. It came as a shock for him to find that he wasn't just pursuing a helpless woman any longer but her husband as well, and that husband was far from helpless. Mr. Hint saw the fist coming and dodged to the side, but not completely out of its path. The fist grazed his cheek, less than the total force of the power behind it, yet it knocked him backward against the wall. Dazed, he managed to raise the pistol he still held in his other hand until it was pointed at Brandon's midsection. He heard the woman scream.

"You knocked the wrong one out of my hands, Mr. Birmingham. 'Tis a shame, ain't it."

Brandon made a move forward, his expression murderous. Heather screamed again and grabbed his arm, pulling back with all her weight to stop him. She couldn't.

"He didn't harm me, Brandon! I got away in time!" she screeched.

Brandon stopped. He looked down at her and some of the violence seemed to leave his face.

"He killed Louisa," she said.

"Aye, I did," Mr. Hint admitted as he grinned at Brandon. "And I won't think twice 'fore shootin' you. But I have my idea you knows what I did already, don't you?"

"Perhaps," Brandon replied. He stepped back a few paces, pulling Heather with him.

"Aye. I know it for certain. I hear you were asking about me in town. You started nosin' around that day you come to my shop, wantin' to know when I comes from England and what sort of fellow I be. What I wants to know is why."

Brandon grinned leisurely as he pulled his shirt from

his shoulders. "My wife made mention of you several times."

Startled, Heather jerked her head up and looked at him closely. He smiled down at her reassuringly, drawing his shirt around her. But his eyes hardened when they fell on the marks left by Mr. Hint's teeth. His mouth went rigid as he touched the spot and the muscle in his cheek twitched violently.

"Aye. I see you've noticed my brand on your wife. She's a small bit of woman, ain't she? Looks real fetchin' without her clothes," he snickered. "That's a hard thing what to admit for a chap in my profession. But 'tis true. There's no one ever I see what got her beauty. And she's a mite more resourceful than most. Got away from me 'fore I had a taste of her charms. Slippery as an eel, she is."

"You'd be dead now if you had taken her," Brandon growled.

Mr. Hint grinned his horrible smirk. "So she told you about me, eh? I didn't figure that. When she run from Willy's shop that night I thought she'd be too frightened to say my name, she a thinking she killed him and all. I didn't figure that she'd talk. But why did she act so frightened when I told her I'd tell you if she didn't buy my silence?"

"I'm afraid my wife knew nothing of what she said to me."

Mr. Hint frowned. "Eh? What's that you say? You don't make sense."

"It's no matter, Mr. Hint. Now if you would be so good as to tell me what my wife gave you, I would be grateful."

"You know what she give me or you know of part of it. I seen you pick up that diamond earring when you stood over Louisa's body." Mr. Hint grinned as Heather gasped and dug in his coat pocket. He brought out the jewels clutched in his hand and displayed them for Brandon. "To satisfy your curiosity, guv'na," he smirked.

"Pretty lot, ain't they? Just like your wife. A pretty thing she is with her silky skin and her black hair. She has teats what I'd wager any man would itch to touch, nice and soft and—"

"Did you also rape and murder Sybil Scott?" Brandon interrupted.

Mr. Hint squinted at him. "Aye, I did. She laughed at me like Louisa. I followed her from Charleston that day and took my pleasure of her in the woods. She weren't nearly so pretty as your wife though."

"You were also in the woods by my mill?"

"Aye. I couldn't hardly help myself that day. I got the feeling in me loins for her what left me aching for a week. When the bartering man sold me that gown, I knew she were here. I tried to find out from him where he got it but he wouldn't say. But in the woods I recognized her right off as being the same little girl what Willy tried to bed. She fooled him too and stuck a knife in him."

"No!" Heather cried. "He fell on the knife when we were struggling."

"Well, she thought him to be dead, but he weren't that is, not 'til I slit his throat."

"You murdered all these people, Mr. Hint, without anyone becoming suspicious of you?" Brandon questioned.

"Aye, and a lot more. I had my time when I had to run from England, but nobody has caught me and nobody were suspicious of me here."

"You must think yourself a very clever person."

"Clever enough to add a few more to my list." He waved the pistol around dangerously. "But I have my wish to please myself with your wife afore your eyes while you still lives. I never had it that way before."

Brandon sneered. "You'll find yourself dead if you lay one finger on her."

Mr. Hint laughed loudly, and his eyes had an unnatural shine to them. "Aye. It'll be most pleasurable. I can just see you now—all trussed up and unable to move while

I have your wife spread on the bed. You'll go mad as you watches me settle myself in her. I'll even make her scream for you everytime I take a bit of her.''

Heather clung to Brandon tightly and buried her face against his chest.

"I'll kill her myself before I'll let you get your slimy hands on her, Mr. Hint,'' Brandon swore. "But you aren't even going to get near her. You'd better take careful aim with that pistol. If you don't kill me with that one shot, you won't live long after you release that hammer.''

He was moving in on the man, pushing Heather behind him.

"Your death can very easily be arranged,'' Mr. Hint warned as he braced himself against the wall. He lifted the pistol until it pointed at Brandon's heart.

With a cry, Heather flung herself in front of Brandon. He tried to push her behind him, but she clung to him fiercely and in her fear for him, her strength exceeded its normal bounds.

"For God's sake, Heather, get out of the way!'' he cried.

"No!'' she said stubbornly. "He only has one shot. He can kill just one of us with it.'' Her voice became pleading. "Let it be me, Brandon. I'd rather die now than have him touch me again. I couldn't bear it.''

"Your wife has a point, guv'na. I can hardly kill you both with one pistol. It'll be interesting to see which one of you I get. You're both so anxious to die for the other.'' He jeered at Brandon. "Now you, guv'na, are a gallant soul. You say you'll kill your wife yourself 'fore I lays a hand on her. What chivalry! A body would gather you think I'm not fit to bed her.''

"You're not fit for her to walk on,'' Brandon sneered. "Do you honestly think that I'm going to let you touch her? I let no man use what is mine, and you, who crawl upon your belly in the mud and slime, think I won't fight heaven and hell to keep her safe from your depravity!''

"You've no choice, guv'na," Mr. Hint smirked. His eyes went over Heather's back. Holding the pistol pointed straight at Brandon's head, he reached for the shirt covering her and snatched it away. He stepped back quickly, grinning as his eyes roamed greedily over her thighs and buttocks. "I likes her better this way."

With a sound close to a growl, Brandon stepped forward, but immediately Mr. Hint's attention was on him.

"Step back or I'll blow your wife's head off with this pistol."

A limb hit the window with the force of the storm outside, shattering the glass and startling Mr. Hint. He looked around in surprise, and Brandon seized his moment. He lunged forward, catching Mr. Hint off guard, but not so much that the man forgot the pistol in his hand. He fired and Heather screamed as Brandon went reeling backward, but he did not fall. He grabbed for his shoulder as blood oozed from the wound down over his arm and chest. He grinned evilly.

Mr. Hint realized his mistake. The man was not dead and he had every assurance that Brandon would keep his word and see to it that life ended for him. He was now the hunted. He had ceased to be the hunter. Terrified, he jumped for the door and was out of it in a flash despite his lameness.

Brandon was after him without a second's hesitation. Heather stood for a moment, dazed and feeling sick. The shock of seeing Brandon reel from the pistol's discharge had almost been too much. She followed out the door, still trembling, in time to see her husband start down the stairs after Mr. Hint. The cripple half fell, half slid down the steps. He glanced back over his shoulder fearfully and she saw froth oozing from his mouth. His tongue flicked vigorously over his fat lips and his eyes were wide with panicking terror. When he reached the bottom level, he turned in circles, not knowing what to do. He glanced down at the pistol he still held in his hand and, realizing it was useless, raised it above his head and flung it at the man coming after him. Brandon ducked and the pistol hit harmlessly behind him. Mr. Hint whirled to run to the door, but Brandon was too quick for him. He leaped from the stairs and flung himself onto the hunchback. They both went crashing to the floor, but Brandon was on his feet instantly, dragging the man to his. With a cruel smile, he sent a fist smashing into Mr. Hint's face. The man flew backward, the blood flying from his face. Brandon picked him up again and slammed him back against the wall with enough force to break the man's back. Mr. Hint screamed. Brandon only looked the meaner and buried his fist into the man's belly. When the cripple doubled over, Brandon brought him up straight again with a vicious blow under his chin. The murderer shrieked and sobbed and pleaded as he tried desperately to free himself, but Brandon had no intention of letting him go.

"You'll not have another chance to sink your teeth into my wife, you slimy bastard!"

Heather was frightened. She had never seen Brandon act so violently. He was not hindered by the wound in his shoulder. He seemed for the moment to have forgotten it. Both men were red with blood, and it was impossible to tell whose blood they wore the most of. It mingled as Brandon continued slashing at Mr. Hint with his fists. Her legs trembled as she crept down the stairs toward them, clutching an arm over her bosom, the other hand down her body.

The man was becoming a bloody pulp, unable to comprehend what was happening to him. He whimpered as Brandon drove in another blow.

Heather could stand no more. She ran to Brandon and grabbed his arm.

"Brandon, stop! You're killing him! For God's sake, stop!"

Brandon, in a daze, turned the man loose and watched him slide to the floor. Mr. Hint groaned and clutched at his middle, but Brandon was no longer interested in him,

and Heather didn't care to see how vicious her husband
could be when he lost his temper. They turned from him
without so much as a pitying glance in his direction. She
began immediately to examine her husband's wound. He
winced slightly as her gentle fingers touched torn flesh.

"We must get you home, Brandon. That ball needs to
be taken out of your shoulder."

He managed a grin. "I'm afraid going home is out of
the question for some time. We'll have to stay here for
the night. The storm makes the journey home unsafe. It
has worsened since I came and probably doubly so since
you ventured out."

"But your shoulder needs tending. And what about
Beau? Who will nurse him?"

He laughed and pulled her to him, unmindful of the
blood he smeared over her breast. "You'll have to tend
my shoulder, sweet, and as for Beau, I sent James to fetch
a wet nurse for him in case we couldn't make it back. A
perfect errand for James since he let you go in the first
place. It was foolhardy for you to leave home in this
storm, Heather, and to go in search of Lulu, doubly so."

"But, Brandon, I couldn't sit there and do nothing to
help," she protested.

They were not aware of the figure behind them creeping toward the door. When a blast of wind and rain hit
them, they both turned with a start to find Mr. Hint going
out. He was dragging himself along, trying to brace
against the wind which was now demoniac in its intensity. Brandon had to struggle against its force to get to
the door. By that time, Mr. Hint was running along the
porch to the side of the house where the horses were tied.
Brandon was not in time to stop him from swinging his
crippled body up onto Leopold's back. He yelled a warning to the man, but his voice was lost in the shriek of
the wind.

Mr. Hint jerked the black horse around, struggling to
keep astride. He was laughing in spite of his unsteady
seat, thinking how he had fooled that giant of a man

behind him. He had taken enough beatings from his father in his youth to toughen his body well against what any mortal man could deal him. He still felt the pain and quivered under the blows, but he was not incapacitated to the point where he could not move. With a hideous peal of laughter he drove his heels into the horse's sides, and the animal lunged away in rage.

Heather was on the front porch, struggling with the wind and rain when he rode past her and down the muddy lane with the large oak limbs whipping dangerously above him. She heard the crack of a limb splitting over the roar of the wind. A torrent of rain drenched her as she fought her way down the front steps against the gale. She became aware of Brandon running past her, his hair plastered to his head, his breeches soaked and clinging to him and the blood from his wound streaming down his body in the rain. He turned to look at her and his mouth moved but no sound could be heard above the storm. He motioned for her to go back into the house. Very near them a bolt of lightning hit and thunder exploded its deafening doom. Another flash tore the sky as Heather turned to see Leopold rear up in fright. Mr. Hint, unable to keep his seat on the slippery saddle, fell as a large limb above him broke its final ties with the tree under the strain of the maniac wind and went hurtling to the ground, crushing him beneath it. Lightning hit somewhere near them and Heather's scream was made soundless by the thunder that followed. She ran toward Brandon, but he was already on the move. He glanced over his shoulder and gestured for her to go back. She stopped and watched as he hurried to Mr. Hint, straining against the wind that tore at him. She saw him reach the cripple and try to lift the limb from him, and when it would not budge, kneel down beside the man. He glanced back, saw her watching and shook his head, and Heather knew by that simple motion that there was no reason to roll the limb from Mr. Hint. He couldn't feel it. Mr. Hint was dead. Justice had been served.

Brandon left the grotesque shape of Mr. Hint under the limb and came at a run toward Heather. Again a bolt of lightning struck nearby as he grabbed her and pulled her along with him to the house.

"Get inside. I've got to put Lady and Mr. Hint's horse in the stable."

"Let me help you. You're in no condition to do it alone."

"No. Now get in there and stay. It won't take me long. Find what you need to care for my shoulder, and I'll let you tend it when I come back."

He thrust her in and pulled the door closed behind her. She hurried off immediately in search of rudiments for tending his wound, finding salve, brandy and clean sheets. She left these upstairs by a bed she made ready, and found several candelabras to place by the bed. Night had descended and except for the flashes of lightning, a deep blackness possessed the mansion. She retrieved Brandon's shirt from the room across the hall and put it on, not wishing to touch a single article of Louisa's clothing.

When Brandon came in, she was waiting anxiously at the front door. The candelabrum she had placed nearby showed her that his face had definitely paled. When he shivered and fell weakly against the door, she hurriedly wrapped him in a cotton quilt. The shot had left no small hole and he seemed now to be in a great deal of pain. She helped him upstairs and down the hall toward the bedroom which she had prepared. When they passed Louisa's room they glanced silently toward the four-poster that was clearly illuminated by the candles Heather had left in her search for scissors. Through his pain Brandon smiled at the satin coverlet heaped on the floor, and Heather dropped her face guiltily and continued on her way with him. When she finally had him by the bed, she reached for the scissors, intent upon snipping his wet breeches off.

"What do you plan for me to wear tomorrow when I

take you home, my dearest?'' he questioned with amusement. ''I assure you I left no breeches behind me when I courted Louisa. Just help me pull them off.''

He dropped a leather pouch on the table beside the bed before giving her assistance. The tight breeches did not come off easily when wet. She gave a deep sigh of accomplishment when he stood relieved of them and hurriedly indicated for him to get in bed. After she had cleansed the wound and examined it gently, she gave him a snifter generously filled with brandy.

''I need no other distraction than what you present for me in my shirt, sweet,'' he teased lightly. ''You're a very fetching healer, and if I drink too much brandy and look at you, I might forget myself and use this bed for something other than sleep.''

She laughed and watched approvingly as he downed the contents. There was adoration in her eyes as she gazed at him and gently she smoothed the wet hair from his brow, her fingers caressingly soft as they moved along his cheek. He looked at her, catching her hand, and pressed it against his lips in an ardent display of affection.

''Brandon,'' she said worriedly. ''I do not possess the strength to hold you, and if I am to remove the ball I must be held still. Jeff needs be here.''

''Do what needs be done, Heather. I will hold still for you. Jeff would have trouble if I cared to move, but for you I will be as still as a grandfather oak.''

He was as good as his word. Sweat broke from his brow, and his mouth and jaw grew rigid, but he did not move once while she probed for the lead ball. Heather showed more pain than he under the circumstances. She clenched her lip tightly between her teeth and knitted her brow and looked as if she might burst into tears if he but groaned.

Finally she located the ball and managed to get a grip on it with the scissors. With sweaty palms she clutched the utensil and pulled the lead out. There was a rush of blood then that soaked through the pads she pressed to the wound. Except for his moist brow, there was no sign of pain on Brandon's face, and she marveled at the control he had over his body. Afterward, when the wound was tightly bandaged, she sat down beside him on the bed and wiped his brow.

"Do you feel like sleeping now?" she asked softly.

He caressed her thigh. "The sight of you banishes all pain and thought of sleep from my mind, my love, and even tempts me to exercise my husbandly rights. I missed you last night, wench."

"Not half so much as I did you," she murmured and placed a warm kiss upon his lips.

He gave her a lusty look that stripped the shirt from her body when she drew back. "It wouldn't hurt my shoulder if you got in bed with me now. I can even hold you if you lie against my good side."

She blew out all but one candle and leaving his shirt on the back of a chair, crept beneath the sheet and snuggled against him, finding the bed a cozy haven with the storm raging outside. She lay quietly for a few moments but her curiosity got the better of her.

"Brandon?"

He dropped a kiss on her brow. "Yes, sweet?"

"Why were you suspicious of Mr. Hint so soon? He said you were asking questions about him the day after we met him at the play. Were you?"

"Yes."

"But why?"

"When you were ill on the voyage from England, you kept repeating things in your delirium. One of those things was Mr. Hint's name. You were obviously frightened of him in your illness, but when I saw at the theatre just how much you really were, I wanted to know more about the man."

She gazed at him thoughtfully. "What else did I say?"

He smiled slowly. "You spoke of your father a great deal, kept mistaking me for him, and of a man named

William Court. What I gathered from your ramblings was that you thought you had killed the man when he tried to rape you. You always spoke his name with Mr. Hint's and expressed fear that the latter would accuse you of murder.''

"You knew of this and yet you didn't tell me?"

"I wanted you to come to me first and trust me to help you."

Heather, swallowed hard, blinking back tears. "I was afraid I would hurt you or even lose you, and I wanted so much to make you happy and not have you ashamed of me."

He smiled tenderly. "Do you think I haven't been happy, and I've known your secret for a long time? You have none from me, you know."

"None?" she inquired gingerly.

"None," he answered flatly. "I even know you wished for a girl to spite me."

She laughed and a light blush spread across her face. "Oh, how horrible, Brandon. And you were so close-mouthed I never even suspected anything. But did you know that Mr. Hint was Sybil's and Louisa's murderer?"

"After I met him I learned that he had been Sybil's couturier, but there was no proof that he was the one who murdered her. When Louisa was killed then I had no doubt, but I needed proof. I was confident Lulu could tell me he had been with Louisa, but Townsend came and arrested me before I could talk to her. Townsend found out Louisa had been paying her bills with money I had given her and suspected that she was blackmailing me for some purpose he thought might pertain to Sybil's death. That's why he was so sure and with a witness who saw me running from her place. . . .''

"Did you tell him of your suspicions?"

"Yes, and when Lulu came to see him of her own accord and told him of Mr. Hint's visit with Louisa, he began to believe me."

"Lulu went to see Townsend?"

"Yes, she crept into the house after she saw Mr. Hint leave and found Louisa. She didn't waste time in making herself scarce until she could get to the sheriff safely."

"That's why you said it was so foolhardy for me to have gone in search for her. She had already given her story to Townsend. I suppose now you think I'm just a brainless child."

"Well—I know you're no child," he teased and then an admonishing tone seeped into his voice. "But I am angry that you gave that scoundrel the jewels which I gave you."

She cast her eyes downward. "I was afraid he would tell you what I had done. And it wouldn't have been right for me to give your mother's jewelry away. I know how fond you were of her. It hurt deeply to part with my own, but it was all I had to give him."

"If you had killed Mr. Court, do you think I would have blamed you? My Lord, the man deserved it!"

"I shouldn't have been so gullible as to believe that he would have gotten me a position of work at Lady Cabot's school, but I was so anxious to leave—"

Brandon turned to her with a start. "Did you say Lady Cabot's?"

She nodded uncertainly. "I was to help teach."

He chuckled uproariously. "Teach what, madam? How to bed a man? My dearest wife, Lady Cabot's is one of the most elite brothels in London. I confess I've been there once or twice. Why, indeed, I might have met you there if things had gone differently—and most certainly I would have chosen you right off to crawl into bed with."

"Brandon Birmingham!" she cried indignantly. "Do you mean to say you'd have preferred it that way?" She sat up in a huff and threatened to leave the bed but he pulled her back down into his one-armed embrace.

"No, sweet," he smiled. "I was just teasing. You should know me better than that."

She pouted. "I didn't have any idea it was that kind of place."

"I know you didn't, and I'm glad that bastard who thought of putting you there met his end. Otherwise I might be tempted to go back and wring his blasted neck. He got what he deserved for trying to rape you."

She looked at him slyly. "You were the one who raped me. What were your just desserts?"

He grinned leisurely. "I received my just rewards when I had to marry a cocky wench like you." He reached for the leather pouch on the table and dropped it on her belly. "Don't let these go astray again, madam. I won't be so forgiving next time."

She grabbed up the pouch and opened it. Her jewels fell out as she tilted the bag.

"How did you manage to get these out of Mr. Hint's pocket with the limb on top of him?" she asked, rather surprised.

"They dropped out when he fell from Leopold. I washed the mud off in the stables. I don't know why he chose to ride Leopold when his horse stood nearby. I think perhaps he had been planning to leave Charleston before Lulu had a chance to talk. But it's strange that he took Leopold."

"Perhaps he thought Leopold was the fastest."

"Well, as William Court received what he deserved, so did Mr. Hint. Let's forget them both now. I've an idea to pay a certain wench back for her cockiness."

Heather laughed playfully, feeling free now of all plaguing doubts and fears, and she curled in a ball against him.

"So, you resort to antics when you know I'm lame in my shoulder and arm. Don't be so sure I can't handle you for teasing me, wench. I'll turn that bare backside up and give you a swat you'll long remember."

Uncertain whether he teased or spoke the truth, she uncurled and looked at him cautiously, but he was grinning broadly.

"Madam, you amaze me. Never once have I laid a hand to you and still you act as if you expect me to. Do you think I would take the chance of bruising my playground? Now come here, my little vixen, and let me use it."

"But your shoulder," she said in concern.

He grinned confidently, drawing her close against him. "Madam, you will ride this night after all."

The worst of the storm had passed when they journeyed home the next morning on Lady Fair. Clouds still chased across the sky, but the rain had ceased and the wind was nothing but a shallow ghost of the past evening's giant. The cloak Heather had worn the afternoon before was damp and stifling now in the late morning heat, and she longed to be rid of it but found Brandon's shirt lacked something of the popular mode.

"Jeff won't mind if you discard the thing, and Hatti is quite used to seeing you in much less," Brandon teased.

Heather cast him a mischievous look and made to undo the enveloping cloak. "If you're sure Jeff won't mind."

He caught her hand and grinned. "He won't mind, minx, but I will. You saw what I did to Mr. Hint for trespassing. I would surely hate to turn against my own brother."

So the cloak remained and they arrived home a few minutes later with Heather literally steaming. Everybody came running from the house to meet them, Jeff looking as if he hadn't slept at all, Hatti crying in her apron.

"Oh Lordy, Master Bran, we done thought something bad had happened to you. Leopold come back in a temper an' we thought sure he done went wild and broke your neck." She turned to her mistress, shaking her graying head. "An' you, Miss Heather, scared me pea green. I nearly killed that James for lettin' you go. I been sick with worry about you, child."

A gust of wind caught Heather's cloak and whipped it from her legs. Brandon snatched it closed again, but not before Jeff and Hatti glimpsed a bare thigh.

"Miss Heather! What happened to your clothes, child?"

"Louisa's murderer tried to put an end to her, too," Brandon replied and swung down from Lady Fair. He grimaced with pain and grabbed for the bandage over his shoulder, turning pale.

Heather slid from her horse and anxiously inspected the bandages. "Oh, Brandon, it's begun to bleed again. You must get upstairs and let me see to it." She turned to Hatti. "I'll need some fresh bandages and water and tell Mary to bring Beau to me please. I hope he's starving at the moment. I have need to be rid of some milk. James, will you take Lady and give her a good rubbing. Luke, please go to Charleston and tell Sheriff Townsend he is needed at Oakley Plantation with a few stout men. Jeff, do come up with us. Brandon will want to tell you what happened last night."

Each went scurrying to do the task presented him, and Hatti chuckled as she bustled along.

"She's a gettin' more like Miss Catherine every day."

In the hall Heather came upon George, who hung his head as she passed him and shuffled his feet in embarrassment. She stopped and turned and raised an eyebrow questioningly.

"George?"

"Aye, mum?" he replied and raised his head. One eye had definitely been blackened.

"Whatever happened to your eye, George? It's all black."

"Aye, mum," he agreed.

"Well?" she persisted.

He looked to his captain and cleared his throat. " 'Twas a matter what needed setting straight in Charleston, mum."

"What matter?"

He glanced around uncomfortably and drew a chuckle from Jeff.

" 'Twas Dickie, mum. You remember Dickie?''

"Aye, George," she nodded. "I remember Dickie. And how many black eyes is Dickie sporting?''

"Two, mum, and he's awfully sorry for the trouble he caused you, mum, and swears not another word, drunk or sober," he said in a rush.

She nodded again and turned to take her husband's arm, but then threw a smile over her shoulder at the servant.

"Two, did you say? Thank you, George."

"Aye, mum," he grinned.

After she redressed Brandon's wound and donned a cool muslin gown, she sat apart from the men with her back to Jeff and put Beau to her breast. As Brandon talked with his brother of their adventures of the previous evening, she glanced around their bedroom, feeling its warmth and friendliness. Her gaze swept briefly to a table beside her then returned quickly. Brandon's miniature portrait of his mother rested there. The green eyes which the artist had painted so well seemed alive, full of impish satisfaction, and Heather wondered at the power of a dead woman to take care of those she loved. It was surely her earrings which had brought everything out in the open and exposed Mr. Hint for what he was. Was it truly possible?

"Don't you agree, pet?"

She glanced up, startled from her thoughts. "What, my love? I'm afraid I wasn't listening."

Brandon laughed. "Jeff is going to buy Oakley and I insist he take the land as a birthday gift. Don't you agree he should?"

She smiled at her husband with something close to worship in her eyes. "Most certainly, my love," she replied and glanced back briefly to the portrait. The eyes had regained their dignified stillness, but Heather wondered if she had imagined the gleam in Catherine's eyes.

They shared a secret, these two Birmingham women, which their men would never know. To the world they seemed frail and in need of protection, but their love gave them greater strength and courage than was believable. From the grave their influence still shaped events. A knowing smile curved Heather's lips and she nodded to the portrait of Catherine Birmingham.

*Wiltshire countryside, England
Northeast of Bath and Bradford on Avon
September 5, 1815*

Lady Adriana Sutton whirled through the gracefully arched portico of Randwulf Manor, spilling effervescent laughter over her shoulder as she deftly avoided the reaching hand of an eager young swain. In copying her lead, he had jumped down from his mount and raced after her in his zeal to catch her before she could dash up the stone steps and escape into the Jacobean mansion of her family's closest neighbors and friends. At her approach, the massive door was drawn open and, with quiet dignity, a tall, thin, elderly butler stepped aside to await her entrance.

"Oh, Harrison, you're positively a dear," Adriana warbled cheerily as she flitted through the spacious vestibule. Safely ensconcing herself in the hall beyond the steward, she spun about and struck a playfully triumphant pose for the benefit of her pursuer who came to a teetering halt at the threshold, causing her to lift a brow in curious wonder. As zealously as Roger Elston had dogged her heels in his nearly year-long quest to claim her for his very own, even intruding when not invited, it seemed as if his dread of the late Lord Sedgwick Wyndham, the sixth Marquess of Randwulf, had actually intensified rather than abated in the months following the nobleman's death.

If there had been occasions when Lord Sedgwick had grown exasperated by the apprentice's impromptu visits, it certainly hadn't been the elder's fault, for Roger had seemed unusually tenacious in his endeavor to win her hand, as if that had been even remotely possible. His gall had reached amazing limits. Whenever formal invitations had been extended to select groups or close friends were enjoying private dinners with the Wyndhams or her own family, as long as she had been a participant, her single-minded admirer would present himself on some pretext or another, if only to speak with her for a moment or two. It made her rue the day she had ever yielded to his first unannounced visit to her own home at Wakefield Manor. Even after his audacious proposal of marriage, which her father had answered forthrightly by explaining that she was already committed, Roger had continued to chase her hither and yon.

As much as she had foreseen the need to issue a stern directive that would have permanently banished the apprentice from her presence, Adriana had not yet subdued the qualms that plagued her. At times, Roger seemed like such a lonely individual, clearly evincing his troubled youth. Whenever she came nigh to severing their association, she found herself inundated with reminders of all the helpless creatures that her lifelong companion, Samantha Wyndham, and she had once nurtured as children. To exhibit less compassion to a human being in desperate need of a little kindness had seemed inequitable in comparison.

"I do believe that dastardly fellow is afraid of you, Harrison," Adriana teasingly surmised, lifting her riding crop to indicate her boyishly handsome admirer. "His reluctance to confront such a man as yourself has plainly led to my advantage. If you hadn't opened the door when you did, Mr. Elston would've likely caught me and made me rue the fact that Ulysses and I left him and that paltry nag plodding along behind us again."

Although Roger had not been invited on their planned outing today, he had nevertheless shown up at Wakefield Manor just as her friends had arrived on horseback to join up with her and a recent female acquaintance. What else could she have done other than politely offer the man a mount? In spite of his

awareness that she was obliged to another by a formal agreement her parents had signed years ago, Roger's perseverance
seemed indefatigable, causing her to wonder if the man actually thought he could, by his own resolve, put to naught such a
contract and win her hand.

In a guise of perplexity, Adriana gathered elegantly arched
brows as she laid a slender finger aside her chin. "Still, as
much as I've tried to rein in Ulysses, I fear he can't abide the
sight of another steed racing ahead of him. He refuses to walk
beside any of the geldings from our stables, as Mr. Elston can
well attest by his efforts to keep up today. Indeed, I wouldn't
be at all surprised if the gray considers it a personal affront to
be associated with them. You know yourself, Harrison, that
Lord Sedgwick used to complain fairly often about the stallion's indomitable spirit."

The steward's ephemeral grin hinted of a humor more often
masked by a dignified mien. "Aye, my lady, that he did, but
always with a twinkle of pride in his eye because of your ability to handle such a headstrong stallion. His lordship took
enormous delight in boasting of your accomplishments to any
who'd lend an ear. Why, he was just as proud of you as his own
darling daughter."

Having been in the Wyndhams' employ for several decades,
Harrison had a fine recollection of the Suttons' arrival at Randwulf Manor in a quest to show off their third and newest daughter. Slightly more than a score of years later, the lady now held
claim to the affection of nearly everyone living on the premises.
As for her riding skill, Harrison had heard enough praise from
his late lordship to be conversant of the fact that the girl rode
well enough to ruffle the pride of equestrians who considered
their own talents unmatched. In view of her present companion's lack of experience in that area less than a year ago, it
wasn't at all surprising that he continued to lose without fail. If
anything, his defeats had strengthened his determination to succeed, to the degree that he usually fared better now than other
participants in their spontaneous races. At least this time he had
been nigh upon the girl's heels when she had darted through the
doorway. But then, considering the long climb from the hitching
posts to the manor, her pursuer's leaping strides had allowed
him more of an advantage in the final moments of their contest.

"To be sure, my lady, no other steed has the heart to match the heroic efforts of the gray . . . *or* those of its spirited rider. Nevertheless, Mr. Elston does seem determined to catch you. Perhaps he will someday."

Long years of service had established Alfred Harrison as head steward of Randwulf Manor, in all aspects a rightly deserved position dutifully carried out with loyal dedication. In the presence of such a respected pillar of the household staff, Roger Elston did indeed feel uncomfortable barging into the manor. As much as he craved to have the lady for his own, he couldn't dismiss the fact that he was taking much upon himself by fraternizing with affluent aristocrats who had grown up with lofty titles and well-respected names. His impertinence had already tweaked the ire of a veritable legion of titled lords vying for the maiden's hand, but months ago he had decided the prize was clearly worth any altercation he'd be forced to surmount. Had not his own sire inherited a sizable woolen mill on the outskirts of Bradford on Avon and bade him to learn its management and the woolen trade, he would never have left the London orphanage wherein he had lived since he was nine and, for the last ten of his eight and ten years' residency there, served as a tutor. Truly, considering his less than humble circumstances, it was a miracle he was even allowed in their presence. If not for the Wyndhams' deep, long-abiding affection for Lady Adriana and their reluctance to embarrass her by questioning the one who trailed in her footsteps, a man of his low estate would have been turned away at the door.

Sweeping off his hat, Roger drew himself up in stilted decorum and sought to claim the steward's attention, if only to remind the man he was awaiting an invitation to enter, but he froze in sudden prickling apprehension as his ears caught the low, muffled growls of the pair of aging wolfhounds that freely roamed the palatial manse and the grounds around it. Months ago, he had learned that when Leo and Aris were afoot, he was not always safe, whether in the house or the grounds around it. Indeed, the two seemed ever-eager to sink their sharp fangs into him. Even if the manners of the family members had always been above reproach, the same could not be said for their two pets.

Elaborately ornamented stonework clearly evidenced the artistry of talented masons of bygone eras in the fluted and festooned archways that on two levels and four sides set apart the enormous great hall located at the heart of the manor from the elegantly vaulted passageways that surrounded it. Two of these corridors began at the vestibule, which was itself spacious enough to accommodate a throng of people. From the entrance, the hallways on both the north and south sides almost traversed the entire length of the manor. The expansive great hall, which they buttressed, was typical of those built in ancient castles, where trestle tables, replete with thronelike chairs, provided dining reminiscent of the Middle Ages. The southernmost corridor offered access to the drawing room, at the door of which the lady and the butler had paused to talk. Just beyond that massive chamber, stone archways similar to those encompassing the great room defined the boundaries of the gallery. The library with its handsomely paneled door was immediately adjacent to it. At the end of the passage was a pair of deeply etched crystal doors that led to the enormous, glass-paned conservatory presently glowing with the reflected radiance of the afternoon sun.

The rumbling growls could have come from any of these areas on the south end of the manse, yet the open stone archways bordering the gallery made it completely accessible to the hounds. It was also a room where the pair could often be found basking in the warm maze of fragmented sunlight.

Cautiously Roger craned his neck as he tried to see into the gallery, though from where he stood it was impossible to view the interior of the room. But then, even had he been standing directly in front, the stained-glass windows lining the exterior wall would have made it difficult for him to ferret out the wolfhounds. Framed within elegantly arched stone casings similar to those on the opposite side of the room, the vividly hued windows presented an impressive collection of artistic memorials. Among ancestors honored for their valiant contributions to the Wyndhams' legacy were battle-garbed knights immortalized for their separate acts of courage, several ladies for their righteous causes, and a gentlemanly scholar holding an olive branch. Yet, in seasons stretching from the advent of winter until the coming of summer, the sun cast its rays upon the leaded panes from mid-afternoon nigh to the approach of dusk, causing strangely distorted configurations of multicolored shafts of radiance to flood into the room, doing much to confuse the eye and muddle the senses of the beholder. It was nearly three in the afternoon now, and already there was a riotous blaze of vibrantly hued streaks stretching as far away as the great hall.

Roger blamed his sudden dizziness on the variegated brilliance imbuing the corridor rather than his own swiftly palpitating heart, but he had cause to reflect upon a possible error in his reasoning when he found himself meeting evilly glinting eyes amid the dazzling array of sunlit colors. Beneath those piercing orbs, sharp, white fangs were bared in fixed snarls. The threat was obvious . . . and immensely terrifying; any moment now the huge beasts might decide to rush upon him and close their steely jaws on his legs or arms, if not his throat. They only awaited some menacing gesture to incite them to attack. For that reason, Roger dared not twitch a brow.

Incredible as it began to seem as the moments flew past, the animals remained rigidly poised for battle where they stood, as if some magical potion had transformed them into two granite effigies, which to Roger's regret he could not trust to remain stationary beyond a second's passage of time. In spite of their frozen posture, their hackles now formed distinct ridges along their backs, conveying their unwavering distrust of him or anyone else they loosely regarded as an outsider . . . except that in this case they had taken up what had every appearance of being a protective stance on either side of a tall, uniformed officer who was standing in the passageway near the far end of the gallery. The fact that he was leaning heavily on a cane indicated that he was just another wounded participant from their war with France, perhaps even from the more recent battle of Waterloo or the subsequent skirmishes still raging in that foe's country. From what could be roughly ascertained, the fellow had been halted by the lady's arrival in the manor, for his slowly exacting perusal seemed riveted entirely upon her.

No reasonable explanation could be found for the wolfhounds' acceptance of this newcomer, at least none to which Roger was privy. Stalwart loyalty of the sort he was now witnessing was normally reserved for the immediate family, as

had frequently been demonstrated by the dogs' fierce devotion
to the late lord. Roger had oft suspected and yet had never
found viable proof to privately convict the marquess of abet-
ting the hostility of his pets in order to deter the many suitors
seeking Lady Adriana's attention. Prior to Lord Sedgwick's illness and death, the hopefuls had been wont to descend in
droves on the neighboring country estates of Randwulf and
Wakefield in their eagerness to be anywhere within close proximity to Adriana Sutton. Not only was the lady breathtakingly
beautiful, but perhaps of more interest to some than to others
was the fact that, upon her marriage, her groom would become
the recipient of a dowry generous enough to greatly elevate his
status from pauper to fortunate gentleman.

The hounds had belonged to the nobleman, after all, and if
Lord Sedgwick had been of such a mind, he could've easily
encouraged their aggression. Although outwardly he had
seemed pleasantly amused by the gallants who had found
themselves genuinely besotted with the lady, he had once
decreed his own son should marry the lady, which in Roger's
mind had seemed reason enough for the elder to use crafty
subterfuge in allowing the dogs to frighten off lovesick swains.

It was still a mystery to Roger why the hounds tolerated the
servants, though some came and went, unless their uniforms
somehow set them apart from visitors and strangers in the
dogs' minds. Having nurtured as many aspirations as the rest
of Lady Adriana's admirers, Roger had followed her to Randwulf Manor on more than a score of occasions, and had concluded that Leo and Aris bestowed upon her alone the same
affection they extended to family members. Bearing that in
mind and considering the dogs' intolerance for outsiders,
Roger was more than a little curious as to what connection this
officer had to those living in the manor.

Unable to bring to mind any definite memory of such a man
from previous visits to the mansion, Roger was put to task to
figure out precisely who this newcomer was. If merely an
acquaintance or a distant relative of the family, then why
would the dogs accept him so readily? As perplexing as that
question was, Roger couldn't shake the impression that he had
seen the officer somewhere before or at least someone who
bore a close resemblance to him. Such a face was unforgettable.

It had all the characteristics he had come to envy: strong, noble features and a handsomeness significantly more manly than his own fine, good looks, which in recent years he had begun to suspect would remain annoyingly boyish far into the future. Although he had recently passed his twenty and seventh birthday, he was continually vexed by people who mistook him for a stripling lad.

If the officer was indeed a guest in the house, Roger had to mentally revile the air of authority the man conveyed, which no doubt stemmed from a haughty attitude or perhaps even his military rank. He certainly couldn't have commanded respect merely by his length of years. At the most, he looked no more than thirty and five.

The stranger's imposing presence seemed highly inappropriate in the late marquess's home. Having elevated a dark brow to a lofty height in some exasperation with the elderly butler, who at the moment seemed oblivious to everything but his own animated conversation with the lady, the officer gave every indication that he was expecting an introduction to the maid, as if he had some indubitable right to receive one. Perhaps, like his predecessors, he had become enthralled by her uncommon beauty, a premise that ofttimes had sorely nettled Roger's mood when he found himself in the midst of her audience of aristocratic suitors.

Who the devil was this chap anyway?

That question was swept from conscious thought as Roger was jostled aside by the late lord's only daughter. After falling well behind during their afternoon race, Samantha Galia Wyndham Burke had only just now arrived at her family's country estate. Much in the manner of her closest friend, she seemed playfully intent upon eluding the man who had given chase, in this case her sandy-haired husband of nearly two years. In tossing a quick glance over her shoulder, she found him closing the distance between them at a rapid pace.

Perceval Burke's height and long, leaping strides definitely gave him an advantage in his pursuit. Amid squeals of laughing protest, he gathered his wife in the crook of an arm and, with a devious chuckle, swept her around to face him. "Now I have you, my lovely."

Dragging off her bonnet, Samantha peered up at her handsome

husband through long, silky lashes as the corners of her soft lips curved coyly. "Should I believe I am in danger, sir?"

Sandy brows arched diabolically above gleaming blue eyes. "The worst kind, I fear."

In sweetly contrived contrition, Samantha lowered her gaze as her gloved fingers toyed with the buttons of his suede waistcoat. Even so, her lips seemed inclined to twitch as she strove to restrain her merriment. "I suppose I must pay penance."

"Aye," her husband murmured huskily, squeezing her arm. "I shall see to it without delay upon our arrival home."

The entrance of the third couple was considerably more dignified than the previous two. For some time now, Major Lord Stuart Burke had been hindered by a particularly painful wound, which he had received in the left buttock during the Battle of Waterloo. Yet his courtliness remained above reproach. Having drawn within his accommodating arm the daintily gloved hand of Miss Felicity Fairchild, a young, immensely fetching newcomer to the small nearby town of Bradford on Avon, Stuart escorted her into the great hall with all the gallantry of an officer and a gentleman, while she, with small, mincing steps and demure little smiles, glided along beside him.

Greatly encouraged by the arrival of the couples, Roger followed in their wake and sought to fortify his entrance further still by the example Perceval had set. Daring much, he dashed toward Adriana with every hope of catching her unaware, for if there was one thing at which he excelled, it was his speed and maneuverability. Having had to fend for himself and his mother amid the squalor of London streets prior to her death and his internment in an orphanage, he had learned the necessity of being swift at a very early age. It had either been that or have the stolen food stripped from his grasp by officials, an incident that had usually ended in a magistrate determining the fate of the thief.

The briskly advancing repetition of metal striking marble immediately claimed Adriana Sutton's attention. Recognizing it as a sound that normally accompanied Roger's every footfall, she glanced around in some surprise. It was as she had feared: The rascal was coming toward her with all possible speed.

In spite of the destructive and painful havoc the metallic

wedges had wreaked upon her slippers and feet in the past, Adriana was far more dedicated to the idea of keeping the apprentice at bay. An unwed maid, she would allow no man the same familiarity Perceval had recently evidenced with his wife. She had *yet* to find *any* man *that* engaging. However disappointed she had been earlier to find herself once again in the company of Roger Elston, she could not bring herself to discomfit him by demanding a halt to his antics in the presence of her highborn friends. Her mother had never been one to abide rudeness of any sort, even when it was bestowed upon one who frequently forced his company on others.

Challenged to defeat the purposes of her indomitable suitor, Adriana spun away from Harrison with a well-feigned, light-hearted laugh, managing by a narrow margin to avoid Roger's outstretched hand. Dedicated to the idea of staying out of the apprentice's reach (as much as he would have had it otherwise), she continued her whirling dervish past the first several archways of the gallery, vaguely aware of Leo and Aris scurrying out of her way. Immediately on the heels of their flight, a wooden object rattled to the floor and then skittered across the marble somewhere ahead of her, making her wonder what the animals had inadvertently sent flying. She was just thankful she hadn't heard an accompaniment of shattering glass. The metallic clacking, which had been nigh upon her heels, ceased abruptly as the hounds leapt from the gallery, where they had briefly sought refuge, into the hallway behind her, forestalling the apprentice's advance. As for what the animals had actually overturned, Adriana's curiosity went unappeased, for in the very next instant she came to a mind-jarring halt against an obstacle firmly rooted in her path, giving her cause to wonder if a tree had suddenly sprouted to soaring heights in the passageway. Taking into account her dazed senses, the notion seemed justifiable as she reeled away haphazardly.

The threat of falling seemed imminent as her booted toe struck the decorative molding at the bottom of an Italianate ornamented archway. Or was it a wickedly twining root over which she stumbled?

In the next instant, a long limb stretched forth from the seemingly oaken structure and clamped about her waist in an unyielding vise. Before her wits had time to clear, she was swept full length against a solid structure, which seemed far more human than any tree could have come close to duplicating. Once upon a time, she had plowed into her family's portly cook in her haste to escape to the stables. The experience had been much like landing upon a pillow, a memory that now convinced her that whatever the nature of the one who currently imprisoned her, one fact was certain: The form was *definitely* not of feminine origin!

Lady Adriana Elynn Sutton had grown up in her family's ancestral home no more than a hundred furlongs away, the youngest of three female offspring and, from her earliest years, a companion and close confidant of Samantha Wyndham. Although in many respects she had always been her father's darling, she had nevertheless caused her mother and sisters untold hours of despair. Not only was she dissimilar in appearance from the three, being tall, ebon-eyed, and dark-haired like her handsome sire, but in a variety of other ways too numerous to mention.

Her mother, Christina, was the quintessence of a lady who had tried to sculpt her three daughters in the very same mold. To some degree she had been successful. The elder two, Jaclyn and Melora, had heeded their parents' counsel and, when it met their mood, could convey a genteel demeanor that observers found both pleasing and attractive, to the extent that Jaclyn was now married, living near London, and the mother of two children. Melora, the second born, was not long from being wed. Adriana, on the other hand, had given every indication that she had been cast from an entirely different mold. Her siblings had even suggested that she was more like her paternal aunt than the family could bear.

Except for a contract of courtship and betrothal that had left her uncertain as to her future, Adriana considered herself as yet uncommitted and wasn't at all eager for that circumstance to change. She was reluctant to assume lofty airs for the benefit of high-ranking guests and, in her mother's opinion, had even seemed rebellious at times when, instead of donning her finest gowns, she'd appear before their visitors in riding attire, offer gracious excuses with enchanting smiles, and then flit out the door in a dizzying flash before any had the inclination to object.

Unquestionably her equestrian abilities ranked among the

best in the area, especially when she rode the proud Andalusian stallion her father had had imported from Spain especially for her. But to achieve such skill as an accomplished rider, she had dedicated herself relentlessly to hours of training, something her fainthearted siblings had been disinclined to do soon after discovering they were not always safely ensconced in a sidesaddle. A tumble or two had made them keenly aware of that fact and abruptly turned their interests toward more ladylike activities.

Her mother had fretted untold hours over the tomboyish ways of her youngest offspring, who had proven far more adventuresome than her siblings, not only while racing Ulysses across the rolling fields or sending him flying over steep hurdles, but in her avid fascination with archery and firearms. Under her sire's doting tutelage, she had acquired a keen eye for both and, from a goodly distance away, especially with the Ferguson rifle he had bestowed on her, could take down a stag or some other game to relieve the monotony of the fare served at the family table or to deliver dressed-out portions to people in need, most often to a couple who had taken in a dozen or more orphans. It was the opinions of her tutors that her doting sire had found most satisfying, however. According to those worthy scholars, Adriana Sutton had an intellect keen enough to be envied by many a learned gentleman.

In spite of such lauding praises from her instructors, her *lack* of certain accomplishments had earned sharp disapproval from her dainty, green-eyed, flaxen-haired sisters, a condemnation greatly strengthened by the fact that she was totally lacking any skill with a needle. She was especially loath to sing or play the harpsichord, at which both Jaclyn and Melora excelled. She was also fairly selective in extending her friendship to those of her own gender, for she couldn't endure twittering little gossips who were forever whispering snide comments in others' ears about this or that young lady who just happened to be more appealing than the little tale-mongers. It seemed deplorable to her sisters that she had far more gentlemen friends than feminine companions. "Why, what would people think?" they complained. Yet, inexplicably (definitely to those who frowned on her flawed, ofttimes unladylike

behavior), Adriana Sutton had been much favored by the late
Marquess of Randwulf, his family, and their loyal servants,
many of whom had watched her grow from a painfully thin
chit to an intriguingly beautiful young lady.

Now, here she was, caught in an unyielding vise that, by
rights, should have made her hackles rise. At the moment,
however, she was experiencing some difficulty in discerning
reality from illusion. Under the circumstances, Adriana
thought she had had every right to entertain the whimsical
notion that a tree had taken root in the hall, for the towering
form against which she had been swept left her inundated with
impressions of a steely oak. The smoothly draped black skirt
of her modish riding habit and its short, double-breasted
Spencer jacket of forest-green velvet, fashionably set off by a
creamy-hued jabot, seemed insufficient protection against the
stalwart frame, for she had cause to wince within the unyielding embrace of the one who clasped her so tightly.

In a sudden, peevish attempt to push herself away and
regain her dignity, she was relieved to find the man's arms
falling away. Upon reclaiming her freedom, she sought to
retreat farther still from the fellow. Alas, her effort to escape
fell far short of her expectation, for in backing away, she
stepped on a stick or some other long, wooden object, which
promptly slid forward beneath her booted foot, throwing her
completely off balance. Her arms flayed wildly about in a frantic attempt to catch herself as the man reached for her. In desperation she clutched the first thing that came within proximity
to her hand, the waist of the finely tailored red coat. Even then,
her feet seemed to twist beneath her. The sole of her boot
slipped, making her lose what little equipoise she had gained.
Her frantic gyrations to recover her aplomb ended abruptly
when her right thigh slammed into the manly loins. Her victim
seemed to choke from her haphazard assault, but that was
hardly the end of her disgrace. Her skirts rode nigh up to her
knee as her left leg slid down the outer side of a hard, muscular
limb, seemingly with the same intent as a skinning tool. It was
difficult to determine who winced more from her outlandish
feats, the officer or herself. Adriana only knew the inside of her
leg felt as if it had been scraped raw after skimming down the
man's smoothly tailored white wool breeches. If any wrinkle

had existed in his trousers, she had no doubt she would've been the first to discover it.

Diligently she sought to regain her modesty as well as her dignity as she strove to unmount the iron-thewed thigh, but, as much as she tried, she couldn't ignore the fact that her softer parts felt sorely abused. Considering her discomfort, she had reason to doubt that she'd be able to grit out a smile, much less laugh at her own clumsiness. She could only wonder in agonized reflection what havoc she had reaped upon the man.

"I'm sorry . . . ," she began, blushing hotly as she endeavored to hide her burgeoning chagrin and distress. She feared her pantaloons had cut creases where previously there had been none. "I didn't mean—"

"Never mind," the officer strangled out. The tendons in his cheeks fairly snapped as he struggled for control. His arm came around her waist once again, and he lifted her easily, shifting her weight off his thigh before settling her feet safely to the floor between his own shiny black boots.

Still struggling to surmount his manly discomfort, the officer closed his eyes and bent his head forward to await its ebbing, allowing Adriana to catch a vague scent of his cologne. Mingled with an underlying essence of soap and an equally indistinct trace of the fine, costly wool of his uniform, the pleasantly aromatic bouquet drifted upward into her nostrils, and twined tantalizingly through her senses. Adriana had never in her life experienced the like of such strangely provocative stirrings. Indeed, the manly fragrance seemed far more intoxicating than a glass of port on a warm evening. As difficult as it proved to be, she sought to lend her attention to what she was actually seeing rather than the warmly titillating ambience through which she had just drifted.

Another painful grimace evidenced the man's continuing discomfort, tightening chiseled features and compressing well-formed lips as he endured the torment in silence. Stoic-faced, gentlemanly decorum didn't seem at all conducive to abating his pain, however, for with a softly muttered apology he reached down between them beneath the protective shroud of her skirts.

Adriana made the mistake of glancing down before it dawned on her just what he was doing, gingerly readjusting the torpid fullness defined by his narrow-fitting breeches. Just as quickly, a breathless gasp was snatched from her throat, and her eyes went chasing off. She suffered through an endless moment of excruciating embarrassment as she tried diligently to banish from her mind what she had just seen and to keep her thoughts firmly fixed on logical matters, such as the reason for this officer's presence at Randwulf Manor. Yet it was impossible to ignore the heat creeping into her cheeks. It certainly didn't help that she felt much like a ship adrift in some strange sea halfway around the world.

Purposefully, Adriana focused her gaze within an area no higher than closely cropped, dark brown hair and no lower than broad shoulders adorned with gold epaulettes affixed to the blazing red fabric of his military blouse. It seemed the only way she could keep her thoughts well in line with what was proper for an untried maid, but she never in her life imagined the alluring quintessence of masculinity could be embodied so completely in just one man.

In the midst of a handsome arrangement of chiseled features, darkly translucent gray eyes were now thankfully devoid of pain, at least enough to communicate some evidence of humor above a waywardly charming grin. Still, white teeth, as perfect as any she had seen in many a year, seemed far too bright to allow for sober reflection. Neatly clipped sideburns accentuated crisply chiseled bones beneath sun-bronzed cheeks. Poorly suppressed amusement momentarily compressed manly grooves that formed deep channels on either side of his mouth. Any woman would've stared in admiration at the intriguing results that perhaps had evolved through the years from simple dimples. Yet those indentations troubled Adriana, for they seemed to pluck at fibers long entrenched in her memory, as if strumming some tantalizingly evasive tune she had heard ages ago but now had difficulty bringing clearly to mind. If some faint recollection of those devilish creases actually did exist, then surely it was no recent memory and in all probability had been relegated to the dark, fathomless depths of her brain, where she could imagine such thoughts and remembrances of forgotten years were now moldering from disuse.

"Considering the discomfort we have shared in this past

moment," the officer murmured in a warmly hushed tone meant for her ears alone, "I think I should at least know the name of such a captivating companion before another calamity befalls us . . . Miss . . . ?"

The warmly mellow tones of her captor's voice were imbued with a rich quality that seemed to vibrate through her womanly being. To Adriana's amazement, the sound evoked a strangely pleasurable disturbance in areas far too private for an untried virgin even to consider, much less invite. As evocative as the sensations were, she didn't know quite what to make of them. They seemed almost . . . wanton. But then, the image that had recently been scored into her brain had undoubtedly heightened her sensitivity to wayward imaginings. If not for the man's sterling good looks, she'd still be struggling to drag her musings away from his loins.

"S-Sutton," she stammered, and could have groaned in chagrin at the clumsiness of her tongue. Her present failure to articulate clearly could in no wise have been due to any painful bashfulness suffered in the presence of men, for hardly a month passed without some new request for her hand being addressed to her or her father. If anything, those pleas had become rather hackneyed, solidifying her disinterest while she awaited some news of the one to whom she had been promised.

Prior to this day in history, she had considered the darkly handsome Riordan Kendrick, Marquess of Harcourt, without equal among those who had petitioned her father. Riordan had definitely seemed the most charming, and although his persistence hadn't equaled Roger's, she definitely counted that a point in his favor. Indeed, his manners were suave and polished. Yet, she couldn't recall a time wherein she had been so completely awed by Riordan's shining black eyes as she was now by the thickly lashed, luminous gray depths presently sparkling with amusement above her own. She hadn't seen eyes like that since . . .

"Sutton?" A well-defined eyebrow jutted sharply upward in what could only have been astonishment. A sort of incredulous awe seemed to spread over the officer's features as he looked her up and down. Still, he seemed hampered by lingering doubt as he thoughtfully canted his head and peered at her more closely. As much as he searched her face, it was as if he just couldn't believe what he had heard or, for that matter, was actually seeing. "Not . . . Lady . . . Adriana Sutton?" At her cautious nod, his grin deepened by nearly the same astonishing degree his arm tightened, crushing her soft bosom against the unyielding hardness of his broad chest. "My goodness, Adriana, you've become thoroughly enchanting in your maturity. Never in a thousand years would I have dreamt that one day you'd be so utterly ravishing."